The House in New Orlea

Ottilie drifted off into imaginings. ~~~ and skin and eyes and hair and ... she quivered. Naughty ideas that made her pale skin blush crossed her mind. The touch of that man's lips on hers; his hands and fingers straying over her breasts and belly; her legs opening and him probing that hungry wet place. Ottilie pulled her thoughts to an immediate stop. What was she doing? How could she, a virgin, think so licentiously. It was almost as if a devil was on her shoulder and a small voice was saying, go ahead. Think and then do. Go ahead. Experience. She squirmed in her seat.

Other books by the author

Odalisque
Handmaiden of Palmyra

The House in New Orleans
Fleur Reynolds

BLACK LACE

Black Lace books contain sexual fantasies.
In real life, always practise safe sex.

This edition published in 2002 by
Black Lace
Thames Wharf Studios
Rainville Road
London W6 9HA

Originally published 1994

Printed and bound by Mackays of Chatham PLC

ISBN 0 352 32951 3

*This book is dedicated
with love to*

*Paul B-S, Eddie A,
Oliver P, Ian M, Philip A,
Andy A, Ronald F,
Stewart C, Graeme H,
Richard and Gil*

Chapter 1

'Whoever he is he's wickedly fascinating,' thought Ottilie Duvier.

Her glance had fallen on a handsome and distinguished looking man in his early thirties. He was sitting a couple of tables away from her in the latest, most fashionable restaurant in Paris. His body language showed that he was paying as little attention to his beautiful blonde companion as she was to Lord Christopher. Ottilie thought he seemed vaguely familiar. She tried to work out where she had seen him before. He looked up at her. His ice-cold piercing blue eyes captured her hazel-green ones and they stayed momentarily fused together. A shiver of excitement ran down Ottilie's spine.

Staring at him she felt as if his eyes held the key to her locked soul and he had seen into her inner depths. This thought made her acutely uncomfortable. She wanted to grip the table to steady herself and gain strength to look in another direction, but she was powerless to make such an obvious move. Instead she took a deep breath, tensed the muscles in her abdomen, pushed her tongue out to lick her lips, and surreptitiously rolled her hips from side to side.

Ottilie Duvier was a rich and beautiful redhead. Neither too tall nor too thin, she had a good figure, full

1

rounded breasts, a tiny waist, a neat bottom, shapely legs with slim ankles and soft velvety peach type skin.

Superbly dressed in a short, dark blue silk velvet cocktail dress, overprinted with metallic pigment and worn with its matching bolero which was lined with red silk, she was sitting opposite her fiancé, Lord Christopher Furrel. Bored with listening to his ridiculous reasons as to why she should marry him quickly and leave France for England, Ottilie was rubbing her fingers up and down the stem of her wine glass whilst surveying the opulent, mirrored, Art Nouveau room. That was when her eyes had alighted on the stranger.

The man let his gaze fall to Ottilie's full bright red lips. He gave a slight smile, raised his full glass of champagne towards her, took a sip, then let his eyes insolently wander from her face to her breasts and return to her mouth. Receiving the full impact of his 'come-to-bed' eyes, Ottilie felt a shock wave. An untamed emotion ran through her. Some invisible hand had plugged her into a massive electrical voltage and she was shaking. She had an overwhelming desire for him to crush her to him and kiss her until she was out of breath. Her heart fluttered at the thought. Goose pimples broke out over her body. Her womb tightened. Her thighs gave an involuntary outward movement as if to welcome the most masculine part of him to her most secret self. Her nipples hardened in a wild fantasy of anticipation and strained against the fabric of her dress. She was glad her clothing hid all evidence of her sudden sexual arousal.

The man leant his elbows on the table and his chin on his hands. Ottilie wondered what the touch of those well manicured hands would be like on her bare flesh; on her neck, on her breasts, playing with her nipples then searching downwards over her belly, between her legs; now damp and swollen with desire, she was aching to be felt.

The man's companion stood up and so did he, bowing as she left the table. As the woman made her way through the diners towards the sign that said 'toilette',

Ottilie realised she was still staring at the stranger, mesmerised like a jack-rabbit in car headlamps. With a sudden, harsh movement she jerked her head away from the mystery man back to Christopher's familiar face. Moments later when she looked back again his table was empty. The man had gone.

'I say old girl are you feeling all right?' asked her fiancé.

'Fine,' she snapped.

Christopher really did have things about him that she found intensely irritating; calling her 'old girl' was one of them.

'Eat up then,' he commanded, pointing to her poached salmon as he attacked his steak and blithely continued with his argument.

Lord Christopher wanted them to marry very soon. Ottilie was not sure 'soon' was a good idea. She said she needed time. He demanded to know why. She said to recover from her father's illness and death. Also, having trained as a singer, she wanted to return to the concert platform. She needed to see if she could still perform, if her flair and ability were still there.

That was when Lord Christopher decided to lay down the law. His law. He said he did not approve of wives working. Especially his wife. In fact he objected strongly, no matter that it was something as refined and socially acceptable as Lieder singing. Lord Christopher was the old school type English aristocrat who married money. Wives, mothers, sisters, did not do paid work. Talent was not something that entered the equation. Ottilie decided she had heard enough for one evening.

'I'm going home,' she announced.

'What! You haven't finished! And neither have I. Ottilie, my steak is particularly good and so is the sauce,' he said.

'So stay and finish it.'

'I can't let you go home on your own.'

'Christopher, I think I can manage to get a cab for myself.'

3

'Yes, but . . .'

'No buts, Christopher. I don't expect you to come with me,' said Ottilie.

'Ottilie, I think you're behaving quite unreasonably.'

'Are you for real!' Ottilie's Americanness came to the fore in an effort to counter Christopher's insufferable and arrogant Englishness. 'Christopher, let me tell you I've listened to you drivelling on for the last hour about what you expect of me when we're married, and I think that's unreasonable.'

'Now look here Ottilie . . .' Lord Christopher began, and his clipped English tones were even more clipped than usual.

'Christopher,' she said interrupting him sharply, 'don't treat me as a child who doesn't know her own mind. I'm going – you finish your dinner.'

'Ottilie, now, really, your behaviour is quite absurd,' he said, exactly as if he was dealing with a recalcitrant child. At the same time he rose from his chair.

'Stay where you are and shut up,' said Ottilie. 'I'm not listening to one more word of your bullshit.'

'Ottilie, how dare you!'

'Goodnight, Christopher,' she said picking up her enormous gold and black fake fur coat which was draped over the back of her chair.

'Very well, if you take that attitude,' he said, sitting down again, and beginning to slice into his steak, 'I shall do just that.'

But Ottilie didn't care what he did. She wanted to be outside. She wanted to be in the open air; to breathe in the night; to watch the waters of the Seine; to calm herself down, and be by herself. It was a long walk from the sixth district, where they had been dining, to her home in the sixteenth, and she would take a cab – eventually. She needed to think.

Lord Christopher watched Ottilie sail out of the restaurant and the moment she had gone he hurriedly left his table for the telephone kiosk.

'Sylvie, Sylvie, is that you?'

4

'*Oui, Cherie*,' said Sylvie Cordonier, chirpily. 'I didn't expect to hear from you yet. Did you have a good dinner and did you manage it afterwards?'

'No,' said Lord Christopher.

'No, what?' Sylvie's voice changed dramatically. She wasn't the least bit chirpy. She was furious and showed her fury. 'Oh Christopher, we rehearsed this again and again. How could you fail? Her butler's away, it's the maid's night off and all you had to do was take her out, get her drunk and screw her. *Mon Dieu!* You are incompetent.'

'Sylvie, stop stop . . . there was nothing I could do. She just walked out on me. Left the restaurant in a huff and went home.'

'What did you say for her to do a thing like that?'

'I was just telling her I wanted us to marry quickly . . .'

'Yes, yes. And what else?'

'I said I didn't want her working, going back to singing.'

'*Imbecile*. Idiot. With all the money she's got she's not going to work, do those awful tours and things . . . For God's sake, why didn't you just say, "of course you can my darling. I love you. Whatever you want is what I want." *Merde*, do I have to tell you everything in minute detail? Where are you now?'

'Still in the restaurant.'

'I don't believe it! Leave this minute and go to her apartment. Tell her you're sorry and you didn't mean it. Tell her you love her. Seduce her, Christopher. Gently. Like I told you. Make love to her . . . then she'll marry you quickly and *Voilà* . . . We achieve our objective. Poor you will have a rich wife. You will get some of her money. I will still be your lover and you give me some of what you get. Perfect, *n'est-ce pas*? So go and do it, *immédiatement*.'

'Sylvie, if it was you, no problem but she doesn't turn me on,' said Lord Christopher. But that wasn't strictly true. Ottilie didn't usually turn him on, but quite suddenly tonight she had. He knew when it had happened. It was moments before she left the restaurant. She had a glow about her when she was telling him what she thought. A glow and bloom he had never seen before. He thought it was because he had never seen her angry. Whatever the reason, for the first time he really did find her sexually attractive. But not as attractive as Sylvie. 'Sylvie, listen to me, I can't just arrive cold on her doorstep and say "I love you darling, come to bed." '

'So, do you want me to suck your cock so that you can fuck her?' said Sylvie, blatantly.

'Yes,' he replied, his prick twitching and rising at the idea.

'Okay, *Cherie*,' she said.

'You will?' The very thought of it increased his hard-on.

'I said okay didn't I? I'll leave my front door open, but don't be long.'

Lord Christopher replaced the receiver and adjusted himself. He then walked straight up to the *maitre d'*, got the bill, paid it and left.

Sylvie's tiny, sparsely furnished second floor apartment was close by in the Rue Bonaparte. It did not take Lord Christopher long to get there. When he pushed open the door and walked into her sitting room Christopher was immediately presented with the alluring sight of Sylvie's luscious bare buttocks. Her lightly suntanned body was fully clothed in a white satin blouse, a slinky white skirt, white stockings and black high heels, but she was bending over a chair, her feet apart, and her skirt was up around her waist. Her splendid large soft bottom was beckoning to his cock to enter her.

'That is a nice fat arse,' he said.

Sylvie didn't say a word, not even a brief hello. She stayed mute and quite still. Christopher came up behind her and stroked her abundant curves whilst undoing his flies. He took out his prick and rubbed it between the tops of her naked thighs. He brought a hand round and began to play with her moist sex.

'And you're wet. You know what happens to ladies with wet pussies, don't you?'

'Yes ...' she whispered, rubbing herself backwards

6

and forwards on his prick and wiggling so that his fingers could probe deeper within her.

'Tell me then,' he said. 'You have to tell me.'

'They get screwed,' she said.

And, as she said the words, Christopher lunged into the warm comfort of her creamy moist opening. Holding her hips to keep his balance he rode her hard and fast. He thrust without stopping until she was gasping, her head was bobbing up and down, her long blonde hair flowing this way and that, and her inner muscles were gripping him as he jerked backwards and forwards within her. And then she came.

'You're a sexy bitch,' he said. 'And now you're going to suck me.'

Sylvie twisted round and knelt before him. He held her sloping shoulders. She took his penis in her hands and placed it in her cleavage embracing it between her massive breasts. She held his balls, caressing them gently. She raised his prick towards her, lowered her head and licked its tip. Christopher gave a long sigh of pleasure. She opened her thick full lips and slid his cock into her mouth. She worked on it, her mouth wandering up and down, up and down along the ridges of its stiffness until she felt his sap rising. Then she held fast to the base of his prick to stop him coming.

'No, *Cherie*, now you go and screw Ottilie,' she said, standing up, pulling down her short slinky skirt and walking away from him.

'Sylvie . . .' he wailed.

'Tell you what, I'll come with you and play with you in the car, that way you won't lose your er . . . impetus . . . but don't forget to give me the cab fare home.'

Lord Christopher looked with continuing desire at Sylvie's sexy feminine figure, admiring her large breasts, her curving hips, and her softly rounded stomach. He put a hand out and touched her olive-skinned face, tracing her thick mouth with his fingers. He kissed each of her large dark brown eyes, and stroked her streaked blonde hair.

'God, Sylvie, why couldn't you be rich then I wouldn't need to go through this charade. We could marry and screw each other all the time.'

'Well I'm not and anyway we do, so why worry?' said Sylvie, putting on her coat. 'Come on, *Cherie*, before it's too late and the silly cow's gone to bed.'

And Sylvie played with him, forcing her fingers past the buttons in his flies all the way to Ottilie's apartment, then, knowing he was highly aroused, she jumped out of the car and caught a cab back home.

Outside in the cold of a late January evening, and intrigued by her own reactions, Ottilie went back over the brief incident with the stranger in the restaurant. She found she was able to recall it vividly. She was quite surprised to discover how much she had taken in in those few moments of eye contact. One thing she realised with certainty: she had definitely seen the man before. But her memory would not be jogged. This annoyed her. Surely she should be able to remember someone so impressive? But then she had gone through the last few weeks in a daze. Her beloved father's death and his funeral had left her numb, almost an automaton. Her mind returned to the stranger again. He was tall – she had noticed that when he stood up – and thickset. The superb cut of his elegant suit disguised just how thickset he was, but he was certainly handsome, in a hard, blond, Teutonic way, and sexy. Sexuality had flowed out from him to her, igniting her loins, inflaming her, opening up channels within her and feelings she had never known; feelings she had never expected to feel, did not even believe in. And more than that, he was ... powerful. Yes, that was the adjective, but one more word popped into her mind. Dangerous. And she wondered if she would ever see him again.

She was surprised that Christopher had not noticed anything amiss. In fact, had she not jerked her head in such an odd way he would have stayed guzzling his steak impervious to the silent challenge the man had issued. But then Christopher was intent only on his own thoughts and desires. He wanted to eat his food and tell her how she should live her life in future.

Ottilie started to walk over the Pont Royal, then leant against the parapet gazing into the murky waters of the Seine below. She lifted her head to drink in one of the most famous views of Paris: the Quai des Tuileries to her left and the twin spires of Notre Dame to her right. She pulled her coat closer as if hugging the essence of Paris to her body. Her Paris. Where she had lived for the past few years. Where she had trained at the Conservatoire of Music. Where she had made her debut as a singer to enthusiastic reviews. And now where her father was buried. The city that Christopher was now ordering her to leave for marriage to him and his home in England. His demands had come as a shock to her. She had envisaged them living in her apartment. It had never crossed her mind that she, that they, would leave Paris.

Ottilie walked on over the bridge and towards an empty taxi rank, hoping by the time she got there a cab would have turned up, but it didn't.

She was torn by a variety of emotions. Anger was uppermost. How dare Christopher dictate to her, tell her what she could and could not do once they were married. She was definitely seeing another side of him. When her father was alive Christopher had been sweetness and light; caring and comforting. Nevertheless her father had had some reservations about the marriage. She remembered how he had touched on the subject.

'Don't rush into anything, *Cherie*,' he'd said. 'Make sure that you really love him.'

'I do Papa,' she'd replied. 'I really do.'

'You know so little of the world, you've had so few experiences,' her father had said sadly, taking her soft long-fingered hand in his thin bony one and stroking it. 'Passion, my little cabbage, is an overriding emotion and I don't think it's one that has touched you as yet. Maybe it will. Maybe it won't. From the moment I set eyes upon your mother I felt a great passion for her and it stayed

9

with me until the day she died. And that sort of passionate love helps through the ups and downs of life. When that crazy unknown drunk sonofabitch crashed into her, killing her, it helped me to know that we had had something special. But the love you think you feel for Christopher is not passion, it's companionship. It's comfortable.'

But comfortable was not something that her relationship with her fiancé was any more. Irritation and annoyance was a far better description. She thought of Christopher, how his brown, almost sandy coloured hair, flopped endearingly over one eye. It had been endearing. She had wanted to smooth it away so that she could see his brown eyes properly. Now it was another source of irritation. Her present response was – why didn't he get a decent haircut? That made her smile. She was recovering her equilibrium.

With no taxi in sight, Ottilie walked through the Palais Royal and turned left into the Rue de Rivoli, oblivious to the sights and sounds and lights of the street. She was totally caught up in her own thoughts and imaginings until a boutique selling menswear caught her eye. She liked well turned out men. Christopher was always well dressed, in a classically English fashion. Ottilie tried to imagine him in a French or an Italian designer's outfit. The idea was so ludicrous she laughed out loud – then stopped sharply. This was not the manifestation of equilibrium. It was more like hysteria.

There was no taxi at the next rank. Ottilie decided to carry on walking. Christopher was a good catch. Her best friend Sylvie Cordonier said he was. He certainly moved in the right circles. But she had yet to visit his stately pile in England. Sylvie had been there. She'd visited it on a long week-end sightseeing trip to England. She said it was built of a lovely golden stone, but was big and draughty and needed money spent on it. Well for Ottilie that was not a problem. Her mother's death had left her rich. And, although she didn't yet know the full extent of his will (she would find that out in the morning) Ottilie knew she was her father's main beneficiary: and that she was now an exceptionally wealthy woman.

Ottilie wondered if her father had provided for his step-son, Elmer Planchet. Or, had he cut him out completely. He had threatened it often enough. Elmer Planchet was a gambler. Although Bernard Duvier could be inordinately extravagant and then suddenly extremely parsimonious, as could his daughter, he utterly failed to understand the lure of gambling. He thought money too important a commodity to be idly thrown away.

Bernard Duvier came from an old Louisiana plantation family. They were more cultured and intelligent than most of their ilk. They had managed not only to hold on to their money through the various declines and depressions in the economy, but also, by judicious property buying and investment (the Duviers did not see this as gambling), and by a series of good marriages, had actually increased it.

Bernard had made a good marriage, although his only and much loved sister, Liliane, had not. She had married the handsome penniless Italian, Frank Delassio, who now preferred to call himself Frank Dale. Bernard thought he was a gangster, a hoodlum, a jumped up jackass wanting to better himself by leaping on Liliane. He had made the mistake of telling his sister what he thought. He had warned her. But she had been too love-blind to heed what Bernard said. He had refused to countenance the marriage. When they had eloped he had refused to accept their union and he had never received Frank in his house. Bernard had watched his brother-in-law get richer and richer and knew it was from nefarious activities. After their daughter, Mary Lou, was born, Liliane caught a virus and grew weak. Bernard had then seen Frank out on the town with a variety of plastic-implanted women with faces coated in make-up, clothed and coiffeured to resemble dolls. He had watched him but had kept his mouth shut. Bernard didn't interfere. Brother and sister both knew she had made a big mistake. During their infrequent but friendly meetings, neither referred to it. She had made a vow. And she kept it. Kept it until death.

Bernard was sensible. He had fallen madly in love with Clarissa, the beautiful daughter of a lawyer who was also an 'old money' plantation owner. When Bernard met Clarissa she was the young widow of a wealthy New Orleans architect who had drunk himself into an early grave. Elmer was Clarissa's son by this marriage.

Ottilie loved Elmer. When she was small, and pale and sickly, Elmer had been her protector. He had taken on the role of big brother and fought anyone who came near her, attempting to bully or torment her. Ottilie looked up to Elmer. They had not seen one another since their mother's death.

Bernard, unable to bear living in the same city, the same state, the same country, as his wife's unknown killer, decided to settle permanently in Paris. Even his dying sister's entreaties had not stopped him leaving the States. Bernard had let his Garden District home (at a peppercorn rent) to Elmer, and had departed for France.

Ottilie had also wanted to leave New Orleans, to go to New York and the Juilliard School of Music. Her father was delighted for her to study. He recognised her beautiful voice and was not one to allow talent, or the ability to make money, go to waste. But, he had not wanted her, a good southern girl, to live in the inhospitable, lonely and hostile environs of New York City. He had suggested she try for the Paris Conservatoire and live with him in the French capital. To her surprise the professors there had liked the timbre of her soprano and had accepted her as a student. And, until cancer and the longing for his dead wife had caught up with him, father and daughter had lived harmoniously together. Very few things had disturbed their well ordered existence, but Elmer had managed to do so on a number of occasions.

Ottilie remembered the first time it happened; how surprised she had been when, on coming home from her music lessons one afternoon, she had found her father in a raging temper. He had received a fax from Elmer telling him that he was in considerable debt and needed help. There were hints about the underworld and violence. Bernard Duvier had exploded. He felt in his bones that his rogue brother-in-law Frank Dale was implicated. Bernard was well aware that Frank had illegal gambling dens amongst his other unlawful businesses. Bernard ranted and raved, saying how Elmer was just like his useless father who had drunk himself to death. A weak strain, he had said. But, rather than let Elmer be prey to the gangster Frank, he had helped him. He had helped him a couple of times just as he had paid his school and university fees. But his generosity came with a health warning. Don't gamble. If you do, I will find out and although I will help you out of scrapes whilst I'm alive, you will gain nothing from my death.

However, there was one thing Bernard absolutely refused to help him with. The house. When Elmer wrote demanding money for new roofing and new wooden boards for the wrap-around balcony, Bernard had refused. By then Elmer had qualified as an architect; Bernard had bought him into his father's old practice. He wrote his step-son a measured letter. He told him that he should be making plenty of money, and that if he wasn't, he was a fool and should get out of the business. If he was, then he was downright greedy. He had to pay so little to live in such a beautiful house that he should be able to afford its upkeep. The faxes had flown thick, fast and angrily across the Atlantic, but Bernard Duvier had refused to budge.

Since then communciation had been kept to an absolute minimum, namely invoices and receipts for the rent of the house. Ottilie had notified Elmer of Bernard's death. She had half expected him to arrive in Paris for the funeral but he had telephoned to say pressure of business and an exceptional work load prevented him attending. Ottilie was disappointed but understood. Work was necessary.

Ottilie crossed the Place de la Concorde and turned into the Champs-Elysées where a taxi was waiting at the front of the station. She jumped in and in her perfect French told the driver to take her to the Rue Pierre Charron.

Watching the streets fly by Ottilie thought she caught sight of her friend Sylvie in a cab going in the opposite direction. Ottilie turned her head but both cars were going too fast for her to be sure. If it was Sylvie, Ottilie wondered where she had been. She hadn't said she was going anywhere. In fact, Ottilie had asked her to join them for dinner but Sylvie had said she wanted a night on her own at home for study.

'Anyway *mon amie*, you must have time with Christopher by yourself,' she said. 'After all you are engaged.'

Ottilie felt sorry for Sylvie. They had met at the Conservatoire. She was pretty but she was fat.

'You'll have trouble getting a man being so er . . . um, large,' Ottilie had said, trying to get Sylvie to go on a diet.

'No I won't, there are still some real men in the world who like big women. Anyway, I'm not fat, I'm voluptuous,' Sylvie had said, 'and in years gone by it was people like me who were considered sexy not the ones like you, slim and looking like a boy.'

'I don't look like a boy, my tits are too big,' Ottilie had protested.

'Yes, they're your saving grace,' Sylvie had replied.

Poor Sylvie, for all her show of defiance Ottilie knew it was going to be hard for her to make a good marriage. And Ottilie never did see her with a man. Sylvie had told her she met somebody from time to time and screwed him, but who it was Ottilie didn't know. They had never been introduced. Somebody wildly unsuitable, and she knows I wouldn't approve, thought Ottilie, finding Sylvie's situation far from satisfactory. Surely Sylvie would want a home, a husband and children. There was small consolation in her being a good violinist. She would be able to make some sort of living from her playing but as her parents were not rich, a wealthy marriage was out of the question.

'Oh, you're such a lucky person, Ottilie,' Sylvie would say, 'and soon you'll have everything. Money, a title and a good looking husband.'

Was Christopher good looking? She had never thought so. She hadn't been immediately struck, as she had with the man in the restaurant, by his good looks. Christopher had been kind to her. She had grown used to his face. She had welcomed it, especially after a bad day with her father. Christopher would be gentle. He'd make an inane remark that would make her laugh. They had become accustomed to one another. Ottilie conjured him into view with her fresh dispassionate eye. He was slim and of average height, had large round brown eyes set in a round face, and a short nose. His top lip was rather thin and the lower one fleshy. He had a well modulated voice, with perfect diction; the sort of voice that Ottilie – brought up in America's deep south and on movies where everyone with 'class' had an English accent – adored. When he had first walked in to her father's apartment – to finalise a property deal – and she had heard him speak, Ottilie had thought it fascinating. Now she found it stilted. Pretentious. Ottilie decided Christopher was presentable rather than good looking. And she could never say that about the stranger in the restaurant.

With a pang of horror Ottilie realised that she had never had the desire to kiss Christopher until she was out of breath, or the urge to have him crush her to him, feel her breasts, stroke her nipples, or open her legs to him. The mystery man, however, had made her instantly want to do all those things.

Ottilie remembered Christopher's chaste goodnight kisses. Thinking about it she realised Christopher did not seem bowled over by passion either. So why did he want to marry her? Ottilie was genuinely amazed by the amount of questions, thoughts and inner turmoil one torrid glance in a restaurant had thrown up.

Christopher was waiting in his car outside her exclusive apartment block when she arrived. He jumped out.

'Where the hell have you been, Ottilie?' he shouted.

'Minding my own business,' she replied haughtily.

'Your business is my business,' he said.

'Oh really? How do you work that one out?'

'Because you are my bride to be.'

'Christopher, didn't you put that the wrong way round?' she asked.

'What do you mean?'

'Shouldn't you have said, I was worried about you because you're my wife to be and I love you. Not "You're my business. You're my bride to be." '

'For God's sake Ottilie, stop quibbling. I've been sitting here for ages worrying, wondering what had happened to you and whether to call the police.'

'I was walking, thinking,' she said, putting her key in the main door lock and stepping into the inner courtyard. Christopher went to follow her in. She put out a foot. 'No, Christopher.'

'Darling, what's the matter?' he said, trying to be conciliatory. 'I'm sorry. I'm sorry if I laid down the law. Came on too heavy. I didn't mean to frighten you. It's just that being American you don't understand the ways of us – us English.'

'Perhaps I don't, Christopher,' she said. 'But I do know when I'm tired and I want to go to bed.'

'Ottilie, look we must talk.'

'Not now. Not tonight.'

'Yes.'

'No.'

'Sweetheart. Old girl . . .' Ottilie drew in an angry breath. Christopher noticed. 'Look what can I say? What can I do?'

'Go home, we'll talk tomorrow.'

'But I feel it's important we discuss things now.'

'You're pushing me Christopher.'

Christopher misinterpreted her words. He thought she was relenting and pushed a bit harder. He took her hand and kissed it. She drew it away quickly.

'Ottilie, darling. Please let me come in. Just for a moment. I don't want to leave you like this. You're angry . . .'

'Oh, you've realised!'

'I want to explain,' he said. 'Ottilie, let not the sun go down upon thine anger.'

'You're very poetic all of a sudden!'

'Not me, somebody else,' Christopher laughed. 'I wouldn't know a piece of poetry if it came up and hit me. At least only the bits I had to learn at school. And that's probably one of them. Ottilie . . .'

Ottilie, surprised by his sudden confession, felt sorry for him, removed her foot and let him in. They took the gilt, mirrored, and rickety cage, that was the nineteenth century's idea of a smart elevator, to the second floor.

Ottilie never failed to feel a sense of supreme satisfaction the moment she stepped on to the shiny parquet floor in the hallway of her home. The glowing colours in the wall hangings and in the Persian carpets welcomed her; the flowers, changed every other day by the maid, bade her hello.

'Do you want coffee, Christopher?' she asked.

'Please.'

'Veronique, Veronique.' Ottilie called for the maid but there was no reply. Angrily she threw her coat on to a nearby Louis quinze chair. 'Well, it'll have to be instant, it's Veronique's night off,' she said, thinking that if she'd remembered there was no way she would have allowed Christopher in the apartment.

Ottilie removed her shoes. She then lifted the lid of a nearby medieval carved sandalwood chest where a supply of slippers were kept. She took out her own monogrammed pair and handed Christopher his.

When he had first visited Ottilie's father to talk about finishing the land deal in England, Christopher had thought this an odd custom. There was no need for it in his vast draughty house with its threadbare carpets, but in Ottilie's apartment it was vitally necessary that the filth from the streets was kept out and the beautiful rugs were not damaged by unsuitable footwear.

Whilst Christopher undid his shoe-laces, Ottilie stalked along the corridor past the closed high double doors of the formal entertaining salons and through to her own section of the apartment.

She opened the door of her private sitting room which was decorated almost entirely in shades of blue. Even the white marble fireplace was blue veined. Looking at it Ottilie wondered whether to light the logs which were sitting in the heavy cast iron grate; the firelighters were ready to hand beside an old fashioned set of tongs, an iron poker, and a coal scuttle. She decided not to. The central heating was enough, soon she would be safely tucked up in her bed.

Waiting for Christopher to join her, dreading the on-coming conversation, Ottilie stood still, enjoying the room and its sense of calm. Pale blue tussure silk was fixed to padded panels on the walls. The woodwork and the ceiling were painted a French navy, with the small bows and curliques of the plasterwork picked out in gold leaf. The heavy, chambray-blue drapes, cascading along and around the long French windows, were patterned with large peacocks printed in their usual colour. The pre-Impressionist paintings carried on the blue theme. Most of them were sea-scapes, but some were of interiors with figures in blueish clothing. Displayed by itself in front of the gigantic mirrored overmantle was a beautiful fourteenth-century Persian vase decorated in low relief and covered with a monochrome blue glaze. The only variance to the blue theme was supplied by a small bookcase holding a variety of brightly coloured dust-jacketed new novels, and the Persian rug. The latter gave the room its real warmth. It was ten foot square and had lions and eagles and imaginary beasts fighting on a field of deepest rose whilst the flowered border was in a variety of blues. It was these blues that had been matched, brought out and shown off in the other fabrics in the room. Christopher came in closing the doors behind him.

'Take a seat, Christopher,' said Ottilie, pointing to a

deep blue-black velvet settee which balanced the shiny black of her Bechstein grand piano. 'I'll make your coffee.'

When she returned with the tray and the coffee she found Christopher had removed his jacket and was curled up comfortably with one of her books.

'There are some sexy bits in here,' he said, putting the book down as she approached.

'Are there? I haven't had a chance to read it yet,' she said, handing him his coffee which he immediately placed on the small table closest to him.

'Haven't you, well let me read some to you,' he said, picking up the book again.

'No, thank you, Christopher. You said you wanted to talk, so talk.'

'Darling girl . . .' he began.

'No, don't darling girl me. I'm tired, I want to go to bed . . .'

'With me . . . come to bed with me.'

'Christopher! How dare you suggest such a thing.'

'Ottilie, you are my fiancée, we are going to be married.'

'Well I don't know . . .' she said, hesitantly.

'What do you mean you don't know! You agreed. Your father agreed. You can't go backsliding now,' said Christopher, his voice raising to a near shout. He didn't want to lose her. Not because he loved her. But because she was his passport to riches.

'Christopher, it's my life you're talking about and if I don't think it's right I will take time to think about it.'

'It was right before so what's changed?' he asked, calming down.

'Me. I told you I needed time.'

'Ottilie, darling, look at me. I love you . . .'

'Do you?'

'You know I do.'

'No, Christopher, what I know is that you say you do. You see, how I figured it is this: if you really loved me, when I said I wanted time you'd give it me without hesitation.'

19

Christopher was silent. Sylvie's words were echoing in his ears. Ottilie found him and his silence irksome. Why didn't he say what he'd come to say and go. She stood up, walked over to the piano, opened it and began to play one of Chopin's Nocturnes.

'That's beautiful, Ottilie,' he said, joining her.

Christopher watched her playing thinking how sexy, almost erotic she looked as her long tapering fingers floated effortlessly across the piano keys. He wanted those fingers clasping his cock.

'Are you going to sing?' he asked.

'No,' she replied, shaking her head.

Her red curls parted and Christopher was made aware of the soft whiteness of the nape of her neck. He wanted to kiss it. He wanted to touch her. His mind darted down dark avenues of longing and desire. Aroused by Sylvie he had to come. He had to have Ottilie. He put his hands on her shoulders. Ottilie tensed, and flinched.

'What is the matter with you?' he asked. The thought occurred to him that she might be rejecting him. That was impossible. He was the leader in this situation. He had offered to marry her, make her Lady Christopher Furrel and give her a good solid English title, something that was hard to come by. There were a number of other heiresses in the world who would give their eye teeth to be his wife. Ottilie carried on playing and didn't answer him.

'I asked you what's the matter?' he said quietly, endeavouring to keep the irritation out of his voice.

'I told you, I'm tired,' she said.

Something in him snapped. Whilst she continued to play he took a step back and undid his flies. Then quickly he came up behind her, gripped her neck, and twisted her head up to his. He kissed her roughly, forcing her lips open so that he could stick his tongue in her mouth. Taken by surprise Ottilie gasped with horror. He shoved his hands down the front of her velvet dress, tearing it in the process, grabbed her breasts and pinched her

20

nipples. Ottilie shrieked. She loathed his touch. She hated his smell.

Protesting, flaying her hands in the air or on any part of his body that she could reach, Ottilie looked about the room wondering what she could do to stop him molesting her. Her eyes fell on the vase. Could she really hit him with one of her father's most prized possessions? That brief moment of inattention allowed Christopher time to pull her off the piano stool and on to the floor. She kicked and scratched and hit and bit and he kept pulling at her clothing, tearing it, trying desperately to manoeuvre himself between her legs whilst keeping his lips firmly planted over hers. Ottilie felt as if she was fighting for her life. This man was not going to get the better of her.

'No,' she hissed, managing to turn her head away from his. 'No, Christopher stop it. No, DON'T.'

'I've waited and waited for you,' he said, holding her down with his legs. 'Now rich bitch I'm going to fuck you whether you like it or not.'

'You are not,' she screamed. 'Stop it. Go now Christopher and we'll pretend this hasn't happened.'

But Christopher was inflamed and angry. He pulled his prick out, forced her skirt up and tore at her pantyhose. She was twisting and turning. She felt his hot stiff member against the flesh at the top of her thighs. He ripped at her tights again, making a gash from waist to thigh. His fingers were pulling and plucking at the silk of her neat, tiny bikini panties. He touched her between her legs. He touched her warm hidden outer lips that had been damp when thinking of the stranger but were now closed and dry.

'No,' she screamed, every part of her utterly repelled by him and his actions. 'No, no, no. I don't want you.'

'You'll take it,' he said, holding his cock, and rubbing it whilst adjusting his position on top of her.

For the first time in her secluded life Ottilie saw a live, erect and engorged penis; about five inches of upright throbbing flesh. Was that it? She thought. Was that the

21

thing he thought he was going to force inside her? No way, she decided. No way. Thoughts tumbled over themselves as she tried to remember what she should do in this situation. Kick him. But first she had to get her legs and feet into the position to be able to do that. She squirmed away from him, closed her legs as best she could and laughed derisively.

Her laughter was such a surprise that Christopher immediately lost his hard-on. In fury he slapped her face, ripped her dress from top to bottom, and squeezed her breasts hard, hurting her. In trying to keep her still he bit her nipples with his teeth. Her stinging skin and painful nipples did not put her off her objective. She quickly brought a leg up and kneed him in the groin. He doubled up, though more with humiliation than pain.

'When I say No, Christopher, I mean No,' she said, rapidly rolling away from him towards the fireplace. She grabbed hold of the poker. 'If you come near me again, I swear, I'll swing for you,' she said, menacingly.

Christopher stared at her. Angry and dishevelled, her bolero still covering her shoulders but her velvet dress torn hanging in strips from her body, her pert, full breasts half in and half out of her brassière, he thought she looked even more desirable. He took one step towards her. She brandished the poker.

'I mean it, Christopher,' she said. 'I'll kill you.'

'Now look here old girl . . .'

'Don't "old girl" me. Just get out. Get out,' she screamed. 'I never, ever, want to see you again.'

Then the door opened and Veronique came in.

'Throw him out, Veronique,' cried Ottilie with tears of relief streaming down her face at the sight of her short squat, and hefty maid. 'Throw him out. And never let him come in here again.'

Christopher looked at the two women and knew when he was beaten. Ottilie was standing with an iron poker pointing at him and the maid, her arms akimbo, was ready to charge. Shamefacedly he adjusted his clothing grabbed his jacket and fled the room. Veronique ran after him. He snatched up his shoes on the way and sped out of the apartment. Veronique closed the door firmly behind him.

When she returned to the sitting room Ottilie was collapsed in a sobbing heap on the floor.

'Mam'selle Ottilie, Oh Mam'selle . . .' cried Veronique rushing over to her young mistress.

'It's all right, Veronique . . . I'm all right. Really. It was just such a shock.'

'Your father always he tell you, no man in the house unless we are here.'

'I know. I know. I forgot it was your night off.'

'*Merde!* Is a good thing the film ends early,' said the maid. 'Come, *ma petite*, go to bed. I will make you something nice for to sleep. What you want, eh?'

'Hot chocolate,' said Ottilie.

'What, no wine, no whisky, no cognac?'

'No, something warm and sweet and hot and soothing.'

'Okay you go to bed . . .'

Veronique put the poker back in its proper place then helped Ottilie to her feet.

'No first I'll take a bath and Veronique, take these clothes and burn them, they are unclean, soiled and revolting,' said Ottilie. She ripped the remnants of her beautiful dress and bolero, her finely embroidered silk brassière, her neat panties, and her damaged panty-hose from her body and flung them in a heap on the floor. 'I don't want to be reminded of this night.'

'Yes, Mam'selle,' said Veronique picking up the offending articles. 'And I'll bring you some special chocolate. The real thing from Martinique, my son he sent it to me.'

Waddling into the kitchen Veronique thought that her young mistress had learnt a useful lesson. Never be alone with a man unless you intend going to bed with him. She had never liked Lord Christopher. She didn't trust him. And she'd said so to her late master.

'I agree with you. I, also, don't think he's all he's

23

cracked up to be,' Bernard had said. 'But a certain way to make sure she runs to his arms and clings to him is to voice my feelings.' Bernard was thinking of his sister, Liliane. Perhaps she wouldn't have married Frank if he'd kept quiet. 'You keep an eye on Lord Christopher for me, Veronique,' he'd said. And she did.

Lord Christopher knew the butler had gone on holiday. And a couple of days before he had asked Veronique which was her night off. He had done it cleverly. Made it seem as if he thought she worked too much and too hard. But Veronique's antennae had been working; she had sensed he was up to something. That's when she decided to see a short cartoon instead of a major feature length film and get home early.

Ottilie lay in her bath a long time in a desperate effort to cleanse the memory of Christopher from her mind and his touch from her body. She gazed unseeing at the mosaic fish swimming through their static sea-scape along the walls and across the ceiling, trying to understand why he should have attempted to seduce her in such a brutal fashion. But she could make no sense of it. Eventually she was disturbed by a worried Veronique banging on the door.

'It's okay, Veronique, I'm coming out now,' Ottilie shouted. She grabbed a huge white bath towel and swathed herself in it then padded across the thick white fitted carpets of her walk-in wardrobe through to her white-walled, and white-curtained bedroom.

From her seventeenth-century carved chest she took out a pale lemon silk and lace night-dress, still wrapped in its shop tissue. She slipped it over her freshly bathed and scented body. She climbed into her high four poster bed, which was elaborately curtained in the heaviest white silk with sprigs of roses embroidered on it. Then she realised what she had done instinctively. She had put on something brand new. She climbed out of her bed, walked through into her wardrobe and threw every article of clothing that she had ever worn with Christopher or that he had ever seen, on the floor. Suits,

24

skirts, frocks, cocktail dresses, blouses, ballgowns, and her entire underwear draw was tipped out.

Veronique came in with the hot chocolate and was surprised by the sight that met her eyes.

'Burn the lot,' said Ottilie.

'Oh Mam'selle, no,' she said aghast at the sight of some of the finest most beautiful clothes in France lying in a messy heap on the floor. 'Please not burnt. Let me give them to charity.'

'Very well, but I don't want to see any of them ever again.'

Ottilie slowly sipped her drink whilst Veronique collected some carrier bags and unceremoniously shoved Ottilie's clothing into them. Then she tidied up the bathroom, taking the used towels away and hanging out fresh ones.

'Veronique, first thing in the morning I want you to go out and buy me a new underwear set and a jogging suit, get it from the first place you come to, I don't care what, just so that I've something real fresh to put on.'

'Yes, Mam'selle,' said Veronique, taking the francs that Ottilie handed to her. 'That's all, goodnight, Veronique.'

'Goodnight, Mam'selle,' said Veronique.

Ottilie settled down between the sweet smelling, freshly laundered, pristine white, Egyptian cotton sheets and Veronique turned off the lights and carried away the bags of clothing.

It took some time for sleep to come. Her mind was a jumble of thoughts and emotions. What was she going to do now? She felt her engagement ring. She couldn't even give it back to him. It hadn't been his to give. It had been her mother's. She twisted it round and around the third finger of her left hand. Christopher said he was getting one made for her at his jewellers in Regent Street, London. But could she believe him?

What was happening to her? She was doubting everything. She had reason to doubt Christopher's sexual gentlemanliness, but his honesty as well? Nevertheless

25

she now thought it odd. Surely he should have come prepared with a ring when he had asked for her hand in marriage? Why hadn't her father said anything? She supposed he had thought she was an adult and capable of making her own decisions even if they were wrong.

Ottilie thought back to the start of the evening and the mystery man in the restaurant. She had been mentally retreating from Christopher before she had seen him. But that one look, that highly charged glance had in one moment broken her engagement. And the realisation made her happy. Excited. She was suddenly free. What was she going to do with her freedom? Sing? She would ring her old agent and talk about the possibility of performances. She would have to do that first thing in the morning. No. First thing telephone Sylvie, tell her what had happened with Christopher. And then there was the reading of the will.

Ottilie put her hands down between her legs. She held herself for comfort. Thinking of the stranger and wondering if they would ever meet again, Ottilie drifted into a dreamless sleep.

Chapter 2

Ottilie's mystery man in the restaurant was Count Helmut von Straffen and he had first seen her at her father's funeral. Knowing he was going to be in Europe, her half brother, Elmer Planchet, had asked Helmut to attend on his behalf. Helmut had gone out of curiosity.

'I'd like to know the old buzzard is dead for real,' Elmer had said. 'And check out my half sister, she got herself engaged to an English Lord. She used to be a quiet, plain-Jane skinny redhead. God knows what she's like now. But she's her father's daughter so she could still be plain, but by now also an A1 pain in the butt. However, miracles do happen!'

It had been a simple service and Helmut had stayed close to the back of the church without letting anyone know who he was or why he was there. Everyone assumed he was part of Bernard Duvier's life: they all knew that he had kept it well compartmentalised. Helmut had got a shock when he saw the beautiful girl that followed the cortège down the aisle. She had the carriage and the elegance that he admired. She had his favourite and most glorious Titian red hair. She had the silky soft skin he loved to touch. She had the beauty that he wanted to possess but he dismissed her from his thoughts. Helmut had other things on his mind.

27

Helmut left the church quickly managing to avoid the other people and thence their questions, which might have been awkward. He went back to his cousin's house where he was staying. His visit was proving more enjoyable, and consequently longer, than he had anticipated. His plan had been two days in Paris and then on to his old schloss in the heart of Bavaria. However, his cousin, Isolde, had provided him with some unexpected entertainment.

Isolde and her husband, Jacques Marnier, had been married for six months. No one thought it would last that long. The twenty-five-year-old Isolde had married the old Frenchman for his money. They had wed on his deathbed, but much to everyone's surprise, and within hours of the ceremony, he had perked up considerably and decided not to die.

'You've made some excellent changes here,' Helmut said to Isolde on his first evening in Paris since her wedding. They were enjoying a late cognac whilst sitting in comfortable easy chairs either side of the high marble fireplace in the sumptuous cream and gold drawing room of Jacques Marnier's double-fronted, detached, town house in the Marais. Both were dressed for bed. Helmut was wearing maroon pyjamas of the finest lawn, a maroon silk dressing gown with quilted lapels and cuffs, and velvet monogrammed slippers. Isolde was wearing a pale pink silk negligée over a dark pink silk night-dress, and was barefoot. Helmut thought she looked charming, serene and happy. She also looked sensual, but her sensuality was not overwhelming, or too obvious.

'Yes,' she said, smiling enigmatically.

'Gone those dreary dark greens and browns,' he said looking around the room. 'But Jacques has never been known to spend money, so how did you manage it?'

'With subterfuge,' she answered, pouring him another brandy.

'And he's looking very well,' said Helmut. 'I think you've given him a new lease of life.'

28

'Could be,' said Isolde, smiling softly.

'And you don't look too bad either . . .'

He looked at her searchingly. Isolde had always been beautiful in a simple cuddly way. She was too short to have the model-like elegance that was fashionable but her figure went in and out in all the right places, with everything in proportion. She had the family eyes – ice, ice blue – but not the blonde hair; hers tumbled down in large black curls. She had very pale skin and an oval face with a short retrousée nose and a full mouth. However, there was a change in her that he couldn't quite place; an ease of movement and expression that suggested a freed sexuality. Surely her old husband had not managed to bring it about.

'Thank you Helmut . . .,' said Isolde, thinking he had been staring at her long enough.

'You must tell me your secret,' he said.

Isolde laughed a sweet tinkley laugh.

'Why?' she asked.

'So when I'm in my eighties I'll make sure I get the same treatment.'

'I'm sorry Helmut, I couldn't possibly tell you,' Isolde replied.

'Why not?' he asked.

'You're far too much of a prude,' she said.

'What!' Helmut exclaimed. The cousins had been close as children but had drifted apart. Her comment revealed how apart they were. The idea of him being a prude! That he thought was quite laughable. 'Isolde, I promise you I'm not a prude and I'd really like to know.'

'Well . . .' she began and then hesitated.

'Please tell me.'

'It's quite simple really. I put him to bed with a night-cap. Jacques and I don't share a bedroom but I always do that. And sometimes he has a very special night-cap. In fact, he's having one tonight. I shall be giving it to him very soon. But first I must wait for the door.'

'Why?' asked Helmut, intrigued.

'You'll see,' she replied mysteriously. And then the doorbell rang.

29

'Won't the maid get it?' asked Helmut as Isolde went to answer it.

'No,' she said.

Moments later Isolde returned with two handsome, very blonde young men. They were dressed identically in tight black leather trousers, which emphasised their genitalia, and leather jackets. Neither wore a shirt but they did wear long fine handmade black leather gauntlets.

'This is Fritz and Heini,' said Isolde. The men gave a short bow. 'Now we go upstairs. Come with us Helmut.'

Helmut was completely mystified. What did his strictly brought up, somewhat reserved cousin have planned? He eyed the two men as they swaggered sexily up the grand staircase. Was she going to screw them? Surely not.

The four of them made their way along a corridor to Isolde's exotic tent-like bedroom. The ceiling was completely covered in deep pleats of light grey silk gathered into the centre and held in place with a cut glass chandelier. Three of the walls were covered in the same light grey silk, but more finely pleated and fixed on to panels. The pleats met at the dado. Where the walls joined the ceiling there was a frieze of a wavy valance of silk in the deeper grey. The wall opposite the bed was one huge mirror with the darker grey silk cascading and looping down either side of it.

Isolde flung open the door and disturbed the pretty plump young maid who was turning down the heavy dark grey comforter on her mistress's high double bed.

'Ah Monique, you are late doing that. I thought I asked for it to be done half an hour ago.' said Isolde, severely.

'I'm sorry Madame,' said the maid, turning to her mistress and bobbing a curtsey. That was when Helmut noticed that the maid's breasts were bulging out of her black satin uniform.

'Monique, you have put on the wrong uniform again.'

'No, madame, I haven't madame,' said the maid.

'I think you have. Look at you, this one is far too small.'

'Sorry madame, it won't happen again, madame,' said the maid contritely.

'It most certainly won't. You are a disgrace girl, a disgrace. What would the master say if he could see you?'

'I don't know madame.'

'You don't know! I know. He'd say "spank her bottom." '

'No madame, no . . .'

'Yes he would. He'd say bend her over and lift her skirt, pull down her panties and spank her bare bottom.'

'Please don't tell him madame, please I beg you.'

'Very well, if Fritz can cover your breasts so that you are decent I won't tell him. Fritz . . .'

Fritz went over to Monique and clasped either side of the fabric and pulled. In pulling the fabric it tore and Monique's large breasts were left completely bare.

'Oh, madame, he's torn my uniform,' said the maid, her lips quivering and quickly crossing her arms in an effort to hide her nakedness.

'So I see. Monique we really can't have this . . .'

'No, madame.'

'Standing there in front of these men showing your breasts to the world. How disgraceful! And such big tits for such a young woman.'

'No, madame, no they're not,' whimpered the maid.

'Are you arguing with me, Monique?'

'No, madame.'

'Then take your arms away and let us see,' said Isolde.

'No, madame, no . . .'

'Are you refusing to obey me?'

'Yes, madame,' said the maid, moving her hands and squeezing her nipples as if she was exciting herself.

'Fritz, take her arms down and hold them by her side,' commanded Isolde.

Fritz grabbed the maid's hands and held them tightly behind her back. Helmut found himself with an immediate erection as Monique stood with her shoulders braced

31

against Fritz's chest, her large breasts bare and inviting, her rounded belly jutting forwards, her legs parted and slightly back and her black satin skirt rising up her legs. Helmut could see naked flesh above her stocking tops and . . . Helmut looked more intently. She wasn't wearing any panties. He could see the tight dark little curls surrounding her pussy. Helmut found that brief glimpse exciting, erotic. And he felt an instant desire to begin fingering her.

'I say those are large breasts and they need to be felt,' said Isolde, interrupting Helmut's salacious thoughts.

'No madame, no . . .'

'Heini,' Isolde went over to the other man and stroked him between his legs. She felt his cock rise instantly. She rubbed him through his leathers. 'I think this naughty little maid is asking to have her tits touched, don't you?'

'Yes, madame,' said Heini, hardening as a result of Isolde's expertise.

'Then I give you permission.'

Heini immediately sauntered over to the held girl and with his black leather-gauntleted hands began fondling her big breasts. Helmut noticed Monique slithering her hips licentiously against the leather of Fritz's trousers. Then he heard a zip being taken down. Helmut moved slightly to get a better view. The maid had put her hands inside Fritz's flies and was playing with his prick.

'Madame, I can feel a stiff cock.'

'Nonsense girl.'

'I can madame, it's very stiff.'

'Let me see.'

Isolde moved and looked between Fritz and Monique. Monique eased Fritz's large pink prick and balls out of their tight black leather casing. She ringed it with her fingers and slowly began to caress it.

'Oh! Not only is it very stiff, it's very large,' said Isolde.

Before she could say anything else there was the sound of another zip being taken down. Heini pulled his prick free from his leather trousers and began rubbing it

32

against the slinky black satin of the girl's uniform. Isolde put a hand over her mouth in surprise.

'You see what you have done by your outrageous behaviour,' said Isolde. 'You have incited these two innocent young men to feel you and stroke their cocks against your body. I will have to tell the master.'

'No madame, please . . .'

'And who taught you to do that?' asked Isolde, watching Monique's hands sliding up and down on Fritz's prick.

'Do what, madame?'

'Play with a man's cock like that?'

'The master, madame,' said the maid sweetly.

'The master!' exclaimed Isolde.

'Yes, madame, he likes me to put my hand under the bedclothes and find his prick and play with it.'

'I see and when do you do that?'

'Every night madame,' said the maid. 'Every night after you've gone to bed.'

'So, my naughty husband makes you play with his dick does he?'

'Yes, madame.'

Isolde put out a hand and ran it along Heini's leg and up round his balls and then she took hold of his long firm upstanding prick.

'Well now two can play at that game. I wonder what he would say if he could see me playing with somebody else's cock.' Isolde rubbed Heini's penis with a deftness that rapidly increased his hard-on. 'And what else do you do for the master after I've gone to bed?'

'I suck him, madame,' said the maid.

'You suck him!' said Isolde.

'Yes, madame, I suck his cock,' said the maid, triumphantly.

'You are lying,' said Isolde.

'No, I'm not, madame,' said Monique. 'I pull back the bedclothes and I take his prick and put it in my mouth and suck . . . just like this . . .'

Monique bent down, opened her mouth and placed

33

Fritz's prick between her lips and then let her head move up and down slowly encompassing his entire member.

'I think you should be punished for performing such a disgraceful act,' said Isolde, still playing with Heini's cock. 'I think I will have to spank you.'

'No, madame, please, don't do that,' cried Monique.

'You can have one more chance. Let me see if your stocking seams are straight. Monique bend over.'

Monique bent over. Her seams were perfectly straight but as she bent down her short skirt rose up revealing her bare bottom.

'You are not wearing any panties!' exclaimed Isolde.

'No, madame, I'm sorry madame. I was in such a hurry I forgot to put them on.'

'Your sex is easily accessible.'

'Yes, madame.'

And to prove Isolde's point Fritz clasped hungrily at her big pink luscious bum, his black leather gloved hand digging harshly into her flesh. And Heini put a gloved finger on her wet sex trailing its specially sewn hard ridges along the wanton lips of her vulva.

'There you see, easily accessible,' said Isolde. 'Do you really want me to tell the master that I found you in my bedroom with your tits hanging out, no panties on and a couple of men touching you up.'

'No, madame.'

'Monique, you know the rules. You must always wear your knickers. An infringement such as this deserves punishment. You leave me no alternative. I will have to tell the master.'

'I won't do it again,' said Monique. 'I promise. But please don't tell him. I will do anything you want but don't tell the master.

'So you will do anything I want, eh?'

'Yes, madame,' said the maid.

'In that case ...' Isolde looked straight at Helmut, noticing his very large bulge. 'We have a guest staying with us, I think perhaps he should have the pleasure of punishing you.'

Isolde took a small whip from a cabinet beside the bed and handed it to Helmut.

'I think she deserves twelve on that big fleshy rump of hers.'

Helmut was delighted by the sudden turn of events. He took the whip and with practised skill, trailed it lovingly over Monique's raised and expectant flanks. With care he let it linger along the crease between her cheeks. Monique took a deep breath. She was waiting for the stripes.

'Twelve, Helmut,' said Isolde.

The maid felt a searing flash of pain. She moaned. The next stripe heightened the pain. She moaned louder. With the third and fourth stripe and the criss-crossing of the welts, pain turned into exquisite pleasure. Her sensitised body was tingling. Just before the last stripe Helmut touched her clitoris and her entire body heaved and every nerve ending throbbed. She longed for the next blow and when it hit, blazing fast and hard, Monique writhed and came, collapsing on to the floor.

'What do you say, Monique?'

'Thank you, madame, thank you, sir,' said Monique.

Isolde took the whip from Helmut and threw it on the floor.

'Monique, you will stay here until I return,' commanded Isolde. 'I will leave Fritz and Heini with you. They will make sure you don't leave the room. And do not allow them to touch you. If they do I will know and you will receive further punishment for your transgression.'

'Yes, madame, thank you, madame,' said Monique, giving another little curtsey.

'Come with me Helmut,' said Isolde. With Helmut following behind her she strode out of her seductive boudoir to the masculine oak-panelled room next door. And there was Jacques sitting up in his high bed his hands moving rapidly beneath the bedclothes.

'I like that girl,' said Jacques, as they entered. He was pointing at the opposite wall. Helmut turned and saw a complete view of the room they had just left. 'That Monique, she's got good tits.' Then he saw Helmut. 'It's a two way mirror,' he explained, adding, 'and you looked as if you were enjoying yourself, Helmut.'

'I was.'

'Well, as you can see your little cousin has been most inventive. It is her inventiveness that has kept me going. Now look at that.'

Helmut turned back to the wall mirror and watched as Fritz knelt over Monique and began to stroke her whip marks with his prick.

'Now that is a good size,' said Jacques, with approval. 'Do you like that one my dear?'

'Yes,' she replied, indicating to Helmut to sit beside her on the long velvet stool at the end of Jacques's bed.

Fritz then pulled Monique to her feet, stood behind her, lifted her skirt up round her waist, tucked the hem into her little apron so that her naked sex was clearly visible and then, with both of them still standing, pushed his prick between her thighs letting it rub backwards and forwards so that anyone watching could see the tip of his cock emerging and retreating, emerging and retreating. Then he began again to play with her breasts. Meanwhile Heini took off his clothes, stood beside Monique, his long prick erect, and she languidly caressed it.

'Well my dear now which one do you prefer?' asked Jacques.

'I don't know yet,' Isolde replied. 'Let's see their performance.'

Intent on watching the three in the other room Helmut's cock had pushed up through his pyjamas and was also standing erect and throbbing. Isolde gave a cat-like smile as she glanced down. She parted her negligée, pulled her night-dress up above her knees and spread her plump white legs. Helmut swallowed hard.

'Jacques enjoys his night-cap,' she said, letting her fingers wander until she had found the gap in his pyjamas. Lightly, and without moving her body so that Jacques

36

could not see what she was doing, Isolde began to stroke Helmut's manhood.

Fritz kissed Monique's neck and tweaked her nipples. Monique was moving her hips round and round in small circles against Fritz's cock. Heini turned and knelt down in front of Monique whose legs were now splayed open. Playing with his own penis he started to lick Monique's pussy. Big licks, so that every movement was taken in and assessed by the onlookers.

Isolde was squirming. Helmut slowly began to stroke her rounded white thighs.

Fritz put one gloved hand down, lifted the hood of Monique's sex exposing her protruding clitoris and rubbed that delicate and excited little point whilst Heini pushed his tongue deeper and deeper into her love channel. At Fritz's touch the maid thrust her hips forward, putting her hands behind her back under her bottom, making her hips jut further forward for Heini's probing tongue. She held Fritz's cock. He then fell backwards on to the bed pulling her with him.

Heini came up between her legs, grabbed her ankles and lifted them high. The whole of her swollen sex was wide open. Fritz's hand was once again relishing the pleasures of Monique's tiny shuddery abandoned movements as he grazed the source of her pleasure with the raised seams of his glove. Softly and gently he moved that finger from side to side, heightening Monique's pleasure. She raised her hips, and her legs went rigid. Heini bent down. She rested the back of her knees on his shoulders. Fritz edged another finger into the warm wet folds of her vagina. Heini re-adjusted his own position so that he was kneeling with his cock poised at the entrance to Monique's sex. Monique was twisting and turning, raising and lowering her hips. Heini slowly introduced his cock into her juicy pink wetness. Monique took a deep breath and waited, rigid with anticipation. With one hard shove Heini thrust into her and Fritz fondled her breasts, his cock gliding up and down along her back, close to the crack of her bottom.

Isolde clasped the whole of Helmut's cock and slowly but firmly began to rub, up and down, up and down. Helmut sighed. She turned her head to look at her husband and saw that he had gone to sleep with a smile of satisfaction on his face.

'And now?' asked Helmut.

'Oh Jacques always falls asleep at this point.'

'And them?' said Helmut, jerking his head towards the threesome in the mirror.

'They get paid for having a good screw,' she said.

'And what do you get?'

'A satisfied husband,' she replied, 'who will leave me all his money.'

'You mean you don't screw any of them?' said Helmut.

'Certainly not,' she said. 'They are our entertainment, our actors, we are the audience.'

'But you'll fuck me?' he said, his fingers had found her soft moist sex lips and he was squeezing their outer rim.

'Yes, you're different, you're audience too.'

'And you don't mind screwing at the end of his bed?'

'No, he won't wake up. And if he does he'll think he's having a wonderful dream.'

Isolde slid on to the floor and lay there with her legs wide open, touching herself.

'So, fuck me,' she said.

Helmut knelt down between her legs and slowly let his cock trail along her thighs. Isolde gasped. He touched her clitoris with one finger. Isolde clenched her buttocks, raising them high, inviting him to enter her. Helmut put the tip of his prick at her warm wet inviting sex and gave a couple of tiny movements, enough to tease her but not to penetrate.

'Oh please, please fuck me,' begged Isolde.

Helmut pushed again at the entrance to Isolde's sex. She opened at his touch. He slid in slowly, very slowly and she took his large cock that was stiff and wanting her. With a gentle rhythm he rode her and then he caught sight of the three in the mirror.

Fritz was lying on the floor on his back. Monique was bending over him sucking his cock while Heini was taking Monique from behind. The sight of this made Helmut thrust with force into Isolde's writhing body. He rode her as fast and as hard as he could.

Later, after they had come and when Monique and Fritz and Heini had gone, Isolde took Helmut into bed with her.

'I must know how you managed it, Isolde,' said Helmut, curling up beside her and holding her breasts.

'Manage what?'

'Everything,' said Helmut.

'It all began when I was staying here last year with his granddaughter. I knew that Jacques had taken a fancy to me, so after she went home I stayed on in Paris and visited him from time to time. Oh all above board. I played chess with him actually. And backgammon, and read him the classics, especially the novels of Balzac. Then it came time for me to go back to Germany, and he begged me not to. He said he'd got used to my visits, liked having me around, and would I marry him. I was quite shocked. I mean, I had a boyfriend, actually still have but that's neither here nor there. Anyhow, Jacques said he didn't expect me to go to bed with him, just carry on looking pretty and reading to him and of course keep playing backgammon and chess. And if I did that he'd make me a very rich woman. I fancied the idea of being a very rich woman, so I said yes.'

'How very sensible of you,' said Helmut.

'But I also said if I was going to live here he'd have to do something about the dreary old decor. Visiting, I said was one thing, living with it every day was quite another. He didn't like that. Told me to wait until he was dead before I started changing things. I said no. We had quite an argument and I said if that was his attitude he could call off the marriage and I stormed out.

'Well I came back. I had to, I'd let my own apartment. I went upstairs to my bedroom and as I passed his door I heard voices. His and a woman's. So I peeped in. And there was Monique sitting on his bed.

'Monique!'

'Yes, Monique. She's worked here for a couple of years you know.'

'What was she doing?' asked Helmut.

'Telling him a bedtime story, only this was one with a difference.'

'What sort of a difference?'

'Don't be so impatient Helmut . . . I'm coming to that . . . She was sitting beside him with the buttons of her blouse undone, her breasts spilling out and . . .'

'What was he doing to her?'

'Nothing. Just listening to her . . .'

'He wasn't touching her?'

'No.'

'What was she saying?'

'She was telling him that she had a couple of friends called Fritz and Heini and how she liked to screw both of them together.'

Helmut felt himself rising again and lifted Isolde's night-dress up so that he could press his cock into the small of her back. Isolde changed her voice so it sounded like Monique's Parisian twang.

' "I'll be sitting between them at the table having dinner," she said, "and then one of them will begin stroking my legs. Then the other one will start doing the same thing. I never knows which one is going to start, it changes each time. Of course, I don't have any panties on. Then one of them will reach my pussy and slide his finger up and down, making it really wet and open. The other one'll take his trousers off. I'll be well horny 'cos the one that's playing with my pussy will be driving me mad going backwards and forwards on my clit but he won't go any further, he won't shove it up, 'cos he knows I'll get well out of my brain if he keeps on teasing me. Then the one what's taken his clothes off stands behind me, puts his hands down my blouse and starts playing with my tits. Then the one fingering me stops and takes off his trousers. Starkers, he slides under the table, letting his prick rub against my ankles, ever so sexy that is, and he begins licking my pussy. And I go crazy with the feel of his tongue, start squirming and writhing all over the place 'specially when he nibbles at my clit. Then the one playing with my tits turns my head and tells me to suck his cock. I opens my mouth and takes it . . ." Monique put her thumb in her mouth and made sucking noises. Then she lifted her skirt and rolled over so that she was lying across Jacques's knees with her bare bottom in the air. "You deserve a good spanking," said Jacques, and he began to pat her buttocks . . .' Isolde stopped suddenly.

'What's the matter?' asked Helmut, his own fingers now playing with Isolde's clitoris.

'Nothing, that's it.'

'What do you mean, that's it!'

'I walked away.'

'You walked away!'

'Yes,' said Isolde, squirming on Helmut's finger, and putting her hands behind her back so that she could clasp Helmut's cock that was pressing large and firm against her spine. 'But don't you stop . . .'

'Why did you do that?' asked Helmut, slowly allowing his fingers to enter Isolde's wet and willing sex.

'Because I saw that Jacques was very excited. And that gave me an idea.'

'And what was that?'

'If Jacques liked hearing about it maybe he'd really like to watch it. So next morning after breakfast I asked Monique if she had any boyfriends. She looked at me in surprise. I'd never taken much interest in any of the servants, didn't enquire about their lives, just told them what I wanted done and they did it. She told me that she had, and then confessed to having two. "Two," I said, "that's greedy isn't it?" She agreed and said that she couldn't choose between them and they didn't mind sharing her. "Sharing!" I exclaimed. "Do you mean you screw both of them?" "Yes," she said. "Not together surely," I said, "Yes," she said. "It's wonderful. I love it." And then I told her I had seen and heard her with

41

Jacques the night before. She didn't turn a hair. "Oh," was all she said. That's when I put my proposition to her. Would she like to bring her two men here and screw them both in front of Jacques. This was a couple of days before the wedding. "Not all the time," I said. "I'd like you to do it on our wedding night. My present to Jacques. Name your price," I said, "and I'll pay." She said she'd have to have a word with the boys. I said, "Okay." '

'So what happened then?' asked Helmut, sliding his prick between Isolde's thighs whilst flicking her stiff aroused little clitoris with the tip of his fingers. 'Did you tell Jacques?'

'No,' said Isolde, 'but what I did say was if I gave him the most marvellous present in the world for our wedding would he get the decorators in.'

'Did he agree?'

'He said, if he thought it was the most marvellous present that was a deal.'

'And then,' said Helmut, his cock gently touching Isolde's swollen and succulent sex lips, exciting her so that she pushed down trying to draw his penis up inside, but he withdrew, and let it lie between the tops of her thighs.

'After the wedding he was very tired. I put him to bed. "Where's my present?" he asked. "It's coming," I said, "just wait a minute and don't go to sleep. First Monique wants to see you. Now, I've got some things to do so I'll leave you with her for a while." I didn't want him to get a hint of what I was up to, or let him know that I'd seen him with Monique. I waited behind the door with Fritz and Heini, and Monique went in. I heard her say that she'd come to give him his bedtime story. Then she sat on his bed, and started telling him the same story ... "I will be sitting between them at the table having dinner and then one of them will begin stroking my legs ... Only Monsieur Jacques tonight I'm going to show you ..." She slid off the bed and sat on the stool by the card table. "Sit up higher Monsieur Jacques," she

42

said, "otherwise you can't see." And then Fritz and Heini walked in in their leathers and sat beside her at the table. She continued talking. And they did exactly what she was saying. First Fritz stroked her legs. Then Heini. "Can you see Monsieur Jacques?" she said. "I'm opening my legs wide because Fritz wants to play with my pussy. He's putting a finger on my clit and he's rubbing it" And while she said that Heini stood up and took off his trousers. Then he stood beside Monique as naked as the day that he was born with a huge hard-on. "Remember what I told you Monsieur – how the other one came up behind me and put his hands down my blouse . . ." Heini came up behind her and put his hands down her blouse, fondled her breasts and rubbed his cock against her back.

'Jacques was sitting bolt upright in his bed and staring unbelievingly at the tableau in front of him. I watched his hands go under the bedclothes.

'Fritz stood up and took off his trousers and slid under the table.

' "I've opened my legs really wide now Monsieur because Fritz is going to suck my pussy. He's going to stick his tongue in and wiggle it around . . ."

'Then Heini turned Monique's head. "Suck my cock," he said.

' "Monsieur," said Monique. "I'm going to open my mouth and suck Heini's cock whilst Fritz carries on sucking me. Can you see what I'm doing Monsieur?"

'Jacques could see very well what she was doing and his hands were moving rapidly beneath the sheets. Monique opened her mouth wide and clamped it close over Heini's manhood. Her head went up and down on his prick. Her hips went up and down as Fritz probed and slurped noisily at her wanton sex.'

'Then what?' asked Helmut, putting one of Isolde's legs up over one of his, opening her swollen wetness with his hands and placing his penis just inside her sex lips.

'Heini lifted Monique off the stool and told her to

crouch on the floor with her shoulders down and her arse up. Then he came up behind her between her legs, grabbed her hips and went straight up her arse.'

Isolde jerked, her voice suddenly rising with the last words as Helmut suddenly thrust into her vulva.

'Carry on telling me,' said Helmut, holding back the leg that was over his leg so that he could penetrate her deeper.

'Fritz came over and lay in front of her presenting his cock to her mouth. After a while the two men changed places. And that's when I walked in. Jacques didn't see me because he had his eyes closed and was wanking himself into ecstasy.

' "Jacques," I said, the moment I saw him relax. "Jacques . . ."

' "Yes," he said, confused, looking beyond me to the three screwing on the floor.

' "Jacques, are you enjoying my wedding present?" I asked.

' "That is your present to me?" he said smiling.

' "Yes," I said, "and don't you think it's marvellous?"

' "Oh yes," he said, watching the three of them writhing and grunting, groaning and sighing and coming on the floor.

' "So now I can have the decorators in?"

' "Definitely," he said.

' "Good," I said, "because what I think would be an excellent idea is if we had that whole wall opposite your bed made into a two way mirror and then we could get them back another time without it bothering you."

' "You're a very clever girl," he said.'

'Oh yes you are,' said Helmut, jerking hard but leisurely into her. 'You're also a damned good screw.'

'I know,' she said, opening and closing her muscles around his penis as Helmut began thrusting faster and faster. 'And so every other day or so Monique gets her friends in and we give Jacques a little performance. Of course we change it. Give him a bit of variety. Monique has an English friend. Daisy. She wants to be a biochemist but they've cut her grant. So she came over here to make some money doing escort work. I pay her to come in from time to time.'

'What's she like?' asked Helmut.

'Beautiful, more like a model than a would-be scientist. Tall and blonde . . .'

'What happens then?'

'Oh, different things . . .'

'How different?'

'We use the sex toys.'

'When's she coming over?' asked Helmut, pounding harder and faster into Isolde at the thought of more sex.

'You'd like to take part in that, wouldn't you Helmut?' said Isolde, twisting her body round so that both her legs lay across Helmut's hips and she could start playing with her own clitoris.

'Very much,' said Helmut.

'In that case I'll have to see what I can manage for you,' she said, tensing her muscles around his cock. 'And Helmut, it didn't escape my notice that you used the whip with considerable finesse and skill.'

'I did tell you I wasn't a prude,' he answered.

'It would seem,' she said, stretching her legs wide and rigid and easing her other hand down, finding his cock, ringing its stiffness with her thumb and forefinger, feeling it as it went in and out of her very wet pussy, and letting her other fingers play with his balls, 'as if we have similar inclinations.'

'It would seem so,' he said, squeezing her nipples hard between his fingers, increasing her pleasure and allowing her to come.

A week later when Monique brought Helmut his breakfast she brought with it a note.

'From madame,' she said. 'She's had to go out.'

Helmut read it quickly. ''Helmut, please pick Daisy up from her home at 13a Rue St Etienne, it's just between Boulevard Montparnasse and Avenue Edgar Quinet, at 8.30. Take her to dinner, at the La Chatte de

Ma Tante. It's an old Art Nouveau place in the seventh district but it's been taken over by some new people and it's the place to be. Dress is formal. Then when she has eaten and drunk her fill bring her here, at 11.00 prompt. But please use the side entrance. I enclose the electronic key and the pass number is 6969 + . Isolde."

Helmut had a variety of business things to attend to all that day. And from one of his meetings it looked as if he might have to forego time at his schloss and return to New Orleans sooner than expected. However, periodically his thoughts went back to Isolde's brief note. He smiled remembering the pass number. He liked that sixty-nine sixty-nine plus. It augured well for the evening. So did the name of the restaurant. When in the late afternoon he went back to the house only the ancient housekeeper was about and caring for Jacques. Helmut bathed and changed, called for a taxi then collected Daisy.

Helmut knew to expect someone tall, pretty and blonde. He was not expecting someone so sexily chic. She was wearing a black chiffon frock with long floaty sleeves but the front bodice was slashed open from neck to navel, revealing a black rubber undergarment. This covered her small pert breasts, went up and around her neck and down over her belly and hips. The bias-cut panels of the full chiffon skirt swirled out as she walked and Helmut was able to see that the tight rubber tubing stopped at the top of her thighs. There was a paler area of what he took to be bare skin. Her legs were encased in fine black stockings. Her feet were thrust coquettishly into very high-heeled side-buttoning boots. She invited him into her neat small apartment.

'Champagne?' she asked, pointing to a couple of engraved crystal flutes and the bottle in the ice bucket on the table.

'Thank you,' he said.

Daisy poured, gave him his glass then sat opposite him. She sat very upright but with her legs slightly apart.

'Cheers,' she said. They clinked glasses. She stuck her finger in her champagne then parted the folds of her skirt, opened her legs wider, and with infinite delicacy lightly touched the outer lips of her pussy.

'I like to make absolutely sure I'm wet before I go out,' she said. 'Perhaps you would care to check.'

'Yes,' he said.

Helmut put his glass on the table and took Daisy's hand, pulling her up. Slowly he inserted a finger in her wet sex but he could not obtain full penetration. Something was blocking the way.

'My love balls,' she said. 'I thought you'd like to know so when I'm sitting opposite you and squirming you'll know I'm preparing myself.'

Helmut smiled, and lightly flicked her clitoris. She gave a quick gasp.

'Yes,' he said, and undid his flies. 'And you can put your hand in there and feel that.'

Daisy did as she was told, finding his cock as stiff as a ramrod. She licked her lips.

'Bend over,' he said. 'I want you now.'

Daisy bent over, the folds of her skirt falling to one side and presented him with her neat rubber covered backside. He edged the rubber undergarment up just enough to allow him instant access.

'Hold yourself open,' he commanded.

Daisy took hold of her bottom cheeks and spread them wide. Helmut grazed his cock up and down her neat, tight, puckered but expectant little hole. She started to move her hips.

'Keep still,' he ordered, 'keep absolutely still.'

Helmut trailed his nails along her buttocks, then slapped her flanks hard. She gasped and moved.

'I ordered you to keep still,' he said and with that rammed his cock hard into her arse and thrust and thrust without pity or feeling for her or whether she wanted to come. It was of no concern to him. Daisy knew and accepted it finding something powerfully erotic in being used without foreplay.

The restaurant was crowded. Isolde was correct, it was all too obviously the 'in' place, and many of the Paris glitterati were there.

'Monsieur le Comte welcome, and Mam'selle Daisy,' said the *maitre d'*, greeting them. 'Madame Marnier booked you in. She said you, sir, had a most refined palette. I have put you over there . . .' The head waiter was pointing towards a heavily ornamented door, close to a sign saying *toilettes*. 'When you want to take your dessert Mam'selle will let me know, n'est-ce pas Miss Daisy?'

'Oui, Armand,' said Daisy.

'And then Claude will serve you.' The *maitre d'* indicated a hefty man standing guard beside the ornamental door.

'Thank you, Armand,' said Daisy.

'Tell me what happens if I should want *hors d'oeuvres* instead of dessert?' asked Helmut.

'That can be arranged, sir,' said Armand, 'but I would suggest you have an aperitif here, perhaps some wine, and then call Claude . . .'

Armand showed them to their table, handed Helmut the wine menu and left them to decide. Helmut ordered champagne.

'So you have been here before?' said Helmut to Daisy.

'Many times. It's a most interesting restaurant.'

'How interesting?'

'Well the food's good . . .'

'And . . .'

'So is the service.'

The wine waiter uncorked the bottle and poured the light corn-coloured bubbly liquid into their champagne flutes. Daisy drank hers fast. Helmut refilled her glass. Helmut glanced around the room. Everyone was exceedingly fashionably dressed, but few were as sexy looking as Daisy. She smiled at Helmut and wiggled. Helmut, remembering the love balls inside her, began to think of what he could do to her when they were alone together. He'd enjoyed their brief screw. He found taking her quickly a turn on. His cock was rising. He wanted to do it again. She was talking to him, something to do with mathematics, but he wasn't listening. She took out a small notebook and began explaining a theory to him. Helmut was not interested. He wanted to know what went on behind that door.

'Daisy, I think it's time to call Claude,' he said, sipping his champagne.

'One moment,' she said. 'I've just had a thought.' And began to jot down a series of equations.

And that was when Count Helmut von Straffen saw Ottilie Duvier for the second time.

It was the colour of her hair that caught his eye: that beautiful Titian-red was glinting in the soft lights of the restaurant. It framed her peaches and cream face in pre-Raphaelite curls. God, he thought, the woman was stunning. A rare beauty coupled with an air of sexual innocence. And an ability to wear clothes. He recognised the designer's hand, and its exorbitant cost, in the dark blue silk velvet dress she was wearing. It was modish and expensively classical but the gold and black fake fur coat draped over the back of her chair showed another side to her. It was outrageously extravagant. Almost exhibitionistic.

Helmut assumed the nondescript sandy-haired man dining with her was her fiancé. Helmut was struck by the boredom of her pose; the lack of passion in her body language. Why had such a beautiful and rich young woman committed herself to such a relationship? The man with her was alternately using his fork to emphasise a point he was making or stabbing at the steak he was eating before shovelling it greedily in his mouth. Listlessly her eyes began to wander round the room. Helmut stared at her well shaped full mouth and felt an immediate desire to kiss it. Helmut glanced at Daisy. She was busy writing. Staring down at the table Helmut willed Ottilie to look at him. And she did. He looked up, and saw her hazel-green eyes staring at him. He met her stare and held it captive. As he did he thought about touching her skin, playing with her, teaching her how to make love; he was convinced she was a virgin. He would open up a world of pleasure to her, give her appetites she had no idea existed, but instinctively knew she would enjoy. He saw her take a sharp breath, open her mouth, lick her lips and move her bottom slightly.

Helmut smiled. He knew then he was face to face with a highly sexual woman who had never been screwed. He raised his glass of champagne towards her then let his eyes roam from her eyes to her mouth down to her breasts and back to her mouth again. And she seemed unable to tear her eyes away from his. That pleased him.

Helmut put his glass down, leant his elbows on the table and his chin on his hands. He wanted to possess Ottilie Duvier. He'd like to lie her out naked, kiss her eyes, her mouth, her neck, fondle her breasts, tease her nipples, languidly let his hands roam over her belly, push her legs apart, then feel her swollen, ripening sex . . .

'Okay, come,' said Daisy, putting her notebook back in her handbag. She raised her hand, waggling two fingers at Claude, the burly waiter standing beside the ornamental door. He acknowledged her by raising one hand and nodding his head.

Daisy stood up. So did Helmut, and bowed to her.

'I'll follow you,' he said, sitting down again quickly.

The spell was broken. Ottilie had turned her attention back to her fiancé and Helmut had a massive hard on. He needed it to recede before he walked through the restaurant.

Helmut downed the rest of his champagne then followed Daisy across the room and through the ornamental door.

Chapter 3

'*B*loody hell,' thought Lord Christopher as he awoke, 'I blew it.'

He was lying in a tangled heap of ancient blankets and dirty coats on Sylvie's uncomfortable lumpy old couch in her apartment on the Rue Bonaparte. His mouth tasted like a sewer, his eyes had difficulty focusing, and his brain bore a strong resemblance to scrambled eggs. Through the mist of recollection he vaguely recalled women shouting at him, but they were all mixed up: women with hair striped red, black and gold; tall elegantly dressed women with wide squat bodies, big red open mouths, large boobs, long skinny arms and short fat legs were telling him he was a fool, an idiot, an imbecile. He lifted his head and the room turned.

'Shit,' he thought, seeing clearly in his mind's eye Ottilie's furious and panicked face.

He stared at the old, peeling, smart in the '70s brown, wrapping-paper wallpaper, and the almost obligatory, faded, curling, not to mention bad, print of Degas' 'Absinthe' fixed on it with drawing pins. He reckoned the dejected look on the woman's face in the picture must be much the same as his. Memories surged into the forefront of his mind. His attempted seduction of Ottilie had gone horribly wrong. Silly cow, why couldn't she have just lain down and opened her legs. The maid arriving and chasing him out of the apartment hadn't helped matters either. Then Sylvie had been beside herself with anger when he presented himself at her door in the early hours of the morning, drunk and dishevelled; his dream of riches gone, disposed of, evaporated – for the moment at least. He'd have to find another heiress.

He toppled off the couch on to the floor, stood up and lurched to the bathroom. He peed then splashed his face with cold water.

Staggering back he passed Sylvie's bedroom and looked in. She lay fast asleep on her double divan bed. One large tit was uncovered. Lord Christopher couldn't resist her luscious ample body. He threw off his clothes and slid in beside her. She had the arousing sweaty odour of morning bed after late night sex. He caressed her breasts. He teased her nipples. He nestled his head into her neck and nibbled along her well rounded shoulders. She stretched out lazily. Then she curled back positioning her naked buttocks against his penis which gave him an instant erection. Sleepily, forgetting how angry she was with him, she wiggled her bottom, feeling it pushing along her crease. She lifted and spread her bottom-cheeks so that his cock could graze along her sex lips. Very slowly he entered her, edging his prick deeper and deeper into her soft wetness. Sylvie stretched out once more, this time with him embedded inside her, and his hands trailed down over her belly stopping when he touched the mound between her legs. He flicked at her clitoris, making it stiffen, and her inner muscles contracted around his gliding prick. Her body moved this way and that, and up and down, taking more and more of him. He got up a steady rhythm and built up momentum until he was charging in harder and faster. Then she woke up and remembered.

'*Va te faire foutre! Cochon!* Pig. What the fuck do you think you're doing, you bastard?' she screamed.

'Screwing you,' he replied.

Swiftly she jerked away from him so that he was out of her and she rolled off the bed.

'No way,' she said. 'You bloody imbecile.'

'Sylvie, Sylvie . . .' he cried.

'Forget it. You try to rape Ottilie then think you can slide in here and fuck me, well no way, schnook, no way. Seduce her, I said, seduce her, not rape her.'

'That wasn't rape,' said Christopher.

'Oh no? What do you call it then?' she asked.

'Coming on strong,' he replied.

'Well the way you described it I would call it attempted rape,' she said. 'And it's a good job I'm broke and thought you were too pissed to drive, otherwise you wouldn't be here now.'

'Don't fool yourself, Sylvie,' said Lord Christopher. 'You love the feel of my cock and can't get enough of it.'

'*Merde*, don't bank on it, *imbécile*,' she said. 'And where did you leave your car?'

'Outside in the street. Why, where should I have left it, half way up the building?' he answered facetiously.

'Move it. Go on. Now, move it fast.'

'Why?'

'Because you're the last person I want here and in any case it's possible Ottilie will turn up any minute to tell me what happened last night.'

'No she won't. She's got the lawyer coming at half ten. Sylvie, don't be cross with me. I love you.'

'Sure, words come cheap. Christopher, I'd like you to bugger off . . .'

'But I'm hungry. Have you got any bread? I'd love some toast.'

'You are a fucking insensitive idiot.'

'And you love me . . .'

Sylvie made them both breakfast.

Ottilie was still sleeping when Veronique nipped out to the bakery for a baguette and croissants and to a nearby boutique for the clothing Ottilie wanted. When Ottilie awoke she immediately telephoned Sylvie Cordonier.

Much to her surprise there was no answer. Even her friend's machine wasn't taking messages. She was still in bed when Veronique came in with breakfast and a beige and black jogging suit and some plain white cotton underwear.

'It's not so wonderful, but it's the best at eight o'clock,' said Veronique.

'They're fine,' said Ottilie, giving them a perfunctory glance and drinking her thick black coffee.

Veronique had set out the breakfast beautifully, a silver tray with a Madeira embroidered traycloth, English Minton china, the croissants fresh and piping hot, home made apricot jam, but Ottilie decided she didn't want it.

'I'm sorry Veronique,' she said, pushing the tray away and climbing out of bed, 'but I seem to have lost my appetite.'

'A pity, mam'selle. It's better that you eat, but . . . Oh, Monsieur Raoul telephoned and said could you possibly make nine instead of half past ten?' said Veronique.

'Actually that suits me better. 'Phone him back and tell him I prefer that,' said Ottilie.

Veronique went off to ring the lawyer and Ottilie bathed and dressed. She put on the new jogging suit, dispensed with any make-up and tied her hair back with an elastic band. She would go to the beauty salon later.

Sitting in her drawing room awaiting the lawyer's arrival Ottilie tried again to make contact with Sylvie. Still there was no answer. Ottilie thought it odd. I bet she's unplugged the 'phone and doesn't realise the answer machine's not turned on, she thought. And decided she would visit her as soon as the lawyer had gone.

Sylvie was her confidante. She wanted to talk to her. She needed to talk to her. Not that Ottilie needed or wanted advice about what to do with Lord Christopher. Their engagement was over. Finished. That chapter was now firmly closed. It was more that Ottilie had to talk, to unburden herself; let her feelings out and tell Sylvie about Christopher's bestiality, his unwarranted attack upon her. But should she tell Sylvie about the stranger in the restaurant? No, that was too personal. Some things had to be kept secret. In any case nothing had happened. Only a torrid glance. Ottilie dismissed it instantly as of no consequence, yet she knew full well she was deceiving herself. It was of the utmost consequence. Whether she saw the man again or not, that look had played its part in ending her relationship with Lord Christopher. If that hadn't happened she might not have discovered those sensual sensations that had made immediate inroads into her sense and sensibility. The excitement it had induced in her; the unfamiliar tingling in her body, in her breasts, her womb and between her legs had . . . Had what? Bewitched her? Or brought her to her senses. Passion. Her father had tried to tell her about passion but she had been deaf to his words.

There was no doubt in Ottilie's mind that that glance had been a passionate glance. And without it she might not have been so forthright with Lord Christopher. He might not have irritated her so much. She might not have left the restaurant in such a huff. He might not have followed her and . . . Ottilie was suddenly tired of the 'might nots'. Lord Christopher was now past. But Sylvie was still present and Ottilie wanted to see her. Perhaps they could go shopping together; she had an entire wardrobe to replace. And maybe Sylvie would like something. She was playing Mendelssohn's violin concerto soon. A couture evening gown for that special performance would be a nice idea. Ottilie decided that's what she would do; she would celebrate her good fortune by buying Sylvie a present.

At nine o'clock prompt the fussy, pompous little lawyer came bustling in and read her father's will. It didn't take long. Apart from some small bequests to servants she was the sole inheritor except for the old house in New Orleans. That was left to her jointly with her half brother, Elmer, with a proviso; if for any reason it was to be sold, on no account must it be sold to Frank Dale. Her father maintained that his brother-in-law would try by fair means or foul to get his hands on it; thwart this gangster at every turn he admonished from the grave. Monsieur Raoul then departed leaving Ottilie considerably wealthier than when he had arrived.

Ottilie wandered into the stainless steel and well scrubbed wooden kitchen where the cook, Bettine was rolling out pastry for a *tarte aux pommes* for lunch.

'Where's Veronique?' she asked.

'Gone to the charity shop with some things,' replied Bettine.

'Oh, in that case would you call Pierre for me, tell him I want the car. I'm going shopping,' said Ottilie.

Within minutes her father's great pride and joy, his British racing green vintage Rolls Royce was at the door of the apartment block and Pierre was ringing the bell.

'Where to Mam'selle,' he said, slightly surprised when he saw her dressed in a cheap jogging suit.

'Faubourg St Honore,' she said, then she changed her mind. 'No, first to Rue Bonaparte.'

She would call on Sylvie, take her with her if she was in. Ottilie sat back in the car feeling pleased with life. It wasn't so bad and she and her friend would have a good day together. She would spoil her; buy her whatever she wanted.

The sight of Lord Christopher's car parked and clamped on the sidewalk near the entrance to Sylvie's apartment came as a rude shock. Ottilie blinked her eyes as if not believing what she was seeing. Then, her mind whirring, she proceeded to make up all sorts of excuses as to why it should be there. Any excuse except that he might be in Sylvie's apartment. But what if he was in Sylvie's apartment? It could be quite innocent. Perhaps he was feeling contrite. Perhaps he'd gone to tell her what he'd done. But why should he do that?

Ottilie steeled herself. There was no point sitting in the car thinking things, better to ring the bell and find out.

'Wait here, Pierre,' she said, 'but if you have to move go round the block and come back.'

'Oui, Mam'selle,' he said.

56

Ottilie rang the bell on the intercom. Sylvie answered.

'Oh, you are there,' said Ottilie. 'I've been trying to ring you. Can I come up?'

There was the tiniest hesitation then Sylvie said, 'Yes, of course.'

Ottilie's basic instincts were now fired up. Sylvie should not have hesitated. That confirmed what she suspected. Lord Christopher was there. If he was there contrite and she innocent, then Sylvie should have said, 'Lord Christopher is here, Ottilie.' But she didn't, she hesitated.

The buzzer sounded to give her access to the building. Ottilie put one foot over the threshold. Did she want to meet Lord Christopher? No, she didn't. Did she want to know what Sylvie was doing with him; had been doing with him? No, she did not. Ottilie stepped back into the street.

Seeing her advancing towards the car Pierre jumped out and held the door open for her.

'Faubourg St Honore,' she said, 'and fast.'

Driving through the wintery rain and hail and along the wet streets Ottilie's mind worked overtime. Sylvie and Christopher. Sylvie and Christopher. Suddenly a lot of things started to make sense. Was he the lover she never introduced? She had visited England as a tourist yet gone to Lord Christopher's house. That wasn't on the tourist map. Various things began to slot into place the moment Ottilie viewed the situation with different eyes. And Sylvie had deliberately not come to dine with them last night. Had she known what Christopher was going to do? No, she couldn't have. That was a mistake. Or was it?

It was now snowing. This made Ottilie feel worse. She glanced forlornly out of the window, and suddenly she saw a sports shop selling ski and climbing equipment.

'Stop,' she shouted to Pierre.

Pierre stopped. Ottilie ran out before he had time to open the door for her.

'I want a bell tent,' she demanded of an assistant the moment she entered the shop.

57

'Yes, madam,' he said.

'Have you got one?'

'Of course, madam.'

'I want it gift wrapped and delivered,' said Ottilie, 'and do you have any tags?'

'Yes, madam.'

'Give me one.'

The assistant gave her one. Ottilie wrote on it. 'Sylvie. Have it as a wedding dress. Hope you and Lord Christopher will be very happy. Ottilie.' Then she gave the assistant Sylvie's address, paid for it and feeling pleased with herself, vengeance had been wrought, she left the shop.

Pierre then drove Ottilie to the beauty salon and on to various couturiers and accessory boutiques. She had a most successful morning's shopping. She bought, or ordered to be sent on to her, brassières, panties, petticoats, stockings, shoes, hats, gloves, handbags, suits, skirts, blouses, day frocks, cocktail wear and evening gowns, all in the most beautiful fabrics and cut in a way to show off any woman's figure, but particularly hers. She also bought jewellery; rings, necklaces, bracelets and brooches. Ottilie purchased everything she desired in an orgy of spending until hunger pangs grabbed at her stomach. She glanced at her watch. It wasn't surprising. It was late afternoon. She hadn't eaten a thing all day. Maybe she would take tea.

'Where to now, Mam'selle Ottilie?' asked Pierre, relieving her of more bags and boxes and stowing them away in the boot.

'The Ritz,' she said.

Arriving at the Place Vendome she was about to climb out of the car when she saw the stranger from the restaurant walk into that beautiful hotel ahead of her. He was laughing and chatting animatedly to the beautiful, dark haired, fashionably dressed young woman who was hanging on his arm. That was the last thing Ottilie wanted to see.

'No. Home, Pierre,' she said, leaning back with a deep

sinking feeling and a suddenly dry mouth. Seeing the handsome stranger with another beautiful woman was the last straw. Her comfort. Gone. Her fantasy shattered. Snap. Her present reality she neither liked nor wanted. So she would change it.

Ottilie spread her hands over the soft pale green leather of the seats. She was thrown, deeply, inwardly thrown. She had been starting to think how fortunate she was to be able to buy whatever she wanted, whenever she wanted. It had helped assuage some of her upset, some of her grief. But now suddenly her delight faded and the full impact of her emptiness, her aloneness hit her.

She would write to Lord Christopher, not necessarily politely, informing him that their engagement was at an end. She shivered slightly at the thought of him. Whatever had possessed her to agree to their marriage? It was over now; all over. She would leave Paris. She would cut the cord. Sharp. Cut. She quickly made a decision. She knew what she would do. She would go to the house in New Orleans.

As soon as she was back inside her own apartment Ottilie locked herself in her drawing room and began telephoning the airlines. She wanted to go that minute but that was impossible. All flights departed in the morning. She booked herself on one which still had a seat in first class. It had one stop-over in Dallas/Fort Worth.

Ottilie called the staff to her room and told them she would be leaving early in the morning. They were to stay on and keep the house in order until her return but she did not know when that would be. No one outside the household was to be told of her decision and she did not want to speak to anyone before she went. And most definitely not Mam'selle Sylvie, or Lord Christopher.

Veronique packed all her new clothing into some old battered suitcases.

'Shall I buy some new ones, Mam'selle?' asked the maid, looking at the state of them.

'No,' said Ottilie, 'they're less likely to go missing if they're old.'

Veronique was instantly reminded of her father. He too could be outrageously extravagant then suddenly make the most extraordinary economies. It seemed to her absurd to have the finest clothes in the world put into such dilapidated luggage. But the rich were a law unto themselves.

'Yes, Mam'selle,' said Veronique, wondering what had suddenly made her want to leave Paris. There had been no hint of it when they left home that morning. Surely it wasn't that fool Lord Christopher? Ah, well, sooner or later she would find out. All Veronique wanted to know was that she still had a job. And Mam'selle assured her she had.

Pierre deposited Ottilie at Orly early next morning. Ottilie checked in, waited for a while in the VIP lounge then boarded. Ottilie gazed out of her window to get her last glimpse of Paris. She never thought the day would come when she would be pleased to be leaving that beautiful city, but she was pleased, and relieved. She took a sleeping pill and did not wake up until Dallas.

There, groggily, she came off the aircraft and went to one of the refreshment bars in the transit lounge. She was sitting having a glass of cool fresh orange juice when she looked up and saw the handsome stranger from the restaurant striding past. Without warning her heart gave a tumultuous leap. Her legs started to tremble. She would have liked to see where he was heading but it was impossible for her to move. She sat as still as possible and waited for the feeling within her to subside. When her flight was called there was no sign of him.

Back on the aircraft, Ottilie closed her eyes, patiently waiting for the people around her to complete their various procedures. She felt someone flick apart the unfastened belt on the adjoining seat then sit down. She kept her eyes closed. It was just over an hour's flight to New Orleans and no way did she want anyone to try and engage her in conversation.

The aeroplane began its slow taxi down the runway. It gathered speed, and suddenly she felt the blood rush that she loved, and others hated, and they were airborne. She was excited. But was the excitement because she was going home or had it been engendered by that elegant, sexy man she had just seen again?

Ottilie drifted off into imaginings. Lips, and skin and eyes and hair and ... she quivered. Naughty ideas that made her pale skin blush crossed her mind. The touch of that man's lips on hers. His hands and fingers straying over her breasts and belly; her legs opening and him probing that hungry wet place ... Ottilie pulled her thoughts to an immediate full stop. What was she doing? What was she thinking? How could she, a virgin, think so licentiously? It was almost as if a devil was on her shoulder and a small voice was saying, go ahead. Think and then do. Go ahead. Experience. Think sexy. Think erotic. She squirmed in her seat.

It seemed no time at all before the intercom was turned on and the pilot began speaking. 'Ladies and gentlemen, we'll be landing in three minutes in New Orleans. On behalf of all the crew I would like to say welcome to Party town at party time. Welcome to the Big Easy ...' And as he continued the usual end of flight spiel Ottilie opened her eyes and got a shock.

The man, that man, the man from the restaurant, was sitting beside her. Fury, anger, disappointment were the first emotions to assail her. What an opportunity she had missed.

He looked at her. Their eyes met. There was a quickening in her heart beat. And she broke out in goose flesh. She rubbed her arms. Damn and hell, she thought.

'You've been asleep a long time,' he said in a beautifully modulated dark brown voice that had a hint of an accent. A dangerous accent.

A dangerous accent? What could be dangerous about an accent? But that was the word and it wouldn't go away. There was something inherently dangerous in this man.

'Yes,' she replied in a half whisper.

He rolled up *The Times Picayunne* and pushed it into his briefcase. She stole a glance at him. Yes, elegant, ruggedly handsome and definitely dangerous. Ottilie wondered who he was and why he was going to New Orleans. She wanted to kick herself for not opening her eyes and finding out who was sitting beside her. Now it was too late. He was the first off the aircraft. And he marched away fast showing no inclination whatever to linger with her or to talk to her. Maybe, she thought, they would meet up again in Baggage Claim. But they didn't. He had no luggage. He went quickly through passport control and was gone along with hundreds of other passengers from short haul flights towards the exit and the City of New Orleans.

Ottilie determined to put coincidences, and the handsome stranger, to the back of her mind. She had no time for erotic thoughts, let alone erotic experiences. She had come to lay claim to her old house and to enjoy Mardi Gras.

Chapter 4

Ottilie was riding down the freeway towards Uptown New Orleans in her Uncle Frank's silver blue limo. She was sitting between him and his daughter, Mary Lou. They wanted to talk but Ottilie didn't. She was dreaming of her house. She just knew Elmer would not have done any of those needy repairs. She was imagining what she would find.

The huge black iron gates at the entrance would be rusty. There would be flaky white paint on the clapboard fascia; the shutters, with their blue paint peeling and faded, would be hanging off their hinges. The treads of the stoep would be rotten, and there'd be holes to fall through on the wraparound verandah. There would be weeds growing through the gravel on the path. The palm and banana trees would have gone berserk and be overshadowing the lawn. The lawn would look more like a field, and the water lilies in the pond would have been choked to death by algae and weeds.

Ottilie knew there would be a lot of work to do. Planning and organising who would do what and overseeing the whole operation would keep her well occupied. She would have no time to dwell on the events in Paris. She would put the whole place back as it was a century ago. But first she would have to buy out Elmer.

No problem there. He was bound to have gambling debts and would be delighted to sell.

'Ottilie?' Uncle Frank's voice, dispelled her reverie. She turned to look at him. His jowly face had gained more rolls since she last saw him. His perfect silk suit was a little too perfect. His protruding eyes were too close together and his smile was unpleasant and vaguely threatening.

'Sorry, Uncle Frank, I guess I must be tired. Paris to New Orleans is a long haul.'

'Didn't you sleep on the 'plane?' asked her cousin, flicking her mane of long blonde hair with her carefully manicured hands and smiling through her well lip-sticked mouth showing the precision of her pearly white and even teeth. 'I did and I was only coming from Cow Town . . .'

'Cow Town?' asked Ottilie bemused.

'Fort Worth,' said Mary Lou, 'not that the upper reaches of their society like to be reminded of that. But I'm Louisiana born and bred. I don't give a pig's trotter for Texan sensibility, so I reminded them – all the time.'

'My little girl was attending a party there,' said her father butting in. 'And when the brothers give parties they only invite the very best people.'

Neither of them seemed to notice Ottilie's silence, Mary Lou continued as if her father hadn't spoken.

'On a 'plane I take a sleeping pill and sleep 'til I get where I'm goin'.'

'So do I but it's still a long way,' said Ottilie.

'So honey you ain't real tired,' said her uncle. 'Good, 'cos I need to talk to you. Sorry your pa's dead and all that but it was kinda fortuitous meeting you at the air-port when all I'd done was gone to pick up my little girl here – I wanna buy your house. Well, you always called it a house. In my terminology it's a mansion. And I wanna buy your mansion, sugar.'

'Don't "sugar" me Uncle Frank, and it's not for sale.'

'No, no, you misunderstand me. I wanna buy your mansion. I want it. I've always wanted it. It's gonna be my baby's wedding present.'

'I didn't know you were getting married, Mary Lou?' said Ottilie.

'She ain't, not yet, but she will be soon. Hey, what about your wedding, when's it gonna be? We read about it in the newspaper. Lord Christopher Furrel. So you got yourself a real live aristocrat from England. When I saw you at the baggage reclaim I thought, Gee, she's here to sell the house and go back and live in this Lord's stately home.'

'No, I won't be doing that. My engagement is off. Finished.'

'You finished with a Lord!' exclaimed Mary Lou, her eyes widening in astonishment.

'I finished with a man,' said Ottilie firmly.

'Why Ottilie hon, if you gotta a Lord in tow you keep him, you can always divorce but you're forever a Lady. And socially that's such a cache,' said Mary Lou.

Listening to her cousin, Ottilie squirmed with embarrassment.

'Anyhow,' continued Mary Lou, 'you can't be real serious.'

'Oh, but I am,' said Ottilie with the utmost seriousness.

'In that case why are you still wearing your engagement ring?' said the highly observant Mary Lou.

Ottilie glanced swiftly down at the third finger of her left hand. There the bauble winked and gleamed at her. Hell, she thought, was that the reason the handsome sexy stranger on the 'plane had not wanted to stay and talk with her?

'This ring belonged to my mother,' said Ottilie, twirling the elongated emeralds and star cut diamonds around and around so that their pure beauty was clearly visible to her cousin.

'Your mother! Your mother!' exclaimed Mary Lou, with added emphasis on the second 'your'. 'What's the matter with the goddamn sonofabitch lord, ain't he got no money?'

'He was getting one made for me and until it was ready I said I would wear this one.'

'So what did you choose?'

'Sapphires and diamonds.'

'Oh, just everybody does that! But I won't. I want one big, one helluva big, hunky diamond. Anyhow, what sort of a design did you have for your sapphires and diamonds?'

'I don't know. I broke off the relationship before I saw it.'

'Well, that was real foolish of you, hon. You break it off after you got the ring, not before.'

'So whatcha gonna do in Noo Awlins?' asked Frank.

'I intend to go see Elmer, buy him out, do up the old house and live in it.'

Frank Dale and his daughter exchanged glances.

'Ottilie,' said Frank, in his now 'be reasonable' voice, 'I want you to think again about my offer. Know something? If your pa's sister had been a man she'd have inherited it . . .'

'But she wasn't and I don't understand your logic Uncle Frank, because if she'd been a man you wouldn't have married her and you wouldn't have gotten it anyway.'

'Ottilie, cut the crap. Name your price,' said Frank Dale.

'Uncle Frank, my house is not for sale. And most of all it's not for sale to you.'

'What do you mean?'

'My father laid down strict provisions in his will. The house is left half to me and half to my step-brother Elmer, we can each buy the other out and we can sell it, but not to you. His will states that if either of us sell the house to you then our inheritance is voided and it's to be left to the local cat's home.'

'But your pa didn't like cats!'

'That's how much my pa didn't like you, Uncle Frank.'

'Jeez, he's even hatin' me beyond the grave.'

'He said you could change your name from Frank Dalessio to Frank Dale but . . .'

'So he hated me 'cos I'm a wop!'

'No, he hated you 'cos you're a gangster and married his sister against his will and he reckoned your ways of living killed her.'

'Well, ain't you just like your pa, shooting straight from the hip. But I want that house, honey and I'm gonna have it.'

Frank Dale picked up his mobile telephone and dial-led a number. He issued orders that at the next stop-off on the freeway another limo was to be waiting for them.

'I've just remember Mary Lou and I have to go some-where and it ain't nowhere you're heading.'

Ottilie smiled to herself. It would be a relief to be rid of them. She never found either of them congenial com-pany. Frank was too tricky and dangerous and Mary Lou was plain hard. Pretty though, no one in their right mind could say otherwise. She was the epitome of the all-American blonde beauty. She should be; her body trainers, the surgeons and the beauty parlour made cer-tain of that. Ottilie never really liked her. The feeling was mutual.

Ottilie was not going to make a fuss about being un-ceremoniously dumped. She was practical. Frank Dale could simply open the door and tell her to walk. But then he did want something from her and initially he would try to be pleasant. Ottilie was under no illusions that that was why he had called up another limo.

After she had changed cars, and given the chauffeur her Garden District address, Ottilie lay back happily gazing out of the window. Although it was mid-January already the weather was warm, the sun was shining and the Mardi Gras hoardings were up; advising motorists to drive carefully and make it to the Party in the Big Easy and not to the morgue. She ordered the chauffeur to slow down. She wanted to savour the scenery, the view, the coming home. She smiled at the gigantic mov-ing hand on the billboard reaching out to clasp a falling necklace. Beads. Soon everyone, men and women and children, would be wearing multi-coloured beads. Booty from the various parades. The thing that made New Orleans Carnival unique. Crowd participation. The people on the floats, the Krewes, bought plastic mugs and plastic crayfish, and plastic lobsters and beads; masses and masses of beads, threaded in different lengths and in different qualities, and threw them to the waiting crowds. Ottilie smiled remembering that there was a special way to hold your hand up to make sure if one, or some, came your way, you were able to grab it. And it was that special way that the hand moved on the billboard. Ottilie relaxed, she was really pleased to be back in her place of birth. She could return to her previous reverie, think, and speculate, but instead of the house her mind turned again to the stranger.

Who was he? He had money, that was evident from her limited view of his life-style, and no man wasted dollars on first class air travel unless he had plenty. He was exceptionally well dressed, and his thickset body was sleek and well cared for. Could he be an athlete? Maybe, but somehow she thought not. He had an accent, a foreign tinge to his voice that she had been unable to place. He was handsome, his elegant saturnine face made more interesting by the hard brightness of his eyes. Those eyes. They had captured her imagination and her soul in the restaurant. And on the aircraft they had again bored into hers as if delivering the most enticing invitation to . . . Ottilie shivered. To what? To sex?

The limo turned into St Charles Avenue and the old streetcar went trundling by. Ottilie's smile got broader. In Washington Avenue her heart gave a leap. She sat upright, as excited as a child. In a moment she would see the house. Her family home. Her step-brother would open the door. Elmer would look at her surprised. He would open his arms and welcome her inside. She would be assailed by the familiar smells of cedar wood floors and polish. And everything would be the same as it ever was; except that her daddy was dead and the house would be dilapidated. But she had the money to renovate it. The house would soon be truly beautiful again.

The chauffeur brought the car to a halt and Ottilie gasped. She looked bewildered. She gazed uncomprehendingly from the tall black iron gates, to the back of the chauffeur's head, and back again to the gates. Yes, right place. Wrong house. No, right house. But what had happened to it? The chauffeur opened the car door.

'There's got to be a mistake,' she said, not moving.

'No mistake, Mam,' said the chauffeur. 'This is the house.'

Staring past the gates up at the house Ottilie swung her legs on to the sidewalk, straightened up, and went over to the brand new brass bell hanging from the gatepost. She pulled it harshly.

Her dream was shattered. This was no crumbling ruin in which she could lose herself making it habitable. This was a rich man's pride and joy. Somebody had spent a vast amount of money making her house fresh, bright, and clean. New paint covered the clapboard fascia, the new shutters, the porch and its pillars, the wraparound verandah and its wooden rails. It was ultra smart, ultra magnificent, ultra everything. And she was furious. Peering through the gates Ottilie jangled the bell once more and noticed the pond had been replaced by a large swimming pool. An air of despair wafted over her. It was all too, too . . . through her anger she tried to find the correct word. As the French windows opened she found it. Californian. It had the hard puritan, almost Germanic coldness of the golden state, instead of the lush greenness of Louisiana.

The big black butler, who in girth, height and features looked more like a retired prize fighter, was resplendent in his uniform, complete with white gloves. He slowly made his way across the porch, down the stoep and along the gravel pathway, but he didn't open the gates.

'You rang?' he said.

'I did. I want to come in,' said Ottilie imperiously.

'That's what they all say,' said the butler, eyeing her up and down, noting the fresh beauty of her face, the fullness of her breasts, the smallness of her waist and the length of her slender legs.

'What are you talking about?'

'Has the Master given his permission?' he asked. 'I was not aware that anyone was due today.'

Ottilie felt something flip inside her brain.

'Now look here,' she said, shouting at him through the gates. 'My name is Ottilie Duvier, I own this house and I want to come in.'

'Well now, that's the best excuse I've heard yet,' said the butler.

'Excuse, excuse!' shouted Ottilie, beside herself with anger.

'Sure, every beautiful woman in New Orleans wants to get behind these doors. Many get the call, you might say, but few are chosen.'

Ottilie looked at the butler and then turned back as if to gain reassurance from her chauffeur but he was inside the car, staring straight ahead, pretending to be oblivious to the argument on the sidewalk.

'I haven't the faintest idea what you're talking about,' said Ottilie, 'but this is my house and I want to come in.'

'If you'd like to give me your card I'm sure the Count will contact you,' said the butler, leering at her.

'Count! What Count?'

'Count Helmut von Straffen. He lives here and he has not left orders for you to be received Miss er . . .'

'Ottilie Duvier,' said Ottilie rattling the gates.

'So I must hope you have a nice day and say, Goodbye.'

The butler turned on his heel and walked back along the gravel path, up the stoep, across the porch and through the long French windows, which he closed firmly behind him.

Devastated, and quite dumbfounded, Ottilie opened the car door, got in and sat down.

'Where to now, Miss Ottilie?' asked the chauffeur.

'Oh, take me to the Fairmont,' she said, thinking she'd get a room, gather her thoughts, ring Elmer's office and find out what the hell was going on. 'It is still there, I presume?'

'Yes, Mam,' said the chauffeur, smiling at the thought of that great hotel, that centre of opulence and luxury going walkabout.

But after checking in Ottilie did not do any of the things she had planned. Instead, finding she was excessively tired and weary, she slipped out of her suit and lay on her bed. Gradually, as she relaxed, she began to think dangerous thoughts. She allowed her mind to wander along specifically sexual highways.

She imagined the stranger, and his hands unbuttoning her soft cambric blouse, forcing her breasts out beyond the captivity of her restraining brassière and her nipples hardening as his fingers toyed with their brown erectness. Shyly Ottilie cupped her breasts envisaging that handsome man's wide mouth clamping down on her nipples and sucking them. She flexed her shoulders back. She let her own fingers squeeze her nipples, enjoying the piquancy of the unknown and the series of quick needle sharp sensations in her sensitised breasts. Then, overcome by a deep sense of guilt, she quickly dropped her hands.

They landed on her bare legs. Her imagination offered her no respite. Lightly she stroked her thighs, and the muscles hidden within the moistness behind her panties, clenched and tingled. She let out a tiny gasp and put a hand down to ease the tingling. In her mind's eye she saw the man's hands sliding past her rib cage, under the waistband of her skirt, over the gentle rise of her belly down to her waiting pubis. His fingers edged their way in under her pantie elastic. He played with her wetness and found a small erect spot that sent a thrill shooting to the very core of her being. Ottilie arched her back. She spread her legs apart, her own hands splaying herself open, her own fingers exploring her soft aroused tender and virginal flesh. She discovered that the delightful quivering in her soft wet opening was kindled by her each tiny stroke. It gave her a high pleasure she had never realised was attainable. Suddenly she stopped. She jumped quickly off the bed as if the furniture itself

71

was seducing and enticing her. Coming from her strict religious background she knew those thoughts and actions were considered evil. Not only was Ottilie a virgin, she had never, ever, played with herself before.

Agitated she stood in the middle of the room. She would ring Elmer. As she picked up the receiver the stranger came into her mind yet again. She tried hard to analyse what it was that she found so fascinating about him, but it completely eluded her. Even though she had endlessly fantasised about him, she would not and could not accept the fact that it was pure, raw, undiluted, sex that attracted her so much. Ottilie dialled Elmer's number.

Helmut had been very surprised to find Ottilie on the same flight as himself. He had also been extremely disappointed to watch her sleep the time away. He had missed her at the stop-over in Fort Worth. By the time they arrived in New Orleans he was in too much of a hurry to make conversation. He needed to see his lawyers fast. He must sign for the land around Bayou l'Extase before Frank Dale realised it was up for grabs and got his greasy hands on it. Anyhow he would know where to find Miss Ottilie Duvier. He could keep tabs on her through Elmer Planchet. Helmut was determined to have her but it was going to be a game and he intended it to keep him amused for some time.

He took a taxi from the airport. He was glad he had no luggage as he saw his mistress Mary Lou at Baggage Reclaim. He wanted to settle in before he had a session with her, besides he'd sent Daisy on ahead and she'd now be safely ensconced in his home. Helmut was pleased that Daisy had accepted his proposition. He liked her body and her complete surrender to sex. She would end up having enough money to continue her course. She could return to England and her studies with no one there any the wiser. He was looking forward to repeating the time spent with her at the restaurant in the more congenial surroundings of his own home. He trusted that his butler Epps had obeyed his instructions and that she would be ready and waiting for him.

Epps met Helmut on the porch with a glass of iced banana daiquiri.

'Mister Elmer called, sir,' said Epps.

'When?' asked the Count Helmut.

'Just before you arrived, sir. Missy answered the 'phone. He said he'd call back.'

'Then I've no doubt he will. Did Daisy arrive?' asked Helmut.

'Yes, sir,' said Epps.

'Has she obeyed my instructions?'

'Oh yes, sir.'

'You found her co-operative?'

'Extremely, sir.'

'She's ready and waiting for me?'

'Oh yes, sir,' said Epps.

'I'll have a bath before I see her,' he said, downing his drink.

'Yes, sir.'

Helmut made his way through the cedar-wood smelling formal dining room and sitting rooms, which led one into another without a hall. He stopped briefly to admire his collection of Shaker furniture. There had been some in the house when he started renting it, but he had spent time and a lot of money acquiring more. Keeping to the spirit of the simplicity of that sect of delightful carpentry and carving he kept the rest of the furnishing simple. Except for the elaborately decorated French windows. These were swathed in three different shades of muslin – cream, coffee and deep brown, the latter falling from large white plaster medallions of Helmut's coat of arms placed above the centre of the windows. Helmut stopped to pour himself a drink then continued on to his own very private quarters via the wide and elegantly curving staircase.

Helmut's bathroom was exceptionally masculine, everything was panelled in mahogany as was his dressing

73

room where he changed after bathing. He put on a white lawn shirt and black fine wool trousers. These were cut in a particular manner. In the front it had three flaps, two at the sides which met at the waist with one button and the top flap came from under his legs to button over the other two. When the top flap was hanging down it left Helmut's cock and balls completely free and unrestricted. He put on his riding boots then marched through into his dark, richly decorated bedroom, sat on his high four poster bed and rang the bell for Epps.

'Tell Daisy I want her now,' he said, when the butler appeared.

Daisy was waiting in a tiny ante-room. Her face was beautifully made up, her eyes rimmed with black kohl, her lips painted a crimson red, but her body was completely naked. The room was bare apart from a small table, a chair and a rough pile carpet. She had been kept there for some time. Left to her own devices she had stared at the only decoration, vulgar and extremely explicit prints of group sex on the wall. They had excited her and from time to time she had rubbed herself between her legs. Then in a drawer in the small table she had discovered a small white dildo. She had spread her legs wide and played it delicately along her wet juicy sex as she imagined the Count screwing her and remembered what had happened to her the previous evening.

Carey, the polite chauffeur had met her at the airport. He was a skinny nondescript man of Irish descent. On arrival at the house she met Epps. He had taken her to her room. Remembering every movie she had ever seen with black butlers in fine Southern houses, Epps was all that they were not. He looked more like a boxer from Brooklyn. He was big, broad and ugly, but there was something fascinating in his ugliness. A sexuality, an awareness of himself as a person that Daisy found a turn on.

Epps and the housekeeper, Missy Lee, had undressed and bathed her. Missy Lee was tiny and delicate and more saffron than any other colour. She was a mixture of Chinese, Japanese, Native American and black. Missy Lee had an air of authority about her and Daisy did exactly as she ordered. When Missy Lee said, 'Undress' Daisy undressed. When Missy Lee said, 'Step in that bath, honey and shower yourself' Daisy showered. When Missy Lee said, 'I am going to towel you dry' Daisy let her. And when Missy Lee's hands went a-roaming round the top of her legs, and her fingers a-searching out through the soft moistness between her fine, blonde-down slit, Daisy let her. And when Missy Lee told her to lie on her back with her legs high in the air and wide open, Daisy did. And, before putting red high-heeled shoes on Daisy's feet, and Missy Lee said, 'Honey, now I'm gonna lick that juicy pussy of yours,' Daisy let her, revelling in the feel of Missy's full dark lips and her tongue a-nibbling at her aroused little point. When Missy Lee decided Daisy's sex was sufficiently swollen with wantonness, Missy Lee stopped. Daisy accepted it. When Missy Lee wrapped Daisy's slim naked-ness in a long fine white shawl, and only in the fine white shawl, denying her her own clothes, Daisy accep-ted that too.

Then Missy Lee had departed and Epps had taken her to the Count's study to meet some of his closest friends.

In the smallish room, lit only by peripheral candles, Daisy was able to make out the body shapes of the men. Some were tall and thin, others short and thin, a couple were big and fat, they were all dressed totally in black. They sat on a row of chairs in front of a pedestal, which had a small rail on the front of it, rather like a conduc-tor's podium.

Epps walked Daisy on to the pedestal.

'Now, please stand quite still,' said Epps, placing her feet apart, pulling the shawl away and moving to one side. The men smiled licentiously at the sight of her tall slim sensuous body naked except for the high-heel-ed shoes which thrust her calves into an elegant shape and her rounded belly slightly forward. Epps nodded his head and in single file the men took it in turn to approach the podium. Not touching any other part of her body they greeted her by running an unhurried finger along her sex lips. This made further tremors of tingling wantonness flow through her. When each man had savoured the feel of her wet sex, Epps came up behind her.

'Please hold on to that rail and bend over Miss Daisy,' he said, politely. Then a bright spotlight was beamed down on them. Epps unflapped his trousers, removed his large black cock and rammed it straight up hard and unexpectedly into her arse.

Daisy gasped. Epps kept ramming. The men seated below had opened the flaps of their trousers. Daisy's eyes looked straight down on a number of cocks, standing white and proud in the residue light coming from the beam trained on her. Each one was sitting playing with himself whilst wondering who Epps was going to choose to be the first to take her after him.

Epps gripped her belly with one hand and her breasts with another and kept shoving hard. Daisy's head was bobbing up and down as she clutched at the rail whilst taking the full length of his big stiff prick in her tight and less-used hole.

In the ante room, remembering the feel of Epp's prick pounding into her, Daisy edged her buttocks off the seat and spread her legs wider, trailing the dildo round to find her other place. She was beginning to insert it when the door opened and Epps walked in with some flouncy clothes over his arm.

'That, Miss Daisy, is a punishable offence,' he said, dropping the clothes on the floor, clasping the dildo and taking it from her. 'However, as you like it, in a moment I'll make certain you keep it there. But I came to tell you the master wants you now, and whenever he calls you, you are to wear these. This is the correct mode of attire when visiting the Count.' Epps held up a pair of Victorian style stays in green satin and black lace. 'Please step into them, Miss Daisy.'

Daisy did as she was told. Epps pulled on the crisscross lacing tightening her waist, making her small breasts swell up enticingly. He put his large black hands inside the bodice, took hold of her nipples, brought them out from their lacy covering and carefully rested them on the outside edge of the lace. He bent down and licked them harshly with his tongue. Then he took a small porcelain pot from his pocket, dipped his fingers in and rouged her erect teats. He stroked her bare shoulders then tied a collar of black velvet embellished with small gold rings, around her white neck.

'Lay down and kindly lift your legs,' said Epps, and rolled lacy-topped black stockings up and over each limb, flicking her juicy pussy with one of his thick black fingers when he arrived at the top of her thighs.

Then he ordered her to step into a bright green satin skirt which was attached to a number of stiffened white silk petticoats. The centre of the skirt, both back and front, was slit from waist to hem. When she walked it would be possible to see not only the lacy tops of her hold up stockings but also that she was not wearing panties. Epps then told her to thrust her feet into a pair of high-heeled ankle boots. Then he grabbed a handful of her lovely blonde hair and twisting it haphazardly, allowing tendrils to escape and fall sexily down her back, he fixed it securely in position with a large black comb. He looked at her, his prick gaining in size. Master and servant both found pleasure in beautiful women, their bodies constrained. In that constraint they found a coquettishness that was highly erotic.

'Now please lie down again,' said Epps, 'only face down and with your bottom up.'

Daisy lay on the rough carpet which tickled her tender flesh. Epps took another small porcelain pot from one of his pockets. Dipping his fingers in its contents he slowly coated her sex, her bottom and her bottom-hole with a sweet-smelling oil.

Daisy swayed gently to the rhythm of his touch glorying in the licentiousness of her predicament. The outrageousness of being prepared for unbridled sex with a man for whom she felt no love, only lust, and being prepared by his big black butler who had so unceremoniously taken her in her arse the night before, excited her; heightening her sexuality and her essential eroticism.

Epps picked up the dildo. Spreading her buttocks apart he eased it into her freshly greased hole. Daisy relaxed her muscles allowing him greater freedom of access. When it was fully in he began moving it up and down, up and down, and her hips rolled with it. When she was panting he slowed down the pace. He then attached long thin leather thongs through rings in the end of the dildo. Parting her skirt he tied the thongs up through her sex and the crease of her buttocks and wound them around her waist. Epps made sure the dildo was securely in place then helped Daisy to her feet.

'Now you are ready for the master,' said Epps. 'Walk.' But Daisy had difficulty walking in the high heels with the dildo strapped firmly inside her bottom-hole. Parting her skirt and gripping the end of the dildo Epps pushed her forward by jerking the dildo up inside her. 'Walk out of this door into the next one.'

Helmut lay on the bed gazing at her as Daisy was thrust jerkily towards him, her stomach pushing against the tightness of the stays. She was beautiful and debauched, a delicious paramour, and he liked that. Epps brought her to the side of the bed. Helmut reached up and touched her rouged nipples. Epps thrust the dildo harder into her backside making her teeter on her high heels and forcing her nipples flat against Helmut's hands.

'Undo your flaps,' Helmut said to Epps, who did as he was told. And his very big stiff prick launched itself forward and up. 'Daisy, turn round so that your rump is facing me and, keeping your legs straight, bend from the waist and suck his prick.'

'Yes, sir, thank you, sir,' she said, her skirt parting, presenting Helmut with the sight of the dildo stuck hard and rigid in her bottom and tied through her crack and sex.

Helmut took hold of the dildo with one hand and his own prick with another and began to move both with simultaneous rhythm. Then he moved to one side so that he could see Daisy's small tongue snaking out of her crimson painted mouth, flicking around the tip of Epps' prick. He watched her dipping gently into the tiny hole at its tip, licking at some of the escaping moisture then, holding the base of his erect black shaft with her white fingers, she eased her mouth down and over its head and gave the big black man exquisite pleasure.

'Are you wanting to be fucked?' asked Helmut, as her bottom swayed one way, her breasts another and her hand charged up and down from prick to balls meeting her full crimson lips.

'Whatever is your pleasure, sir,' said Daisy, taking her mouth away from Epps' cock but continuing to use her hands with a sure pressure.

'Were you fucked last night?' asked Helmut.

'Yes, sir.'

'Do you know by whom?'

'No, sir. I was fucked from behind.'

'Someone fucked your ass?'

'Yes, sir.'

'Who fucked her, Epps?'

'I did, sir.'

'Did she enjoy that, Epps?'

'I think so sir, because I just found her trying to fuck herself with the dildo.'

'You did what!' exclaimed Helmut.

'Found her in the ante room, trying to stuff it up her own ass, master.'

'Is that true?' said Helmut, shoving the dildo harder and harder into Daisy's second opening.

'Yes, sir,' she replied with downcast eyes.

'Were you given permission to play with yourself?'

'No, sir, but I was left alone and found the dildo, sir.'

'That is a punishable offence,' he said, and began to

slide his hands over her bottom cheeks. Then he stopped and marched across the room, leaving Daisy still bending and sucking Epps' prick.

Helmut noisily opened a cupboard drawer. He brought out a number of whips, dildoes and vibrators and carefully laid them out on his bed: the crop, the whip, the tawse, with its flayed end, and a variety of both black and white different sized dildoes and a couple of small vibrators.

'Come here,' said Helmut. 'Epps prepare the bed'.

Daisy stopped sucking Epps' cock, and stood beside Helmut. He parted her dress and ran a hand over her belly.

'Hold your skirt aside, put your legs apart, and keep silent and very still,' he commanded.

Daisy did as she was told straining her legs back so that her sex was jutting forward. He ran a hand up along her calves and thighs and then over her freshly oiled and fragrant sex lips. The leather thongs, holding the dildo in position, were cutting harshly into her moist squashy flesh. The sight of it excited him. Helmut lifted the hood of her vulva and with the lightest of touches he began to tease her prominent excitable little point into view. Daisy caught her breath, but that was the only movement she made. Slowly, the sweetest sensations started to devour her. Her womb clenched and unclenched as a trickle of energy within her gathered momentum. Helmut knew before long she would not be able to remain either silent or still. He picked up the smallest vibrator, switched it on and handed it to her.

'Use it,' he said, his fingers seeking out her wet furls and entering her thick pink and creamy wetness.

Standing, with the seated Helmut's fingers embedded in her, and the tiny motor exciting her clitoris, Daisy's legs began to shudder. Epps came up behind her, parted her skirt and let his penis rub along the rounded flesh of her buttocks, and his black hands encircle her pale breasts. Daisy closed her eyes. She wanted to take and relish every moment of her wantonness. She forgot the order to keep still. She swayed and sighed.

'That was foolish,' said Count Helmut.

Daisy's eyes flew open. Helmut stopped playing with her sex and picked up the crop. He stood in front of her, thickset and powerful, his muscles rippling and his penis hard and erect.

'I gave you an order,' he said. 'You disobeyed. Epps hold her.'

Epps quickly changed his position and clamped a pair of handcuffs on Daisy's wrists. The handcuffs were then tied to chains attached to the bed posts, which had been hidden by heavy tapestry fabric. Then a blindfold was put around her eyes.

Full of apprehension, Daisy waited, tense. But instead of the crop landing on her buttocks, hands spread her thighs and a tongue began its journey along the swollen moistness of her pussy. Opening her. Making her more responsive. More licentious and wanton. Then she felt soft wet leather trailing seductively through her tingling expectant sex. Her muscles tried to clasp it and draw it inwards. That was when he struck her. Six severe strokes of the crop across her dimpled backside. And Daisy screamed. She yelled. It was searing and unexpected and the lash caught her unawares. The pain, the exquisite agc ʌy ʾook her higher than Helmut's fingering. She twisted on her chains. Then Helmut turned her to face him. He removed her blindfold. He ran his cock along her inner thighs. He opened her pussy with his prick. He licked her nipples. Daisy sighed with pent up desire and longing. The moment she wanted had almost arrived. The feel of his thick stiff prick deep within her. The burning of the lash marks on her backside only adding to her extreme pleasure. Pushing her against the end of the bed, he took her standing up.

When Helmut had finished he buttoned-up the flap on his trousers. He told Epps to bring him some food and Daisy to rest.

'Tonight, I'm giving a small dinner party,' he said. 'I want you there, dressed as you are now. You will rouge your breasts and your sex and you will be open for any of my friends male or female who want access to you. Is that understood?'

'Yes, sir,' Daisy replied, the thought of it giving her a further rush of licentiousness.

'However, whilst you are resting, Epps and Missy have my permission, their other duties permitting, to come in and use you for their pleasure. Is that understood too?' he asked caressing the livid marks on her white bottom.

'Yes, sir.'

'Now, go to your room and sleep.'

It was while Epps was in the kitchen talking to Missy, and putting together some light refreshment for the Count that Epps heard the harsh jangling of the bell on the gate.

When he went out to answer it he was surprised to find a beautiful Titian-haired girl waiting there. He was even more surprised when she demanded to be let into the house, insisting it was hers and telling him her name was Ottilie Duvier. Nice name, nice girl, he thought, sexy but obviously a basket case. He sent her on her way and went back to the kitchen.

Epps took a plate of sticky barbequed spare ribs, a water bowl, salad and french bread and laid it out in the dining room. Then he went upstairs to tell the Count his food was served.

'Oh, and sir, we just had a visitor, a girl, a redhead, said her name was Ottilie Duvier and wanting to come in,' said Epps.

'Well, where is she?' asked the Count.

'I sent her packing, sir.'

'You did WHAT!' exclaimed the Count, to Epps' amazement. 'That, Epps, is the one woman I want, and you sent her packing.'

'How was I to know, sir?' said Epps, feeling put out and aggrieved. He turned to stare out of the window. He saw Elmer Planchet climbing out of his car.

'Very true,' said the Count, calming down. It was unreasonable of him to expect Epps to read his mind. He hadn't yet had time to tell him what had happened in Paris.

'She stood there saying she owned the place . . .'

'Oh really!' said the Count.

'Mister Elmer's just arrived, sir,' Epps said. 'Shall I let him in?'

'Yes,' said the Count. This was going to be a most interesting encounter. 'Bring another plate, we'll eat and talk. Oh and Epps, Daisy is in her room . . . so whilst I'm discussing business with Elmer you can take an hour off.'

'Why thank you, sir,' said Epps.

Epps ushered Elmer in, and then, with his cock rising in anticipation, he went up to visit Daisy.

Chapter 5

*I*t was early evening and Elmer Planchet was still in his top storey, stainless steel and primary colours office at Planchet & Sietz architects, in Poydras Plaza. Until recently the company had been known as Planchet, Seitz & Cates. But due to Elmer's foolishness Norwood Cates had left the business.

The deep orange sun was going down leaving the sky flushed indigo blue streaked with pink and yellow. Staring out of the huge windows Elmer could see most of New Orleans. But he was not appreciating the view. Cash, and the flow of it into and out of his hands, was worrying him. He had hoped when Bernard Duvier died that he'd be a reasonably rich man. The call he had received that morning from his lawyers told him he was not. As the man of the family, Elmer had expected to be left the house in Washington Avenue. It had come as a severe shock to discover that his sonofabitch step-father had left the house, the one thing he thought would be his, jointly to him and to Ottilie. Elmer conveniently forgot that Bernard had told him he would not bequeath him a thing if he continued to gamble. According to Bernard's lights, in leaving him something, he had treated his profligate step-son extremely well. Elmer didn't see it that way. Elmer was seriously short of money.

However, he did have a lucrative sideline. But even this was threatened by the lawyer's news. Elmer had let Bernard's house in Washington Avenue to Count Helmut von Straffen. The Count had wanted to buy, but nobody was selling, not in the Garden District. He had offered to rent it and had given Elmer extremely good terms. Having obtained it, the Count had then spent a fortune doing it up to his own very particular specifications – which Elmer didn't mind a bit. His company had got the contract; he'd made good money from it and it looked superb. But the renting agreement was up for renewal. What was Elmer going to do about that now? He didn't think it'd be legal if he got Helmut to sign immediately whilst pretending he didn't know Ottilie was part-owner?

What was the house to Ottilie? She was an heiress and she had other properties. She lived in Paris, was going to marry an English Lord, and showed no signs of returning to the Crescent City. It was many things to Elmer – mainly a constant source of income which he desperately needed. If he went ahead with a fresh agreement and she disagreed, and if she decided to fight him it would take ages to get to court. He could continue raking in the money whilst the lawyers wrangled. Elmer decided it was worth the risk. He'd go see Helmut and have a word with him. He picked up the telephone and dialled the house.

The housekeeper, the weird yet wonderful Missy Lee, answered. She seemed to possess the knowledge of strange religions derived from the many cultures of her ancestry and Elmer was a little afraid of her. Curtly she told him that if and when the Count appeared she would inform him that Elmer had called and wanted to speak to him. Elmer said he would call again later anyhow. Vexed, he replaced the receiver thinking it was a pity he couldn't buy Ottilie out and be done with it. Unfortunately there was no way that he could do that. The gambling debts he'd run up with Frank Dale had used up practically all his finances. That's how he saw it. To others he was still rich, but what they regarded as luxury he thought of as necessity. Elmer had need of a lot of money.

Elmer's thoughts were interrupted by the arrival of his new secretary, Josephine.

'Excuse me, Mister Planchet,' she said, in slightly clipped tones. Her accent was not that of the deep south. It was harder but not unpleasant, and her vowels were less elongated. 'I've photocopied those plans for you, sir, and arranged the meeting with the committee for the St Jacques Arts Community for three o'clock tomorrow afternoon. You didn't have any appointments for then and I hope that's okay with you.'

'That's just fine, Josephine, thank you,' he said. 'But shouldn't you have gone home by now?'

'Yes,' she said. 'The truth is I had a date but it got cancelled and my flatmate's got a gentleman caller. She asked me not to come home too early. So I thought as I'm new I'd take the opportunity to learn a bit more about the office. Do some filing and things. Have you anything in particular that needs doing?'

'Well yes, Josephine, I have,' he said. 'All those old files belonging to my previous partner need to be sorted. And then parcelled up and sent to him.'

'I'll be happy to do that now, sir,' said Josephine. 'Where are they'

'Over there in that cupboard.'

Elmer pointed to the wall of bright yellow stainless steel. He had had the cupboards painted in red, blue and yellow. Easy to find things. Easy to refer to. He reckoned it made him more efficient, and consequently his staff as well.

Josephine opened the cupboard door and began taking out the many files stacked there. Elmer sat down at his tubular steel and glass desk and pretended to write. He was actually looking at the girl.

He didn't know why he'd chosen her over the other candidates. She wasn't his usual type. All his secretaries, all his women, had been good looking long-legged blondes. Josephine was nothing special, short with light brown hair and she wore spectacles. He supposed she was pretty; fortunately she didn't wear too much make-up. She had a nice smile, and was also rounded: cuddly; big boobs; sloping shoulders, small waist but large hips. She didn't seem too bothered about not being the archetypal beauty. Maybe that's what he liked about her. She was comfortable with herself.

Josephine was wearing a trim white cotton blouse. He could see her brassière outline. Her formal office wear grey skirt was a wrap-over. When she bent down one of the wraps spread out slightly and he could see her chubby thighs and her dimpled knees. Elmer found those knees unbelievably attractive. Their softness appealed to him. He stopped pretending to write and stared fascinated; every time she moved, taking a file out, putting it down, her skirt flipped sideways and he caught another flash of those knees. They didn't seem to have any bones in them. Just rounded flesh and dimples. The longer he looked the more he was captivated. Elmer had a strong desire to touch them. To caress them. He started to imagine his hands revelling in their shape, feeling like a sculptor with wet malleable clay. He wondered if she was wearing stockings or pantie-hose. His cock began to rise. Elmer put his hands down under the desk and gripped his balls. No. Definitely No. Josephine had only been with him one week and she'd proved a good worker. His better instincts told him not to go mess things up. His wayward dick had caused enough trouble for the time being. His dick was another reason for his present impecunious state.

If only he hadn't screwed his partner's wife. Elmer re-adjusted his thoughts. If only he hadn't got caught screwing his partner's wife. Elmer pretended to be writing again, vividly recalling Sharon Cates marching into his office demanding to see her husband, Norwood.

She'd stood in front of him in her bright red suit, the jacket buttoned to the neck and the skirt short. She wore red high-heeled shoes but no stockings, and her permed hair was tied up with a gaily coloured bandanna.

'Norwood's gone to a meeting,' Elmer had told her.

'How long will he be?' she'd asked, in her simpering whispery voice whilst sitting on his desk and crossing her legs.

'A couple of hours,' he'd answered, watching her skirt rise and her tanned thighs appear.

'Time enough for you to fuck me then,' she'd said. And he had gulped.

'Don't tell me you haven't wanted to.'

'Well, yes . . .' he replied.

'I thought so. I've seen those big brown eyes of yours staring at my tits and wondering . . .'

Then she'd leant across the desk pulled on his tie, bringing his face towards hers, and kissed his lips.

'Elmer you're a handsome man,' she'd said. 'And I like men who are handsome, lean and mean . . .'

This statement did exactly what it was supposed to do. It puffed Elmer out with pride. Lean he certainly was, stick of liquorice lean, but mean – no. He'd always wanted to be. But Elmer could never be accurately described as mean. Stupid, foolish, thoughtless, plodding were the more usual epithets for Elmer. However, he decided, there was a first time for everything and he liked the idea of Mean Elmer. His cock twitched and started its inexorable rise.

'Norwood's gone to seed,' Sharon continued, 'too fat for his own good and he can't give me a good time, not any more. You know I have to give him a blow job before he can get it up. And then once he's got it up I have to sit on him. Sit astride that great bulk of his 'cos he's too fat to move. Now, Elmer what I want is a real man. Somebody who's gonna be on top and screw the living daylights outta me. And I reckon you's just the guy to do it.'

Sharon undid her suit buttons whilst she was talking. When Elmer's hand reached up his fingers were surprised to meet bare flesh. No brassière. Just pert smooth breasts with long hard nipples. Sharon swung her legs over to his side of the desk and the next moment her skirt was up round her waist, her legs were wide apart and he was faced with bare pussy. Then she took off her suit top and swivelled round so that she lay full length along the desk.

'So fuck me,' she said.

Elmer could not get his trousers off quick enough and his cock had gained several inches with her words. Sharon hitched her skirt higher and began stroking herself. Elmer jumped up beside her on the desk.

'That's a real nice cock,' said Sharon, leaning forward and taking hold of it. Bliss, he thought as her hands encircled his throbbing member. Pure bliss. His body started to shake, and the familiar tightening in his balls and twisting feeling in his gut started to overcome him. The difference a woman's hands make, he thought. It wasn't the same doing it to yourself, wasn't the same at all. Pleasurable for sure, but not the same.

Elmer had been celibate for three weeks. His last girl-friend had found someone else when he made it quite clear he did not want to take their relationship further.

Elmer had been lusting after Mary Lou – Ottilie's cousin, Mary Lou. Elmer suspected she was having an affair with the Count. Mary Lou was the epitome of his type of woman. She was a tall, good looking, long-legged blonde. And he wanted her. Elmer had wanted her for some time. He thought he was making real head-way, taking her out to dinner, to the theatre and con-certs, then she had stopped 'phoning him. Stopped taking his calls too. One day he saw her out on the town with the Count. And they were very friendly. She'll soon have had enough of him, Elmer had thought. When she finds out exactly what he's into she'll run a mile. But so far she hadn't. Not that Elmer knew for sure what it was the Count was into. But he had ordered some odd things for the house. Special sound-proofing for one room and he wasn't a musician. The rumours were rife. Sex romps and sex orgies. Those were the rumours. He couldn't see

Mary Lou taking part in any of that. But imagining her taking part in it had kept his night time fantasies going. But now Sharon was handling his dick, doing all the right things to it. And if she wasn't careful he'd spurt before he could screw her.

'Stop,' he said. 'Sharon if you don't stop I'll come.'

'We can't have that, honey,' she whispered. And opened her wet sex for him. Elmer positioned himself between her outstretched legs, his prick at her entrance, and lunged.

Elmer pounded into her. She lay gasping but not moving, not really, just taking every thrust he gave her.

Elmer was about to come when Norwood walked in.

'What the hell!' exclaimed Norwood. 'Sharon you goddamn whore I'll divorce you for this, and Elmer, I quit this business right now. You can have a mega scandal or you can just sign the termination and pay me what I want. Whichever way, you'll hear from my lawyers in the morning.'

And he had. Documents had arrived, almost as if they had been drawn up ready and waiting to be sent and signed. Norwood had departed taking some of the firm's best clients with him. But he hadn't divorced his wife. He and Sharon were still together. A couple of times in recent weeks Elmer had wondered whether the whole episode was a put up job. Had Norwood, for some reasons best known to himself, wanted out? If he had then by catching Elmer with his pants down he'd sure got the best terms. Yet Elmer had to face the fact, if his goddamn prick hadn't reacted, they couldn't have done it. So he wasn't going to react now. He was going to turn off fantasising about his new secretary. What he had to do was concentrate on getting Mary Lou into bed.

'Oh Mister Planchet, where do you keep the ladder?' Josephine's pretty lilting voice burst in upon his lustful thoughts . . .

'In the cupboard in the bathroom,' he answered, not offering to get it in case she saw his state of arousal.

Josephine returned with the ladder. She stood on it,

climbed half way up and began removing files from the top shelf. Every time she stretched her arms, her skirt went up. And Elmer saw those knees again and got a real thrill. Elmer sat at his desk fixated on those knees, day-dreaming just how he'd touch their rounded softness and those dimples. He was so busy concentrating on their shape that it took him a moment to realise that the knees were moving, not upwards or downwards but sideways. Out into the air. And the ladder was going another way. It dawned on Elmer that Josephine was falling. He rushed over, caught her, and the two of them landed on the floor in a tangled heap of legs and arms and files. Elmer was entranced by the soft squashiness of her body against his. He moved his arm as if he was trying to extricate himself from her, but actually held her closer.

'Oh . . .' she gasped.

'Oh, Josephine,' he said. 'Are you hurt?'

'I don't know, sir,' she said a little breathlessly, turning her innocent young face to his and gazing into his eyes.

Every good intention Elmer had made was blown apart. Josephine's spectacles had come off during the fall and he was staring into the most beautiful violet eyes he had ever seen. What with her eyes and her knees, and her mouth perilously close to his, Elmer could not resist the little voice within him that said, kiss her, Elmer.

That was when the telephone rang. Saved from his own lust by his urgent need to talk to Helmut, Elmer gently pushed Josephine to one side and sprang up to answer it.

Josephine was extremely disappointed by the unexpected sound. She had spent some considerable time and energy planning on how to be seduced by Elmer. She had decided that he was the man she wanted, and she was going to have him. Hurriedly she adjusted her clothing and got to her feet whilst Elmer took the call.

'Elmer . . .' It was Ottilie's voice.

'Oh! Ottilie!' he said with surprise.

'Elmer, I have just been to Washington Avenue ...'

'You're in New Orleans?'

'Yes, Elmer, I'm in New Orleans. I couldn't have gone to the house otherwise. Elmer what have you done to it?'

'Um ...'

'Elmer, why the silence? I asked you a question. What have you done to the house?'

'I let it to Count Helmut von Straffen.'

'Now, Elmer that house is yours and mine and before that it was my pa's and I don't recollect him giving you permission to rent it out.'

'No that's true Ottilie he didn't.'

'Well now I suggest you get that Count whatever he calls himself out of there because, Elmer, I want to live in that house.'

'Ottilie, I don't think I can too readily do that.'

'Why not?'

'We have an agreement.'

'Which as from now is null and void, Elmer. So you'd better go see this man and tell him to quit the premises.'

'Ottilie ...'

'Yes, Elmer ...?'

'... that'll be mighty difficult ...'

'Elmer, I am tired. I'm planning on having a quiet evening to myself and be early to bed. But in the morning I'll be at your office at nine sharp and I'll want to know this man has had his order to quit. Then I want the two of us to talk money, Elmer.'

'What sort of money, Ottilie?'

'I'd like to buy you out.'

'Ottilie ...'

'I don't want to discuss anything else right now. Goodnight.' The telephone clicked off.

'Shit,' said Elmer.

Every goddamn thing he touched concerning the house went wrong. Still it had stopped his bad intentions towards his sweet little secretary.

'I think it's time I was going home now, sir,' said Josephine.

'Yes,' said Elmer. 'I'll lock up and see you in the morning.'

'Yes, sir. I'll be here, nine on the dot.'

Josephine departed. Elmer went into the bathroom and tidied himself up. He would go to the house and see if Helmut was there. It was vitally necessary the two of them had a plan of action. He had to have something to say to Ottilie next morning.

Elmer was welcomed by Epps who showed him into a downstairs salon. Every time Elmer came to the house he appreciated more and more the things the Count had done. He'd kept the essence of its old fashioned elegance and had been guided by its proportions for the various changes he'd made. It was all so very different to the frusty drapes and over-the-top furnishings Bernard Duvier had left behind. Elmer sat in one of the four Shaker chairs and glanced about him feeling the essential puritanism of the room. It was sparkling clean and utterly free of clutter, each item of furniture beautiful in its own right. It was a masculine room, no frills or fripperies. One large vase of fresh seasonal flowers, a display of exotic feathers and the three layers of different coloured muslin drapes were the only lightly decorative and vaguely feminine things to be seen. After a few moments Helmut came in.

'Elmer, good to see you,' said Helmut. 'What'll you have to drink? Whisky, Southern Comfort, wine or a cocktail?'

'Southern Comfort.'

'Fine,' said Helmut opening up a cabinet and pouring that thick sweet brown liquid into a glass for Elmer and getting a whisky for himself. 'I'm having a small dinner party tonight so I can't be too long ... Missy told me you'd telephoned and your voice sounded urgent.'

'It is,' replied Elmer. 'I've had some news today. My step-sister, Ottilie, you know the one I asked you to check out in Paris. Well she's here in New Orleans.'

'Is that so?' asked Helmut, keeping to himself the knowledge that she had been to the house and demanded entry.

'By the way, did you get to see her in Paris?' asked Elmer.

'I did,' replied Helmut.

'And? What was she like?'

'I only saw her briefly. Didn't actually get to meet her. Not to be introduced. You told me she's engaged to be married, to an English Lord. Is that engagement still on?'

'I suppose so. I haven't heard any different. Why?'

'Idle curiosity,' said Helmut.

'Oh! Well anyhow, I've got a problem which could also be your problem,' said Elmer.

'How's that?'

'Remember my step-daddy died? Well he left me something in his will.'

'Wasn't that unexpected? I thought he said he wouldn't.'

'It would almost have been better if he hadn't,' said Elmer. 'He left me this house but not all of it, half to me and half to Ottilie. She rang me and is well pissed off because you're renting the place. Says she wants you out. Now I want you to stay. So I was thinking can we draw up a new agreement and get it signed before she starts her nonsense? Present her with a fait accompli.'

'If your step-sister owns half the house I don't think that would be legal,' said the Count. 'But Elmer, why be hasty. A good income for you is also good for her . . .'

'Yes, but . . .'

'Listen, Elmer, wouldn't it be better if you introduced us, then we could have a little talk together, just the two of us. Maybe she'd agree to renting the house to me and everything then would be just fine.'

'But she'd take half the rent!'

'That's for sure but Elmer, half is better than none at all, isn't it?'

'Yes . . . but the thing is Helmut, she says she wants to buy me out and live here.'

'Oh does she!' said Helmut, thinking that did not suit him at all. 'No, Elmer not a good idea on her part. That wouldn't work for either of us. So I think perhaps we'd better work out some other arrangement.'

'Maybe you could seduce her and get her to agree!'

'Elmer that is a wildly immoral suggestion.'

'But it's a good one isn't it?'

'It has definite possibilities,' said the Count, a lascivious smile hovering around his lips.

'Ottilie said she's coming to see me at nine sharp tomorrow, so what say you if I bring her here about half nine?'

'I'd say that's an excellent idea,' said Helmut.

The jangle of the front door bell hit Elmer's ears. Out of the corner of his eye he saw Epps disappear through the long French windows. Moments later he saw him again and caught a flash of blonde hair and long suntanned legs.

'Who's he got in there with him?' Elmer heard Mary Lou ask Epps.

'Mister Elmer, Mam,' said Epps.

'Cousin Elmer! Why I must just go in there and say howdy,' said Mary Lou.

Before Epps could restrain her Mary Lou was walking into the salon. And Elmer gasped. He had never seen Mary Lou look so outrageously sexy. She was dressed in a short leather skirt with a tight leather jacket and round her neck she wore a leather necklet decorated with metal studs. She wore no stockings but very high-heeled black leather shoes.

'Helmut, darling,' she said striding towards him and kissing the top of his head. 'And Elmer!'

Elmer stood up and Mary Lou kissed him on both cheeks. Elmer flushed as he smelled her scent. He didn't know what it was but it sure was potent. Mary Lou sat on the edge of the Count's chair. He was sitting opposite Elmer. Mary Lou crossed her legs, wiggled, then she uncrossed her legs and Elmer got a flash of blonde pussy. No panties. The Count let his hands trawl along Mary Lou's legs.

'Did I interrupt you honey?' she asked.

'You did,' said Helmut. 'We were discussing business. Apparently Elmer's step-sister's in town.'

'I know.'

'How do you know' asked Elmer.

'I met her at the airport,' replied Mary Lou, changing her position slightly so that the Count's hands could ride further up her legs without hindrance. Elmer sat mesmerised as the Count's hands blatantly searched out her golden pussy and gently played with it. Elmer felt his cock stirring. The two of them were being deliberately provocative.

'Elmer tells me she now owns half this house and wants to buy Elmer out and come and live here,' said Helmut.

'Yeah,' said Mary Lou, squirming as the Count's fingers touched her clitoris. 'She said something like that to me and my daddy.'

Then Elmer remembered the Count's previous query regarding Ottilie's engagement.

'Did she come here with her fiancé?' asked Elmer.

'Hell, no,' replied Mary Lou, rolling her hips round and around as Helmut's fingers were gliding into her moistness. 'She said her engagement was over. Finished. I told her she was a fool. Well fancy letting go of a real live English lord.' Helmut jabbed harshly into her as she said that and Mary Lou squirmed and gasped. 'Elmer, can you see what the Count is doing to me? He's put his fingers up and is playing with my pussy.'

'I can see that,' said Elmer swallowing hard, and trying to keep his cock down.

'Isn't that just something you've always wanted to do?' said Mary Lou, shamelessly.

'Yes,' said Elmer.

'Then I think you should,' said the Count. 'Elmer, come over here. One should always do the things one most wants to. You want to feel Mary Lou, then I give my permission. Mary Lou, please hold your skirt up, right up.'

Mary Lou stood and wiggled her skirt up over her hips so that it was bunched up around her waist. The Count stayed seated, his hands still running along her thighs as he thought about ways of seducing Ottilie.

'Open your legs, my dear,' he said.

Mary Lou stood with her legs braced apart.

'Elmer, I don't think this is the moment to be shy,' said Mary Lou, beckoning him towards her.

Elmer stood beside her. Mary Lou pulled at his zip. She put her hands inside the opening in his trousers, encircled Elmer's prick and then eased it out from its fabric imprisonment.

'Hold it, Elmer,' said Mary Lou. 'I wanna see you hold your prick.'

Elmer clasped himself.

'Rub yourself, Elmer,' said Mary Lou. 'I wanna see you wank.'

Elmer held his prick just under the rim of its cap. Violently and quickly he rubbed himself as the blood surged through into his veins pumping his cock into a good and effective size. And the Count's fingers continued to glide in and out of Mary Lou's wet and wanton pussy.

'I think I'd like him to suck me,' she said.

'The lady wants you to suck her,' said Helmut. 'And in this house we do not deny ladies anything. So kneel down Elmer and lick.'

Elmer knelt down in front of Mary Lou, the Count removed his fingers from her sex and Elmer, still holding his own prick, put his tongue at the entrance to Mary Lou's moist opening. He knelt slightly to the side and let his cock trail along the inside of Mary Lou's legs as his tongue nibbled and found her engorged clitoris. He used long thick strokes with his short fat tongue and Mary Lou began to sigh. Then she swayed and jerked and gasped.

'He does it too good,' she said to Helmut who was caressing the cheeks of her backside. 'How about letting him fuck me?'

'No,' said Helmut. Annoyed by her request he slapped her bottom hard, leaving a bright red imprint on her pale white buttocks. 'And it'll be a long time before you get screwed. Your uncontrollable wantonness will have to be punished.'

Mary Lou was excited by his words. She opened her legs fractionally wider as if in silent acceptance of judgement.

Elmer, who was still licking and slurping at Mary Lou's soft wetness, felt the tiny muscles quiver and wondered what the Count meant by that. What sort of punishment? After all he had been in favour of Elmer sucking her pussy.

'But I would hate to let a friend leave my house unsatisfied,' said Helmut. He picked up the bell on the table beside him and rang it.

Elmer could not believe what was happening to him. He was kneeling on the floor his cock sidling along Mary Lou's legs, sucking Mary Lou's pussy with the Count fondling her bottom and promising her punishment for letting Elmer suck her when Epps walked in.

'You called, sir,' asked Epps, not turning a hair by the sight that met his eyes.

'I did, Epps, I did,' said Helmut. 'Would you bring Miss Daisy down?'

'Yes, sir.' said Epps.

Elmer felt a sudden closing of Mary Lou's muscles as she flinched.

Who the hell is Miss Daisy, Mary Lou wanted to ask but didn't dare. She knew too well that Count Helmut von Straffen was a law unto himself. He did not brook questions about the women he invited into his home. But Mary Lou was jealous. This woman might supplant her in the Count's affections.

'And some of my toys,' said the Count.

'Yes, sir, anything in particular?'

'No, bring a selection,' said Helmut.

'For yourself, sir?' asked Epps.

'No, not at the moment. As you can see Mister Elmer is enjoying himself.'

'Yes, sir, he seems to have a very good technique, sir. It looks to me like he's giving Miss Mary Lou a real good tonguing.'

'Oh he is Epps, he is . . .' said Mary Lou, enthusiastically, knowing this would annoy Helmut. Then she put her hands down so that she could pull her thighs further apart, allowing Elmer's tongue to go deeper.

'On second thoughts, Epps,' said Helmut, giving Mary Lou a harder, harsher, more stinging slap on her bottom. This made her jerk forward and Elmer's tongue lose its position on her clitoris. 'Bring me my special box.'

'Yes, sir,' said Epps, and left the room.

'So my dear, Elmer is giving you an excellent tonguing is he?' asked Helmut, his hand gripping her flanks, his fingers digging into her flesh.

'Yes,' she gasped.

'I see,' he said.

Elmer caught a hint of a threat in the Count's words. But it didn't deter Mary Lou getting wetter and wriggling her hips under the onslaught from his tongue. Elmer's cock was needing attention. It needed to be enclosed, it was yearning to be surrounded by warm flesh. He took it in hand and rubbed it against the calves of Mary Lou's bare legs.

It didn't take long before Epps was back.

'Miss Daisy, sir,' said Epps some few minutes later.

Elmer looked up from Mary Lou's pussy and saw a tall blonde woman being ushered into the room. It was Elmer's turn to gasp as Epps led her across the room to stand before the Count.

Daisy was blindfolded with a black silken strip over her eyes. She was wearing a tight basque with her breasts spilling over the top and her nipples placed on the outer edges of the lace. Her full ballooning skirts were slit from top to bottom. As she walked Elmer could see her stocking tops and the fair down covering her sex. Her hands were held together over her belly with leather bindings.

'Kneel,' said Helmut. Epps helped Daisy to kneel. 'Pleasure me,' he said, undoing the flap of his trousers. 'Keeping your arse up.' Epps guided Daisy between Helmut's legs, so that her back was horizontal, and her bottom up and easily penetrable. Epps parted her skirts

99

making certain her crop marked and rounded flanks were clearly visible. Then he put her hands up to Helmut's large, waiting and very erect member. With as much mobility as the bindings allowed Daisy reached out and caressed Helmut's balls with one hand and encircled his penis with the other. Then she brought her head down over the tip and her wide bright red lips took the head of his member into her mouth. And she began to suck.

Helmut, enjoying the sensation of Daisy's expert mouth rubbing up and down along his prick, continued to caress Mary Lou's bottom with one hand, the other hand hovered over the box that Epps now held in front of him.

'Ah, these two I think,' he said pointing.

Epps took from the box a whip with a flayed end and a large black double-ended dildo which met in the centre with a couple of large imitation testicles.

'I think Miss Mary Lou can have this,' said Helmut, handing the dildo to Epps. Mary Lou licked her lips. 'Oh Elmer, the lady sucking my prick is Daisy. As you can see she has a delightful motion, and she also has a pussy just waiting to be entered. And as I can see from the size of your erection you need to enter a good pussy. You have my permission to screw her right now.'

Elmer, excited by the idea of screwing an unknown and blindfolded woman, edged away from Mary Lou's sex but before he could turn round to put his legs between Daisy's he saw the butler had got there before him. Epps had his big black hand running along Daisy's open swollen sex lips. Her hips were moving to the rhythm of Epp's fingers, just as her head was moving to the rhythm of Helmut's prick.

'The lady is very wet,' said Epps. And sidled away leaving space for Elmer to come between Daisy's legs.

Elmer looked at the sight that was presented to him. A young woman sucking one man's cock, her bottom high in the air, her sex open and juicy and about to be taken by him. It excited him almost beyond endurance.

His penis had gained inches it never had before and was throbbing with a new intensity. He swallowed hard in an effort to relieve the tightened sexuality that was flooding into his stomach, his loins and his mouth. Elmer positioned his prick at the pink swollen opening that was waiting to be plundered. He heard Daisy give a slight gasp as his prick began its journey into her luscious wet wanton folds. It was his turn to gasp out loud when her muscles closed around his member and drew him in, and let go, then closed around his member again and drew him further in and in and in. And then he slid backwards and forwards fast, gripping her hips as hard on the outside as her inner muscles gripped him on the inside.

'Now Mary Lou . . .' said Helmut.

Elmer slowed his rhythm down. Once more there was that threatening note in Helmut's voice. Elmer looked past the Count to Mary Lou standing at his side.

'Epps has a present for you, haven't you Epps?'

'Yes sir.'

'Turn your back to Elmer and bend over my dear, and touch your toes.'

Mary Lou did exactly what Helmut asked. Helmut rubbed her rump.

'Epps, the dildo, please.'

Epps stood behind Mary Lou who was still wearing her leather jacket and had her leather skirt up round her waist. Elmer, whilst screwing Daisy, watched Epps slowly insert the leather member into Mary Lou's expectant opening. When it was up as far as she could take it he began moving it up and down. And Mary Lou's hips were going round in small circles as she took it.

'You may stand up now, Mary Lou,' said Helmut.

Elmer found the sight unbelievably exciting as Mary Lou stood up and the end of the dildo was hanging down from her sex. Helmut reached out a hand, caught hold of the hanging end and slowly eased it up and down inside her.

'Now, Epps, let her feel your cock,' said Helmut.

101

Epps undid his flap and his huge black prick stood erect.

With his own prick thundering backwards and forwards inside Daisy, watching Mary Lou being screwed by the dildo and then her hand encircling the black man's member, Elmer's mouth went completely dry with unbridled excitement. He began to move faster and faster within Daisy.

Mary Lou loved the feel of the hard leather inside her, the touch of the soft leather balls along the erogenous zones of her upper inside thighs and the strength of Epps' thick and throbbing cock.

'Bend over again, my dear,' said Count Helmut, handing the whip he had chosen to Epps. 'And stay bending over until I give you permission to do otherwise.'

Elmer was quite mesmerised by Helmut's tone towards Mary Lou. It was more of master to servant than lover to mistress. He was even more amazed that Mary Lou not only accepted this but appeared to revel in it.

Helmut caressed Mary Lou's bottom, gave her a few more jerks with the dildo, then held up his hands to Epps. He spread five fingers on one hand and his forefinger on the other and silently mouthed 'Six'.

With the flap of his trousers hanging down and his penis standing rigidly erect, Epps stood to one side, raised the whip and brought it down with swinging force on Mary Lou's bare rump. She jumped and squealed.

'Keep still. This is for your impertinence,' said Helmut, in command but writhing to the feel of Daisy's mouth still working on his penis. 'How dare you suggest that Elmer fuck you. I fuck you. I allow others to fuck you but you never, ever make suggestions to me, do you understand?'

Before Mary Lou could answer the next five hits of the lash came down hard in quick succession.

'Do you understand, Mary Lou?' asked Helmut once more, trailing a finger along the stinging bright red marks on her bottom.

'Yes,' she said.

'Yes what?' asked Helmut, his hand now searching for her tight puckered bottom hole.

'Yes, master.'

'Hold that leather cock inside you. Now, on your knees, shoulders on the floor, and show me your pretty little arse,' said Helmut. Mary Lou obeyed. 'Now Epps will fuck you. Epps . . .'

Epps came up behind her and without ceremony rammed his prick hard into her other hole, the dildo still occupying her wet sex.

Elmer, who was screwing Daisy with a steady but hard rhythm, now gathered momentum as he watched Mary Lou being assaulted by the black man's penis – and the dildo hanging between her legs moving backwards and forwards with every thrust Epps gave her. The scene he was witnessing gave Elmer a sexual high he had never known. It was so mannered, so formal, so blatant and so erotic. The whole of his body was shuddering. Every fibre within him wanted to possess the girl he was screwing more and more violently. The harder he took her the more she moved her hips and moaned and the faster her head went up and down as her mouth sucked on Helmut's cock. And then Elmer came. He fell back exhausted. And so did Epps who immediately left the room. But Helmut was still stiff and aroused. He wanted more and he was going to have more.

'You,' he said to Mary Lou, leaning over and catching hold of her by her pubis. 'I want you to continue to entertain us. Screw Daisy.'

Mary Lou, slipped out of her leather skirt, slipped off her leather jacket and stood naked except for the leather collar about her neck. With one half of the dildo still hard up inside her she let the other half lie along the crack of Daisy's bottom. Then she bent over and rested her breasts with their erect nipples against the back of the kneeling and blindfolded Daisy. Mary Lou then brought her arms round and captured Daisy's nipples between her thumb and forefinger and squeezed them,

103

caressed them, rubbed them, whilst Daisy buried her head in Helmut's balls, and continued to suck his prick.

Epps re-appeared and held a bowl of iced water in front of Mary Lou and she plunged her hands into the freezing water.

Daisy, whose tactile senses were more alert because of the blindfold, was surprised when Mary Lou's warm hands stopped touching her breasts. She gave a loud gasp and squeal of pleasure when her juicy red sex, as swollen and as wanton as when she was ushered into the room by Epps, was assailed by the other woman's freezing cold and supple hands. The icy touch was deeply unexpected. Momentarily Daisy's openness closed, then as Mary Lou's cold fingers found first Daisy's clitoris then, travelling deeper within her wet folds, found that other special point of pleasure that causes a shuddery glow to suffuse the whole body, her sex opened and then opened more and more. That was when Mary Lou stepped back, positioned the dildo and lunged.

It was a lunge of force driven by jealousy. She wanted to give the Count his vicarious pleasure but she also wanted to hurt the unknown blindfolded girl. She was a rival. Mary Lou did not tolerate rivals.

Daisy was surprised by the harshness of the attack. She had felt soft breasts along her back and had expected a gentle motion, a sexual and licentious caress. The fierceness of the dildo's entry stopped Daisy's flowing rhythm and the swaying of her body. She let out a tiny agonised cry.

'Enough,' said Count Helmut, sensing what had happened and why. He raised Daisy's head up. 'Mary Lou, stop. Go upstairs and prepare for my guests.'

Mary Lou looked perplexed. Helmut had never told her to stop before.

'What? What have I done?' asked Mary Lou, knowing full well.

'I'm tired of your performance. Give me the dildo and go,' he replied, coldly.

104

Meekly Mary Lou did as she was told then left the room. Elmer thought she looked almost as if she was afraid.

'Epps, put my toys away,' said Helmut. 'Elmer, as I told you I have guests coming for dinner. So, if you will excuse me. And I'll see you tomorrow morning as arranged.'

With Germanic haughtiness Helmut stood up, took hold of Daisy's hand and led her out of the room.

'Mister Elmer, allow me to show you to the door,' said Epps.

Elmer, not quite understanding the many implications in the emotional undercurrents within the house, fixed his clothing and followed Epps.

'I'll be back in the morning with Ottilie,' said Elmer, because he was embarrassed and felt the need to say something.

'Yes, sir,' said Epps, closing the door on Elmer.

Elmer made his way down the stoop and along the gravel path back to the high iron gates. He had had the most extraordinary evening but for the life of him he could not see why Helmut's attitude had altered so suddenly. Why had sexual warmth and general licentiousness so quickly turned to a threatening coldness?

He walked determinedly towards his car and did a mental re-run of the various happenings, convinced that the rumours concerning the Count were true. For the first time in his life he'd had multiple sex, and he'd never seen a dildo, let alone a double ended one in his life before. He thought about the blindfolded girl, and Mary Lou dressed in leather. And Mary Lou's bottom receiving a lashing. Elmer found that quite a turn on. Then, in his mind's eye, he saw Josephine's knees. His gait became less determined, more jaunty. He'd be seeing her again in the morning. That pleased him. Even the possibility of a battle with Ottilie did not take the jauntiness out of his step. Working was going to be a whole heap nicer now he realised Mary Lou had lost her mystique and that he was exceedingly hot to trot for

Josephine. Elmer opened his car door, got in the driving seat, turned the key and drove away. He did those things automatically.

His mind was totally occupied with thinking of the different ways of seducing his sweet innocent and cuddly secretary.

Chapter 6

The early morning sun was bathing the streets in a shiny glow after a brief and heavy downpour of rain and the sky was a cobalt blue.

Ottilie was searching through the wardrobes in her hotel room attempting to choose an outfit. She smiled a knowing smile. She remembered New Orleanian weather. Rain, sun and then a slight breeze that by mid-morning would have moved on out to the Gulf leaving a damp stickiness in the city.

She thought about her day to come. It was going to be formal: part nice, part nasty. Nasty was the probability of arguing with Elmer about their house. But after that it would be fun.

She'd buy an automobile. A big automobile. Maybe second-hand. Now she was back in America Ottilie didn't feel the tasteful restraint of Europe. She was going to take back her own inheritance – America. She'd always adored big flashy Detroit monsters with fins. A real automobile. Not a stretch limo that reminded her of her uncle Frank Dale. That was ostentatious. If she could find a 1950s roadster she'd buy that. In good condition they were hard to come by. It would be a gas guzzler for sure, but cost she wasn't counting. That would shock everyone who knew her father. It might shock a few people who thought they knew her, too. Then, when she'd bought it she'd drive to City Park and Bayou St John. There she'd be able to sing in the new small concert hall.

Ottilie had not known a thing about that until, after her talk with Elmer and feeling angry and unable to sleep, she had telephoned her old school friend Bonnie Maitland.

Bonnie and her brother Beau had both been musical. She had played the cello. He had played the violin. It was music that had cemented their childhood friendship. But when she had gone to the Paris Conservatoire she had lost touch with them.

Bonnie's brother Beau had answered the telephone. He told her that Bonnie had married, gone to Seattle, was now teaching music and had three young children. He also told her that he was co-owner and manager of New Orleans' latest cultural venture, the St Cecilia Chamber Music Hall.

'Oh, Beau, that just sounds too marvellous,' Ottilie had said. 'Listen, do you think I could come and practise. I'd pay of course, but right now I'm living at the Fairmont and out of suitcases. No piano, and I'm just longing to give my vocal chords some work.'

'Ottilie, it's good to have you back in town and why not visit tomorrow?' he'd said.

'Sure, great idea, what time?'

'Whenever, there's nobody practising or playing for a few days. It's Mardi Gras remember, it's jazz time in the Quarter. So just turn up.'

'Beau, that's real good of you. I will,' said Ottilie, excited at the prospect of seeing a friendly face and singing. It dawned on her that nothing really wonderful had happened since she'd arrived back in the Big Easy.

Her uncle and her cousin were only nice because they wanted something. A strange butler hadn't allowed her access to her own home. And Elmer hadn't been exactly wild with enthusiasm when she had called him.

Ottilie scanned the rails of clothing but couldn't make

a quick choice. She took out a few garments and threw them on the bed. Naked, and holding up each one in turn, she paraded in front of the mirror. A khaki-green and deep brown suit? Too sludgey. A stark black and white suit? Too harsh. Okay for Elmer but not for the concert hall afterwards. The soft flowing pink silk geor-gette, overprinted with a Japanesey bird design in soft greens and blues that buttoned down the front? Ottilie decided on the latter. It came with a light sleeveless coat in a darker shade of pink. That would make the outfit formal. It would also keep her warm in the breeze and under the relentless air-conditioning which she knew El-mer would have in his office.

Ottilie took a bath, using some of her special herbal bath salts and washed her glorious red hair. Then she put on pale pink silk underwear; the low cut brassière, that showed off her cleavage; the tight bottom hugging high cut bikini panties and the half slip all of which were decorated with fine ecru lace. Over her shapely legs she drew on hold up stockings. Stockings were a must for all business meetings but at least her thighs would be able to breathe and she did not need to wear a suspender belt. She thrust her feet into black suede high-heeled shoes, and chose a matching black suede shoulder bag.

Dressed, she put a towel around her neck, sat at the built-in dressing table and carefully made-over her face with protection cream and foundation lotion, powder, mascara, and rouge. She shaped her eyebrows with a brush, and outlined her lips with a pencil then filled in the colour with a deep shade of luminous pink.

Ottilie decided to wear her hair up. She fixed it in place with some beautiful French combs. This showed the pale skin of her swanlike neck to great advantage. The only jewellery she wore was her favourite French watch and diamond stud earrings. She looked cool and elegant and was ready to face whatever the day might bring. It was only as she rode in the cab the short dis-tance from the hotel to Poydras Plaza that Ottilie realised that she had not once thought about Lord Christopher, Paris or even the beguiling handsome stranger.

Ottilie arrived at Elmer's office on the dot of nine o'clock. She was greeted pleasantly by a pretty, plump young woman who introduced herself as Josephine, Elmer's personal assistant.

'Mister Planchet is here, Miss Duvier,' said Josephine, 'but he's gone down to bring the car to the door. He said he'll ring when he's there.'

'Why didn't he call for valet service?' asked Ottilie. 'Anyhow our meeting's supposed to be here.'

'Mister Planchet said he thought it best if he drove you to Washington Avenue. I think he wants you to meet the Count,' said Josephine.

'But I don't want to meet the Count,' said Ottilie.

The telephone rang on Josephine's desk.

'Yes, Mr Planchet, she is,' said Josephine picking it up. 'Yes, Mr Planchet, I'll tell her.' Josephine replaced the receiver. 'That was Mr Planchet, Miss Duvier. He said would you please go down and meet him in the foyer.'

Ottilie breathed a sigh of pure frustration. If this was the start of the day what would the rest of it be like? Ottilie had the distinct impression that she'd been hi-jacked and was puzzled as to why. Unless Elmer was bringing up re-enforcements. Two against one. Two men against one woman. Well, she'd be ready for them. There was no way she'd give in. She wanted that man out of her house. She wanted to live in it. And that's precisely what she was going to do. Nothing, just nothing was going to deter her from her decision. Ottilie wished Josephine a good day and strode out of the office and into a waiting elevator.

Downstairs and in the street, Ottilie thought how smart and prosperous Elmer looked as he held the door open for her to climb into his limousine.

'Good to see you, Ottilie,' he said, kissing her on the cheek.

'Is it?' she asked, returning his brief peck.

'Sure,' he replied, closing her door and walking round to the driver's seat.

'Elmer, tell me why exactly are we going to Washington Avenue?'

'I want you to meet the Count.'

'And I wanted you to organise him out of the house, not take me there to meet him.'

'Unfortunately the Count and I weren't able to talk business last night. I said you were in town and he suggested you go meet with him this morning.'

Not best pleased Ottilie sat beside Elmer in silence for the rest of the journey.

When they arrived at the mansion Elmer rang the bell at the high gate and the ugly big black butler she had seen the day before came out to welcome them.

'Ah, Miss Duvier,' said the butler, smiling. 'I did tell the Count you had called, yesterday. He was very sorry to have missed you. I do hope you have forgiven me for being so ...' continued Epps, then floundered for the word.

'Rude?' said Ottilie not mollified in the least, walking past him with the air of ownership, along the gravel path, up the stoop, over the porch and through the open main door.

This door opened straight on to a large salon. Ottilie was instantly met by the familiar smell of cedar wood floors and the drone of an overhead fan. There familiarity ended. She was astounded by the renovation and the sparseness of the furnishings. It seemed very alien to her. Yet it was American, though more Northern than the Deep South. Her thoughts when she had first seen the outside of the house, with its precision and cleanliness, came back to her. From the Persian carpets, the French Empire furniture and the heavy drapes of the house of her childhood, she was presented with almost Puritan austerity. Yet it was beautiful. Ottilie knew what made it so, it was the simplicity of the design and the joy of making that exemplified the Shakers, their work, their carpentry.

Ottilie stood quietly surveying the room. It was almost a shrine to Shakerdom. The walls were plain white,

111

the skirting board and the doors, all the woodwork, was in a deep green or blue. There were no pictures on the walls but a rail fitted with hand-turned pegs ran at a height of six feet on each wall. Hanging from the pegs was a delightful series of beautifully made household objects. An eighteenth-century broom, pails in red and ochre and green, a skimmer, and a selection of skillets, candle holders and a maple wood clock with Roman numerals. Displayed on a blue stain workstand between a fern plant sat a couple of 'nice boxes' in red and ochre. A fine simple grandmother clock stood near the arch leading to the dining room beyond. Through the arch Ottilie could see a twelve foot long pine dining table with chairs around it similar to the rocking chairs in the room where she was standing.

These rocking chairs were dotted about, sometimes clustered together, and at other times set close to a wall. The one point of design they had in common was the four slats in the back; some had scrolled or rolled arms, others cushioned arms, some had seats of rush, others of woven straw or weaved tape. Most were made from maplewood but a couple were in cherry and walnut. One had a shawl rail at the top of its slats. Ottilie chose to sit in that one which had been placed beside a spinning wheel. There were no carpets on the highly polished floor but drapes of flowing muslin – white, pale blue and yellow ochre – swathed the long French windows.

'Count Helmut offers you his sincere apologies,' said Epps. 'Unfortunately the long distance call he had been waiting for since the early hours came through just before you arrived. But he will be with you in a moment. Would either of you care for some coffee, or tea?'

'No thank you,' said Ottilie. She was not at all pleased to be kept waiting. She wanted the whole matter cleared up quickly so that she could go to the concert hall and sing.

'Yes, please Epps, coffee,' said Elmer, and Epps bowed out of the room, the personification of the perfect southern butler.

Elmer smiled to himself. He watched the departing figure, thinking how the previous evening that same man had screwed Mary Lou and whipped her bare bottom. And then he remembered how he had watched Epps' coal black hands stroke the blonde sex of Daisy, the blindfolded semi-naked girl. Elmer swallowed hard, his cock began to twitch as he also recalled how she had sucked the Count's cock whilst being screwed by Mary Lou with the double ended dildo. In the quiet calm of this room, no one, least of all Ottilie, would have believed that. Or, that he, Elmer, had screwed that young woman without having properly seen her face. He wondered if and when it would happen again. Elmer squirmed in the chair and began to rock.

Elmer's rocking was contagious. Without thinking Ottilie also began to move backwards and forwards in her chair. The leisurely movement eased her sense of anger and frustration but she saw no reason to let Elmer off the hook.

'Elmer, if this man doesn't come soon, I'm leaving,' she said.

'Oh I'd hate you to do that,' said a voice from a doorway behind her.

Ottilie turned quickly and received a shock. A shock that was like an earthquake trembling through her own private fissure. There was her man. Her handsome stranger. Her fantasy man. And the same thing happened to her as had happened in the restaurant in Paris. A shiver of excitement enveloped her. Her heart fluttered and her womb tightened. Her nipples hardened and a tingling rushed through the softness of her hidden self leaving a moistness between her legs. Ottilie immediately stopped rocking, put her knees together and her hands neatly in her lap and, though she tried not to, she gulped.

Helmut was composed and controlled. He knew he was meeting her. Ottilie didn't and she began to shake nervously, more so when she felt her erect nipples straining against the silk of her dress, betraying her

113

sudden inner turbulence. As he advanced into the room, Helmut looked from her shining hazel-green cat's eyes, to her wide luscious red mouth, to her hard nipples piercing the smooth outline of her frock, to her knees held fast together and her hands clasped with white knuckles in her lap, and then back to her red mouth. He was aware of the telltale signs of her sexual stimulation and enjoyed it.

Helmut had watched Ottilie arrive from an upstairs window. He had been enchanted by her bearing, her upright carriage and her air of self-containment. Also by her beauty. Whatever it took, however much he had to lie, twist and turn, manipulate his diary, he was utterly determined to have her. And have her in every possible way. Ways he didn't think she had ever dreamed of. The Count found himself excited at the thought of licking her fine body, her neck, her breasts, her thighs, between her thighs, opening up her secret hidden lips and allowing his tongue to travel up, supping at her juices. He thought of the constraints he would put about her body and caressing her under those constraints; exciting her, taking her higher, inducing in her erotic thoughts and ideas that he would play out.

Helmut was so inflamed at the thought of making love to Ottilie that he marched into Daisy's room, where she was sleeping on a pallet and chained to the wall as he had ordered, turned her bare buttocks towards him and took her swiftly.

As he lunged into the half sleeping, passive girl, Helmut thought of how he had dealt with Mary Lou for violating his code. He smiled. Her punishment was the last thing she had expected.

Quickly physically satisfied, Helmut went back to his room, finished dressing, drank his coffee and strode downstairs to meet Ottilie.

When she turned to see him Ottilie was surprised to find him dressed for the country rather than a formal business meeting. He was wearing white riding breeches, a white short sleeved polo shirt and shining

114

brown riding boots. In these sportive clothes she could see that though he was as tall as she had remembered, was still as blond with a sense of power and his ice blue eyes were as icy blue and cold as ever – though now she noticed they were fringed with long black lashes – his chest was broader and deeper, and his legs were longer. He was far more athletic; the tight breeches allowing her to see his rippling thigh muscles. Once again she had the feeling of danger; as if faced with a jungle animal. Only this was the king of the jungle. The lion. And he was on the prowl. Ottilie had the distinct feeling she was the prey.

That insight forewarned her. She must remember why she was here: that he had something that was hers. She wanted it returned and had every intention of reclaiming it. She was not going to fall for his charm. His very sexual charm. She smiled at that thought. What an anomaly, that this man, who provoked such an incredible sexual furore within her, should have a collection of Shaker furniture, the sect that denied sexual intercourse to its members.

'Miss Duvier,' said Count Helmut, with that slight foreign accent she had noticed on the plane. He bowed, picked up her hand and brushed his lips over her finger tips. His touch seared her. Momentarily, electricity fused their flesh.

'Forgive me for keeping you waiting.'

Ottilie inclined her head, anything to get away from that stare and those eyes that could see into her soul, and quickly, with a sharp jerk, she pulled her hand away from his.

'Ottilie, this is Count Helmut von Straffen,' said Elmer, jumping up to meet him.

'I thought you might be,' said Ottilie.

'Did you?' said Helmut, smiling straight at her then turning to greet her step-brother. 'Elmer, good morning.'

Ottilie found herself staring at the Count's rear, thinking how neat and high and well shaped his bottom was.

She noticed it had hollows in it where other men's filled out. It was a trait in the opposite sex that, combined with a barrel chest, Ottilie had always found particularly attractive. She had the strongest desire to trace that curve and hollow with her fingers. She pursed her lips, drew in a sharp breath and told herself to stop her ridiculous thoughts.

Epps came in bringing coffee for Elmer.

'Miss Duvier said she didn't want anything,' said Epps, handing a china cup of black coffee to Elmer.

'Nothing?' queried Helmut, raising one eyebrow quizzically.

'No. Thank you,' she answered, firmly.

'Miss Duvier . . .' Helmut began, as he seated himself in a maplewood swivel chair. 'Elmer tells me that you want me out of this house as soon as possible. That is understandable, if inconvenient. Elmer's and my agreement has three weeks to run. I had wanted to renew the lease. However, I shall bow to your wishes and remove myself. I do hope that in the circumstances you will bow to mine and allow me the next three weeks here.'

Angrily, Elmer slammed his coffee cup down on the saucer. He was devastated by the Count's announcement. What was the man playing at? He had not brought Ottilie to the house for Helmut to capitulate before negotiations had begun. The bastard! Helmut knew only too well that continuing to rent the mansion was a vital necessity for Elmer's ongoing cash flow. But then he calmed down. He knew the Count well enough to know he would not roll over and be killed without a fight. He must be playing another and very different game. But Elmer still felt sore. Something had to be said to let the Count know.

Ottilie was also somewhat taken aback by the Count's offer. It took the wind out of her sails. She lay back in the chair and began to rock. The movement was smooth and easy. She smiled at Helmut.

'Is that acceptable to you, Miss Duvier?' asked the Count.

'Yes,' she answered, simply.

'Elmer?' asked the Count.

'It'll have to be won't it?' replied Elmer, standing up.

'I thought you'd see it like that,' said Helmut.

'I have some appointments,' said Elmer, sulkily. 'So, if our business is concluded for the day I'll leave. Ottilie ...?'

Helmut had not expected Elmer to react so strongly to his suggestion. He wanted Ottilie with him for longer.

'Oh, Miss Duvier ...'

'Please call me Ottilie,' she said.

'And I'm Helmut. Ottilie, as Elmer has to go ... I do hope you don't feel the need to rush away with him. I would like to talk to you, perhaps show you the house. It is yours after all. Elmer, we won't keep you if you're busy.' Helmut stood up, and almost telepathically Epps opened the main door, mentally ushering Elmer through it. 'We'll talk again soon,' said Helmut, shaking Elmer's hand. And Elmer was outside on the porch with the door shut fast behind him before he realised he had been thoroughly outmanoeuvred. Helmut turned back to Ottilie who was gently rocking in the chair.

Every bone, every fibre of her body told her to get up and run. Don't stay. If you stay you're lost. But she was fascinated, not only by the Count but also by her reaction to him, and the fascination was stronger than the warning. There was a desire to find out how far she would travel with the danger. She was quite certain he was as attracted to her as she to him. She could feel the intensity of that attraction in his glance. The thought that he would touch her gave her goose pimples. When would he touch her? Ottilie squirmed slightly in the chair, her hiddenness was swollen and damp but her mouth had gone completely dry. Now that Elmer had departed a part of her was afraid. She decided discretion was the better part of valour. She would give the house a quick once over and then go to the concert hall and meet Beau. And sing.

'I don't know what you have planned for the rest of

the day,' said Count Helmut, sitting back in the swivel chair, 'but as you can see I am not dressed for the city. I have to go out to the country. There's some business I need to attend to. It won't take long. If you'd care to come for the drive I'd be delighted for you to accompany me.'

'I'd like that,' Ottilie heard herself say. Every intention gone, overtaken by her desire, her curiosity. Her wild sexual curiosity. Her virginal body screamed, go with him. Take him and everything on the wing. To hell with the consequences.

'Good, now will you join me in a coffee, or orange juice.'

'Thank you, orange juice,' she said.

Helmut smiled and rang the bell for Epps.

'A large orange juice for Miss Duvier please Epps. And I'll have some sparkling water. Oh by the way, did Elmer introduce you two? Miss Duvier, this is my great friend, companion and helper, Epps. Epps, Miss Ottilie Duvier.'

'How do you do, Miss Ottilie,' said Epps, grinning, his eyes scanning her body approvingly.

Ottilie felt herself tense under his scrutiny. His big powerful ugliness affected her. He seemed to be undressing her, removing her clothing in front of the Count. She gave a wan, hesitant smile.

'Miss Ottilie has agreed to come with me to the country,' said Count Helmut.

'I'm sure the two of you will have a very good day, sir,' replied Epps. 'Are there any instructions for the house?'

'Not really, Epps,' said Helmut. 'Take the day off but make sure you're here this evening. We could be busy.'

'Yes, sir. Thank you sir,' said Epps, bowing out of the room.

'Where are you going?' asked Ottilie as soon as Epps had departed.

'*We* are going out to Baton Rouge and then into Cajun country. There's a lawyer in Baton Rouge and some land out on a bayou. I need to see both today.'

'Oh . . .' she said.

Epps reappeared with two large glasses, one filled with freshly squeezed orange juice, the other with sparkling water complete with a slice of lemon.

'For you, Miss Ottilie,' he said.

'Thank you,' she replied, drinking it quickly.

'Right, that's done,' said the Count, downing the water. 'Now we'll go.'

'But,' said Ottilie, 'Helmut, you might be dressed for the country, but I'm not.'

'Miss Duvier, you look perfect, utterly charming and I assure you what you have on is absolutely right for where we're going.'

'It is!'

'Oh yes,' he said. And Epps smiled a secret smile as he watched Helmut guide Ottilie out to the back of the house where his large gleaming black open-topped automobile was parked in the shade, waiting for them.

The ride to Baton Rouge was hot, breezy but uneventful. And they went to great lengths not to touch one another. They talked about art and architecture, books, and music. Helmut put on a selection of tapes, from Mozart to U2 to Thelonius Monk and then Zydeco. Ottilie wondered if he had a universal taste in music or if he kept different types of music for seducing different women. She smiled to herself. It was a real bitchy thought. Helmut caught her smile.

'I amuse you?' he asked.

'No, it's a beautiful day, I'm home in my own country and I'm happy. That's a good enough reason to smile, don't you think?'

'Yes,' he said, but wasn't absolutely sure she was telling the truth.

Ottilie was drumming on her thighs thinking how apt it was to be playing Cajun and Zydeco driving along past the old plantations and the swamps in the humidity and heat of midday Louisiana. All the time she'd been in Paris she hadn't touched her old tapes. They were somehow out of place. Not just amongst

119

her conservatoire friends but even in her own home. The atmosphere was not right. Here it was. Ottilie reckoned certain wines and certain music don't travel well. Clifton Chenier's classic song 'Eh Petite Fille' came on and Ottilie, knowing it well, joined in. The rhythms and the words, the notes and the tones were a second language to Ottilie. Her classically trained voice automatically changed gear and she was singing as good as any country singer.

Helmut complimented her on her voice.

'I should be practising now,' she said, off guard.

'Oh, where?'

'At the new concert hall near City Park,' she replied.

'Oh yes, it had a grand opening not so long ago.'

'A friend of mine co-owns it and is the manager. He said I could come in some time today to practise,' she said, endeavouring to cover over her mistake. She did not want Helmut to think she had put off somebody else for him. He was so self-assured his ego didn't need any further bolstering.

When they arrived in the state capital Ottilie stayed in the car whilst Helmut quickly dealt with the lawyer then they proceeded out to swamp country. Ottilie hugged herself with joy. Since childhood she had loved the earthy lushness of Louisiana. She was driving through the primeval landscape she adored with a man she fancied like crazy; and she didn't know exactly where she was heading. It was exciting. And everywhere she looked the sky, the trees, their branches, their leaves, even the man beside her, everything had a sharp clarity; outlines and colours were heightened as if during her absence they had grown in intensity.

Ottilie put on the other side of the tape and continued to sing as they drove through small villages, which were not much more than a collection of wooden shacks. It was another world, far removed from the sophistication of Paris. She smiled when she saw French names nailed up over the bars and heard French spoken when they stopped for an oncoming truck. She relaxed back in the thick leather seat, gazing at the sun glinting through the cypress trees and listening to the cries of animals, familiar and unfamiliar.

Helmut turned from minor roads on to dirt tracks, then through the trees and parked the car on a small landing stage at the edge of a creek.

'It's by boat from here,' he said, pointing to a small craft.

'That?' she queried, looking from it to the greeny brown water and wondering how many alligators were lurking in its depths.

'Yes,' he said, 'and you're to put some of this on.' He gave Ottilie a small jar of oil. 'Oil and lemon juice, a sort of vinaigrette sauce. Mosquitoes hate lemon, but I'm sure you know that. Don't forget your ankles.'

Whilst Ottilie coated herself with the oil, Helmut climbed out of the car, opened the boot, and retrieved a couple of ice boxes.

'Lunch,' he said, 'prepared by Missy Lee.'

'Who's Missy Lee?' Ottilie asked.

'My housekeeper,' he said. 'She's many things, including a marvellous cook.'

Helmut lowered the ice boxes carefully into the boat, then stepped in himself.

'Come on get in,' he said, holding out his hand for her. She hesitated. He reached out, put his hands around her waist and lifted her lightly up. His touch made her tremble. She laughed, nervously. He placed her carefully on a seat, then undid the rope holding the boat, pulled the throttle of the outboard motor and they were away.

In the steamy heat Count Helmut aimed the boat upstream, away from the dark green stagnant pools where serpents and alligators lay basking in the dappled sun, and towards his hideaway on Bayou l'Extase.

Ottilie felt as if she was in an enchanted land. And enchanted lands are always dangerous. Birds flew overhead, there was the swish of tails in the water, the drone of the outboard motor and there was the smell of the

121

bayou mingled with her own smell, of French perfume and lemon juice and oil. She lay back in her seat and sighed, a happy, lazy, erotic sigh. She was floating between dreams and reality.

Helmut steered through the brown swampy water. Speckles of sunlight beamed through the canopy of black interlocking branches, heavy with trails of silvery grey Spanish moss, exposing the glistening damp contours of Ottilie's sensual body. Sunbeams emphasised her hard, erect nipples, and Helmut's desire for her deepened.

He wanted her soft smooth body. He wanted it yielding to his passionate embrace. He wanted her lips on his lips. He wanted her breasts crushed against his chest. He wanted her crouching over his mouth. But Helmut knew the power of anticipation and kept the boat on course.

Some twenty minutes later he brought it in beside a broad landing stage. Ottilie gazed up at the precarious muddy and green slimed wooden steps. In her high heels getting out of the boat was going to be difficult. She looked down at the outline of shadowy menacing shapes in the murky water. Ottilie was frightened of alligators. Seeing her hesitate, Helmut lifted her high on his shoulders and carried her up the steps over the porch and into the rough log cabin with its roof covered with palmetto leaves.

Inside the dark room Ottilie felt his hot breath on her neck as he put her down. Leaving her trembling from his touch, he went back to the boat for the ice boxes. Her mind reeled off into a whirr of lascivious fantasy. Every part of her, every nerve ending, was aching and waiting to be caressed. Helmut came back and lit an oil lamp and candles. Immediately the cabin, so crude on the outside, was transformed into a wonderland of exotic drapes, cushions and carpets.

'Please sit down and be comfortable,' said Helmut, indicating a large cushion covered in slippery maroon satin close to the wall. There were no chairs in the room, just cushions of every size and shape. Ottilie curled up, with one foot sticking out and one under her, and the cushion moulded to her body.

Helmut opened up the largest of the two ice boxes, taking out two crystal flutes and a bottle of her favourite champagne. He then sat languidly opposite Ottilie and held out a glass of the light corn-coloured fizzing liquid he had just poured. With a shaking hand and her heart thumping she took it.

'To us,' he said, and leaned across a low table between them so they could clink glasses.

'To us,' she repeated. Thinking to herself, Oh my God, now what? And every portion of her body screamed touch me but was frightened of him doing it. Frightened because she wanted it but couldn't escape. She didn't want to escape; she wanted him. Ottilie was a turmoil of emotions. She avoided his eyes. She sipped at the wine, then not knowing what to do with herself she sipped again and again, faster and faster until the glass was empty.

'The heat has made you thirsty,' he said, reaching for the bottle and re-filling her flute.

'Yes,' she said hoarsely.

His voice had that special timbre, that slight accent that conveyed the danger she found so exciting.

'Perhaps you are hungry, too?' he asked.

'No ... I mean yes ...' she said.

'Let's see what Missy has prepared,' he said, opening the other ice box. First he removed a white table-cloth and two napkins. Then he took the vase that stood on the table with a fine display of feathers in it and put it on the floor beside him. Then he covered the low table with the table-cloth and gave Ottilie one napkin, putting the other on his own lap. Then he peered into the ice box again. 'Ah, caviare, and smoked salmon. Do you like that?'

'Yes,' she whispered, sipping at the wine again, telling herself to go slowly, not so fast, or she'd be drunk.

'And home-made brown bread. Missy makes it. There's cheese here too ... And cucumber.' Helmut held up the large hard stiff green vegetable and stroked it lovingly before placing it on the table. 'And carrots, and bananas ... And lettuce, tomatoes, and here we have a jar of mushrooms à la Grec ... What would you like?'

'Smoked salmon,' she answered, moving her body towards his hand holding out a plate.

As Helmut took her plate their fingers met. Shaking with anticipation Ottilie gave a slight gasp. Helmut pretended he hadn't heard and served her with the pink smoked fish. He knew exactly what he was doing. He wanted Ottilie at a fever pitch and his not touching her increased her frustration and desire. She would have to make the first move towards him. Only then would he know she was ready – for anything.

Helmut opened the small kilner jar of mushrooms, and began to spoon them on to her plate. Ottilie realised she had pins and needles in the leg that was curled under her. She moved the leg. Helmut dropped some of the mushrooms and the sauce on her ankle.

'Oh, I'm so sorry,' he said, taking a sparkling white damask napkin, removing her shoe and dabbing at her ankle.

Ottilie held her breath and swallowed hard. His touch sent exciting tingling messages along every part of her skin.

'There, that's better,' he said, and lay back on his cushion and finished his glass of champagne.

But it wasn't better for Ottilie. Her sexual desire was heightened, she was aware of every nuance in her body, every movement, every tremble. And he appeared oblivious to her feelings. Ottilie decided she would give herself some caviare. She stretched across his legs and her breasts pressed into his thighs and knees as she scooped out the sturgeons eggs.

'More wine, I think,' said Helmut, leaning over her and retrieving her glass.

Ottilie moved her head, knocking Helmut's hand. A couple of cool drops hit the back of her neck. His fingers stroked where the liquid had spilled. She froze, suspended between desire and fear.

124

'Would you give me some caviare?' he asked, standing up.

Ottilie did as he asked then turned towards him holding out the plate. He took it and her hand, and their eyes met. Never letting his eyes leave hers Helmut put his glass down, and pulled her up towards him. In one swift movement he had clasped her fast to his body. She could feel the strength of him. The exciting hardness of his penis erect and pushing against her belly. Ottilie held her breath. His lips came down on hers. She closed her eyes.

Every dream she had ever had of this moment sprang to life as the red wide softness of his yielding mouth touched hers, his tongue and his taste excited her. With the heat and damp of the day and the heat and damp of their bodies they were locked together in a languorous embrace. His tongue pushed past her lips entering into the tiny cavern beyond her teeth, with controlled pressure. His lips travelled from her mouth to her cheeks to her ear lobes and back again to her mouth. Then he nuzzled her neck and a quick spasm, a rash of goose pimples, broke out where his lips met her flesh. Erotic desire flushed through her.

When his tender kisses touched her vibrant skin the whole of her body quivered with pent up longing. Each kiss found her more heady, as if she had taken the most potent drug. The wet heat of his lightly clothed body melded with hers. Leisurely, his lips started their journey again, brushed her ear, her throat, the delicious curve of her neck. Exquisite sensations flooded into and out of her womb. Her mind ceased to think, to plan, to observe. It no longer functioned as a rational instrument. Emotion and desire were paramount. Respond. Respond, cried her tongue, her mouth, her breasts, her arms, her legs and her opening ripe sex.

Ottilie wound her arms around Helmut's neck.

'I want you,' Helmut whispered in her ear.

His potent words let loose her womb, she felt the swelling and the moistness of her inner self increase with her desire to have him lay her down, fondle her breasts and lie between her legs.

His hands strolled down from her neck to hover over the buttons covering her cleavage. He made no attempt to undo them or remove her frock. Instead with infinite delicacy the tips of his fingers touched her hard erect nipples. Ottilie gasped, the sensation was extreme.

It was as if he had turned a key in the core of her body. Ottilie lay back taking his tongue, entwining hers with his, giving it affirmative answering messages. His fingers gradually increased the pressure on her nipples so that from gentleness the feeling progressed to heightened pleasure. Then to pain. Then to a combination of the two. And Ottilie could not tell where one sensation ended and the other began.

Helmut bent her back, down amongst the cushions.

'Open your legs,' commanded the Count, pulling at the hem of her frock.

Ottilie did as she was told. Helmut eased the soft floaty silk up along her thighs.

'Spread them wider,' he said, his fingers winding under the elastic of her panties, lingering with the lightest of touches on the swollen moistness of her wet labia. Tiny currents of torment rushed through her as he squeezed her sex lips together, not entering, just a pressure and a squeezing. The yearning within her to be taken and ravished by him grew stronger. Her breasts were aching to be fondled, and her own hands wanted and needed to caress him. He was playing her as if she were a musical instrument. He was the master player tuning her up. Tuning her way above her known capacity. The candles slowly going out, leaving them in increasing darkness, helped Ottilie discover her innate licentiousness. Very slowly Helmut's fingers began pushing into her juicy wet folds. Ottilie's body moved this way and that, dancing to the incessant tune of his fingers inside her. She found her own natural rhythm. Her hips rising and lowering. The muscles within her opening and closing about his exploring fingers.

'Put your hands above your head,' Helmut commanded.

Ottilie lifted her hands up and back beyond the cushion and found her flesh touching iron.

'It's a ring, hold it,' said Helmut.

Ottilie clasped it.

'Grip it hard, and don't move,' he said. Then he poured some more champagne into a glass and lifted it to her lips.

'Drink,' he commanded. And Ottilie drank the fizzy liquid, becoming more heady, more abandoned than she was before.

'I want to make love to you,' he said, nibbling at her ear lobes. 'I want to pleasure you. Would you like me to do that?' And he delicately pressed her nipples between his thumbs and forefingers. 'I want an answer from you Ottilie. Say yes or no. Do you want me to pleasure you?'

'Yes,' she whispered.

'Yes, is that all you can say? Tell me what you want me to do to you?'

'I . . . I don't know . . .' she said, confused.

'Would you like me to kiss your breasts, suck your nipples, or go down between your legs . . .' Ottilie drew in a sharp breath as he said that. 'I see, so you want me between your legs. But Ottilie do you want my tongue or my cock?'

Ottilie was silent.

'My dear, if you cannot choose I must choose for you, but I must do it my way. And that means you submit to my every whim. Whatever I want to do to you I'll do. Do you agree to that?'

'Yes,' said Ottilie, who had no real idea what he meant but wanted him to caress her more, fondle her breasts, wanted him between her legs. And she wanted to touch his penis. Feel its strength and erect hardness.

Helmut reached into his pocket and drew out a long piece of black silk fabric.

'Lift up your head, I am going to blindfold you.'

'Blindfold me!' she exclaimed.

'Your sense of touch will be heightened by the deprivation of your sight. Also you will not know which part of your body I will touch next and I think you'll find that exciting. If you don't you will tell me and I will stop and remove the blindfold.'

Helmut gently kissed her lips then tied the dark material around Ottilie's eyes. He knelt beside her, swiftly unzipped his trousers and took one of her hands from the iron ring.

'Hold it,' ordered Helmut, placing her hand over his penis.

Ottilie's hand had been aching to hold the stiff warmth of his prick. She encircled it, then let her hand trail its length, finding his balls, letting her fingers glide over his testes she took her hand back up again, under the hood, then played up and down between the rim of the cap and the head. Each stroke she gave him gave her pleasure. She had a wild desire to take its erect fullness into her mouth.

'Suck me,' Count Helmut demanded.

Ottilie turned and put her head down to meet his prick. She opened her mouth and took its urgent roundness in between her soft red lips.

Helmut took hold of her hands and put them back on the ring. With the blindfold about her eyes Ottilie could not see the strips of leather hanging down from the ring. Firmly, but giving her plenty of leeway, he tied Ottilie's wrists. Then slowly one by one he undid the buttons on the front of her frock. When each button was undone, he sensuously stroked her skin. When he laid bare her breasts, he bent and licked them. Then, taking a feather from the vase he caressed her erect nipples. She kept his prick in her mouth, and with a natural inborn rhythm she stayed sucking his cock.

Helmut undid every button on her frock and let the fabulous soft fabric fall to one side. He pulled off her silk half slip. Without undoing her brassière he lifted her breasts from their enveloping silk and lace, revealing their beautiful white swell and contours. Deftly he mass-

128

aged her nipples, enjoying the sweet sound of her sexual whimpering. Then he took the feather and swept it down over her belly to her panties. Snakelike he eased his hand under the waistband. With his middle finger the advance guard, he found her hidden but aroused clitoris. In one fast movement he spread his whole hand over her sex, gripped and held her hard, only the middle finger continuing its salacious work. The slowness of the feather and the swiftness of his action caught Ottilie unawares. She gasped and felt the moisture and dampness increase between her legs. His fingers slid inside her. They skimmed on her silken wet sheen that was lightly covering her palpitating and swollen inner flesh. The sensation Ottilie experienced with his fingers gliding inside her was beyond anything she had ever imagined. She was completely lost to all reality except the fever his fingers wrought within her.

Helmut changed his position, so that his knees were either side of Ottilie's head. His cock remained in her mouth, where she was busy practising her newly acquired skill. Helmut pushed the leg of her pantie elastic to one side and she felt his tongue licking her thighs and then the outer swollen lips of her sex.

Her entire body was trembling. Tiny tremors of pure excitement shuddered through every nerve ending and every part of her body, whether she had ever considered it sexually erotic and arousable or not. Ottilie was amazed by this discovery. Sex did not stop in and around the top of her legs but was made up and heightened in each particle of her living being.

Helmut slid her panties down her legs and removed them.

'Spread your legs wide,' he commanded.

Submissively Ottilie did as he ordered. Helmut smiled a secret smile delighted by her instant and total acquiescence to his every command. He was pleased, very pleased. Everything he had thought about her from the first moment he saw her was coming true. She had a pure and natural love of sex that so far was unsatisfied, certainly untapped and definitely unknown. He put his head between her legs and the next moment Ottilie felt the most delicious sensation fire through her taut body as his tongue enjoyed the soft sweet sea-smelling tissue of her inner body, probing its way further inside her soft warm, wet folds. But it was when his tongue came up and flicked at her clitoris that her mind and body exploded simultaneously, not with an orgasm but with uncontrolled sexual abandonment. She writhed and squirmed and gasped and sighed and visions of total erotica flooded into her brain. She didn't care what he did as long as his tongue didn't stop its extraordinary work. And she stayed sucking his prick.

Helmut slithered away from her mouth, down the length of her body and took hold of her feet. He removed carefully positioned cushions hiding ankle fetters in the floor. He put her feet into the shackles and quickly snapped them shut. Ottilie now lay blindfolded and spread eagled; her arms tied above her head, her legs apart and manacled, her sex bare, her breasts billowing over her brassière, and her nipples erect. She was longing to be fondled and fucked.

'Lift your bottom up high,' he said.

Ottilie raised her hips. Helmut put three cushions under her buttocks. Then he removed all his own clothes and stood in front of her, naked with his penis erect and throbbing, admiring the beauty of the Titian-haired girl he now had at his sexual mercy. He sat down beside her, and with one hand he began caressing her aching nipples, with the other he took an oily mushroom from the jar and trailed it through her sex before eating it.

The cold wet squashy feel of the unknown object dipping into her sex was so unexpected that Ottilie tensed then opened wider, wanting more, wanting that strange feeling again. She rolled her hips and moaned with delight.

Helmut denied her her wish. Instead he took hold of the cucumber and, with infinite care, began to insert it at her soft pink opening. He watched her sex clasp it like a sea anenome, her muscles gently accepting its hard coldness. When he had thrust the tip in he left it hanging lasciviously from her sex and took another mushroom and rubbed it up and down on her clitoris, stimulating her hard little bud. Then he fastened his lips on Ottilie's warm erect nipples.

The lascivious pleasure of his assaults on the aroused membranes of her sex and on her body was bringing Ottilie to the point of climax, but Helmut wasn't ready for her to come. She had to know more, experience more before she would be allowed her release.

Starting at her toes Helmut slowly sucked and licked his way along her body. Ottilie felt his prick pressing against her legs, her thighs and then as his hands and his tongue went higher and higher, his cock stayed at the top of her legs. She could feel the hardness of the unknown something just inside her hidden wet entrance and the urgent warmth of Helmut's penis on her inner thighs. The whole of her was crying out for him, his cock, his prick, his penis, to enter her, penetrate her, dominate her.

'Please,' she moaned, 'please take me.'

'Take you?' he asked. 'What do you mean take you?'

Ottilie hesitated. Could she say what she meant? Could she say the word?

'You must tell me what you want?'

'I want . . . please will . . . please fuck me,' she whispered.

Helmut smiled and watched her tongue licking her lips, flicking in and out like a snake's. He leant his body over hers. Ottilie gasped. She had been longing to feel the strength of him against the yielding rounded softness of herself. Helmut took the cucumber from her ripe wet folds. Then he positioned himself carefully between her open legs and his cock at the entrance to her love channel. With his arms outstretched taking his weight, slowly he drove forward into the dark pink depths of her wanton sex.

There was an agony in his taking her. She had waited so long that her bladder had filled up and each time

Helmut's pelvis met hers the pressure sent an exquisite piercing through her vulva and her womb. Helmut edged his body to one side, put his hand down between their sticky damp bodies and touched her clitoris.

Then Ottilie knew she was on fire. His touch seared her. He pounded into her inner depths with two fingers massaging her hard over-excited little point and she felt she would burst; not only with love juices flowing down from her womb but with water needing to flow out from her bladder. She tensed in order to stop it happening. Helmut knew full well what she was doing and increased his pressure on every part of her that was affected. She could only moan and sway.

Then he put his other hand under her bottom and gripped it hard. He dug his nails into her rounded flesh, and continued to pound into her. Ottilie was twisting and turning on her bindings like a woman possessed.

Then she felt other hands take hold of her hair and push her head back so that her mouth was opened. A glass was held to her lips.

'Drink,' said Helmut. And she sipped but her head was tipped back and she was made to take the glassful of champagne. Now she was heady with the wine, heady with the pounding she was taking, and heady with her own ribald and erotic thoughts. She thought she must be so drunk that she had lost all sense. Nobody else could be in the room with them. Nobody. Nobody. Nobody knew they were there.

She was dreaming wild and fantastic dreams. Of men holding her down, licking her, sucking her, screwing her back and front. All inhibitions had evaporated.

When another cock was placed on her lips, Ottilie opened her mouth willingly and slowly took its great length in and sucked.

Helmut's fingers continued to play with her clitoris and her buttocks. The other hands reached for her breasts, oiling them, encircling them, tweaking their rosebud nipples. She was powerless to do anything except let her body go with its outrageous desires.

132

The shackles on her ankles were sufficiently loose to allow her to put her feet flat on the floor, raise her hips higher, and take the pounding penis within her deeper.

Without warning both cocks stopped moving and were removed. Ottilie was left a vibrant shudder of emotions with an awakened sensitised body. Hands rolled her over. She lay on her stomach. Now her bottom was raised high. Hands oiled her buttocks. The same hands occasionally slipped round and entered her sex. Then she felt something long, thin and supple, she was reminded of a leather belt she sometimes wore, and this was trailing along the soft tingling flesh of her vulva and her arse. Hands came up and gripped her bottom holding it open. Ottilie had little time to register her sense of mortification as she realised her tiny hidden puckered place was on view. Suddenly and without warning that same small forbidden hole was being flicked with the leather strip. Flick and then her sex was stroked. Flick and her sex stroked again. She was opening and closing, the flicks were strange but oddly pleasurable. Then the strength of each tiny lash stroke was increased. Pleasure became pain. In between the pain there was a sudden stab of pleasure as fingers searched inside her sex, playing with her. She was wet and open and could do nothing except sway and moan and cry out with the unexpectedness of the extreme desire she was experiencing.

More oil was poured on her buttocks. Two sets of hands rubbed it into her naked rounded flanks. She could feel the hardness of two warm cocks either side of her digging into her waist. One set of hands travelled along her back. Massaging, massaging. The other set of hands had stopped. Then all hands stopped. That cold hard something, which she thought could possibly be the cucumber, was inserted into her moistness and thrust backwards and forwards, backwards and forwards, loosening her, sending wafts of licentiousness surging through her body. And the next moment she felt the fire across her oiled bottom as thin leather scorched her bare buttocks.

Ottilie cried out. She did not know whether she was crying with pleasure or pain or whether it was a mixture of the two that led her to yell.

Soft hands immediately came down on her buttocks and more oil was massaged into her rounded raised bottom. The massage eased the pain of the stripe. But then she was turned over and those same hands began to press on her belly, on her full bladder and the cold hard elongated thing within her was moved up and down, up and down.

'Please,' she moaned. 'No, please don't do that.'

'Why not?' asked Count Helmut, increasing the pressure so that she was almost at the point of spilling out her water.

'I might . . . I might . . .' Ottilie faltered.

Unexpectedly Helmut kissed her lips.

'You might what?' he asked.

'I might not be able to hold my water,' she said.

'Oh but you must,' he said, and began to play with her sex, stimulating her again. 'If you don't I will have to lash you once more. I must say, your bottom looks very pretty, a neat red line across just waiting for others to join it.'

Ottilie was completely bemused. Who was this man who had her at his mercy? She recognised the voice but not his intentions. She shivered, partially with fear and partially with the pleasure of expectation and excitement.

Once more she was subjected to the twin sensations of the acute pain of the hand pressing on her belly whilst the thin leather strip was trawled through her sex. A mouth began its work along the lips of her labia. A tongue licked and flicked at her clitoris. She raised her hips to take that tongue deeper. And a cock was put beside her mouth. Hands pulled back her head and the cock pushed through her open lips. She sucked. Enjoying the motion and the feel of the prick in her mouth she relaxed and the pressure was increased on her belly. She forgot the discomfort and her water eased out, marking

134

the maroon satin with a dark stain. And once she started she couldn't stop. And she felt herself flush with shame.

'Ottilie,' she heard the Count's voice. 'You disobeyed me.'

The prick in her mouth was removed and hands turned her over once more and oils were rubbed into her buttocks.

'I will have to punish you,' he said, and she felt the quick hard flicks of the thin leather on her bare rump.

'No,' she whispered. 'No.'

'Ottilie, it is my pleasure to whip you. And you will say, "Thank you, master." Do you understand?' Helmut touched her wanton hard aroused clitoris with his tongue and wiggled the cucumber inside her. 'Do you understand?'

'Yes, master,' she said.

'I shall give you six lashes and when I've finished you will thank me, do you understand that too?' He licked her clitoris again. Ottilie writhed with the sensual pleasure of his tongue.

'Yes, master,' she said.

Helmut put another couple of cushions under her bottom.

'Let your buttocks go loose,' he said, wobbling them with his hand whilst massaging more oil into her skin.

'And you will not make a sound. If you do I will give you another six.'

He brought the lash down with swiftness and expertise, criss-crossing her white flanks with bright red weals.

She moaned but did not cry out as the sharp piercing blows left her with a greater sense of abandonment and opened her up to the pleasure of humiliation and total unabashed wantonness.

And then Helmut took her again. He thrust into her hard, and she responded with a glorious wildness. Her yoked hands and feet twisting and turning, her arms and legs shuddering, her head moving with a fluency of motion as he obsessively and with urgency immersed himself in her, blending her body with his. They were completely one.

They slept. Helmut curled himself around her marked and shackled body and they drifted into a deep and satisfying sleep. Helmut awoke first. He re-lit the candles then untied her wrists and unlocked her ankle fetters. He kissed her warm bruised lips.

'You did well,' he said, smiling.

Ottilie stared at him slightly bemused. She was still half dressed. He was naked. The first time she had seen him without clothes. His thick broad chest, his slim hips, long legs and his penis, which even in repose she noticed was large. She looked around the room. Had there been someone else there or had that been her overactive imagination?

'What's the matter,' Helmut asked, stroking her hair, and her neck. 'Are you hungry or thirsty?'

'Thirsty,' she said.

'Wine, water or orange juice?' he asked.

'Orange juice,' she replied.

Whilst Helmut poured her drink Ottilie looked around the cabin. There was no evidence of anyone else having been in the room.

'You are an extremely sexual woman with a wonderful body,' said Helmut, handing her the orange juice. 'Turn round, let me see your bottom.'

She turned and he lifted her silk frock and gazed at the weals.

'They'll be gone by the morning,' he said, fondling her buttocks. 'But they look very pretty.'

He pulled her down beside him and kissed her mouth. His hands began to roam over her body. She reacted instantly. Her nipples hardened. He caught them and squeezed them. She gave a sharp sigh.

'Lie down and open your legs,' he commanded. 'I want to fuck you again.'

Ottilie, excited by his choice of words, did exactly as he ordered. She wanted to watch. She wanted to see him entering her. He climbed on top of her and positioned his prick at her entrance. She gave a series of short gasps as she felt his throbbing member push past her folds.

Slowly, slowly he pushed inwards. She lifted her head so that she could see his cock penetrate and dominate her. Then he put his lips over her lips and suddenly rammed into her, fast and furiously. She raised her hips to meet every thrust. She twisted and turned beneath his sweating body. She ran her hands up and down his back then clasped her ankles over the small of his back and he kept thrusting until all their energy was spent.

Later, after they had eaten and made sure all the candles were out, and the oil lamp was made safe, he drove her home.

It was a pleasant drive. They didn't talk much. Neither of them said anything about the sex they'd enjoyed together. It was as if it was a secret not to be shared in the open air.

Ottilie found her legs were shaking. She was unsteady on her feet. And she was tired. She wanted to sleep. She decided she would go to see Beau Maitland another day. She'd ring him, she'd say some unexpected business came up and she'd see him tomorrow.

'I'll call you,' said Helmut, dropping her at the door of the hotel.

'Yes,' she said, smiling happily.

Helmut drove away and Ottilie walked into the hotel lobby and collected her key.

'Oh, Miss Duvier,' said the hotel clerk, 'there's a letter for you.'

Ottilie took it and noticing it had a New Orleans postmark opened it quickly. It was from Lord Christopher. He was sorry for his behaviour and had come to the Crescent City to claim her as his bride.

Ottilie tore the letter and the envelope into tiny pieces and dropped it in the trashcan.

The hell he will, she thought.

Chapter 7

'Mary Lou, you's my baby girl and I don't give a rattlesnake's ass who the hell you fuck, but unless you wanna be living in direst poverty for the remainder of your natural – you's gonna do what I tell ya and marry Beau Maitland.' Frank Dale was speaking to his daughter. They were sitting in the morning sun on the terrace of his house opposite Audubon Park having coffee after breakfast.

'But I don't understand why, Pa,' whined Mary Lou, more than a little aggrieved.

She had always wound her father round her little finger, but now he was being obdurate in the extreme. She didn't find it congenial or amusing. Mary Lou was not used to being thwarted. Neither was her father. And he held the purse strings.

'I'll tell you why, honey child,' said Frank. 'Beau Maitland ain't rich, not like I'm rich but he is ambitious and he is squeaky clean. Now that young man wants to be governor of this state. And I wanna see he achieves his ambition. You's gonna be the governor's wife, and I's gonna be the governor's father-in-law. And that, my pretty one, is a real neat place to be. It's called power, and in case you ain't realised, power is something I appreciate. You might say relish. But I do not relish being hampered in my ambitions for this young man, by nobody, least of all you.'

'No, pa.'

'You're a clever girl,' said Frank. 'I just knew if I explained the position you'd understand. And I want you to go down and spend some time with him at that concert hall . . .'

'Oh, Pa, classical music ain't exactly my thing.'

'I realise that, honey, but Beau likes it, and you's gonna have to learn to like it. That concert hall is part of my investment for your future. And so far Beau Maitland has been a good and upright partner in that venture. I want it to stay that way. Also we got the St Jacques contract coming up.'

'The Arts Complex? What's Beau gotta do with that?'

'He's in the consortium with me and Norwood Cates.'

'Is he?'

'Sure he is. It's all legal. Totally legal. Whichever bits bend Norwood and me take care of. Especially now we got that fool Elmer outta the way. That guy has a mighty fine ability to ask the most awkward questions at the most right time. That's why Norwood had to leave the company. Not that I could believe it when he told me how he was gonna do it. So it didn't cost him, but it would cost Elmer. And it did. You know that? He sent in Sharon to drop her drawers and the idiot fell for it. Norwood came in on cue. Elmer was giving her the once over. Divorce and scandal shouted Norwood. And Elmer paid up.'

'Pa, isn't Elmer after the same contract?'

'Sure is. He, and nobody else don't stand a chance. We got the preacher person all sewed up and in our pocket. It's the preacher what's awarding the contract. But I want you to get better acquainted with Beau. Go find out how the concert hall's run. Offer to help him.'

'Pa, are you plum crazy?'

'No, child. A governor's wife has to take an interest in all parts of the community. Especially the cultural activities. This goes down well with the blue rinse gals. And it's their votes that count. But first he's gotta be married. And second he's gotta have a suitable wife – otherwise he don't get those votes. Simple eh?'

'Pa, why now? There's only just been an election.'

'We's laying the foundations for the next one. And your cousin arriving here has slightly speeded up the process.'

'Ottilie! Why?'

'Because, she's rich, and free and she and Beau have been friends a long time and having a sharp eye to the main chance he might decide that she is a real good proposition. And that don't suit me. So you gotta go out there and lay claim to him. Do what you do best, seduce him.'

'Jeez pa!'

'Hell, Mary Lou, don't you go annoying me now. It ain't like I was asking you to screw the hunchback of Notre Dame. He's a helluva good looking fella.'

'But I don't love him, pa.'

Frank Dale burst out laughing.

'That some sort of a joke, Mary Lou? You don't love no one so quit the bullshit.'

'I love the Count,' said Mary Lou.

'You lust after that perverted sonofabitch. He ain't nothing in this town. Nothing.'

'He's got the house,' said Mary Lou.

'No he ain't got the house. He rents the house, that's all. Talking of which – Elmer. Maybe you can delay your visit to Beau and go see Elmer.'

'To do what Pa?'

'Get him to sell his portion of the house to me. And I ain't interested in how you do it, just do it. I got the feeling he had a fancy for you.'

'Yes pa he did.'

'Did? What did? What changed? Oh Jeez, Mary Lou you and your sex drive. When you need something for real keep your legs closed and your panties on. How many times have I told you?'

'I didn't know we'd need Elmer for something,' said Mary Lou.

'Shit! Okay, tell him I'll cancel his gambling debts.'

'For real, pa?'

'Sure. And hon, do me a favour, drop these in at Norwood's place on the way.'

'Metairie's hardly on the way but I'll do it.'

'Good girl,' he said, giving her a sealed package. 'I know I can trust you.'

Mary Lou left her father's house and drove the very long way round via Norwood's house, where she gave the package to his housekeeper and then on towards Elmer's office.

Mary Lou decided that she was going to pull out all the stops. She was going to have Elmer. She was wet between the legs and randy as hell. Normally she'd have turned up at Helmut's and he'd have screwed her rigid. But Mary Lou was well pissed off with the Count. She had no intention of going to see him for a few days. Not until the Mardi Gras orgy that he'd planned. Mary Lou thought Helmut was well out of order, taking sides with the Daisy girl against her.

Mary Lou remembered what had happened the previous evening. After Elmer had sucked her, Epps had fucked her in the arse, and with the dildo stuck up hard inside her, she had screwed the blindfolded girl with it, and Epps had lashed her with the whip. After that, Helmut had sent her upstairs to prepare for the evening.

She was standing in the all-mirrored bathroom brushing her hair when Helmut came in. He had the girl, Daisy, with him. He unbuttoned his trousers and handled his sex sword.

Mary Lou gasped. She wanted it. She wanted him. She wanted to be laid out on the floor and pounded by his prick. Telling Daisy to stay by the door, Helmut stood behind Mary Lou, lifted her skirt and pushed his prick between the tops of her legs without entering her wanton wet sex.

'Take off your top,' he ordered.

Recognising the commanding tone in his voice, Mary Lou immediately did as she was told. He fondled her breasts. His prick could feel the moistness of her sex lips opening, her muscles trying to ease his cock upwards and her hips gyrating just as he wanted them. Helmut put his hands between Mary Lou's legs and his fingers touched her clitoris. He began to stroke and excite her ravenous little point. Mary Lou gasped louder, in sharper shorter puffs, and her inner muscles clenched. Her nipples had become hard. Helmut tweaked them. He could see her face in the mirror and her tongue flicking in and out of her mouth.

'So, my dear, you want to be fucked?' he said. 'Answer me.'

'Yes . . .' she said, and he saw her face flush with anticipation and excitement.

'Very well, remove your skirt then bend over, keeping your knees straight and your legs apart and hold on to your ankles.'

Mary Lou wriggled out of her leather skirt. Licentiously she bent down, her sex open, swollen and wanton. Helmut fondled her naked buttocks. His hands wandering between the crease and grazing her sex lips. With each caress he could feel her shudder, feel her open further, more moisture dampen his fingers. He saw her glands swelling, and her tissue suffuse with a deep pink glow. He put his penis at the entrance to her vagina and with infinite care allowed only the tip to enter. Mary Lou found this unbearable. She moved back endeavouring to take the rest of it but he pulled away.

'Atonement, Mary Lou,' said Helmut.

'Atonement?' she queried softly, her voice shaking.

'Yes, your earlier performance was not satisfactory,' he said. 'Stand up straight.'

Mary Lou stood naked in front of him. He kissed her nipples. Then nipped them with his teeth and held his prick against her abdomen and rubbed it up and down.

'Step into the shower, Mary Lou,' said Helmut.

Mary Lou stepped into the small white tiled cubicle.

'Lean your back against the wall.'

Mary Lou leant her back against the wall, feeling its

icy coldness along her shoulder blades and on her freshly marked bottom.

'Push your pelvis forward and hold yourself open.'

Mary Lou obeyed him. Helmut stood in front of her
and rubbed her clitoris with tiny enticing circles so that
her wanting was increased to a painful level. Then he
took a step back and aimed his cock at her sex. He di-
rected a jet of his warm water at her open soft folds, and
watched it hit her excited point then stream down her
legs.

'Now please step down and follow me,' he said,
pressing a button so that part of the wall slid away. A
room was revealed that Mary Lou had no idea existed.
In the middle on a dais stood a small vaulting horse
with handcuffs hanging from chains on a pulley above
it.

'Mary Lou, please put your hands into these handcuffs,' said Helmut, bringing the chains down and fixing
them around Mary Lou's wrists. 'And lie with your
belly over the horse.'

Full of trepidation Mary Lou lay down, her bare white
rump uppermost. Helmut stroked her inviting buttocks,
letting his fingers move into her sex, playing with it,
teasing her, bringing her up to a state of tremulous desire.

'Come here, Daisy.'

Daisy walked awkwardly into the room. There
seemed to be something odd about her outline. Mary
Lou raised her head. Daisy stood beside Helmut. Helmut parted Daisy's skirts. And Mary Lou gasped.

'As you can see, Daisy has a rubber prick strapped on
and, my dear, I am going to allow her to fuck you,' said
Helmut. 'But first, I have to tell you that if you come
before I give you permission I shall hand you over to
Missy for the rest of the evening. So, unlike earlier this
evening, you had better control yourself.'

Helmut gave her bare buttocks a few sharp slaps with
the palm of his hand.

'Daisy, you can do whatever you want with her but

143

do it very slowly,' said Helmut, knowing full well that Mary Lou was almost at crescendo and the slowness of a dildo fuck would increase her desire to come, not alleviate it.

Helmut then positioned a small footstool between Mary Lou's legs and Daisy stepped on to it.

Daisy's long cool hands began playing with Mary Lou's sex. Against her will she began to move her hips and moan. Then Daisy put the dildo at the entrance to Mary Lou's tingling, expectant and willing sex and slowly moved in. In and out. In and out. Mary Lou took it, enjoying it, loving it and desperately trying not to come. Then Helmut came up behind Daisy and thrust his prick between her legs, and entered her rosy pink vulva. Every time she moved into Mary Lou, Helmut shoved into her. And slowly a momentum was built up. Helmut put his hands around Daisy's breasts and fondled her nipples and kissed her neck. This made Daisy thrust harder and Mary Lou moan and groan and sigh and whimper as the rubber prick prodded along her inner walls.

'Play with her clitoris, Daisy,' Helmut ordered. Obeying him she put her cool hands round, lifted the fleshy hood and lightly massaged Mary Lou's glistening bud.

This was more than Mary Lou could bear, she trembled as shock waves coursed through her womb and love channel. Losing all control she let out a cry and came. Helmut stopped thrusting and pulled Daisy away from Mary Lou.

'You have caused me displeasure for a second time today,' he said harshly, and left the room taking Daisy with him, leaving Mary Lou attached to the chains and bent naked over the vaulting horse.

They had been gone some minutes when Epps came in and sluiced down Mary Lou's rump and legs. When he had finished he oiled her backside with fragrant oils and departed.

She was left on her own for quite a while before Missy Lee came in. Mary Lou felt a frisson of fear as Missy Lee approached her. She knew the strength in those tiny delicate hands. She also knew Missy Lee's proclivities. Missy did not speak to her, but unhooked one of the chains above her head and attached them to the heavy leather belt around her waist. Then she unhooked the other one and attached that to the same belt.

'Please, come with me, Miss Mary Lou,' she said politely. Mary Lou knew she had no option. She could see the large bull whip in Missy Lee's hand.

Missy guided the naked and chained Mary Lou out of the bathroom along the corridor to the blacked out room adjoining Helmut's bedroom. She sat her down on a large chair covered with a rough cut velvet which grazed her soft skin.

'Please stay here,' she said, and unhooked the chains from her belt and attached them to a hook on the wall. Then she took the handcuffs and locked them to small chains hanging from the arm rests. When she had done that she took Mary Lou's ankles, spread them apart and locked them to the chair legs. From her apron pocket Missy took a tiny vibrator, switched it on and clicked it into a small holder in the chair between Mary Lou's legs. Missy opened Mary Lou's sex lips and placed them around the vibrator, positioning its tip on Mary Lou's excited protuberance. Missy turned it on. The friction of the vibrator polishing her hard bud and gliding on the juices within her soft fleshy folds caused a pleasurable shudder through the whole of Mary Lou's body. Missy gave Mary Lou a sharp shove in the back forcing her buttocks forwards.

'Please sit up straight,' said Missy.

Mary Lou was delighted to obey, the vibrator was then pressed harder on her moistness making her more sensual and sexy. Missy moved a slat in the back of the chair and locked it firmly behind Mary Lou. This meant the captured girl could not move backwards and avoid the ministrations of the vibrator on her sex, even if she wanted to, which she did not. Missy Lee put her arms over Mary Lou's shoulders and excited her nipples.

Rubbing them with a sure fast rhythm. Mary Lou braced her shoulders back and pushed her breasts forwards wanting more of Missy's hands. But that didn't happen. Instead Missy covered them with a harsh tweed fabric, tying it around her neck and under her breasts so that its roughness aggravated her stiff nipples. Then Missy departed.

Mary Lou was left in a constant state of agony as her clitoris was aroused more and more by the shuddering object and she was unable to touch herself. She licked her lips and thought erotic thoughts. She wondered what Missy would do with her when she was unlocked from the chair. Who would have her? What would Helmut do with her? What would her punishment be?

Some while later she heard the sounds of pleasure and pain coming from the next room. The door opened. Mary Lou caught her breath with anticipation. Now she was going to be freed. Mary Lou could see naked figures in the room beyond: a woman bending over and being screwed by a man. She could see another woman outstretched on the Count's large bed and a man crouched over her face. Missy Lee came in and closed the door. Without saying a word, she untied the rough tweed fabric and let it fall over Mary Lou's belly. She took some thread from a pocket in a black uniform and tied it around Mary Lou's nipples, attaching that thread to the arm of the chair. Then manipulating those brown teats with a sure scissor movement Missy enticed Mary Lou's nipples to a greater fullness. When she had done that and there was a terrible ache coursing through Mary Lou's body, Missy Lee covered her up again with the tweed, changed the battery in the vibrator and left.

And there she had remained throughout the night. Her torment and her punishment was to listen to the sounds of pleasure and pain and not be allowed to participate. Denied everything. Even the vicarious joys of watching other people screw. She had had to stay there shackled and alone. Slowly the battery had run out and she had eventually fallen asleep. At some stage during the early hours of the morning someone had undone the fetters and had driven her home. She didn't know who or how, but she had awoken in her own room. Furious, Mary Lou decided she could not forgive Helmut for his sadism. She wanted her revenge. Angrily she had gone down to breakfast where she had met her father. He had then informed her that she was going to have to marry Beau Maitland. That was too much. Somehow, Mary Lou decided she had to get her own back on both of them, her father and Helmut.

Mary Lou was determined to seduce Elmer, and seduce him real good. To hell with her father. Then she thought again. She'd screw Elmer for fun and tell him that Frank would cancel his debts. Nobody would find out. Round one to her. But how could she have her revenge on Helmut? She'd think hard and sooner or later some idea would come her way.

Driving down Magazine Street to buy some odds and ends at the health food store Mary Lou caught sight of Elmer's automobile parked outside his apartment block.

How very fortuitous, she thought, pulling in behind it. If he's home all the better for what I have in mind.

Elmer, in a temper, and deeply angered by the Count's capitulation to Ottilie's demands for vacant possession of the house, had gone home.

As soon as he arrived at his apartment he had telephoned a disappointed Josephine telling her he had unexpected appointments and would not be coming to the office. He asked her if, when she had finished dealing with the morning's mail, she would deliver the plans and the various papers to do with the St Jacques project to his apartment. Elmer gave her his address, telling her to bring his front door keys with her – they were in his desk drawer – and use them. He might not be in. Elmer had a great desire to go gambling. But he'd wait a while. No good doing that in a temper. Calm down. Get centred. Think winner.

He sat in his sitting room with a large glass of whisky.

147

His apartment was as comfortable and as impersonal as a furniture showroom. It wasn't that he cared little for his surroundings. He did, sometimes. He liked it frugal. Operational. His home was somewhere he came back to after the office. Somewhere to wash and bathe, sleep, watch the television, occasionally screw and even more occasionally read a book. There weren't many books about. And there were only two pictures on the walls. One was of an old plantation scene. He thought it could have been his grandfather's and he'd had it for ages. He kept meaning to chuck it but never did. The other was a present from Ottilie, years ago. A Paris scene. That too should have been chucked. Elmer was quite good at chucking. The only permanent things in his apartments were the fitted kitchen and the fitments in the bathroom.

For the last three years Elmer had lived with hi-tech black and white and cool grey. Before that it had been the era of rustic. Now it was cool cream and beige with a touch of yellow. He'd come home after the Norwood Cates débâcle, looked at his possessions and telephoned the thrift store. Not one in particular – Elmer was not altruistic – but the first one that answered the telephone.

'Come and clear my apartment. Take everything,' he'd said. 'The day after tomorrow.'

That gave him time to go to Maison Blanche, choose and order and have delivered his new furniture. With no plan. Whatever took his fancy the day he set foot in the store. That and that and that and that. He'd point to settees, and easy chairs, a dining table and its chairs, beds and wardrobes, occasional tables. Bedlinen and table linen, television and hi-fi. The lot. Everything gone, everything replaced. And if he didn't like the carpets with the new furniture they'd be ripped up and thrown out and new ones laid. Elmer didn't bother with curtains. Shutters on the windows served him well enough.

Elmer sat with his glass of whisky and thought. He was in real shit. His gambling debts were high, his income was dwindling. Everything in his life seemed to be falling apart. The business. His love life. He had wanted

148

Mary Lou. And he had had her. Sort of. Not as he'd imagined. He wouldn't mind doing it again. It had given him quite a thrill. Sucking her, fucking the other girl. How many women did the Count have in that house. And Epps? What was his true role? He'd always appeared as the perfect butler but he'd screwed Mary Lou's arse without a qualm and whipped her bottom with evident expertise. And Missy Lee? She was a dark horse. Was she a housekeeper for real? And the manner in which the blindfolded girl was dressed was bizarre. Her breasts jacked up over her basque. Her skirts made so that her sex and her bottom were instantly accessible; able to be had and fondled whenever the Count so desired.

Then there was Josephine. Her rounded body excited him. Her big breasts, her large hips, her pouting mouth, her big violet eyes and her dimpled knees. He imagined Josephine in the blindfolded girl's situation. He envisaged her wearing a bodice with her big tits on display, and him parting the split skirt caressing her wide arse. Elmer imagined her rounded mound. She'd have soft downy light brown hair. Elmer thought of his hands stroking that mound and then pulling back the hood to reveal her bud. These thoughts gave Elmer real pleasure. It was heightened by the knowledge that he would do no such thing, because she was a good secretary and he did not want to lose her. He was sure going to learn from his past mistake. No way was he going to drop his pants. Leastways not for Josephine. Mary Lou maybe. She was something else. She was into sex in a big way. Elmer liked that.

Elmer finished the whisky in his glass, turned on the radio – he wanted some music – and poured himself another drink.

He knew he should be thinking about the afternoon's presentation for the St Jacques Arts Complex. But he was in no mood to concentrate on business. Sex. He was far more interested in sex. He wanted sex badly. His cock had grown stiff with thinking about Mary Lou and

Josephine. And he was hungry. Hell and Goddamn. Should he have a wank or get himself some food? Eat. He took some bread and lettuce and cheese from the fridge and made himself a sandwich. Then he turned off the radio and turned on the television. He channel hopped. He wanted a person, not a cartoon, in the room with him. Didn't matter who or what, old movie, new comedy, but someone had to be there with him, sharing his repast. Eating was a social occasion. Living by himself Elmer did something he would never do living with someone. He watched television when he ate. He had to. Then he didn't feel so alone.

Elmer finished his sandwich, ate an apple and still felt out of sorts with himself. It was no good. He needed more than food. He sat in his most comfortable armchair and unzipped his flies. His cock sprang out from its imprisonment. Thick and sturdy. Elmer cradled it lovingly. He pushed his trousers down around his thighs and caressed his balls. With a pressure that he was used to he began to rub from the tip down to the base. Then he held himself under the cap and rolled the skin up and over its head and back again. Squeezing, letting his thumb press on the inside of his fingers, roaming on the outside; he was playing his own flute, opening and closing the holes for different notes. The tiny hole in the top began to ease out moisture and he took this and ran it along his penis as lubrication. He held his sack, juggling the balls between the fingers of his other hand. Sweet joy. His stomach contracted. The muscles in his buttocks hardened. His legs stretched out, his heels holding their place on the rug on the floor. The blood in his prick kept it hard, rigid, erect. And thoughts were flooding into him. Dark erotic thoughts. If he wasn't careful he'd come too soon. He wanted more of himself.

Elmer stood up, took off his clothing and put on a fine cotton kimono. That was better, easier. No constrictions.

The doorbell jangled. His penis shrivelled at the sound. He wouldn't answer. He'd carry on. The doorbell

150

went again. Jeez. Josephine. He'd have to answer. Thank God she hadn't used the key.

Elmer tied the kimono sash loosely around his body and opened the door.

'Mary Lou!' he exclaimed, when he saw who was standing on his doorstep.

'Hiya, Elmer, can I come in?' she said.

Elmer leant back against the door and she ambled passed him into his lounge. He watched her closely. She was wearing a loose fitting black top, white ankle socks, white stiletto high-heeled shoes and tight blue jeans. He ran his eyes the length of her legs. His eyes saw. His brain whirred and his cock shot up. The Triangle. Embarrassed he tried to push his prick down as he walked behind her.

Elmer was fixated. He stayed staring at the great turn on: that place of space at the top of a woman's thighs that drives men wild. And Elmer was no exception.

Her thighs were neatly encased in jeans that held her meeting flesh away from her legs and produced the wishful wonder fuck. He wanted to push his fingers through that space; he wanted to push his cock through it. Run it along the ridges of her jeans, push it through one side and out the other. Jeez, he thought, how many goddamn turn on points do I have? Josephine's knees and Mary Lou's triangle.

'Take a seat Mary Lou,' he said. 'Can I give you anything – a drink?'

'Sure, what have you got?'

'Most things, what'll it be?'

Mary Lou noticed the whisky glass on the small table, picked it up and sniffed it.

'Whisky, same as you,' she said.

Elmer poured her a large whisky and gave himself another one.

'What brings you here?' he asked, handing it to her.

'My pa. I was driving over to your office when I saw your car outside. Maybe he's home, I said to myself. I'll ring the bell and see and here I am,' said Mary Lou.

'Your pa brought you here!' said Elmer. 'For why?'

'Well now, he said if you'd like to sell him your portion of the house he'd cancel your gambling debts.'

'Bullshit,' said Elmer.

'No, for real,' said Mary Lou.

'And your name's Lady Luck! That it?' said Elmer.

'Look at it this way,' said Mary Lou, 'maybe your luck's in. Makes a change for you, doesn't it Elmer.'

And Mary Lou stood in front of the window sipping her whisky with the light shining through the triangle at the top of her legs. And Elmer squirmed.

'So what d'ya say to my Daddy's suggestion?' Mary Lou asked.

'I say it bears contemplating,' replied Elmer.

'It sure does,' said Mary Lou. 'And while you're contemplating, let me ask you if you had a good time last night?'

'Yeah.'

'I did not,' she said. 'Wanna know why? Because I wanted you to fuck me, Elmer. And Count Helmut doesn't like any of his women wanting someone else. Doesn't mind if he says they can be fucked, or sucked or whipped, whilst he looks on but 'cos I made the suggestion he was real mad. That goddamn sonofabitch made me pay for it.'

'What did he make you do?' asked Elmer, amazed that she should discuss it with him and also intensely curious.

'Well,' said Mary Lou, sitting down on the settee and patting it for Elmer to sit beside her, 'he made damn certain I didn't get fucked at all.'

'How did he do that?' asked Elmer, gulping down his whisky.

'Sadistically,' said Mary Lou, her hand resting on his knees. 'He took off my clothes, and had that damn Missy Lee take me naked into a room where she locked me on a chair.'

'Locked you on a chair!'

'Yeah. Spread my legs apart, and chained them to the

chair legs, yoked my hands to the arm rests, and then guess what she did?'

'I can't guess,' said Elmer, swallowing hard. Mary Lou's hands were now stroking his thighs.

'She put a vibrator on my clit. Can you believe that? Put it just here,' Mary Lou opened her legs and rubbed herself through her jeans. 'And left the battery running. Know what, that's some sort of hell. 'Cos my clit is mighty sensitive and when you have something like that vibrating just there, and nobody doing nothing to stop it, it's hell. Elmer I can tell you it's one helluva punishment. And all 'cos I wanted to fuck you.'

As she said that Mary Lou's hands moved further up Elmer's legs and on the last two words her hands encircled his cock and his balls.

'My, Elmer that's a real good hard-on,' said Mary Lou, letting her hand drift up his shaft and over its cap and back down towards his balls. Her expert caresses increased his blood rush. Elmer's prick was standing rigid and very proud.

'Elmer, would you have any objections if I put that beautiful cock of yours in my mouth?'

Elmer sighed his reply. Her cool hands had just the right pressure, his sort of pressure, and she was driving him wild.

Mary Lou bent her head and Elmer watched as she slowly took the entire length of his phallus into her mouth. And then she began to suck. Taking his skin up, letting her tongue wander around the lip of its head, staying playing with the cap as she took the skin back down again, letting her tongue find the tiny slit in the top. Her hands held his balls. A couple of fingers strayed, finding the tender skin before his bottom-hole, Mary Lou delicately made the tiniest of blissful circles on that special sensitive spot. The fingers of her hand that held his prick splayed out over the top of his balls, capturing them momentarily before starting her work on the same route all over again.

Elmer's hands moved under her loose blouse, found

153

her brassière, unhooked it at the back and embraced her pert breasts. Her head was bobbing up and down as it sucked at his prick and her blonde curls had fallen either side of her head leaving the back of her neck exposed. A slim thin neck with smooth skin spread taut and white over the vertebrae. Entrancing Elmer. He bent and kissed it.

It was such a gentle loving touch that it sent shivers of excitement surging down Mary Lou's spine. And a sudden rush of damp through her love channel.

Mary Lou slipped from the settee on to the floor and knelt in between Elmer's thighs.

'Lean back and put your legs on my shoulders,' she said.

Elmer was more than happy to do as she asked. Her hands then stroked his belly, one lingering over his cock as the other gripped his buttocks. He liked that. She noticed his reaction and dug her nails into his flesh. He liked that too. Mary Lou reached up and pulled the sash from his kimono and tied it around the base of his penis. Then she licked its head and gently juggled his balls.

Elmer pulled her black top off over her head and removed her brassière. Her jeans remained fastened and tight. She was moving her hips, as she playfully used her fingers and her mouth to excite him more and more.

Elmer wanted her badly. But first he wanted to put his naked sex sword through the gap at the top of her legs. He wanted to feel the ridges of the jeans on his phallus as he rubbed backwards and forwards in that place of the wishful fuck. He ran his hands through her hair.

'Turn round and kneel showing me your arse,' he said, masterfully.

Mary Lou quite surprised by the tone in his voice immediately obeyed him.

Elmer looked at her as she knelt, her back straight, her tits falling forwards, her arms rigid and outstretched. She looked like an erotic artist's sculpture for an erotic table. And the triangle was still there, only added to by the forcibly flattened curves of her backside.

Elmer knelt between her legs and positioned his cock

at the space where he knew her sex began and slowly he began to rub. The ridges of the seams excited him. She squirmed as he moved. He bent over her back and clasped her tits. She held her position but moved one arm and put her hand up to meet his thrusting penis as it ventured to the other side of the gap in her trousers. She ringed her thumb and forefinger so that his prick slid into it after passing along the fabric and the seams.

Elmer wondered if anybody had ever done this to her before. Did she like it? Had the Count fucked her, or even whipped her with her jeans on? Thinking of the Count reminded him of earlier and Ottilie; he wondered what they were doing now.

'I wonder if the Count will seduce Ottilie,' he said, without thinking.

Instantly Mary Lou froze. Jeez! The Count and Ottilie! Those two together! What! He wouldn't! Does hell suck? He would. Mary Lou knew he would. Her desire for revenge against the Count was almost overwhelming. First the Daisy girl and now Ottilie. Shit! That was too much. She'd go see Helmut. She'd have the whole thing out with him. Either she was number one or he could go rot. Mary Lou was aware she might be cutting off her nose to spite her face but if he was screwing Miss God-damn Prim and Prissy Ottilie she wasn't going to take part in any more of his orgies. And who else was he going to find in this town to take her place? Hookers, yeah but someone with real class? Rich and classy. No-body, that was for sure. Mary Lou knew hookers were not Count Helmut's scene. So she'd got him well by the short and curlies.

'Mary Lou?' questioned Elmer. He was aware that her attention was rambling away from him. Her responses had changed; her movements were almost non-existent.

'What do you mean?' she asked, carefully keeping her jealousy under control. 'They don't know one another, do they?'

Her duplicitous nature got the better of her and she rocked again on his penis.

'They didn't but they do now,' he said.

'How?' Mary Lou asked, rocking and grateful that Elmer could not see her face or the effort she was making to sound normal.

'I took her there to discuss the house,' said Elmer. 'And the bastard . . .'

Elmer stopped in mid-sentence. If he told Mary Lou exactly what had been discussed he might not be able to get the deal out of her father. To get his debts paid was a mighty fine incentive to discretion.

'What did the bastard do?' asked Mary Lou, making the hole with her thumb and forefinger smaller so that Elmer had to use greater force to thrust through it.

'He managed to get rid of me double quick fast,' he said, 'said he'd like to show Ottilie the house.'

'I bet he didn't show her all of it!' said Mary Lou. 'There are a few rooms in that house that just ain't for public viewing.'

'The ones where he had the sound proofing put in?'

'That's them but how do you know?' asked Mary Lou.

'You forget I designed it. I thought it was odd. He's not a musician, so what's he want with sound proofing?'

'Maybe one day you'll find out,' said Mary Lou, thinking of the delicious times she had spent in the Count's dungeon. This made her wet. She wanted to be fucked and fucked hard. Mary Lou rolled over and undid the buttons on her jeans. Elmer still had the sash tied around his penis. It was causing him a delightful agony. He sat up and helped Mary Lou ease her jeans down over her hips.

'Don't take them off,' he said. 'Not yet. Let me suck your pussy.'

Mary Lou stood in front of the seated Elmer. She thrust her pelvis into his face. He wound his fingers under the elastic of her panties, held it to one side and let his tongue travel along her labia, opening her moist sex lips. He lifted back the hood and nibbled on her enlarged clitoris. He liked her standing waiting for his tongue. It was an outrageously erotic stance: her willing

156

body bent slightly back as his tongue foraged amongst the furls of her sex. He pulled her jeans down a fraction more.

'Lie beside me, head to tail,' he said. 'But don't take your jeans off.'

Elmer found the rise of her bare bottom coming up through the compressed half off, half on jeans utterly irresistible.

He lay full length on the settee. She lay on top of him, positioning her sex over his mouth. She took his tumescent phallus in her hands and guided it into her wide red mouth. She tightened the sash from time to time to increase the pressure at the base of his prick to prolong his orgasm.

Elmer nuzzled into her wet folds. He spread her bottom apart and let a finger run up and down along that fine puckered skin. She heaved with each touch. He gave an answering shudder to her muscles. She pulled on the sash. He went deeper into her, one finger beginning to enter her other hole. The two of them lay completely abandoned. Totally enraptured by the joy and the excitement they were giving one another.

They failed to hear the doorbell ring.

Josephine had dressed most carefully that morning. She knew that Elmer found her attractive. If it hadn't been for the telephone ringing at the most inopportune moment he would have kissed her, even tried to seduce her. She wouldn't have let him. Not first time round. But she wanted him. There was something vulnerable about Elmer that appealed to Josephine.

Josephine boarded in a nice white district of nice white middle class Metairie. She wanted to stay in the French Quarter but tales of rape and guns and drunks had frightened her. She'd met a woman on the plane who'd told her, 'Live in Metairie, that's where all the nice people of New Orleans live.'

Josephine Mattsey was an Okie. Her father was a farmer back in Oklahoma. Her mother kept house. She was the only child. They were God-fearing people. And as soon as she could, Josephine took the greyhound bus and left for the city. But the cities of that state didn't appeal. She worked as a waitress, she studied in the evening. Secretarial work. She made enough money to take a plane to Louisiana, New Orleans. Sin City the Okies called it. And that intrigued Josephine.

A city where sin was allowed. Indulged. A city of laughter and party time. But it wasn't all like that. The church – whichever church, it didn't matter – the church was strong. It held sway. It pronounced on things spiritual and material. It had something to say on every topic, and it said it loudly. It proclaimed it from hoardings in the streets and – especially at Mardi Gras – on people's backs. 'Repent and be saved.'

Josephine had been planning on leaving Metairie. There was little music to be heard. Everything was neat and clean and white. It was dull. Even duller than the farm. Leastways there she had the sun in the morning on the yellow-gold corn. Sure the sun was bright on the luxuriant foliage in people's backyards but there was something else. A feeling of oppression in the attitude of the residents of Metairie. People were judgmental, and whatever they were judging, there was no room for leeway. Whether it be blacks or whites or unmarried mothers, they were firm in their belief that they were right. Whatever right was.

The previous evening, after leaving the office, Josephine had wandered through the Quarter. Not down Bourbon Street with its sleaze and crap T-shirt shops; she ambled along Royal with its antique shops and its old houses – their wooden balconies bedecked with gold, green and purple bunting. Streamers flapped from windows, silently telling everyone who passed by to have a happy Mardi Gras. She wound her way as the will took her, backwards and forwards into Chartres, down St Ann, into Dauphine and up Ursulines. There she stopped for a coffee and a slice of gateau in a pretty cafe, and got talking to a young couple seated at her table.

They told her they were leaving, going back north to New York City. They'd been in New Orleans long enough and had to go. They'd seen Mardi Gras three times, and now work called. They had a place on Elysian Fields Avenue close by Burgundy Street.

'Isn't that where Blanche Dubois lived?' she asked.

'You mean Tennessee Williams's heroine?' asked the young guy.

'Yes,' said Josephine.

'Supposed to have done,' he said. 'Anyhow we got the run down half of a duplex through room, with gays in the house on one side, blacks on the other, a dyke club on the corner, across the highway on the other corner there's a gay bar. And next to the gay bar a supermarket. Everything you could ever want.'

Josephine felt in her bones that's where she had to be. That was the New Orleans she'd come to find.

'Oh, and don't forget Her Majesty the Right Reverend Queen Otavia Wanja dos Rios Santos,' said the young woman.

'Who is she?' asked Josephine.

'The local Voodoo Queen.'

'Oh wow! And you're leaving? Anybody taking over your place?'

'No, 'cos it's a dump,' said the guy whose name was Richard. 'Our landlady who lives the other side of the duplex, which is great, had a goddamn limey husband who married her for citizenship, then when it came through, went and left her for pastures new.'

'Not so much pastures, more like the young cows in the pastures,' said his partner, Gil.

'And the mother's demanding half of all she's got.'

'What?' said Josephine.

'And he can, 'cos this is Louisiana. Anyhow, that's why the place stays the way it is. If it's half he wants, he gets that half.'

'Sounds like just the place I wanna be,' said Josephine. 'If you're leaving can't you take me there, let me see it, introduce me . . .'

'What d'ya think,' said Richard.

'I think why not. Suzi needs the dough. You'd have to pay rent up front.'

'That's fine. I've got a good job.'

'Lucky you.'

It was a one storey nineteenth-century house, with a small garden, high palms, a banana tree, and a mass of busy lizzies in an ancient huge porcelain sink by the porch. At the back were the old slave quarters. Six foot wide and five stories high – room for them to sleep but that's all. They were being done up by property speculators, to be rented out as studios.

They entered not through the front door but via large white garage gates. Beyond the porch Suzi was sitting smoking, talking to Walter and Scott, her gay neighbours. She was in her early forties, and looked and sounded like a young Lauren Bacall.

Richard and Gil introduced Josephine, and said she was looking for a place to stay. Suzi looked her over and said, 'Okay, see if you like it.' And they went back the way they'd come to the side passage on the other half of the duplex.

It was a mess: old furniture piled together with bicycles and washing machines; old paint on the walls; an ancient claw footed bath but the hot water worked; a huge kitchen with an enormous wooden table; bare boards. But there was one room that was habitable, with a futon, pictures on the wall, a chaise longue and a big noisy fan.

'We live here,' they said. 'We ignore the rest, except for cooking and peeing.'

'I'll take it,' said Josephine.

Josephine felt like she was breathing again; like she was returning to reality. She took it, then went back to Metairie, gave her notice, packed up her meagre belongings and was ready to leave at first light.

She'd spent a night of half sleep, excited at the prospect of her new home. Also at the thought of Elmer. Josephine wasn't absolutely sure what it was that attracted her to Elmer. She had pondered it every night since her interview. She had an idea but wasn't certain. She was determined she'd soon find out.

Josephine wasn't a virgin. She'd lost her cherry in one of the cities of the plains after a long night waitressing. A guy had seen her back to her rooming house. She was drunk. He was drunk. He had a packet of condoms on him and she'd thought, what the hell, let's give it a try. It hadn't been marvellous or earth shattering or even particularly good. But it had been safe so she gave it what she could. Saw a stiff prick for the first time. She'd seen them plenty on the little boys down home – hanging loose, a sweet appendage – but never rampant. Wanting. The whole experience had been nothing special but Josephine was glad she'd done it. She felt less vulnerable. And since then there had been the odd one night stand, when she'd been passing through, and always under the same conditions. Always she felt a lack of engagement, emotionally speaking. But Elmer was different. She wanted to kiss him. Not just open her legs and have it shoved up as if releasing some natural cleansing fluid through her body. And she did feel cleansed after one of her encounters. She was able to function better and was more rational.

Josephine felt Elmer needed looking after. He needed to be guided by a firm hand. Her parents were like that. Father brought home the money. Her mother ruled the roost. He said everything that needed to be said. He laid down the law while mother did exactly as she pleased. She would always say that that was the way he wanted it. Anything, it didn't matter what it was, was prefixed by 'Your father said'. And Josephine knew he never had said a damn thing. But that was the game they played and by osmosis she understood that way of operating. She recognised it, and saw that Elmer needed it. Yes, a firm hand. Josephine knew she'd be good at that.

One of her men had introduced it to her. In a motel. They had been screwing when suddenly he produced a cane from his luggage.

161

'Use it,' he'd said.

'Where?' she'd asked in total ignorance and innocence.

'On my ass,' he'd replied.

'What for?' she'd asked.

'Because I like it,' he'd replied.

He had lain on his belly on the bed and waited. She had stood by the side of him in her bra and panties feeling stupid. Hitting somebody for no reason seemed to her against all reason. She tapped him with the cane on the rise of his buttocks.

'For fuck's sake!' he'd exclaimed. 'Hit me hard.'

Wanting to burst into tears, but thinking that was real dumb she'd brought the cane down with surprising ferocity on his bottom. He'd jumped up and squealed, partly with the unexpected pain and partly with delight. She jumped back, afraid she'd hurt him.

'That was better,' he said. He took his own belt from his jeans and wrapped them around his wrists.

'I can't get away see. I've been a bad boy and you've got to punish me,' he said.

Click, went Josephine's brain. Click. Click. Click. A game. A new game.

'Oh yes you have,' she said, a threatening tone in her voice as she advanced towards him. 'Tell me what you've done.' She brought the cane down hard on the bed beside him. 'Tell me.'

'I was wanking. Wanking, mistress. I was watching this girl undress and I was wanking.'

'How many times have I told you, wanking is not allowed. Answer me. How many times?'

'Many, mistress, many,' he said cowering.

She turned him over and took his half mast phallus in her hands.

'Miserable little thing,' she said, and flicked his balls with the tip of the cane. His penis sprang to life.

Josephine trailed the cane along his inner thighs, rubbing his cock, feeling it stiffen under her attentions. When it was very hard, and droplets were oozing from

162

the tiny hole in the top, she pushed him over, back on to his belly.

'So, you've been wanking many times?'

'Yes, mistress.'

'And what is the punishment for that?'

'Whatever is your pleasure, mistress,' he whimpered.

'Speak up,' she said and let the cane come down savagely on his rump.

He wasn't expecting that and curled up foetally and squealed once more.

'Speak up and lie flat,' she said.

'Yes, mistress,' he replied.

'My pleasure is . . .' she let the cane wander over his backside, through his crack, and poke at the hidden hole. The man held his breath.

'Twelve strokes . . . at least.'

And Josephine brought the cane down. First hard. Then soft. Then hard. Then soft, then harder and harder until there were eighteen livid weals criss-crossing his buttocks. And with every stroke she felt power. Power and control oozing from her hand, her mind and her sex. In one short lesson Josephine learned the enjoyment of the dominatrix.

'What do you say?' she asked when she had finished.

'Thank you, madam,' he said, and slid off the bed and knelt at her feet. 'Thank you, madam.'

'Suck me,' she said, pulling the wide legs of her loose panties to one side.

'Yes, madam,' he replied, and put his tongue at her soft folds and supped at her juices until she came.

'Will madam allow me to fuck her?' he asked.

'Madam will not,' she replied. 'Under no circumstances. But I will give you permission to wank in front of me. Hold yourself and do it properly. If it is not done to my liking I will think of something else. I will lash your cock, so wank, and wank good.'

The man had rubbed himself like a dervish, coming almost instantly, spurting into the air.

He'd wanted to see her again but she left that night

163

for another town. A lesson well learnt. But she hadn't put her learning into practise since. She'd just filed it away until the time was right. And Josephine reckoned the time was going to be right with Elmer.

Josephine had gone to her new abode early and she'd found a posy of flowers on the kitchen table with a note saying 'Welcome'. There she had dressed for the office. On top she'd dressed for the office. Underneath she'd dressed for seduction. She'd put on a black lace brassière and wide-legged black silk knickers. Easy for a hand to slide up, easy for eyes to see pussy when accidentally bending over. And a black straight skirt that would rise up, and a V-necked black cotton blouse which revealed the lace and the swell of her breasts.

She had gone to the office confident, looking forward to the day. Because if not today then tomorrow she would have Elmer, and meanwhile there was the fun of anticipation. And then he had telephoned saying he was not coming to the office. Her heart had dropped. Landing somewhere beyond her stomach.

'Bring the files over to my place,' he had added. 'The keys are in my desk drawer.'

Josephine had rung the bell. No one had answered. She felt a keen sense of disappointment again. Perhaps he did have an appointment somewhere she didn't know about. Maybe that's why he said drop the files round. He'd be too busy to go to the office before his meeting with the preacher on the St Jacques project.

Josephine let herself into the apartment, and the moans and groans of lovemaking hit her ears, and guided her to the sitting room. She stood silently in the doorway watching Elmer's head buried between a long-legged blonde's legs, whilst the blonde, sucking on his cock, was pulling on a sash that was wrapped around his prick. Josephine smiled inwardly. Her instinct was correct. Elmer would just love having his bottom tanned.

Josephine stood there silent. She was in a slight quandry. Should she make herself known or slip quietly away? There were certain advantages in both courses of action. However, she reasoned, he would be more at her mercy if he knew she had seen him sixty-nining some woman. She would make herself known. She coughed.

'Oh Mr Planchet, I've brought the files,' said Josephine.

Chapter 8

Ottilie's body was sparkling and alive, like a clear stream on a summer's day in a temperate climate. Bubbly and transparent.

Having had a leisurely bath, Ottilie, wearing an oyster satin negligée, lay on the bed thinking back to what had happened out on the bayou. She was wonderfully tired and stretched out happily, lazily. She had dismissed Lord Christopher's ridiculous letter, with his stupid comment about claiming her as his bride, from her mind. Her thoughts were all of Count Helmut and her awakened senses. Ottilie found it almost impossible to believe how much her body had responded to his hands, his tongue, his penis.

The telephone rang beside her. Its shrill sound made her jump. With a degree of caution she picked up the receiver.

'Yes?' she queried, warily.

'Ottilie!' It was Beau's voice. 'So you are there. I've been waiting for you here.'

'Sorry, Beau,' she said, 'something came up.' She suppressed the desire to giggle. It was a perfectly ordinary comment that suddenly took on another connotation.

'Oh well are you coming?'

'Um . . .' she hesitated. Her sense of humour had better not get the better of her.

'I really want to see you.'

'I've had a business meeting today,' she lied. 'I'm tired right now. What say you if I come over in a couple of hours?'

'Fine,' he said. 'Oh, Ottilie, are you doing anything over the next few weeks?'

'Why?'

'I need some help here. I've got other things to see to and wondered if you could take over for me?'

'I don't think so, Beau,' she said.

'Think about it,' he replied. 'You know the music scene, temperamental singers, viola players who think they're God's gift. It wouldn't be anything heavy. Just admin stuff. But I need someone I can trust. Give me your answer when I see you. Oh, and Ottilie, the place will be closed so go down the side to the artist's entrance. Ring three times on the bell and I'll know it's you.'

'Okay,' she said.

'And whatever your answer I'll take you out for dinner. That fine by you?'

'Sure is, thanks Beau,' she said.

Dinner with Beau that evening was fine but Ottilie had no intention of wrapping up any other time. She wanted every available moment left open for the Count. He'd ring her soon. He'd tell her what a wonderful crazy time they had together and ask when they could repeat the process. She wanted to be free for him.

From the first moment she had seen him Count Helmut had provoked in her a deep and tremulous desire. Being with him, driving to Baton Rouge and then through Cajun country, had only increased her longing. By the time they had arrived at the cabin that longing had turned to hunger. When, eventually, he had touched her the contact was so electrifying she had thought she would shatter into fragments. Ottilie tried to recapture those exquisite sensations; the feeling in her mind and on her skin as the Count had explored her breasts, her nipples and her mouth, and her mouth taking his penis, but she found it almost impossible.

167

Realising that thinking erotic thoughts had made her feel sexy she undid the ties of the negligée. She let her hands drift across her nipples, down over her belly, to find her own mound. She was wet with desire. Moist with sensuous thoughts.

Her fingers parted her labia. Her newly discovered self was eager to be stimulated again. Her dampness was yearning to be stroked. Needing to be felt. The tiny nerves in her rosy flesh were tingling and asking to be calmed. It was as if her flesh at one and the same time was begging to be opened and then have something occupy the space left by that opening. Slowly she let her fingers glide along her sex lips. Sighing with pleasure her body roused itself and emulated some of the sensations the Count had aroused in her.

Ottilie found her own behaviour extraordinary. She who was normally so prim and proper had been wild and indiscreet. Consumed by a wanting, she had been led into a maze of strange desires. The careful Ottilie had gone. She was free and freed. Passion had beckoned her and she had welcomed it with outstretched arms and open legs.

She put the soles of her feet together and, when she tensed the muscles in her buttocks, her knees rose up like butterfly wings. She pushed her fingers firmly into her inner being. Hard and searching, straying where the Count had strayed. She touched her bud, her centre of extreme experience. A thrill shot through her. She touched it again. Massaged it. Loving the feeling. She saw herself as she had been. Blindfolded and shackled. She saw herself outside and felt herself inside. The willing participant in her awakening. The discovery of her sexual appetite. She felt again the Count moving over her body. She experienced once more the delights of the mushroom trailing through her sex. The Count's prick hard against her body. Against her mouth. In her mouth. Hands exploring. Her own hands increased their pressure on her extended protuberance. She was once again in the darkness of the world behind the fabric on

168

her eyes, and hands were investigating her curves, her mound, her furls and crevices. Four hands. Two pricks. She stopped. Shame.

Shame overcame her. No. It was fantasy. Sexual ardour had been overtaken by erotic fantasy. Her fingers again sought out her softness. She allowed her imagination full play. There was more than one man feeling her wanton body. She was a whore. Degraded. Degradation. Her degradation. Her shame. And those two emotions combined with her heightened sexuality excited her. Her inner need was greater than her outer sense of shame. With sensuous precision she kneaded her own soft flesh. Thoughts, sexual erotic thoughts flooded her mind. Bizarre ideas and visions appeared to her.

Men were licking her, supping at her essence. Taking her. Fucking her. The more she thought the harder her little point became and the more it demanded greater pressure from her fingers. The more the pressure the more eroticised she became. Her shame evaporated. Out on the cabin on the bayou she had been bound by fetters on her hands and feet. Powerless. She imagined that happening again: being in a situation where before she knew it she was bound and gagged and blindfolded. Men were doing whatever they wanted with her. Using her for their pleasure. And hers. She had a cock in her mouth. She had a cock thrusting at her sex. She had a mouth licking her buttocks. Men were enjoying her. She was enjoying their attentions.

Someone would turn her over. Raise her bottom high. A cushion would be put under her belly. A mouth would lick her wet lips, her furls. Leather would be trailed through her sex. Tiny flicks applied to her moist hard bud. She would feel the lash of the whip across her naked flesh.

Ottilie squirmed at the thought. She raised her buttocks higher. Wanting more. Visions tumbled out of her as she continued to excite herself. She could amost feel the cock move within her mouth; her shackled hands opening and a penis placed in both. She was given the order to play with them. She was lashed again. She wanted it all. In her imagination.

But had there been someone else with her and the Count out on the bayou?

No, never. Her mind had played tricks on her. Her over stimulated body had reacted to the sense of sight being denied. It had conjured up someone else with them. Ottilie knew it was daydreams. But what would she do if . . .?

What would she do if more than one man, someone other than the Count but with the Count, real men, and not imaginary, touched her. If two or even three men began caressing her body? Would she allow it to happen or would she stop it, roll away, shamed.

Even by herself she blushed as she thought of those other hands, surely imaginary, exploring her belly, and her womb. She would have told the Count to stop. She knew she would. Never would she have allowed more than one man at a time to know her body. That was an outrageous thought.

In any case who could it have been? There was no one there when they arrived. No one knew they were going there. Except Epps. Epps! No. Ottilie froze. That ugly man could never have touched her breasts, her womb. She could never have sucked his cock. A licentious thought assaulted her. Imaginary or not it had been a beautiful shape, thick and long and powerful and thrusting. She had enjoyed it in her mouth.

Ottilie had her eyes closed. Both her hands were working her sex. One hand was hugging the flesh between her legs arousing her near the part that went round towards her backside. The other was inside, and had found the most tender spot in her soft pink walls. Her thumb was on her clitoris. Her head was moving from side to side. Her legs were rigid and shaking. She was coming. A long slow series of convulsions shook her, her very essence bottled up in the kernel of her womb exploded out, to be lost into the world. She collapsed. Exhausted.

Ottilie set her alarm clock for an hour's time and slept. When she awoke she found a plan had formed in her mind. There was no need for the Count to give up his tenancy. They could share the house. Live there together. He must have fallen in love with her as she had with him. Without love no one could make love in the fashion they had. Love led to marriage. She had the house he wanted. He was the man she wanted. Ottilie was utterly sure that she was the woman he wanted. Therefore all their problems were solved. But she had to make the first move. She had to tell him she would draw up a fresh tenancy agreement. Even Elmer would be delighted by that. He'd get some money. She picked up the receiver to call him, then remembered he had not given her his telephone number. It didn't matter. She would call there on her way to see Beau.

Ottilie sang as she dressed. She hadn't practised for days. She sang the scales. In perfect pitch. She searched through her wardrobe, wanting something eveningy and elegant but not too dressy. She carried on singing without thinking. She had a quick shower and continued to sing. She stopped to put on black silk bra and panties, and hesitated whether to wear stockings or not. She decided it was warm enough not to, then chose and put on a bottle green long-sleeved fine mesh top over a silk chiffon tunic of the same colour and its matching ankle length knitted silk cardigan coat. She brushed her hair, as she curled it up and fixed it with her favourite jewelled combs she started to sing again. Suddenly Ottilie was aware of a subtle difference in the timbre of her voice.

A conversation with her old singing teacher came back to her.

'Are you a virgin, *cherie*?' she'd asked.

'Yes,' Ottilie had replied.

'I thought so,' said Madame.

'Why?' asked Ottilie.

'Because *petit chou*,' explained Madam, 'a virgin has one voice, a married woman another.'

171

'What do you mean?' Ottilie had asked.

'We don't know why, but I have my own explanation,' Madam had said, 'but something seems to happen to a woman's voice after she loses her virginity. It is somehow rounder. More effective and affecting. I believe it's because some part of them is made whole. Humans are not meant to live without sex or in isolation. *Et voila*, when a girl has sex, she is at one with her body.'

Ottilie thought how true that was. For the first time in her life she felt truly at one with hers. She really did feel whole. She smiled, content.

It was on her way down in the lift that she realised that not only had she not visited Beau, she had not bought herself an automobile. That was a nuisance. She'd do it tomorrow. Tonight she'd take a taxi.

'Washington Avenue, and wait for me, then Bayou St John,' she told the cab driver.

Ottilie was about to ring the bell at the gate of the house when she was amazed to see Mary Lou trotting down the pathway, her blonde curls bobbing up and down. Her breasts were moving sexily from side to side under her black top, her nipples erect and easily seen, betraying her lack of brassière. Her long legs were encased in tight jeans, and though her white high heels made her totter slightly, her gait was nevertheless easy. It was the walk of someone who had recently enjoyed some real good sex. The two women saw one another at the same moment. Mary Lou waved.

'Ottilie,' she called. 'Ottilie . . .' Before Ottilie could pretend she wasn't about to ring the bell and make a quick getaway Mary Lou had opened the gates. 'Hiya hon, great to see you.'

Mary Lou kissed Ottilie on both cheeks. Ottilie was quite taken aback. Mary Lou was the last person she expected to see.

'Have you come to see the house or Count Helmut?' Mary Lou asked, then seeing Ottilie hesitate before answering added. 'If it's the Count he's not there.'

172

With glee she watched Ottilie's crest-fallen expression. She kept her own face quite impassive.

'Oh,' said Ottilie. 'Um, yes, it was the Count.'

'What a pity. You missed him by five minutes. He's gone to the airport.'

'Is he meeting someone?' asked Ottilie ingenuously.

'Hell no, hon,' said Ottilie, 'my fiancé is on his way to Dallas/Fort Worth.'

'Your fiancé!' stammered Ottilie.

'Yes, Count Helmut von Straffen is my fiancé. He's gone to buy me the one thing I wanted. Remember I told you, if ever I got engaged I wanted the biggest goddamn diamond? As you know everything is bigger in Texas so he's gone there to get me one.'

Ottilie was dumbfounded, as Mary Lou expected her to be. Ottilie could hardly hold back the tears. Her wonderful world had instantly fallen apart. So had her body. She could feel her throat constricting. She could feel her stomach heaving as if she was about to be violently sick but the bits of her in between had disappeared. There was a gaping hole of nothingness around her heart. How could he! How could he make love to her and ask Mary Lou to be his wife? It wasn't possible.

'When did this happen?' Ottilie asked, making her voice controlled and calm. She refused to betray her real feelings.

'This evening,' said Mary Lou. 'Aren't you going to congratulate me?'

'No,' said Ottilie. Mary Lou looked at her sharply. 'It's the man you congratulate, Mary Lou, not the woman. To do otherwise is the ultimate in bad taste.'

Ottilie turned on her heel and climbed into the taxi leaving her cousin standing on the sidewalk.

'Bayou St John. The St Cecilia Concert Hall' she said, imperiously. 'And fast, I'm late.'

Ottilie sat in the car shaking. Her emotions were running riot. Betrayal, anger, sorrow. They were all mixed up. Well that was that. No way would she see 'that man' again. He could go whistle down the wind before she'd let him have one minute longer in the house than that specified in Elmer's agreement. She would keep her word as far as the arrangements she had made with him earlier. But that was it.

There wasn't much traffic about and the taxi pulled up outside the hall before Ottilie had finished ruminating on the situation. She wasn't calm but she was calmer.

Beau must have been waiting for her just the other side of the door because no sooner had she pressed the bell with the three rings signal than he opened it.

'My, you've changed!' she said when she saw him.

He had become incredibly good-looking. The sort of good-looking you see on hoardings, advertising things. Tall, bronzed, with flashing white teeth, short well cut black hair and deep brown soulful eyes. A bow shaped mouth – must be a Libran, she thought – a nice slim body and elegantly dressed. He was wearing darkest grey trousers, pale blue sea island cotton shirt and a deep rose pink fine wool blazer. She wasn't expecting this – in London or Paris, but not New Orleans. When they were conservative they were very conservative. She had thought he'd be wearing a pin-striped suit. The jacket was a real nice surprise. She also noticed Beau had an aura: self-awareness, self-confidence and sex. And something else. She couldn't put her finger on it. It was ambition.

'So have you!' Beau exclaimed, holding her hands out and gazing at her admiringly. 'Hey, Ottilie, when you left you were a skinny redhead kid who still had braces on your teeth.'

'I know,' she laughed, 'I nearly died, arriving in Paris with all those super looking people and me gawky with those goddamn braces.'

'Come and see my pride and joy,' he said, guiding her along a passage then onto the stage.

She stood beside the piano and looked around. The hall was small and very modern, tasteful though and exciting visually. She lifted the lid of the piano and gave herself a note. Then she sang. The acoustics were excellent.

'Oh Beau, it's marvellous,' she said enthusiastically. 'When could I give a concert here?'

'Come to my office and we'll sort it,' he said. He was delighted she was pleased. It occurred to him that Ottilie Duvier with her very large bank balance would be an excellent choice as a patron. If he was to grant her an appearance, he would induce in her a certain loyalty. Then, when he put the proposal to her she would naturally accept. That would help the concert hall's ongoing finances.

Then another thought crossed his mind. Ottilie was unattached. He'd heard about her engagement but had also heard it was off. She would make an excellent governor's wife. She had the right background, old plantation money, and masses of it. Just what he needed for his campaigns. And she was beautiful. Even sexy. Ottilie had been an angular creature when she'd gone to Paris. Now she was standing in front of him, a svelte, softly rounded woman with a glorious mane of red hair. Beau definitely fancied getting his hands on Ottilie's body. Almost as much as he fancied getting his hands on her bank account.

In his soothing, cream and pink office, Beau checked out his wall chart.

'There's a date next month,' he said. 'Could you get something together by then?'

'I'll sure try,' she said, extremely pleased with the way things were turning out.

A concert in her home town was something Ottilie had wanted for years. The wanderer returns, triumphant.

'Fine, I'll pencil you in,' said Beau, marking the chart. 'You ready for dinner?'

'Sure am,' she said.

The excitement of the discovery of the hall with its fabulous acoustics had assuaged some of Ottilie's feelings of despair. She was not one to dwell on negative things. She must go forward. If the Count wanted Mary Lou, let him have her. Ottilie had her career. She'd put

175

everything she had into that. Meanwhile, a very handsome man was about to take her out to dinner. What more could she want?

'I didn't book 'cos I wondered if there was something particular you wanted to eat?'

'New Orleanian,' she said. 'Gumbo file and Jumbalaya. I want the best in town. Only when I've eaten that will I know I'm truly home.'

'There's a new place opened on Royal. I tried it the other night. 'Twas real fine.'

'Let's head out there,' she said, her mouth watering. She couldn't wait to taste that delicous soup with duck and crab and powdered sassafras leaf. And then Jumbalaya. Crayfish, lobster, chicken and rice and spicy sausage all mixed up with special Creole spices.

Beau drove them in his smart European car which he parked outside his apartment on St Peter's. They walked the short distance to Royal. The restaurant was cool and the service friendly. They had cocktails whilst they ordered. Tequila sunrise for Ottilie with real fresh orange juice. Beau had a Kir Royale.

When they were ordering a middle-aged man came over and greeted Beau. They talked briefly about this and that and Beau introduced Ottilie.

'The daughter of Bernard Duvier?' asked the man whose name was Ray Miller.

'Yes,' said Ottilie.

'My condolences,' he said. 'But tell me Miss Duvier, what are you doing in New Orleans. Just visiting or . . .?'

'This is my home town,' said Ottilie huffily. 'I'm here to stay and reclaim my family home, which was let out without my Papie's consent by my cousin Elmer.

Ottilie felt very pleased with herself for saying that. That would teach that man, Helmut von Straffen, to mess with her.

'And,' said Beau, butting in, 'Miss Duvier will be giving a concert at the new St Cecilia Concert Hall, in a month's time.'

'May I quote you, Miss Duvier?' asked Ray Miller. 'As

176

Mr Maitland knows, I'm a reporter for *The Times Picayunne.*'

'Of course you may,' said Ottilie. No point in saying anything else. She'd said what she'd said and wasn't going to deny it. And if it got in the newpapers, what the hell!

Ray Miller left the restaurant and Beau and Ottilie both ordered Gumbo, done, as every restaurant says, to its own special recipe. It was real good. Then Beau had blackened swordfish and Ottilie had the Jumbalaya which she pronounced 'fine but not as good as mine'.

'You cook?' asked Beau, somewhat surprised.

'Not often,' she replied, 'but my Jumbalaya is to die for. It's about the only thing I ever make. When I was little, Beulah, our cook, taught me how. I made it in Paris. Reminded me and my Papie of home. But you need the Creole spices so I had to have them sent. Like everything you evolve your own way of doing things. I make mine my own special way which I know everybody just adores. So I cook it, but at special times.'

'Will you cook it for me some day?'

'Sure will,' she said.

Beau ordered a good vintage Chablis, which went down so fast they had another bottle.

Beau and Ottilie were telling each other stories of mishaps in the musical profession. Soprano stories. Opera stories. Viola player stories and laughing. Beau had just picked up her hand and was telling her what a stunning operatic heroine she'd make when the flashlights popped.

And the next day they made the papers with the headline 'Is Beau heiress's beau?' There were quite a few people real angry when they saw that. Not least Frank Dale. There were quite a few people even angrier when they read Ottilie's in quotes comment about her reclaiming her house.

'Ottilie,' said Beau, turning the full beauty of his soulful brown eyes on her. 'I heard you were engaged to be married.'

'I was,' she replied. The combination of tequila, and wine and a solicitous old friend made her want to confide in him. 'I broke it off. I discovered he was not quite the gentleman I thought he was.' She stopped and laughed. 'Know something, Beau? The stupid idiot decided not to take no for an answer. He's only come here to New Orleans. Staying at the Hotel Justine, said he's sorry for what he did . . .'

'What did he do?' asked Beau.

'We won't go into that, sufficient to say he leapt on me when I didn't want to be leapt on. Thinks it's good enough to say sorry. "I've come to claim you as my bride." The hell he has! I couldn't believe it when I got that letter. I mean, when a gal says no, she means no.'

'I understand that,' said Beau. 'But I can also understand him not wanting to lose you. You are very beautiful, Ottilie.'

Ottilie blushed.

'And even more beautiful when you blush,' he said, taking her hand. Which she did not pull away from him.

Ottilie was confused. The wine had gone to her head and she was feeling sexy again. Well why not have Beau? He was good-looking and an old friend. The episode with the Count was now behind her. She was a free woman. It might be nice to put into practice some of the things she had learnt earlier in the day.

'Dessert or cheese or both?' Beau asked.

'Nothing,' she said.

'Coffee?'

'Um . . . I'm not sure,' she replied.

'Say, Ottilie, what about a walk through the quarter and have coffee somewhere else?'

'Yes,' she said. Fresh air might do me the world of good, she thought.

The two of them wandered out into the night. Beau took Ottilie's arm. She was a little unsteady on her feet. Sounds of music came out from the various cafes, bars and clubs. Mardi Gras revellers were out and about. Beads were everywhere: on the ground, hanging from

178

balconies, about people's necks. People were dancing inside the clubs and outside in the street. Ottilie got the rhythm and swayed with it. The two of them laughed, and sometimes sang to the songs being played. Soon they were outside Beau's apartment on St Peter.

'How about coffee here?' said Beau. 'Or shall we carry on walking and . . .'

'No,' said Ottilie, all caution thrown to the wind. 'No, here's fine Beau.'

Inside his elegant apartment in a large old house with windows that opened on to a large garden, Beau made the coffee whilst Ottilie sank down into a large Chesterfield and fell asleep.

'Ottilie,' said Beau, waking her up, and putting a tray of coffee down on the large glass table in front of her. 'Ottilie, coffee.'

'Oh yes, thank you, Beau.'

'Look, are you okay? Do you want this or shall I drive you home?'

'No, I'm fine.'

'Sure?'

'Sure,' she said reaching for the cup. Her head was swimming. 'But I could do with something for my head.'

'I'll get you a pill. Maybe you should stay here,' he said.

'Maybe I should,' she replied. She really didn't fancy the idea of walking into her hotel drunk.

Beau gave her a pill. Ottilie swallowed it. She drank her coffee. He drank his. Then he lifted her up and carried her through to his dark bedroom. Through the slatted shutters the moonlight hit the expensive copy antique furniture in strips. Ottilie could see it was a tasteful room and bland.

'Where are you gonna sleep,' she said, as he took off her shoes.

'On the Chesterfield,' he replied.

'Oh Beau, that's not necessary,' she said. 'I'd hate for you to have an uncomfortable night.'

179

It was odd, she thought, how his not touching her, being a gentleman, not taking advantage of her made her want him. She patted the bed.

'Beau, we're adults,' she said removing her cardigan and then getting the mesh top stuck half on half off her head. Beau came to her aid.

He helped her off with her top and then the silk tunic. She lay on the bed in her bra and panties looking delectable and delicious. The soft moonlight was playing on her soft skin and the dark silk of her underwear, causing havoc with Beau's desires. He wanted her but was very wary. If he rushed her now everything could be lost. This woman with her huge bank account was worth waiting for. He mustn't pounce. He gently rolled her to one side and lifted up the comforter and the pure white sheets. She rolled back in between them. Beau went to the bathroom. He undressed, cleaned his teeth, came back into the bedroom and slid in beside her.

'Ottilie?' he said. There was no answer. She wasn't asleep. There was just the whisper of irritation within her. Why didn't he kiss her, touch her gently, seduce her. She wouldn't be lying in his bed if she hadn't tacitly given permission for him to embrace her. What was his problem? Why was he hesitating? He who was so assured – surely he didn't think she didn't want it? It was almost as if he was calculating his next move, and calculation and passion did not go together. Not hesitant calculation, not in Ottilie's new book of sex.

He snuggled down and curled into her naked body. She had taken off her bra and panties whilst he was out of the room. He put one arm around her waist and pulled her buttocks back against his stomach. And his prick leapt into life.

Feeling the strength of his member hard against her back Ottilie gave a slight wiggle. His cock stiffened more. She wiggled again. He brought his hand up and lay it on her breast. She pressed her backside closer into his stomach and her nipple hardened. He kissed the nape of her neck. Lazily, she moved her body so that his cock was now along her thighs. She lifted one leg so that his penis could move between her legs. She clenched and unclenched her buttocks. Sleepily they moved together, backwards and forwards. She was moist. Slowly his cock began to penetrate. She moved again enabling him to enter deeper. With his hands holding her breasts they had a long slow comforting but passionless fuck. Neither of them came. They both fell asleep.

Ottilie awoke at first light. She bathed and dressed and kissed him goodbye. Beau grabbed her hand.

'Ottilie, don't go now. I'll take you home.'

'No, I must go. I've a lot to do,' she said.

'Will you come to the hall later?' he asked.

'Yes,' she said.

'Ottilie, I didn't mean that to happen,' he asked.

'No, neither did I,' she replied. Thinking that wasn't strictly true. But she felt she had to say it. She didn't want to seem to be the protagonist.

'Oh Ottilie, we didn't talk about you and the admin job. Will you do it?'

It was the question she'd been dreading. She didn't know if she wanted to. To sing there was one thing but to be in charge of the organisation was something else.

'I don't know, Beau. I mean what's so important?'

'Well my partner and I have another deal we're wanting to consolidate on. It could mean big bucks. I need big bucks, Ottilie. I didn't tell you but I'm planning on running for Governor.'

'You are!' she exclaimed.

'Yes,' he said.

'Jeez, that's gonna take a lot of money,' she said.

'I know, that's why this other deal is so important. It'd only be for a couple of weeks, Ottilie. I need someone I really trust to run the place. Someone like you with integrity. And maybe you and I could continue seeing one another. I'd like that, Ottilie. I'd like that a lot.'

She looked at him so handsome and sleepy. And although she felt a fondness for him she was fully aware that the passions aroused in her by the Count were completely missing in him. The sensible part of her told her that Beau was offering a long term relationship and she should accept, but the wayward side of her, the newly awakened highly sexual side of her, screamed no.

'Who is your partner?' asked Ottilie.

'Frank Dale,' replied Beau. He had no idea what a bombshell he would drop when he said that name.

That answer clinched her thoughts.

'I'm sorry Beau,' she said. 'I don't think I'm the right person for you. On any level.'

'What do you mean?' he asked, annoyed by her sudden change of demeanour and attitude.

'For the concert hall and for your private life. I'm not the one. You'll have to find somebody else.'

'But I don't understand . . .'

'And you can cancel my proposed concert.'

'Why Ottilie, why? What have I done?' he asked perplexed.

'Beau, didn't you know that my father and Frank Dale were sworn enemies. And that there is no way I will have any contact with him.'

'Well yes, I'd heard a rumour. But your father's dead and . . .'

'But I'm not. Frank Dale is rotten, a gangster, and I will not touch any business, any thing or person who is associated with him. Sorry but that's the way it is. Goodbye Beau.'

Ottilie quickly left the apartment and walked through the early morning misty streets.

She had forgotten it was Lundi Gras – red beans and rice day. People were already out on their balconies and in their gardens preparing for the day ahead. They shouted to her. Threw baubles at her. By the time she arrived back at her hotel Ottilie was laden down with a mass of brightly coloured beads.

'Goddamn it,' said Frank Dale in fury, shaking the morning paper over his sleeping daughter's head. 'Mary Lou, you stupid little whore. Look at this.' He crashed the offending journal down on the pillow beside her. 'What did I tell you? What did I tell you to do? Go see Beau, that's what. You didn't did you?'

'I did Pa,' she said, raising herself up on her elbows. 'He wasn't there.'

'When I say go see I mean go see. See and talk. Look at this. Look.'

Frank shook the paper in front of her. There was the picture of Beau holding Ottilie's hands in the restaurant.

'See what it says? "Is Beau Heiress's beau?" Where were you, eh? You should have been with him. Not that goddamn snob Ottilie Duvier. I warned you, Mary Lou. Poverty is gonna be your close companion unless you get that guy to marry you. I've given you everything that money can buy. In return you're gonna give me what I want. So, where were you?'

'Pa, it was you who told me go see Elmer.'

'Elmer!'

'Yes, pa, Elmer. You said get him to make over his share of the house to you in return for cancelling his debts.'

'And?'

'Well, he took some persuading,' said Mary Lou, remembering the feel of Elmer's cock.

'Persuading! I'd've thought the goddamn mother would have jumped at it. Did he agree?'

'In the end, yes.'

'Good. Now what we've got to do is get Ottilie to sell.'

'Huh! Rattlesnakes don't rattle and skunks don't stink!' said Mary Lou picking up the newspaper and glancing at the story beneath the photograph. 'See what she says here. The house was rented without her consent and she's planning on taking it back. Pa, there's no way you can get that house.'

'My will's stronger than hers,' said Frank Dale. 'I will get that house. Mary Lou, I'm gonna go see Beau and you's coming with. So move your butt and put on some clothes. I've got business to discuss . . .'

'How did the meeting go yesterday with the preacher?' she asked.

'Just dandy,' he replied, smirking. 'Reckon we've got that all sewed up. But I've gotta talk a few details through with Beau. Be ready in ten minutes. No jeans. We're going to a concert hall, and you's gonna be the next governor's wife. You's gonna look like the next governor's wife. Elegant, Mary Lou, not goddamn white trash.'

Mary Lou bathed and put on her favourite suit. White gabardine with green and purple and yellow sequins on the lapels. She wore a purple silk blouse and her white stilettos.

'Now you's my baby girl,' said Frank admiringly, tousling her long blonde hair. 'Now you's looking like a lady.'

The chauffeur had brought the limo to the front of the house. The two of them got in. They drove in silence to Bayou St John and the concert hall. Frank was thinking about the little plan he'd formed and the little speech he was going to give Beau.

Mary Lou was thinking how Ottilie must have gone straight to Beau's last night and cried on his shoulder, ostensibly about her ex-fiancé. Mary Lou bet a dime to a dollar that it was more about the bombshell she had dropped about Helmut going to Dallas/Fort Worth to buy her a diamond.

Mary Lou was delighted with herself and her performance: Helmut was repaid for taking Ottilie to the bayou; Ottilie had decided to keep clear of Helmut; and her pa well pissed off 'cos she hadn't jumped to his tune and made an instant play for Beau. There was time for that. She'd check Beau out. Sure she'd play hard to get. That'd please his goddamn ego. She'd carry on screwing Helmut and enjoying his 'private parties'. She'd be the perfect Southern Belle for Beau. Even if she wanted to suck his cock; she wouldn't. She'd do just as her daddy said. Keep her legs closed and her panties on. That'd drive him wild. Might even be fun for her. No way was she going to settle for poverty. She looked at her pa sitting beside her and squeezed his hand.

'I think today's gonna be real fruitful, daddy,' she said.

'I have no doubts about it, baby doll,' he replied.

Beau was not in the best of tempers when he got to work. He'd had a perfectly okay evening with Ottilie which had taken a bad turn come morning. He hadn't screwed her exactly in the way he'd thought of screwing her but it was nice enough. She had a good body. She'd moved well, and didn't seem to have any inhibitions. That had surprised him. She just lay there happy to be had from behind, without too much preamble. It dawned on him he hadn't even kissed her. He gave a grim half smile. Fucked her but not kissed her.

He thought he'd had everything worked out fine. Ottilie would help him with the admin. She'd give a concert. She'd become patron. She'd put money into the project. They'd spend a lot of time together. They would become an item. They would marry. She'd put money into him to become governor. He'd win the next election. Then he tells her who his partner is and the whole goddamn edifice, his entire thought process as far as she's concerned, goes tumbling down.

Ottilie could go to hell. There were plenty of other rich women in the city who'd be pleased to be his wife. He was a handsome guy going some place. Women liked that. He'd choose and he'd choose good. Beau rubbed out the pencil mark on the wall chart for Ottilie's proposed concert.

He was checking his mail when Frank Dale stormed in, his daughter behind him.

'See ya had a good time last night,' said Frank, waving the newspaper at him.

Beau glanced at it.

'Reporters!' said Beau, 'they got it wrong as usual.' Beau wasn't about to tell Frank the ins and outs of his evening.

'I'm glad to hear it,' said Frank, ''cos she's a goddamn poisonous bitch.'

'I hear she loves you too, Frank!' said Beau.

Mary Lou laughed. Frank Dale didn't.

'I was comforting an old friend,' said Beau.

'How much comfort did you give?' asked Frank.

'Apparently,' said Beau, deliberately avoiding Frank's question, 'her ex-fiancés in town.'

'He is!' said Mary Lou, suddenly all ears. 'We've got a real life Lord in town!'

'The guy's broke Mary Lou,' said her father, dimissively.

'How d'you know?' she asked.

'I made a few enquiries,' said Frank, 'checked his status. Basically he ain't got none. He's got a title, sure. He's also got a crumbling mansion in England and a French mistress in Paris and he wanted Miss Ottilie Duvier for her money. Now, he did something wrong, 'cos he blew it. I'm thinking maybe we can help him blow it back again.'

'Why, what's he to you, pa?' asked Mary Lou.

'Where's he staying?' asked Frank, ignoring her question.

'Hotel Justine,' said Beau.

'Call,' said Frank. 'I'd like to talk with him.'

'Why?' asked Beau.

'Well now, after my meeting yesterday with the preacher man from St Jacques, it looks like we've got that project in the bag. There's a few wrinkles gotta be sorted and I'll discuss that with you later. What we've gotta do next is get hold of Ottilie's house and the land that goes with it. Prime land, Beau. Prime land. Just perfect for re-development. That's gonna be the new leisure centre. The newest, the most up-market leisure centre in the whole of New Orleans.'

'You'll never get planning permission for that, not in the Garden District,' said Beau.

'Sure I will,' said Frank, utterly confident. He knew who to bribe. That part of the procedure was of no concern to Beau. Nor did Frank want it to be. Beau had to be kept squeaky clean. But in Frank's debt.

'Now Beau, tell me,' said Frank, 'you didn't happen to discover why Miss Ottilie cancelled her engagement, did you?'

'Um, yes,' said Beau.

'Was it money?'

'No, he tried it on when she didn't want it,' replied Beau. 'Leastways that's what she told me.'

'Yeah, could be the truth,' said Frank. 'And is easily sorted. What I propose is we get this young man to a meeting and offer him money. Real money. Tell him we'll pay his hotel bill, his drinks bill – and he don't have no dry season. And give him more to walk away with. All he's gotta do is get Ottilie to agree to marry him.'

'Why?' asked Mary Lou.

'Because, in this state, once married what's hers is his. Then he gets her to sell her part of the house. I'll give him a good price for it. And Elmer's already agreed. So I get what I want. No problem. All we've gotta do is get this jackass to play ball. And money is the key. We'll give him money to court her, like a lady should be courted.'

As Frank was talking Beau was looking at Mary Lou. Her father's words were ringing in his ears. 'What's hers is his.' Of course. He didn't need to go looking for a wife. One was being presented to him that very moment. She was sitting opposite. He'd have to do something about her dress sense. But money she had. More than enough to make him governor. Truly Ottilie Duvier could go to hell. He was gonna make a play for Mary Lou. Why hadn't he thought about her before? Maybe because Frank had never spelled it out. Not that he was spelling it out for him. It's just that he was thinking on his feet. Beau turned the full charm of his eyes and smile on Mary Lou.

'This talk must be very boring for you,' he said. 'With your pa's permission I'd like to take you out for lunch.'

'Why thank you, Beau,' said Mary Lou.

'And you have it,' said Frank Dale. He was delighted.

His little speech had hit the spot. This guy would make a good governor. He knew what was what. And he knew it fast.

'I'll ring the Hotel Justine,' said Beau.

'Ask for Lord Christopher Furrel,' said Frank. 'Tell him lunch at my place. We'll talk later about St Jacques. Don't see me out. I'll leave you two together.'

Frank departed, well pleased with his morning's work.

Mary Lou gave Beau her most dazzling smile. She crossed her beautiful long legs and modestly attempted to pull down the hem of her short skirt over her knees.

That simple small gesture whetted Beau's appetite. He watched her, thinking she was the all-American girl personified: blonde and healthy looking, slim and rich. She seemed a trifle brash but her father will have kept her on a short lead. She could be a virgin and he might have trouble seducing her but seduction wasn't the endgame. Marriage and access to Frank's millions was.

Beau picked up the telephone and called Lord Christopher who was well ensconced at the Hotel Justine.

Chapter 9

Count Helmut von Straffen sent out a number of invitations. Some had gone by mail. Some were hand delivered. Some said one thing. Some said another. Frank Dale's and Elmer Planchet's were sent. Lord Christopher's and Beau Maitland's were hand delivered. All four received an embossed card which said the same thing:

> Count Helmut von Straffen
> Invites you and a partner to his
> Mardi Gras Morning Barbeque.
> 1.00 a.m.
> In the Marquee on the lawn at his house
> On Washington Avenue.
>
> *Menu*
> Smoked salmon and corn fitters
> Barbequed Spare Ribs
> Cranberry and Apple Charlotte
> String Cheese and Biscuits
> Champagne and Fruit Juices
>
> Dress Formal
> RSVP

Mary Lou and selected friends from home and abroad received theirs. Their embossed card read:

> Count Helmut von Straffen and his Household
> Invites you without a partner
> To a Masked Fancy Dress Ball and Cabaret
> On the evening of Lundi Gras
> 8.00 p.m.
> At his house on Washington Avenue.
>
> Do not reply.
> Arrive on time with this card.
>
> At 1.00 a.m.
> There will be a Mardi Gras Barbeque
> In the marquee on the lawn.

Ottilie received hers via a bellhop after it had been delivered to her hotel by Epps. Its arrival threw her into a state of panic.

She'd already been faced with a dilemma when the Fairmont's receptionist had given her four telephone messages from Fort Worth and had handed her a fax from the Wetherington Hotel in that city which had said simply, 'Need to see you. H.'

As far as the Count was concerned Ottilie's emotions were all over the place. Downcast and in a quandary she had taken the elevator to her room. She had butterflies in her stomach but thought it wisest to eat and ordered a full breakfast. She undressed and lay soaking in the bath, thinking that the man was a complete bastard. But was he? There were a number of questions to which she'd like answers. After all, she reasoned, she only had Mary Lou's word that he was her fiancé.

Why should Helmut call her repeatedly if he was engaged to Mary Lou? Why hadn't she gone up to the house and checked it out at the time? Was she frightened of finding out the truth? Which truth? That the Count was engaged to Mary Lou or that she, Ottilie, had screwed somebody else as well as the Count out on the bayou? And that somebody might have been Epps. She hadn't wanted to face Epps with Mary Lou standing beside her. She was embarrassed. Shamed. Was she running away from herself and her own desires and needs? Her own sexual self? As she lay in the warm enveloping water Ottilie let her hands stray and began to caress herself.

There was a deep ache inside her for the Count. Only for him. This she had discovered when fucking Beau. She'd been wet. She'd sort of responded. But nothing special. It was Helmut who set her alight. Her body and her mind were left glowing rosy by him and by the thought of him. She could feel her wantonness returning. Her secret flower opened up to her probing fingers.

The four telephone calls from last night and then the fax sent in the early hours led her to believe that he wanted to see her as much as she wanted to see him. Her hunger for him must be matched by his for her. But what was Mary Lou's game? Why had she said the Count was her fiancé? Why was Mary Lou warning her off? Surely she hadn't been having an affair with him?

When Count Helmut's invitation arrived Ottilie didn't know what to do. Of course she wanted to go. But should she? What should she wear? How fancy was fancy dress? Masks weren't a problem. She'd go down into the Quarter and buy a real good one.

She could attend the ball incognito. She didn't have to formally accept. She could just go and pretend. Be someone else. Her hair would give her away. She'd buy a wig. No, better than that, go to the hairdressers. Have Mardi Gras colours woven in, disguising it.

Ottilie realised the water had gone cold when the waiter banged on her door with her breakfast. She stepped out of the bath, wrapped herself in an enormous bathrobe and let him and his trolley into the room. Once he had gone she lifted the silver lids, looked at the food and knew that whatever she thought she should do, she couldn't eat it.

Instead she threw open her wardrobe and searched through her evening clothes. There, sitting pristine amongst her couture outfits, was one that she had bought on a strange whim. Not her usual style, this one was Baby Doll, re-vamped courtesy of a French designer. Ottilie took it down. Palest softest lemon yellow organza, with a darker shade of silk lining; puff sleeves; a Peter Pan collar. Waisted with a full skirt, it buttoned from neck to its mid-thigh hem. It was so un-her that Ottilie decided it was perfect for her disguise. She would wear it with shiny stockings of the palest purple and deep lemon-yellow satin sling-back shoes. The colours were right for Mardi Gras. She needed green. She'd get the hairdressers to add masses of green streamers to her hair. Ottilie rang the hotel's hairdresser and booked herself a late afternoon appointment.

Her earlier gloom had disappeared. She was totally involved in working out her clothing for the evening. Which undergarments should she wear? She decided to slip on the frothy garment. Its delicate gossamer caressed her sensitised soft skin. She sashayed across the room. The fabric touched her breasts and buttocks, reminding her of the Count's feather light fingertips. The feel of the silk was wonderfully sensuous against her naked body. Ottilie took a daring decision. She would not wear any underclothes, no panties, no brassière. That way she would keep feeling sexy throughout the evening.

Having taken care of the evening's wardrobe Ottilie dressed herself in a minty powdery blue classic fine wool suit with a white cambric blouse. She tied her hair up in a couple of light and dark blue crinkled muslin scarves. She thrust her feet into navy blue Italian shoes, slung the matching bag over her shoulder and went to buy an automobile.

She bought a 1950s pink Pontiac Sedan, which the salesman said, when she pointed out the various dents, 'had a history' and mentioned Hollywood. It was more or less exactly what she wanted. Big, huge fins and lots of chrome. An outrageous automobile. An exhibitionist's automobile. She drove it to Washington Avenue. There she left it as close to the house as she could. Ottilie had decided that come the evening she'd take a cab, but she did not want to be dependent upon anybody for getting back. Forward thinking. This way she could walk away at any time and drive herself home. Having parked it she caught a bus on Magazine Street to the Vieux Carré.

It was on Decatur, close by the French Market, that she found a small shop selling fantastic masks. She bought one that she knew would exactly match the organza evening dress. It was made from stiffened purple silk, studded with diamanté and had high green and pale lemon yellow feathers. This done she ambled through to Jackson Square, sat down at a cafe with an inside and an outside, and had a beignet and a coffee. Although she had everything prepared she was still worried. Should she or should she not go to the ball? She was thinking she would go back to the hotel and sleep, make her decision before going to the hairdressers, when a piece of paper fluttered by from the street and landed at her feet. She picked it up and read it. It said:

> Do you need help with your life?
> Then visit the
> Voodoo Queen
> Otavia Wanja dos Rios Santos
> on Elysian Fields Avenue.

Ottilie decided that help was needed. She looked at the number and knew it was only a short walk from where she was sitting. She finished her coffee and her beignet, and departed.

She found the Voodoo Queen in a terra-cotta coloured camel-back house close by Washington Square. Ottilie apologised for not having an appointment but asked through the intercom if it was possible to consult the priestess. A melodic voice said, 'Yes,' and the door swung open.

Queen Otavia Wanja dos Rios Santos was a massive woman, with skin that was ebony blue-black. She was strikingly beautiful, and she was wearing white. Pristine white. A fine blouse with a drawstring neckline and puff sleeves, that was embroidered with the finest of hand embroidery: leaves and flowers all in white. Her full skirt was spread over a crinoline cage. Masses and masses of petticoats, all white, were covered by a beautiful white skirt, embroidered with the same motifs as the blouse.

She smiled, showing her big white teeth, and her face lit up.

'Child,' she said, 'you have a problem?'

'Yes,' replied Ottilie.

'Then take your shoes off and come in, let me see if the old Gods can help you.'

Queen Otavia Wanja dos Rios Santos led Ottilie along a dark corridor into a huge room with a sky light. This too was white. Against one wall was a plinth, and on it stood a gold and white throne. Beside this in an enormous vase stood branches of sweet smelling myrtle. The Voodoo Queen sat on the throne and picked up some of the Myrtle branches and fanned herself.

'My price is a cockerel,' she said. Ottilie looked completely bemused.

'But, I don't have a cockerel,' she said.

'I do,' said the Voodoo Queen. 'I kill it, you replace it.'

Then she handed Ottilie the branches.

'Take these, and the rest from the vase and spread them over the floor,' she ordered, and moved her great bulk off the throne and waddled out of the room.

Ottilie did as she was told. Some time later the Voodoo Queen returned holding a bowl of what looked like entrails and herbs and put it down on a small spirit filled container.

'You are wearing blue so we will ask the God who is the patron of blacksmiths and warriors to help us. That is his colour,' she said. 'I feel you are asking about a man. A man who works with iron or steel.'

Ottilie was about to deny this when she flushed red as she remembered the handcuffs on her wrists. The Voodoo Queen gave a short laugh. Then she started to sing. A strange song. A click song. As she sang her great form began to sway and her feet began to pound into the myrtle leaves and branches the smell of which was pervading the room. Hypnotically the Voodoo Queen moved and then reached out her hands to Ottilie. The two of them danced together in that high white room. Danced and danced, and all the while Queen Otavia Wanja dos Rios Santos sang her song with its click.

Then she stopped. And so did Ottilie, though her brain was reeling. She watched the woman take a box of matches and light the small container. It flared. Flared high. And made them both jump.

'Fire,' said the huge black woman. 'You have fire in your heart for this man. But you must beware. When the God lets his fire rush he's telling you to be careful. You have enemies. Not this man. Another.'

Then as the smell of cooking, the herbs, the garlic and the offal rose up, Queen Otavia Wanja dos Rios Santos plunged her hands into the mixture and threw it on the floor at Ottilie's feet. They both stared at the mess; Ottilie amazed and fascinated; the Voodoo Queen intently, looking for signs.

'You must go tonight,' she said. 'It's imperative you go. You will discover your enemy but again, see, there is a cauldron and flames. Fire. Beware of fire where you eat. The man you love will bind you to him. You will be shackled to him. He loves you.'

'He loves me,' said Ottilie in a whisper, this was what she wanted to hear. Not the warnings. The Voodoo Queen had answered her question. Answered both her questions. Should she go tonight? Yes. Does he love me? Yes.

Smiling a smile that was almost as broad as that on the black woman's face Ottilie turned to her and thanked her.

'Remember everything I told you,' said the Voodoo

Queen, guiding her away from the room back along the corridor. 'Everything, not just what you want to remember.'

'Yes,' said Ottilie in a dreamy daze. 'How much for the cockerel?'

Queen Otavia Wanja dos Rios Santos told her the price. Ottilie paid her and went outside into the bright sunlit streets and caught a bus back to her hotel, happy that the decision was taken from her. The god had told her everything she wanted to know. She would have a good sleep before attending the hairdressers to have the metallic strips woven into her hair.

Elmer received his invitation when he arrived at the office. His immediate reaction was to throw it in the trash can and not go. Elmer was not a happy man.

The meeting with the preacher from St Jacques had not gone well. In fact it had gone extremely badly. He'd given an appalling presentation. The Reverend didn't like it and said so.

'Sorry, Mr Planchet, but what you've designed just ain't what I had in mind.' That's how he'd put it. And he couldn't be much plainer than that.

Then of course there was Josephine arriving just when he had his tongue stuck up Mary Lou's pussy. And she was gobbling his cock. Jeez had he had a shock! And it had showed – instantly.

Josephine had plonked the files down and left. Mary Lou though was unabashed. She had brought his dick back to size and they'd screwed.

Elmer sat at his desk turning his pencil up and down, up and down, desperately wondering whether Josephine would arrive for work. Not that there was much to do. He'd been banking on that job to get the company back on its feet. Elmer was at a loose end.

He thought back to Mary Lou and how he'd taken her jeans off; eased them down her long legs; made her sit astride him. She had rubbed her pussy along his cock, exciting it. Then once it was stiff she had lowered herself, slowly at first, on to its tip. Catching it between her labia, she'd used her inner muscles to grip it. Then she'd raised herself off only to start again. Each time she'd lowered her pussy she'd taken him deeper. One time she had lifted up, played momentarily with tiny pushing movements on its head, then come down forcibly. She'd taken him to the hilt. Taken him to the top of her womb. Rode him up and down. Squirmed her hips round and round. And he had held her neat breasts. Squeezed her nipples. Harder and harder. She was rocking and she was rolling. The sweat had streamed along their bodies. He had clutched at her buttocks. She had ridden him like a woman possessed.

He was thinking how that was what he'd like to do to Josephine when, on the dot of nine, she walked into his office, a cup of steaming hot coffee in her hand.

'Good morning, Mr Planchet,' she said, as if it was an ordinary morning. No reference in her demeanour to his activity the previous day.

'Good morning, Josephine,' he said, unable to keep out the feeling of relief from his voice.

She was looking highly desirable, intrinsically sexy. She wore a black and white check suit with a short wrap-over skirt. Elmer's eyes glanced down at her knees. Her wonderful dimpled knees were now sheathed in sheer black stockings. The sight of them performed the same attack on his senses as they'd done before. His hands itched to stroke them. His cock moved with desire. She was also wearing a high necked black cotton jumper with a large metal zip running its length, and extremely high heels. Long thin spiky heels. That was a turn on. There was a dull pain in his abdomen. His prick surged upwards. She was carrying a large black bag which she slid off her shoulder.

'How did the presentation go?' she asked, putting the coffee on the desk.

'It was a disaster,' he replied.

'Oh dear,' she said. 'And whose fault was that?'

'Mine,' he replied.

'You didn't do it properly,' she said. It was more of a statement than a question.

There was something in her voice that held his attention; that sent a thrill through his stomach and groin. She began to unbutton her jacket.

'What did you do wrong?' she asked.

Elmer didn't answer immediately. His eyes were watching her red nail-varnished hands. Each button she undid revealed more of her enticing feminine shape. Elmer swallowed. Josephine removed her jacket and hung it on a peg beside the office door.

'Mr Planchet,' she said, seriously. 'I have checked the files here and you don't have much work. In fact, now you've lost this contract you don't have any real major projects.'

'That's true, Josephine,' he said, contritely.

'I like your designs,' she said, bringing up a chair and sitting opposite him, with her legs tightly together. Her knees on show. Her knees. Turning him on. 'You're good Mr Planchet. This business should be the best and I'm gonna help you make it so. Tell me, why did your partner leave?'

'He caught me, er ... fucking his wife,' he said.

'Mr Planchet, if you don't mind me saying so that was real stupid.'

Josephine moved in the chair and her legs parted. He caught sight of her stocking tops. His prick made a further leap.

'Now, Mr Planchet, yesterday when you should have been working I saw you engaged in the act of eating pussy. You were stretched out on your settee with a sash around your penis. A blonde hooker was lying over you, her jeans half on and half off. Her bottom, which I noticed had whip marks on it, was up in the air. Had you whipped her, Mr Planchet?'

'No, no ...' he answered quickly.

'I see. But you did have your tongue in her cunt whilst she was sucking your cock. Can you tell me, Mr Planchet, where that got your business?'

Elmer was unable to say anything. He was staring at Josephine thunderstruck. She was using the rudest words but treating him like a child. It was the most thrilling thing that had ever happened to him. Instead of answering he put his hands under the desk and adjusted his stiff prick.

'You don't reply!' she said. 'Well now, I can tell you. It got you nowhere fast. It lost you another contract. You made a bad presentation. You told me so yourself. It was a disaster. Those were your words. Were they not, Mr Planchet?'

'Yes,' he said, slightly hoarse. She was driving him to distraction. Everything he had ever thought or fantasised was embodied in her. He wanted her. He wanted her real bad. His cock was stiff and he was tense. What else was she gonna say?

'In other words, you were a bad boy.'

Elmer took a sip of his coffee and tried to clear his throat.

'Do you know what happens to bad boys, Mr Planchet?'

'No,' he said, staring at her, completely mesmerised. Her voice had got slower, more languid. More sexy.

'They get punished,' she replied. Elmer quivered. He held his balls. His cock was straining against the fabric of his trousers, begging for release. And she knew it.

'Come here,' she said, her tone altering. It was more of a command.

Elmer stood up. Josephine pretended not to see his hard-on.

'Come here and stand in front of me,' she ordered.

Staring not at her face but at her knees and wondering when he could touch them, Elmer obeyed her.

Josephine followed his glance down.

'So you want to touch my knees, do you?' she asked.

'Yes,' he said hoarsely.

'Touch them and stroke them?'

'Yes.'

'Very well, you may,' she said. 'But you'll have to do

it my way. Kneel down and don't move until I give you permission.'

Elmer knelt in front of her. She put her legs close together.

'Put your hands in my lap and close your eyes,' she said.

Quivering with delight, Elmer closed his eyes. Josephine pulled her skirt up so that when he knelt and put his hands in her lap he was touching her skin through stockings. He made tiny little circles on her thighs. She smacked his hands hard.

'In my lap and keep them absolutely still,' Josephine commanded.

The backs of his hands tingled from her slap. His fingertips were tingling from where he was feeling her warm skin through the silk of her stockings. His entire body was tingling from anticipation. Very slowly she undid his shirt buttons. Almost as if she had forgotten to take it off completely she slipped the collar back and the sleeves down to his elbows, severely reducing his freedom of movement. But Elmer didn't care. She was stroking his chest and neck. The touch of her red nailed fingers sent shivers of delight down his spine.

'Keep your eyes closed,' she said.

Josephine unzipped her handbag and took out a pair of handcuffs. A fraction of a second before she clapped them on his wrists Elmer heard the steel chains jangling, felt that hard cold substance touching the fine hairs on his arm, and it gave him goose pimples. He guessed what she was about to do and a rush of excitement flushed through his loins. He let out a quick sharp sigh when she locked them shut.

Josephine delved into her bag once more and drew out a black leather hood.

'Bow your head,' she ordered.

Willingly, submissively, he obeyed her. She pulled it over his head. It had an opening over the nose and mouth but none for the eyes or ears. She wiped her tongue along his lips protruding from the hood. He pushed his tongue out to meet hers. She nipped it. He quickly closed his mouth. Josephine smiled. He instantly understood. He did what she wanted. Not the other way round. She pushed his hands down along her thighs so that they were placed one on each knee. She allowed him to fondle them, feel them, find the dimples.

Josephine leant forward and undid Elmer's zip. She pulled his trousers and his boxer pants down around his knees immobilising him. His prick was not quite fully erect. She opened her handbag and took out a small, hard rubber ring.

Elmer gave a tremulous shudder as he felt her long cool fingers grasp the tip of his penis and stretch it as far as possible. Then as she delicately caressed his prick he felt her roll the ring of rubber the length of his shaft. Elmer's hands were increasing their pressure on Josephine's knees. He tried to let them wander further up her legs but was slapped hard for his trouble. When the ring was firmly in place she stroked his inner thighs, then took his sac into her soft, gentle and manipulating hands. Elmer gave little moans of pleasure. She brought up one knee and laid it against his chest, slowly pushing him away from her. Then she brought up her other foot. He felt the spikes of the heel digging into his nipple. She gave a sharp thrust with her foot and Elmer fell backwards.

Josephine left him on the floor. She placed one foot on his stomach, pressing the heel hard down into his skin. She undid the zip of her jumper and threw it across the room. She pulled at the waistband of her skirt. The fastening gave way easily. She threw that across the room too. Josephine stood in front of the hooded Elmer dressed in a PVC corset. Her great melon breasts were stuffed into cups ending in harsh, hard points. Her tiny waist was laced firm, accentuating her large hips and the roundness of her belly. A buckled flap was placed over her sex. The PVC extended down over the tops of her thighs to meet her stocking tops. But at the back she had left the half studs undone to reveal the dimples at the base of her spine and her enticing full bare bottom.

Josephine removed her foot from his stomach and pushed the toe of her shoe into his side, indicating to him to turn over. Which he did. She then arranged him so that his head was leaning on his handcuffed hands and his bottom was high in the air. She pulled off his trousers and his underpants, his shoes and his socks.

She searched again in her bag and brought out a number of instruments and laid them carefully on the floor beside him. Then she took a jar of oil and, standing between his thighs, she slowly massaged his buttocks. Gradually moving her hand down and around, she coated his scrotum with the same oil, and then his penis.

His prick grew quickly under her tender ministrations, and the ring at the base was giving him an extra sensation. It seemed to him that his cock was larger and more sensitive than he had ever known it. Her hands knew exactly where to go to heighten every nerve, to make him her complete slave.

She parted his buttocks, and with the same infinite care she began to rub oil around his small tight hole. Round and around she went, exciting and teasing the sensory muscles surrounding his tight, puckered little place. Then she put on skin tight rubber gloves and coated them with oil. Taking his prick in one hand and fondling it, she slowly penetrated his anus with a gloved finger.

The feel of her rubber encased hands wandering up and down along his engorged prick and entering his arse was utterly exquisite. Elmer licked his lips and held his breath. She stopped still. She squeezed his prick but did not push any further upwards nor rub any further downwards. He waited, quivering. She gave the minutest wiggle inside his rectum. Enough to entice him. Then stayed still again. With the hood on he could neither see nor hear. He was desperate for more. He waited. Nothing happened. Then he pressed down. Opening himself, allowing her deeper penetration. And he rocked. He rocked hard backwards and forwards as she rubbed on his prick and thrust into his arse.

Elmer's body was alive, tingling and wanting to feel Josephine's body. Elmer had discovered the joy of domination. His muscles were beginning to contract. She pushed harder. He wanted to expel her. She thrust in harder. His hand itched to hold her flesh: touch her tits, grope around her legs, feel her wet sex. She kept him in suspense and kept thrusting.

She moved her body. For the first time Elmer felt the sticky coolness of the PVC against his flesh. Through his hard tumescent prick the blood surged again. Touch, any touch, but especially her touch was taking him to spurting point. His entire body was moving snakelike, dancing to the tune of her expert hands.

Josephine put her mouth beside his covered ears.

'I am allowing you a great privilege,' she said. 'You must thank me.'

She removed her fingers from his prick and put her legs either side of his head. She trailed her rubber gloved fingers across his mouth. She bent down, stuck out her tongue and licked his mouth. Elmer thought he couldn't possibly take any more, she had to stop the attack on his senses. Josephine had no intention of stopping.

'You say, thank you, madam,' she said.

'Yes, madam. Thank you, madam,' he said.

'I told you bad boys are punished,' she said, and raised his flanks higher. 'Stay exactly as you are.'

Josephine walked away from him. There was a silence. He could not see or hear her pick up the paddle. But the next moment he felt its delicious sensation as its flatness came down hard on his buttocks.

'Naughty boys need spanking,' she said, and brought it down once more with considerable force on his rump.

Sparks flew in Elmer's brain. With each blow she gave him, questions and answers flooded into his brain. Was this why he had chosen her as his secretary? Had his senses, his body chemistry picked on something inexplicable that his logical self had missed? He'd puzzled for days as to why he'd chosen her. She didn't have his favoured colouring nor his body shape. She had much more than those surface attributes. She had a skin as soft as down that oozed sex. She had a smell, a sea shell smell that oozed sex. She had a quiet dominance, now activated, that oozed sex. She was sexuality incarnate. She was his goddess. He was her slave. He would be hers forever. She hit him again. For ever and ever. She hit him again and again. Harder and harder. His tingling buttocks clenching and unclenching were now a delightful bright red. He wanted to kiss her. Kiss her feet, her legs, any part of her that she would allow. Elmer was floating in a mesmeric state of desire. Which part of his body would she touch and stimulate next? Elmer was ecstatic.

She told him to remain on all fours. She lifted his head. Then she crawled in front of him presenting her naked buttocks to his mouth and the sea smell of her and the PVC hit his nostrils. She pushed her bottom into his face. He licked her. She pushed harder, spreading her crease so that his tongue was forced to find her small back hole. He wanted his tongue to trail downwards to find her other feminine hole but his way was barred by studs and more PVC.

Deciding that for the moment she had been pleasured enough, Josephine stood up. She picked up the crop and ran it through his crease. Excited, he stiffened, waiting for the blow. But she was teasing him. Instead she stopped, bent down and rubbed his tumescent throbbing cock. Then she fitted a heavily seamed leather sheath over its erect length. The front was attached by a short tie to a belt which she fastened around his waist. She secured it by taking the back tie and drawing it up through the crack in his bottom and fitting it to the belt.

'Naughty boys must receive a very good spanking,' she said. 'What do you say to that?'

'Yes, madam,' he said.

'And you've been a very naughty boy, haven't you?'

'Yes, madam.'

Josephine began to rub his cock whilst plying his

backside lightly with the crop. Elmer was shaking from top to bottom. The leather covering his prick, her hand rubbing it and the feel of sharp exquisite pain as she wielded the crop on his fleshy expectant bottom was sending him delirious with pleasure. She was wickedly tormenting him and the ring, tight at the base of his cock, was delaying his climax.

He wanted to pleasure her. He wanted to suck her. He wanted to feel his tongue slobbering at her furls, voyaging inside, finding the spot that would make her squirm. He wanted her squirming. He wanted her crouching over him. Queening him. His bottom was stinging from the crop and his prick was blood-surging and throbbing.

'You are going to change your attitude, aren't you Elmer,' said Josephine, juggling his balls between her hands.

'Yes, madam,' he said. He didn't know what attitude he had to change but he'd agree to anything she demanded.

'You will agree to anything I want, won't you Elmer?'

'Yes, madam.'

'Tell me then, say "I will agree to anything madam wants" and say it loud,' she said, swishing the crop across his flanks so hard that he screamed and fell flat on the floor. She gave him an extra hard thwack for good meaure. He jumped and curled into a ball.

'Tell me,' she demanded.

'I will agree to anything madam wants,' he whimpered.

'Good,' she said, 'Stand up. I'm going to remove your hood.'

Elmer stood up, his buttocks stinging violently. She covered them with oil. She took off his hood. For the first time Elmer saw Josephine in her full dominance. He almost came with surprise. He had smelled her and PVC and even felt it grazing against his flesh but he had no idea she was totally encased in a corset. He couldn't wait to feel her tits. Those huge breasts that were crushed inside and bulging outside the shiny fabric. He didn't know which part of her to grab first. Then he realised that without her permission he couldn't touch her at all.

She stood beside him and played with his prick and his balls.

'Kneel down, undo my buckles,' she said, pointing at the fastenings over her sex.

Elmer knelt in front of her. With difficulty, as she had not loosened his hands from their manacles, he undid the buckles.

'Suck me,' she said, thrusting her sex at his mouth.

His tongue came out and licked her moist labia, he brought his hands up and parted her sex lips. He lifted the hood to reveal her enlarged clitoris. He flicked it with his tongue. She sighed a long drawn out sigh. She allowed his hands to wander so that while his tongue was busy his fingers began their probing search into her inner depths. Her hips began to roll.

Her moisture was easing out over his tongue. She was swollen and wanton. She wanted more than his tongue. She wanted his prick. Wanted it hard inside her.

Josephine pushed him away. She lay on the floor. For a moment he looked non-plussed. Had he done something to displease her?

'Fuck me,' she said, opening her legs wide so that he could crawl up between them.

Elmer lay over her body. He put his shackled hands above her head. He trembled as he felt her huge breasts flatten against his chest.

Josephine held his leather encased prick. She placed it at the entrance to her sex. She wiggled with desire as she felt the raised seams scraping against her moist walls. She tensed her arse and lifted her hips.

'Now,' she said.

Elmer plunged into her. He took her in one savage thrust, up to the apex of her womb. He ploughed her with every ounce of his pent up energy and desire. She brought her hands round and slapped his seared and marked bottom as it raged backwards and forwards.

The stinging sensation on his buttocks, her hips gyrating, the moistness of her vagina, his leather casing, her PVC, the ring around his cock, everything conspired to make him fuck as he had never fucked in his life before.

She turned her mouth towards his mouth. Their lips met. Bliss. Their tongues entwined. Soldered together wherever they touched, in a dizziness of emotion, almost an annihilation of the senses, they climaxed simultaneously.

It was later after Josephine had adjusted her clothing and Elmer had gone to the bathroom that she noticed the invitation to Count Helmut's barbeque on his desk. She decided that she and Elmer would go together.

Lord Christopher was screwing Sylvie in the Hotel Justine when Beau Maitland's telephone call came through. He hesitated before answering. Then he thought it might be Ottilie responding to his letter and picked up the receiver.

'Hello?' said Lord Christopher, in his hot potato in the mouth voice.

'Hi,' said Beau. 'My name's Beau Maitland and I'm a friend of Ottilie's uncle, Frank Dale.'

'Frank Dale?' queried Lord Christopher. 'Never heard of him.'

'Well if you haven't you soon will. Everybody in this town knows Frank Dale. He was married to Ottilie's father's sister.'

'Oh really,' said Lord Christopher, bored and wanting to get on with fucking. He nibbled Sylvie's shoulder and gave a small thrust inside her to remind her he was there.

'Yes, really,' said Beau, irritated. He didn't like Lord Christopher's arrogant turn of phrase. 'And Frank Dale would like to meet you.'

'I rarely meet with people I don't know,' replied Lord Christopher.

'He has a business proposition for you.'

Business. Proposition. Those two words were open sesame to Lord Christopher's avaricious brain.

'Tell me more,' he said, tweaking Sylvie's nipples.

'How would you like your hotel bill paid, your restaurant and bar bill paid plus some extra?'

'I'd like that very much but what do I have to do for it?' asked Lord Christopher warily.

'Marry Ottilie Duvier,' said Beau.

Lord Christopher laughed. The man on the other end of the telephone was a clown.

'How fascinating,' he drawled.

'No, not fascinating,' said Beau, 'interesting's a better word.'

'Tell me,' said Lord Christopher, 'why a man I've never heard of should want me to marry my fiancé?'

'Your ex-fiancé,' said Beau, pointedly.

'We won't split hairs,' said Lord Christopher. 'I can only assume that Ottilie has something that this man wants. Now, if this man, what did you say his name was . . .?'

'Frank Dale.'

'Oh yes, Frank Dale, a very ordinary name. I must try to remember it. If he wants something that Ottilie's got, it's just possible I might want it too. Especially if I'm married to her.'

Beau took a deep breath. Jackass, Frank Dale had called him, but he was a goddamn clever jackass. The Brits hadn't ruled half the world without being damn smart. And this one had it in his genes. Well, he hadn't been smart enough to keep Ottilie when he was in Paris. He might not be smart enough to get her to marry him now he was here. Beau reckoned that for all his attitude the guy was still in need of help. Besides, when Frank Dale did a check up on someone he did it real thorough. If he said this goddamn limey was broke, whatever he sounded like – he was broke. And money talked. Yeah. Beau would get him to do what Frank wanted.

'I see there ain't no fooling you,' said Beau. 'But, what she's got that Frank Dale wants, I don't think would interest you. However, the proceeds from its sale I'm sure would. And nobody would give you as much money for it as Frank Dale.'

'What is it?' asked Lord Christopher, his mind rapidly going through an inventory of Ottilie's possessions.

'You'd have to wait for Frank to tell you that. He suggests you go meet with him for lunch at his place.'

'And where's that?'

Beau gave him the address.

'What time is he expecting me?' asked Lord Christopher. He was intrigued.

'You'll go?' asked Beau.

'My dear fellow I'll go almost anywhere for a free lunch with booze. He will have booze, won't he. He's not one of these teetotal Joes?'

'He'll have liquor,' said Beau. 'And he's expecting you at one sharp. Oh, and Lord Christopher, Frank Dale is not on holiday. Time is money for him. If he says one sharp that's what he means.'

'Punctuality, dear fellow, is the politeness of princes and of the English aristocracy. I wouldn't even keep my tailor waiting.'

'Fine. Maybe I'll see you there, good luck and goodbye,' said Beau, putting the telephone down.

'You did real good,' said Mary Lou, smiling at him, and giving him another one of her wonderful, 'oh you are so brilliant' smiles.

Beau liked her more every minute.

'Sounds like a goddamn asshole to me,' he said.

'Perfect for our Ottilie,' said Mary Lou, bitchily, putting her handbag over her shoulder and rising from her seat. 'I'm hungry.'

'Yeah, time to go.'

'Oh Beau, do you know Count Helmut?'

'No.'

'He's a friend of mine and he's giving a barbeque party tonight. Would you like to come?'

'You going?'

'Sure am.'

'In that case, yes.'

'Mind if I use your telephone. It's invitation only. I'll get one delivered to you.'

Mary Lou rang the house and spoke to Epps who agreed to have one sent to Beau's office.

Mary Lou and Beau left for a quiet luncheon together. He wanted to eat Japanese. She didn't. They ended up in a Creole restaurant. They ordered cocktails. She had a Highball. He had a Hurricane. Whilst they were sitting waiting to be served Blackened Redfish, Crawfish Etoufée, and Alligator Gumbo, Mary Lou's thoughts strayed to Ottilie and her Lord. She decided it might be fun to see this man for herself. On the excuse of going to the rest-room Mary Lou rang Epps again and asked him to send out another barbeque invitation. 'For Lord Christopher Furrel,' she said, giving his address at the Hotel Justine. Epps said he'd have to consult the Count when he got back from Texas. When he did, Count Helmut was highly amused at Mary Lou's request. He told Epps to get one delivered.

Lord Christopher found the invitation waiting for him upon his return from his visit to Frank Dale. He decided he would go minus a partner. He would not take Sylvie. In fact, armed as he was with loads of dollars courtesy of Frank Dale, Lord Christopher took another course of action. He sent Sylvie back to France, putting her on the next plane out of New Orleans to Paris, telling her it was for the best. His plans were about to come to fruition but if Ottilie caught even a whiff of Sylvie's perfume the whole thing would blow up in his face. Sylvie understood and went.

Lord Christopher's plan was that if he should fail in his objective – if his charm did not work on Ottilie – then at Count Helmut's barbeque he might find another heiress.

Having accompanied Sylvie to the airport Lord Christopher's next stop was the best jeweller's in town. He bought a sapphire and diamond ring; the sort he'd told Ottilie he'd have made for her. Then he went off and booked himself into the Fairmont. Staying at the same hotel meant he would have easier access to Ottilie's room. He would not need to go via reception.

210

Lord Christopher was certain his mission would succeed. He was chirpy, almost singing as he made his way down Canal Street, past the Mardi Gras stands and the people covered in beads and making merry, and the street cleaners picking up the trash.

Mary Lou sat at the table with Beau Maitland thinking, sure he was beautiful but beauty ain't everything. He was talking high-faluting talk: concerts and sopranos, violins and orchestras, conductors and divas which Mary Lou didn't give a shit about.

Jeez, she thought, my pa doesn't know what he's asking of me. I'd die of boredom before I inherited one cent. That'd make me a goddamn rich corpse.

Not exactly Mary Lou's idea of fun. She had to do something about it. She excused herself once more from Beau's company.

'Is it something you've eaten?' he asked when she said she had to go the rest-room yet again.

'No,' she said flashing him one of her sweet and brilliant smiles, thinking, no way sunshine, just the person I'm eating with.

Mary Lou did not go to the rest-room but to the telephone booth. From there she made a series of calls and as a result was too late for Helmut's Lundi Gras party.

Chapter 10

Ottilie was standing naked in her hotel room thinking about the Count whilst admiring the coloured metallic strips the hairdresser had woven into her hair, when her day dreams were interrupted by a loud sharp knock. Quickly she covered her nakedness with a bathrobe and opened the door.

'Christopher!' she exclaimed in astonishment, seeing her ex-fiancé standing there. 'What the hell are you doing here?'

'Came to see you, old girl,' he said.

Ottilie winced as she always winced at those words. Lord Christopher didn't notice her expression. It was her essence, her sensuality which struck him like a bolt of lightning. Something about her had changed. There was an openness, a freedom, a real, not covert, sexiness. He wanted her.

'I say you do look rather super. Even if all that metallic stuff is a bit over the top. Going to a Mardi Gras Ball, are you?'

'Mind your own business,' she said.

'Anyhow I didn't just pop in to say hello. I wanted a few words . . .' he said.

'I thought,' she said patiently, 'that I made it crystal clear that I never want to see or hear from you again.'

'Ottilie, you're being foolish. You don't really expect me to believe something that was said in anger, do you? We'll let bygones be bygones. I know I did wrong. I know you were angry . . .' he said, putting one foot in the doorway so she couldn't close it on him.

'Not "were", Christopher, "am". I *am* angry with you,' said Ottilie.

'And you have a perfect right to be. I was a boor. I shouldn't have done that but you inflamed me. I thought I was going to lose you.'

'You did,' she said.

'Ottilie, I'm sorry.'

'So you said in your letter.'

'But truly I am. Look, I've got something for you,' he said pulling out the small beautifully wrapped package that contained the engagement ring, bought with Frank Dale's money.

'Whatever it is, Christopher, I don't want it,' she said.

'Darling heart,' he said, 'forgive me.'

'I forgive you, Christopher, now if you'll excuse me . . . Goodbye,' she said and tried to close the door. 'Move your foot.'

'Sorry, old girl, seems to be glued to the carpet,' he said.

'Are you harassing me?'

'No, wouldn't dream of it,' he said, smiling. 'I just want you to listen to me. A few moments of your time . . .'

'No.'

'Ottilie . . .'

'No. Whatever it is – no. Understand me, Christopher. I don't want to see you. I don't want anything to do with you. I want you out of my life completely, now fuck off.'

'Ottilie! How coarse. If this is the effect America has on you the sooner I take you back to Europe the better. Ottilie, I love you.'

That was the last straw. How dare he! He hadn't the slightest idea of love. What it was. How it worked. How it changed one's perception of people and the world.

How it gave one a clarity to see people as they were. And Ottilie saw Christopher with a great clarity. As he stood there in front of her, smiling, elegantly if conservatively dressed, she saw him in all his meanness. His avariciousness was paramount.

'How's Sylvie?' she countered.

'Sylvie?' he asked, raising one eyebrow as if he hadn't the faintest idea who she was talking about.

'Your mistress,' said Ottilie.

'Darling girl,' he said patronisingly, 'you've made a major error there. Sylvie's not my mistress!'

'Christopher, quit the bullshit,' said Ottilie, angrily. Jeez, the guy couldn't even admit that he'd been screwing Sylvie.

'I want to marry you, Ottilie,' he said.

'I don't believe you!' said Ottilie. 'But you're persistent, I'll give you that. What you want is my money and you've figured you'll get your greedy hands on it if you marry me. Well, Lord Christopher, this woman ain't co-operating. You do not love me. You love my money. Also you don't *want* to marry me, you *need* to marry me, or you think you do. Christopher, listen and listen real good, 'cos in a minute I'm gonna call reception and have you thrown out. I wouldn't touch you with the Empire State Building, and I wouldn't marry you if you were the last man on the planet.'

'Come now, Ottilie,' he said, 'I think you're exaggerating.'

'Move your foot.'

'Very well. But I must say, I had no idea you were this angry, old girl.'

'Go, Christopher,' she said, glaring at him.

'We'll meet again,' he said. 'I don't give up easily. You will marry me.'

He turned on his heel and Ottilie closed the door fast.

And that, thought Ottilie, pleased with herself, was the end of him. She had managed that well. He was dismissed. No way would he come back for more. She turned her mind towards other, far more pleasant things: dressing herself for the ball.

214

She took down the frothy lemon yellow organza garment from its hanger. She put it on her pampered body, feeling the softness of its silk lining caressing her skin. She pulled on the long hold up pale purple silk stockings, their lacy tops finishing high, close to her sex, but leaving a small gap of bare thigh. She thrust her feet into the high sling-back darker lemon yellow shoes. She made up her face, paying particular attention to her mouth, emphasising it with brown pencil before applying the bright red glossy lipstick. Then she fixed the high feathered mask in place. When that was done she surveyed herself in the mirror. She liked what she saw. And she liked how she was feeling. Sexy. She knew her decision not to wear anything under the dress was the right one.

However, she did not want anyone beyond the Count to take advantage of her so she made one alteration to her planned attire. She took down a full length deepest purple silk velvet cape and draped it over her shoulders. Picking up her tiny evening bag, containing only some money, a small bottle of her favourite scent and a lipstick, she departed for the ball.

Walking tall and erect through the main hall of the hotel she drew gasps of admiration. She heard the 'Oohs' and the 'Aahs' and the whispers about going to Mardi Gras Ball. Outside the doorman hailed a cab. Within minutes she was in the Garden District.

Ottilie clanked the bell on the gate. Moments later a beautiful, tiny, delicate woman of many races, dressed in a severe black frock with a small white lace-edged apron, came down the stoep and along the path. Ottilie handed her the invitation, the woman scanned it – and her – then led the way into the house.

Ottilie noticed that, although a huge marquee had been erected on the lawn and decked out with Mardi Gras coloured fairly lights, there was nothing about the house itself to indicate festivities. In fact she noticed that all the curtains were drawn closed. No lights could be seen at all.

Inside it was a different story. There were candles everywhere and gentle, seductive music was playing. And she could hear people laughing and chattering. It was a good happy noise and Ottilie who had been tense, relaxed.

'Ah, Missy Lee,' said Epps, coming forward and taking Ottilie's huge cape.

Ottilie gave the woman a quick glance. So that was Missy Lee. The cook. She had imagined her to be a big fat woman, not slim and delicate. Missy Lee locked the door then disappeared through an archway. Epps handed Ottilie a card.

'You're number 27,' he said. She glanced down. That's what it said: written in classic German script, the number 27. The card came with a tiny safety pin attached. 'Shall I pin it on or . . .?'

Ottilie stared at his hands. Big soft hands with long fingers. She wondered if they were the hands that had felt her body in the cabin. He was about to take the card from her and pin it over her breast when she stopped him.

'No,' she said, with a nervous breathlessness. 'No, I'll do it.'

'As you wish,' he said, bowing.

When she had pinned the card on Epps guided Ottilie through to the room she had sat in previously with Elmer and the Count.

It had been transformed. Gone the stark harshness of the Shakers. Now it was awash with flowers, narcissi, iris and lilies, filling the room with a sweet pungent odour. Many candles of differing heights flickered, suffusing the room in a dreamy light. People of every shape and size sat or stood in a circle. They all wore fancy dress. Everyone was masked and covered in Mardi Gras beads.

Ottilie noticed amongst the people talking happily and drinking champagne that there seemed to be a preponderance of eighteenth-century fashions. Mozart and Madame de Pompadour reigned supreme, but there

were some Roman slaves. In the middle of the circle was
a tall blonde dressed as the ubiquitous Madame de Pompadour. She was wearing a tight black and white striped
corset with her breasts jacked up high and her nipples
just peeping over the edge of the lace. Her wide pan-
niered skirt, worn over layers of lace-edged petticoats,
was of a dark green- and black-striped shiny satin. She
wore a high feathered Mardi Gras coloured mask and
around her eyes someone had tied a strip of black silk.
She looked exceptionally exotic. Ottilie stared at her
wondering why. Then realised that she had plaited
waist length strips of shiny black nylon string into her
pale blonde hair. This was literally the added extra. One
of the Roman slaves was turning her round and around.
Ottilie thought she caught a flash of leg, as if her skirt
had been carefully slashed from waist to hem. But she
couldn't be sure. The slave stopped turning her. The fold
of her skirt fell modestly back into place and the blonde
pointed at a man. Everybody looked to where she was
pointing.

'Fifteen,' they all shouted, staring at the number on
his lapel. And the lithe Number 15, dressed as an eighteenth-century gentleman, left the room.

Epps handed Ottilie a glass of champagne and held a
chair back for her to sit down. She felt slightly foolish.
Everyone else was almost over the top in their beads
and in their dress, she should have made more of an
effort. She should have dressed in something other than
a modern gay Frenchman's fantasy for a woman.

'That is the most fabulous outfit,' said the man who
was sitting close to her. She didn't recognise his voice
but his comment was reassuring.

'Thank you,' she said, sipping her drink.

The woman in the middle was being twirled again.
She stopped and pointed. This time her finger alighted
on a woman. A Roman slave.

'Twenty-two,' somebody shouted. A bandanna was
tied around twenty-two's eyes and she was escorted
from the room.

Ottilie was longing to find out where they were going but she realised that sooner or later her number would be called and she would discover.

She finished her champagne, her glass was quickly refilled by Epps and the music was changed. It was no longer gentle and seductive but loud, rhythmic and sexual. The woman in the middle of the room was twirled again and again and gradually the room emptied. Ottilie noticed a pattern emerging. Those dressed as eighteenth-century men and women were not blindfolded. Those dressed as slaves were. And all the people whose names were called did not come back. Ottilie's curiosity was growing by the minute.

Then came the moment when the woman's finger pointed at her.

'Number 27,' shouted the few left in the room.

Now Ottilie was in a quandary. Everyone else had got up with assurance. They knew what to do. She had no idea. She was neither an eighteeth-century grandee nor a slave.

'Come with me,' said a voice behind her. Her heart lurched. It was the Count's voice. She twisted in her chair. He was dressed in eighteenth-century costume and wore a heavily bejewelled mask. He held out his hand. She stood up. The other people clapped as he drew her into the middle of the room and slowly tied a black bandanna around her eyes. Then he turned her round and around, disorientating her before guiding her forward and out of the room.

Ottilie knew she was being taken from one room to another but the combination of the feel of Helmut's hand on her elbow and the unaccustomed darkness left her not knowing quite where she was. But wherever she went the loud sexual music was a constant. Its deep bass and its throbbing drum excited her. Apart from that, the only sound she could hear was the clack clack of her heels on the bare polished floorboards.

'Now stand very still, don't move whatever happens,' said Helmut, jerking her to a stop.

Ottilie felt the Count's breath on her neck. She felt him lift the hem of her dress. She drew a quick sharp breath. Her bare buttocks were naked to his gaze. She waited, trembling, wondering what he would say. Would he be pleased to have found her so wanton? Or would he punish her?

'A beautiful sight,' he murmured, caressing her firm cheeks. She moved her hips. 'Keep very still, I said. Or I will punish you. Yes, a very pretty bottom. And what a wanton girl not to wear any panties.'

She felt his hands move slowly between the crack of her buttocks, finding the sensitive skin hidden there. He stroked it. Then those hands moved to caress her soft wet flesh, and her lips that were opening, ripening like fruit in the sun to his touch.

'A naughty girl to be so wet and open,' he said. 'Tell me, were you naked like this last night when you were in the restaurant with that man?'

Ottilie was completely taken aback by his question. She had forgotten about Beau and the reporter.

'Epps showed me your photograph in today's paper. He greeted me with it upon my return. Did he run his hands up your legs,' said Helmut, his hands moving down over her thighs. 'Did he touch you in the restaurant.'

'No,' she said.

'Did he feel your pussy?'

Ottilie hesitated.

'Did he feel your pussy, Ottilie? Did he do what I'm doing now?'

Helmut's hands opened the lips of her sex and thrust his fingers into her moist flesh. Ottilie gasped.

'Ottilie, did he feel you, did he put his head between your legs? Did he fuck you?'

Ottilie felt the colour of shame flooding her face as she remembered Beau's cock searching between her thighs in the moonlight of his room.

'Yes,' she whispered.

'This man screwed you?'

'Yes, but ...' she desperately wanted to explain that she had been furious with him, and that she'd thought, when Mary Lou had said he was her fiancé and had gone to Forth Worth to buy her a huge diamond, that he was playing with her emotions.

'No buts Ottilie,' said Helmut, his fingers moving up and down within her. 'You opened your legs for this man?'

'Yes, I was angry,' said Ottilie.

'So was I Ottilie, very angry,' he said, taking his fingers away from her sex. 'When I saw a picture of you looking so beautiful, telling the reporter you'd returned to New Orleans to claim your inheritance – and kick out the man who was wrongfully occupying your house. And I looked at your face in that picture, so sexy, so sensuous. I knew he would take you to bed. Knew he would lie you down and put his cock between your thighs and enter your wanton sex.'

As he said that she felt his cock. His warm rigid penis lightly touched the bare flesh between her stocking tops and her sex. The feel of him was so delicious that she sighed and almost came on contact.

'Oh yes, Ottilie, your delicious, wanton and licentious sex,' said Helmut, his accented voice silky but menacing. 'You displeased me. For that you will have to be punished.'

His cock was slowly entering her. She licked her lips, her mouth had gone dry with excitement whereas her inner self was vibrant. Waves of fine shivery tingles suffused her swollen squashy moist red flower. She endeavoured to take him further into her, but he resisted her enveloping muscles.

'You see, my dear, I chose to fuck you, and once I've done that you are my woman ...'

His woman. Those two words would normally have sent Ottilie into a towering rage. The idea of her belonging to anybody other than herself was anathema to her. But now with Helmut's cock rubbing along her sex lips all she could think of was, 'Yes, I'm your woman. And don't stop, please don't stop.'

'. . . And,' he continued, 'I do not allow you to fuck someone else unless I agree to it. Perhaps that should be your punishment. I will watch you being fucked by a man of my choice.'

Ottilie found what he was saying so outrageous but so thrilling that her sex muscles contracted with excitement.

Sensing her sudden and intense arousal and wanting to tease her more, Helmut withdrew his penis. He lifted her skirt higher and pushed his prick along the crease of her bare bottom. He brought his hands round and laid them over her breasts. Very slowly he began to caress them. Leaving one hand to massage her nipples, with the other he undid the buttons of her fine organza frock. He carried on unbuttoning as far as her waist. He pushed the fabric aside completely exposing her breasts. He clasped them, holding them up and out as if displaying them as objects of great beauty for all to see.

'Bend over,' he said. And willingly she obeyed him.

He put his hands under her armpits and, holding her breasts again, let his cock glide along her fresh wet opening. She was glistening with her sex moisture. And the more he rubbed the more she moistened. She began to roll her hips.

'No, keep still, keep very still,' he whispered.

His fingers took her nipples and with infinite care he massaged them, slowly increasing the pressure. At the same time he increased the pressure of his cock along the tops of her thighs – never entering, just teasing, allowing her sex lips to open further and further, become wetter and wetter, feeling her glands swelling, and the tenseness of her body wanting him.

Ottilie wondered where everybody else was. The music was still playing but she could not hear other people. There was only her and the Count in the whole world. This was what she wanted. Him and her together. She wanted to stroke his fine soft hair, to feel his wide and willing lips on hers, to hold his hard and throbbing penis and his large balls. She wanted him to kiss her, to suck her between her legs, to take her. She desperately wanted him to thrust his prick into her wet sex harder and harder and harder.

'Stand up straight, but keep your arms down by your side. Do not attempt to touch me,' said, Helmut, moving his cock away from her legs.

Ottilie sighed but did as she was told. Then he was gone from behind her. The hem at the back of her dress had fallen back over her buttocks. But where he had shoved the unbuttoned fabric to one side it stayed open and gaping, showing off her large breasts with their hard erect nipples.

She felt him kneeling in front of her, undoing the remaining buttons of her dress, his hands opening her sex. One of his fingers was gliding along its lips while another finger was pushing past its folds and entering her creamy wetness. Her hips were straining towards him. With every caress he gave her she opened further hoping to receive him.

Then she felt his tongue. He was holding her sex lips wide apart and his tongue touched her. He trailed it up and down. He lifted the soft hood and found her stiff excited little bud. His tongue rested on it, then flicked over it, again and again and again.

It was the tongue that worked the magic. That was the instrument of witchcraft. The tongue that was the sorceror's wand in Ottilie's dream behind her silken blindfold whilst she moaned songs of love and desire. Turgid dreams washed over her as that tongue increased its power on her senses. She was the sea, the sweet smelling sea, and her breasts were the waves and her nipples were stars pointing their way to the heavens and her sex was the hidden treasure. She was as moving, as undulating as the tides bidden by the moon. She was in motion and dancing the dance of life. Dancing with the tempest of her lust.

Her mouth was open, her own tongue flicking out snakelike into the air to proclaim its existence and that it wanted somewhere to go. It wanted to feel, and so did her hands. They fluttered. As if he knew she was about to reach for him those hands were imprisoned. Held. Held fast to her side. Handcuffs were snapped closed about her wrists and then she felt iron on her ankles and heard the sound of chains. Iron and chains. Binding her. Binding her to him and she remembered the words of the Voodoo Queen. He loves you. He will bind you to him. Ottilie knew at that moment she was lost. She was his forever. His searching tongue had her in its spell. The magic and the music, the touch and her own mind created dreams. She dreamed of tongues and hands and cocks taking her, exploring every nook of her body.

Ottilie did not know when she became aware of the reality of the hands. Hands holding her haunches. Hands taking her teats, squeezing her nipples. Hands stroking her legs and her thighs. Hands spreading her labia wide so that the searching tongue could travel deeper within her. When she did, she was too far into the dream to care. Continue. Don't stop. Every pore, every nerve ending screamed out the same message.

When she felt a cock pushing at her sex from behind, felt it gliding along her hungry flesh at the top of her thighs she knew it was no dream. She wanted to take more of the tongue and the cock but she also wanted to see who was fondling her. If Helmut was sucking at her sex, who was trying to fuck her? It was this thought that caused her to almost lose her balance. She put her own hands out and touched the head that was bent supping at her juices. That was when she realised the person kneeling between her legs was not Helmut. The hair that she was touching was not fine and silky; it was coarse, almost waxy.

Quickly before anybody saw what she was about to do Ottilie lifted her arms and tore the blindfold from her eyes.

She was the centre of everyone's attention. She was on display, exhibited. Her body, her breasts, her sex, her ability to perform was being watched and enjoyed. She was standing in a pool of light, surrounded by half-clothed masked men. All of them were in eighteenth-century costume. All of them with the flap that should have been covering their sex gaping open. Each one of them with an erect penis. Each one of them their hands on her body. Ottilie had the desire to reach out and grab one of the rigid members and play with it. She couldn't, her hands were handcuffed in front of her. She looked down at the person kneeling between her legs, expertly sucking at her sex.

It was Missy Lee. Missy Lee, her hair undone and wearing a black leather suit that covered most of her body and her legs, was enjoying Ottilie's folds and juices. Ottilie found this unexpected sight both depraved and exciting. Its depravity excited her and she pushed her red-gold mound further towards Missy Lee's face. As she moved Ottilie saw that Missy's outfit had large cut-outs leaving her breasts, her sex and her bottom completely bare. Ottilie found it unbelievably sexual. She had another deep and shameful desire. To touch Missy Lee's pert saffron coloured breasts.

Missy Lee leant backwards. Ottilie saw her bare shaven sex. Then she had the intense desire to nestle her head between Missy Lee's legs, put her tongue out and lick her. Taste her. Arouse her as she had been aroused.

Ottilie's pale skin blushed with shame as those wicked thoughts flooded into her brain. She turned her eyes away from the kneeling woman.

In the semi-darkness Ottilie could see a long table and was able to make out partially clothed figures lying on it and some sitting on chairs up to it. But she couldn't see more than that. Where was Helmut? Wildly, with panic rising, her eyes darted around the people. She saw him sitting on a chair, fully clothed, except his large penis was erect, jutting forth from his trousers. The blonde who had stood blindfolded in the circle had his penis in her mouth, her head going backwards and forwards giving him pleasure whilst he was watching Ottilie.

Ottilie was about to cry out with a mixture of jealousy and sexual excitement when she saw the whip in Helmut's hand. She stifled the sound and turned to see whose cock was still gliding between her thighs. She almost knew before she turned to look. She knew she had felt that massive cock before. Out on the bayou. And there he was – Epps, big and ugly, his huge, urgent prick pushing at her labia from behind. And the idea that he was going to screw her again thrilled her. She opened for him.

'I want to watch you being fucked,' said Helmut. 'And I'm giving Epps permission to fuck you. So bend over.'

With her hands chained and her feet fettered Ottilie knew she had no alternative but to obey.

The other men moved away as Epps put his big black hands around her waist and held her. Missy Lee took hold of her hands and pulled them to the floor. Epps tipped Ottilie forward. Missy Lee slid between Ottilie's and Epps' legs so that her pussy was level with Ottilie's head. Epps took hold of his huge prick and rubbed it along the crease of Ottilie's buttocks then round to her open wet and willing sex.

He opened her sex lips that were tender and swollen. He touched Ottilie's hard engorged clitoris that was begging to be felt again. He massaged that little bud until she was shaking and heaving with desire. Ravenous, she wanted to be taken, plundered. She wanted her hunger assuaged. She wanted to feel his prick deep and hard within her. But he knew her craving. Her appetite. He was also under orders from the Count to heighten her longing. Increase her need. Epps was enjoying the feel of her body responding to his smallest, tiniest touch. Missy Lee brought her arms up and started to fondle Ottilie's breasts. At first she used large sure movements then bit by bit she reduced the area she was covering until only Ottilie's nipples were being caressed and played with.

Then Missy Lee lay back, put her heels against her own buttocks, let her knees fall open and raised her hips presenting her sex to Ottilie's face.

'Suck her,' ordered the Count. 'Put your tongue on her clitoris and lick her.'

As he said that Ottilie felt Epps cock starting to thrust at her moist opening. The touch of him on her tingling sex was like an electric charge. She moved back to take him. And Missy Lee took hold of Ottilie's head, and placed it between her open legs.

Epps' cock was filling her up. She was expanding as he thrust. Her nostrils smelled the enticing sea shell sex odour of the woman lying in front of her. Missy Lee brought her hands round and opened her sex further. Ottilie's tongue came out and Epps thrust hard into her. Ottilie's tongue hit Missy's large hard bud.

Then she felt another body, a leather covered body grazing silkily against her legs. She felt a hand come up to touch her labia; a hand enfolding Epps' cock, taking his balls into the palm of the hand as he moved within her. The same hand's fingers were touching her, finding her swollen excited clitoris, as Epps continued to pound her inner walls. With sweat and lust and desire Ottilie continued to polish Missy Lee's over developed clitoris whilst her own was being played with and enjoyed.

The music was playing louder and more insistently. A singer was singing about rocking and rolling. She saw a flash of green and black shiny satin fall over Missy Lee's belly. Ottilie raised her head and saw the blonde with the black string plaited in her hair crouch over Missy Lee's face. Ottilie groaned and moaned with pleasure. Epps took her more slowly. The finger playing with her clitoris moved more slowly. Her mouth, avidly searching through the folds of Missy Lee's sex changed its rhythm too. Ottilie felt the pleasure of control as the delicate small boned woman whose clitoris resembled a tiny penis heaved and swayed beneath her tongue.

Ottilie was lulled by the changes. Her ripeness did not explode as she thought it would. Epps took her back from the brink. His and hers. He gripped her hips and then slowly pulled her to the floor.

Enveloped in sensations of exquisite licentiousness Ottilie squirmed as tongues licked her outstretched legs. Her whole body was alive. Vibrating. Wanting. Her entire being was sexual; there wasn't one part of her that didn't crave attention; there wasn't one part of her that wasn't getting it. Someone began sucking the toes on her left foot from little toe to big toe. Someone else started in the reverse order on her right foot.

Ottilie continued to sup at the honey oozing from Missy Lee. A wet and well oiled hand began worming its way between her back and Epps' moving belly. Down that hand came over her buttocks. Each time Epps lifted to thrust, that hand travelled further along the crack of her bottom. Then as Epps lifted high on his hands to thrust hard, that creeping hand found her small tight puckered aperture. It began its measured push into her other more secret hole. Ottilie gasped. Her entire senses met the heavens. The touching, hers and others; the smells, hers and others; the odours, bodily perfume and rich heady manufactured scent intermingling with the sweetness of spring flowers; the sight of opened legs, firm muscles, moving limbs and soft folds of wet flesh; it all threw her mind into a whirl of rapturous, audacious desire. She let out little sighs of joy that gained in intensity with the probing of the finger and the insisting thrusting of Epps' cock. Her sighs became songs of sex and violation. Her head was moving fast, taking, drinking at Missy Lee, and her hips were gyrating in a primeval dance in rhythm to Epps' cock.

From somewhere in her depths her essence coiled and tensed waiting to be sprung. But Helmut, the master of ceremonies, knew this and stopped the dancers dancing.

He took the blonde girl away from Missy's mouth. He pulled Missy away from Ottilie's mouth. He told the men sucking Ottilie's toes to cease. He made Epps stop his thrusting and told the man beneath her to leave.

Helmut lifted Ottilie up. He held her slight frame in his arms, the delicate organza of her frock floating over his strong body, and he walked with her to his chair. He sat her on his lap, holding her high until his stiff cock was neatly positioned under her sex. Gripping her haunches he eased her body down allowing her to take

227

its full hard length. He kissed her wet open sexual mouth and caressed her aroused breasts.

Ottilie felt the fire roar through her as his cock pierced her and thrust into her burning, wanton sex. Him, she wanted. Him, she adored. Anything. Just anything she would do for him. She wanted more. More of everything. Her open tingling salacious body was ripe for the picking, the taking, the flaying.

'You felt pleasure?' he asked, whispering into her ear.

'Yes,' she replied.

'Pleasure from Epps' cock?'

'Yes.'

'Pleasure from his thick hard black prick pounding into your cunt?'

'Yes,' she said hoarsely, excited by the word she would never use.

'Pleasure from his big hands holding your fine white skin so that he could enter you further and further?'

'Yes.'

'Pleasure from Epps fucking you?'

'Yes,' she said, riding him faster.

'Pleasure from Missy Lee's mouth?'

'Oh yes.'

'Pleasure from the men's hands stroking your body?'

'Yes.'

'Pleasure from the feel of their cocks on your skin?'

'Yes.'

'Now look around you,' he commanded.

She looked beyond him to the other people in the room. She saw the blindfolded Roman slaves lying on the table, which was lower, narrower and considerably longer than a normal dining table. The women had their tunics pushed up showing their sex, and pushed down showing their breasts. The men had either their tunics pushed up and their sex erect or were lying on their stomachs, their bare buttocks acting as serving dishes. All of them lay with hors d'oeuvres dishes beside them.

The grandees in eighteenth-century costume were sitting on high stools at the table. Ottilie noticed that the women's bodices seemed tighter and their breasts and nipples had spilled out over the top of the lace. As she went up and down on Helmut's cock she watched the women taking food from the plate. If it was an olive or a mushroom or a prawn, or a carrot, a cucumber or a courgette, it was trailed between the sex lips of the closest prostrate female slave. If it was a cream dip it was smeared over their breasts and licked. If it was a male slave the cream was smeared over his erect penis and licked, or across his bare buttocks and licked. Whilst they were eating the men and women were chatting together. Ottilie could not hear what they were saying, but their conversation did not include the slaves. They were there simply as objects. They were live serving dishes. Occasionally someone stood up, and that meant everyone moved round.

It was then that Ottilie saw that every woman's full skirts were split down the middle and hitched up at the back and the front leaving their sexes and bottoms immediately accessible. And the men's trousers did not cover their manhood. Their cocks were proudly displayed and as thick and hard and erect as those of the slaves lying passively on the table. When they changed places the men and the women used the opportunity, and the immediate availability of each other's exposed sex, to either play with or suck or fuck one another.

Ottilie decided what she was witnessing was the most decadent scene she could have imagined. It sent a deep and licentious rush through her body. She wanted to be up on that table with someone, anyone, man or woman, known or unknown, smearing and licking food and cream from her breasts and her sex.

Helmut looked up at her face as she rocked backwards and forwards on his penis. He saw the wanton expression flit across her face. He knew she wanted to be a part of it.

'Does that excite you?' he asked.

'Yes,' she said.

'Do you want to be a slave or a mistress?'

Ottilie hesitated. He was giving her a choice she would rather have been without. She preferred him to decide.

'Would you like to be strapped down on the table with people feasting from your body or do you want to do the feasting?'

Still she hesitated.

Helmut kissed her mouth then took a piece of silk from his pocket and wrapped it around her eyes.

'My slave, I think,' he said.

And her muscles quickened, tightening their hold on his thrusting cock and he knew that was what she wanted. 'My willing slave.'

He accented the willing. He wanted her in no doubt. By silence she had left the choice to him. By silence she had acquiesced. He was making sure she knew what she had done.

'My willing slave,' he said again. 'What do you say?'

'Yes, master,' she whispered, trembling with excitement.

Helmut lifted her up and away from his prick and stood her on the floor. Someone unlocked her handcuffs and her ankle-locks. Her frock was removed. Her stockings were rolled down and taken off. She was naked and blindfolded but the high feathered mask was left in place. Helmut stood up and passed her to other hands. Hands which roamed over her body smearing her with thick warm strawberry smelling cream. Her breasts, her nipples, her belly was covered. Then hands travelled down between her legs, coating the sensitive skin at the top of her thighs.

The hands changed and so did the sensation. Her burning body was assailed by freezing cold cream, thick dollops of it were squashed into her hungry open sex. The icy sharpness brought her swaying body to a sudden stop. Meeting her inner warmth the ice began to melt and dribble down her thighs.

She was lifted up and deposited on the table. Conversation came to a halt as the insistent and highly sexual music was turned up to a deafening pitch. She was laid flat on her back, her arms out in front of her, her wrists tied with leather bindings to the rings at the edge of the table allowing her hands to hang free. Her legs were stretched apart, her feet tied to rings and a large hard cushion was placed under her buttocks forcing her sex to jut upwards. She was wide open and on display. Anybody could take her, do what they willed with her, look at her, suck her, feed from her or fuck her. As the iced cream oozed out of her sex intermingling with the gooey cream smeared over her thighs she felt hands parting her, small fingers exploring her, finding their way into and along her most sensitive wall tissue, exciting it, finger fucking her. Then those fingers withdrew and something long and hard was inserted. She opened to receive it. Hard and cold. It stayed cold within her. Penis shaped, this hard cold object slowly travelled upwards, never taking on her own warmth. Jade, she thought. Only jade stays cold. A jade prick was entering her inner sanctum. And hands caressed her breasts and her nipples. Thick warm tongues licked the cream away from her body and more cream was poured over her.

Hands bunched her tits up, squeezing her nipples, scissoring them with their fingers until her nipples were rock hard and tingling. Then a fine cotton was tied around her nipples and pulled tight. Ottilie gasped. Exquisite pleasure seared through her, joining her breasts to her womb to her vagina in one living aching silken inner cord.

More and more ice cream was spread over and around her sex. On her belly. Between her thighs. As soon as one layer warmed and began to melt, another layer was slapped on. One tiny finger played with her clitoris. The sensation was extreme. The finger massaged and polished her tiny bud with the most delicate of caresses. Ottilie's hips were rising and falling. She was moaning, her head was moving, her nipples were hard. Then she felt the jet stream: one endless flow of warm water aimed at her engorged clitoris. She felt hands pushing again at the jade prick within her as the body-warm water continued its flow, dissolving the ice cream and the cream, leaving her in a pool of liquid. She squirmed, delighting in the licentiousness of it; in the sensations hitting her body and oozing from her. Pleasure pleasure pleasure. She squirmed and writhed.

'I love you,' said Helmut, kissing her face, her mouth, her ear. His admission was so startling that it made Ottilie break her rhythm. 'I love you, and I have given you pleasure. Have I not? Answer me, and answer me properly.'

'Yes, master,' she said.

'And you are my willing slave?'

'Yes, master.' His face was beside her, but someone else's hand was between her legs. She could feel the finger once more playing with her clitoris and another taking hold of the jade prick and moving it deep within her.

'I told you when you first arrived that you had displeased me, didn't I? I told you you would have to be punished. You are mine and you fucked someone else without my permission. You did, didn't you?'

'Yes, master,' she said, softly.

'So now you must be punished.'

'Punished . . .' she stammered.

'Yes. You had pleasure when you took Epps' cock. You had pleasure when you felt Missy Lee's mouth. You had pleasure when hands coated you with cream and finger fucked you. Now it is my turn for pleasure. And my pleasure is to have you whipped. I want to see you writhe. I want to hear you moan with pain. I want to see your pretty little bottom bright red. I want you to know my pleasure.' Helmut placed his stiff cock in her hand. 'And afterwards when your beautiful buttocks are striped and marked I will lie you down and fuck you. But first the whip.'

'The whip!' she gasped.

'Yes, my darling,' he said reaching for her nipples, tweaking them, and pulling at the cords surrounding them. 'The whip. And don't beg for mercy. If you do, I will strike you harder.'

232

Helmut signalled to a group to attend him and turn Ottilie over from lying on her back to lying on her front.

Ottilie felt the thongs binding her wrists loosened. Then she was hauled to her feet. She was creamed and oiled, then laid flat again, her head facing the other end of the table. Two large cushions were placed under her belly. Her bottom was raised high. But it wasn't high enough for Helmut. He called for two more cushions. He shook her buttocks, making sure they were soft and wobbly. Ottilie lay still. Every nerve ending was tense. Her arms were pinioned to the side of the table, and once again her hands were allowed to flutter free. Someone underneath the table pulled on a piece of wood and her breasts fell into two holes. Small weights were tied to the fine cotton encircling her nipples, pulling her heavy breasts down with a seductive agony. And the jade prick was hard inside her sex keeping her open and vulnerable.

She waited tense and trembling almost feeling the lash before it came, anticipating the stroke. But Helmut was the master. He knew the rules of the game.

He was standing to one side of the table, the flap of his trousers open. Daisy was kneeling before him sucking on his erect cock and he held the whip in his hand, not touching anyone. He pointed to Missy Lee and silently told her to stop playing with a voluptuous dark haired girl and kneel on the table between Ottilie's outstretched legs. He wiggled his tongue indicating that she should suck Ottilie.

Ottilie's raised arse and open sex were pure joy to Missy Lee. She settled herself comfortably between her thighs and nestled her face in Ottilie's crotch. Then that tongue began its salacious work. It started to lick at the base of Ottilie's spine, gradually moving along her crease then round to her open swollen and hanging lips. There she used the jade dildo to play on the inside of Ottilie's folds. Missy Lee brought up her fingers and played with the luscious juicy petals of Ottilie's vibrant quivering flesh.

Ottilie jumped when the tongue hit her clitoris. Exquisite pain, exquisite pleasure, excruciating sensations surged through her. Missy's tiny effortless touch, the tip of the tongue on the tip of her engorged insatiable clitoris sent Ottilie away, beyond the realms of reality.

Missy concentrated on the one spot. Sharp and needle-like, incandescent drops of pain were in every dainty flick of Missy's tongue. The whip when it struck was hard, searing and forceful. Ottilie writhed and jerked upwards. The weights on her breasts forced her back down again. She attempted to struggle against the bindings. All that happened was that the next stroke missed her rounded bottom and caught her across her thighs. Ottilie clenched her teeth, her hands and her buttocks.

'Go loose and thank me,' commanded Helmut.

'Thank you,' she whispered. 'Thank you, master.'

He plied the whip again, a blazing rip across her bare flesh. Again and again. Six times. Then she felt the cool of ice cold water thrown over her burning flanks. She gasped, jumped, twisted and turned with the suddenness of it.

'Twelve,' said Helmut. Ottilie knew there was no point in protesting. He would have his way. She was the slave. She loved him. He could do with her whatever he wanted.

She was moaning, she was crying. And the pain changed. Altered to another state. Exalted pleasure. An exquisite torture she had never known, a mystic pleasure, a fanatical pleasure, an inquisitional pleasure. The pleasure of the penitent. Helmut continued to burn her bottom with the whip. She gave herself up to the centre of the pain and pleasure; and found a new and special freedom.

Then Helmut kissed her mouth. He removed the blindfold and gently kissed her neck, stroking that soft elegant curve that frequently excited him. He ordered her wrists, her ankles and her nipples to be untied. He lifted her from the table to lie beside him on a large velvety rug. He removed the jade from her sex.

Impervious to the others, aware only of her sore, stinging bottom, she clung to him, opening her legs for him as he moved on top of her. He entered her quickly and took her fast.

And tears of joy and pain and sex and sensuality mingled with her kisses. She loved him. He took her from the front. Then he turned her over, lay against the marks on her bottom, and took her from behind. He took her arse. And she writhed under him with unmitigated joy and pleasure.

Occasionally she opened her eyes. She noticed that everyone in the room was fucking. Fucking or sucking. Men to men, women to women and men to women. Twos and threes or fours. The music continued from hidden speakers and so did the music of the sound of sex. Moans and groans and long drawn out sighs as one by one each person had their orgasm.

Helmut took Ottilie to her pinnacle. He had moved her across his body, her buttocks resting on his pelvic bone, his prick hard up inside her anus, his hands opening her vagina, playing there, playing with her swollen engorged sex lips and her hard excited bud. Their skin, their sweat, their senses, their emotions and their bodies completely united in a great rush of ecstasy.

It was afterwards, as she was lying peacefully in Helmut's arms, and the other revellers were either asleep or had gone to another room, that Ottilie realised she was in a dungeon. Or at least a replica of one.

'I had it specially made for parties,' said Helmut, noticing her wide-eyed stare. 'It's soundproofed and difficult to find. I had lots of false doors put in to stop uninvited guests investigating.'

'Very wise,' she said, cuddling into him.

Chapter 11

'*I* wanna suck your cock,' said Mary Lou, blatant as the sun at high noon.

Lord Christopher stared at her incredulously.

'Allow me to introduce myself. My name's Mary Lou. Mary Lou Dale. Frank Dale's daughter.'

'Right.'

That was all Lord Christopher could think to say.

'So, why don't you let me in and take down your pants, let me see what you've got between your legs before I put it in my mouth,' she said.

It wasn't often that Lord Christopher was lost for words but he was now.

'I'll sure as hell give you a real good time,' she said. 'Man, I give the best blow job in the whole of Louisiana, maybe even in the whole of the South.'

'Frank Dale's daughter, you said?'

'Yep.'

'And you want to suck my cock?'

'Yep.'

'Why?'

''Cos I wanna. And I do most things I wanna.'

'Oh!'

Lord Christopher had always thought Sylvie was pretty forthright but this woman, this all-American

236

beauty standing in the doorway of his hotel room was outrageous.

'Are you sure you haven't got the wrong room?'

'Hell, man, I'm not a hooker. You are Lord Christopher Furrel, yeah?'

'Yes,' he said.

'So I'm in the right place.'

Mary Lou stretched out a hand and put it over his crotch. Her words had their intended effect. His prick was stiff and excited and straining, wanting desperately to be let out.

'You seem to be carrying some mighty fine baggage.'

Mary Lou took her hand away, pushed the amazed Lord Christopher to one side and walked into his room.

He stood bemused. There was nothing subtle or subdued about her. Her shapely body was encased in an outrageous evening frock. Made of black silk jersey, it had a strap over one shoulder, the other was bare. It was short at the front and long at the back and the short front was slashed up to the top of her thighs. The bodice was slashed down to her navel. There was a large golden safety pin across her sex. Two large safety pins across her full breasts, one green, one purple, pulled the fabric tight but left it gaping, enhancing her breasts. She wore incredibly high-heeled black shoes, and no stockings over her long, tanned legs. Her blonde hair waved seductively over her shoulders.

'Ain't ya never seen a woman before?' said Mary Lou, strolling round the room.

'Look here, I really do think there's been some mistake,' said Lord Christopher.

'Hell man, I'm offering you the classiest bit of pussy south of the Mason/Dixie line and you stand there like yesterday's piece of Chitt'lin.'

Mary Lou stood beside him, smiled up at his face, and pulled down his zip.

'There, that wasn't so terrible, was it?' she said, her hands groping for his prick. 'Sure ain't terrible for me. You got one helluva hard on.'

Mary Lou slithered down his body. She took Lord Christopher's erect tool from its hiding place, caressed it, then put it in her mouth.

Lord Christopher was remembering this extraordinary introduction as he sat beside her in one of her father's chauffeur driven stretch limos. He turned to look at her. She smiled back at him, like the cat who got the cream. He reached out and put a hand on her thigh. She leant back in her seat, stretched her legs and lifted her hips. He let a finger glide on her wet pussy.

'So,' he said, continuing to play with her, 'it was you who arranged for the invitation to be sent to me.'

'Sure was. I wanted to meet you. Then I thought, why wait until tonight. You might not turn up. That's when I rang the Hotel Justine and they told me you'd moved to the Fairmont. Everybody knows me there, so it was no problem getting up to your room.'

'And you know these people well that are giving the barbeque?'

'Oh yeah, very well,' said Mary Lou.

'What sort of people are they?' he asked.

'Decadent, mostly,' she replied.

'Decadent?' he said, probing her sex more deeply.

'That's right, decadent. 'Course, there'll be some there who ain't. Just come 'cos they is fascinated by the Count's reputation.'

'And what's that?' asked Lord Christopher, intrigued.

'Licentious,' she replied.

'Oh really!' he said. 'And have you been a recipient of his licentiousness?'

'Oh no way man,' said Mary Lou, lying through her teeth. 'But I had a friend who was. And the things she told me went on in that house! You would never believe!'

'I wouldn't!'

'You sure wouldn't.'

'Try me,' said Lord Christopher, his cock up and erect once more.

'I couldn't. As you know,' said Mary Lou, opening her

238

legs wider so that his fingers could travel further along her glossy thighs and find her wet and open sex. 'As you know I can be forthcoming, but what she described . . .'

'Tell me,' he said, undoing his flies and putting her hand in the gap.

He sighed as she got hold of his prick and began to play with it.

'How long have we got 'til we're there?' he asked.

'Not long enough,' she said.

Mary Lou was determined to keep Lord Christopher on the boil. She hadn't screwed him yet. She'd played with him. She'd driven him crazy letting him play with her, suck her, finger fuck her sex and her anus. She'd decided she'd screw him after the barbeque. She'd missed the Count's orgy but she didn't care. She'd been to plenty of those. She'd never sucked a real live English Lord before. Mary Lou was not one for missing a chance.

'Pity,' said Lord Christopher. 'Anyhow tell me more.'

'I'll tell you this,' said Mary Lou. 'The Count's got a couple of servants. One is a big black guy and the other is a tiny Chinesey woman. Now my friend told me that she only likes women. Gives them a real good time with her tongue, that's what she said.' Mary Lou squirmed on Lord Christopher's moving fingers as she remembered the times Missy Lee's tongue had expertly sucked at her clitoris. 'And the Count likes to watch his big black friend screw. He gets everybody dressed up in outrageous costume. You know, corsets with their tits jacked up, and full skirts slit at the back and the front so that he or his servants can touch them up whenever they feel like it.'

'Oh really!' said Lord Christopher, swallowing hard. His mouth had gone dry at the thought. His cock was thick and throbbing. And Mary Lou kept rubbing.

'But that's not all,' she said. 'He likes them to do it all together.'

'You mean an orgy?'

'Yeah, an orgy. And . . .' She bent over and licked his

tumescent prick. 'And, sometimes he puts handcuffs on them and blindfolds them and then he whips them.'

Mary Lou felt his body shake, felt his cock stiffen and throb more, heard his breath come in short gasps. She saw the juice easing out of his tiny slit. She cupped his balls and held him hard at the base of his prick. She didn't want him to come, not yet.

'Whips them!' he exclaimed, thrilled at the thought.

'Yes, my friend told me he's got a fine selection of whips.'

'And you've never wanted to try?'

'No . . .' she said lingering on the word, and looking up at him. 'Never before now but with you I might.'

Lord Christopher almost came at that idea.

The car was slowing down. The chauffeur began to park.

'We're here,' she said, kissing his cheek.

The two of them adjusted their clothing and stepped out of the car.

The gates to the house were unlocked. Mary Lou pushed them open and they walked towards the marquee dressed all over in Mardi Gras lights.

Josephine had told Elmer he was taking her to the barbeque. They had arrived not long before Mary Lou and Lord Christopher. They were sitting on gilt chairs inside the marquee, sipping champagne and smiling at each other.

'Remember, Elmer,' Josephine whispered. 'This is the first day of your new life. You do everything I tell you.'

'Yes, Madam,' said Elmer obediently.

'And if you don't do it fast enough, what's going to happen, Elmer?'

'You're gonna slap my little botty,' he said.

'No, Elmer,' she said, 'I'm gonna slap your little botty – hard.'

'Yes, Madam,' said Elmer, thrilled with their secret world. Nobody would know anything. He looked at Josephine. She was neatly dressed in a black suit. It was

240

severe, almost unsexy. The skirt was her usual wrap-over design above her knees. Those delightful dimpled knees, a turn on whenever he looked at them. The jacket was buttoned modestly to her neck. Only they knew that Josephine was not wearing a thing under the suit. And only they knew that Elmer was wearing a nappy under his.

Josephine had put it on at his home. She had plied the crop to his bottom for not sucking her fast enough when she had given the order. Afterwards she had rubbed oil into the weals. Then she had chosen which shirt and suit he was going to wear.

'Where's my underpants?' he'd asked.

'You're not wearing any,' she'd replied.

'But . . .'

'You, Elmer, are going to wear this.'

From her handbag she had taken out a large baby's nappy. She had made him lie on the bed, had put a dummy in his mouth, then lifted his legs. Playing with his cock and balls she had wrapped the nappy up and between his thighs, securing it firmly in place with a large safety pin.

'Elmer?'

'Yes, Madam?'

'Did you have a pee?' she asked.

'No, Madam,' he replied.

'Well now, that's too bad,' she said. 'Cos if you wet yourself when we're out I'll have to smack you. Smack your lovely little butt, Elmer.'

'Yes, Madam,' he said, trying not to show his eagerness.

'Is your glass empty, Elmer?' asked Josephine, interrupting his reverie, showing him her empty one and smiling at some people who passed.

'Not yet,' he said.

'Drink up,' she said.

'Yes, Madam,' he replied, downing his glass. His bladder was already full and now she wanted him to take more.

'Control, Elmer, is very important,' she said. 'And if you can't keep control, if you wet yourself, maybe it'll be today I'll pull down your pants and show everybody what a naughty boy you are. How'd you like that?'

'Don't know Madam,' he said, a thrilling fear running through him. He'd made a bet with himself, would it be today she'd do it? He knew one day she would. But which day? On that she kept him guessing.

'Hi Elmer,' said Frank Dale, waddling over to them through a mass of unknown people, 'and who is the lovely lady you've got with you?'

'Hi Frank. Meet Josephine.'

'Hi Josephine,' said Frank, scrutinising her, thinking she wasn't his usual type and wondering where he'd found her. 'Well Elmer, I hear you didn't do too good with the Preacher.'

'No . . .' began Elmer, almost apologetically.

'Oh we're not worried about that crazy old project,' said Josephine, much to Elmer's surprise. 'We've got other, much better ones in the pipeline.'

'Have you now!' exclaimed Frank Dale, laughing. 'And what would that be – a home for old flying pigs?'

'No sir,' said Josephine returning his smile. 'Large stone rest-rooms for short fat turds.'

Both men were surprised by her retort. Elmer hurriedly sipped some more champagne. Frank glared at her, opened his mouth to say something, then thought better of it. A remark like that deserved more than a passing rebuff. He'd think of something real bad. He'd hit them both where it'd hurt. Frank Dale lit up a cigar blew some smoke in Josephine's face then marched away.

'Josephine!' exclaimed Elmer.

'I think I hit the spot!' said Josephine, gleefully.

'D'ya know who that was?'

'Sure. The gangster, Frank Dale. And I think he stitched you up with that goddamn preacher man. He ain't gonna do it again.'

'No, we might be dead before he gets another chance!' said Elmer, gloomily. 'Josephine, I owe that man.'

'Yeah, reckoned you did. Gambling, huh?'

'Yeah.'

'Like I said, Elmer. Control. You ain't gonna gamble no more. You got me. And you and me we want another drink.'

'We do?'

'Yes, Elmer, we do, especially you. You do.'

'Yes, Madam,' said Elmer, knowing that what he really wanted was a pee but that he was on the first day of his new life. And he was gonna learn control.

Frank Dale spent some time searching for Mary Lou. He saw Beau and had a word with him about this and that. He said 'Hi' to the Count, but didn't stay long talking with him. Frank Dale was wary of the handsome German. He had an aura that Frank couldn't quite explain. Frank wouldn't have recognised real sexuality if it jumped up and bit him. He'd never had a decent screw in his life. He was a five second wonder. The only screwing that he was intent on was screwing money out of people. Epps, the Count's butler, gave him a drink.

Frank Dale meandered between the guests, sipping his drink and feeling pissed off. He was annoyed on a number of counts. He didn't like a chit of a girl like Elmer's Josephine getting the verbal better of him. He hadn't expected that. He hadn't expected Elmer would land himself with a bit of pussy that had fire in her belly either. He'd have to watch out for her. And that goddamn English Lord hadn't contacted him. He should have done. That was the arrangement. Frank had told him to report back that night.

'I wanna know what that uptight Ottilie bitch has to say,' he'd told Lord Christopher. 'Most of all I wanna hear the word, yes.'

And he wanted to know where the hell his daughter was. He'd expected her to arrive with Beau. Beau said he hadn't seen her since lunchtime. Neither had Frank. She hadn't even come home to change. Not that that meant anything. She could have bought herself something new and gone to the beauty parlour for a make over. But Frank didn't like it. Something in his bones told him Mary Lou was up to no good. He had a real sneaky feeling that whatever she was up to right now was bad for him.

Then he saw her. Brazen as could be walking across the lawn with Lord Christopher. That was not what Frank Dale had in mind. Frank tipped his drink out on the ground and rushed over to his daughter, totally ignoring Lord Christopher.

'Mary Lou, where've you been?' he asked.

'Visiting friends, pa,' she said, then added, aware that he was rudely ignoring Lord Christopher, 'Lord Christopher's standing beside me pa.'

'Hi,' said Frank. 'I thought you and me was gonna talk tonight.'

'The night's not over yet,' said Lord Christopher.

'So talk. What you got to tell me?'

'Um . . .' said Lord Christopher, indicating Mary Lou.

'Mary Lou, go find Beau,' said her father.

'Sure pa,' she said, smiling at Lord Christopher.

'Oh and Mary Lou, why haven't you been home?'

'Oh, but I have pa, you'd gone,' she replied, waltzing off.

'Okay, what did Miss Uptight Bitch have to say? You did get to see her?'

'I did, and the answer was no.'

'What d'ya mean?'

'No. No means no. Actually what she said was that she wouldn't touch me with the Empire State building, or if I was the last man on the planet.'

'Yeah, well I don't blame her . . . Now, look, there's another way. She's here . . .'

'Ottilie's here?'

'Yes, and to my mind it seems like she's drunk. Never drink Boy, it clouds your judgement and it ain't too good for getting your leg over either. But maybe you Brits ain't too fussed about that.'

Lord Christopher wasn't drunk but he was suddenly

filled with indignation. He had never been referred to as 'Boy' before, neither did he appreciate a lecture on drinking.

'I don't need you to tell me . . .' he began, irritably.

'You'll listen to whatever I tell you, 'cos you've taken my money,' said Frank, lighting another cigar. 'You're my pawn Boy. And I want you to find Ottilie Duvier and make her marry you. 'Cos like I said, I want this house and its land and I intend to have it. Understand?'

Full of his own importance the little fat man walked away. Lord Christopher, somewhat forlorn, ambled his way towards the bright lights of the marquee. He was worried and so just followed the pathway without looking up. If he had he would have seen a stunning firework sculpture arranged beyond the tent. Each year Count Helmut had one. It was lit at dawn to signal the end of the party. This year's was a beautiful and intricate design of beads falling from a crown into a hand.

Lord Christopher was bitterly regretting taking Frank Dale's money. Bitterly regretting having anything to do with him. However, he would go through with the nasty ignorant man's demands because he'd agreed to. He would ask Ottilie again to marry him. A part of him hoped she'd say no. He didn't like the idea of being a gofer for a gangster. Lord Christopher had realised that with his attitude that's all Frank Dale was – a rich gangster. Also Lord Christopher realised he didn't really want to marry Ottilie. If he was going to marry anyone, up till that evening he would have chosen Sylvie. But now there was Mary Lou. She had everything. Sex and money. A great pity she was Frank Dale's daughter.

The marquee was full of people in formal evening wear but both the men and the women were wearing layer upon layer of multi-coloured necklaces. A large black man came up to him with a tray of champagne-filled glasses. Lord Christopher took one. The man bowed. Lord Christopher looked at him. Big and ugly. He must be the butler. The man who joined in the Count's sex orgies. He appeared to be the soul of obsequiousness. Lord Christopher decided that the whole tale was a little unlikely. A complete fabrication from the fevered imagination of over-active female hormones. It was obvious Mary Lou's friend was pulling a fast one. He smiled at Epps and went off to where the spare ribs were being barbequed.

Ottilie could not have been happier, even though her bottom was tender. It was a reminder of how she was now bound to the Count. She sipped at a glass of champagne. It was a warm balmy night. There was plenty to eat and drink. The music was playing Mardi Gras songs and she didn't give a damn who had fucked and sucked her. She'd had a great time and the Count had said he loved her.

He was busy mingling, playing the charming, perfect host. Many of the people from the orgy had stayed. Other people had arrived. Some she knew. She saw her uncle Frank – and avoided him. She saw Beau. And wondered why he was there. She didn't think the Count knew him. Maybe somebody else had brought him. Frank Dale, perhaps? She sat at the table and nibbled at the smoked salmon and corn fritters, thinking.

Ottilie was back to her usual elegant self. The Count had bathed and dressed her. Her frothy organza frock, untouched by any of the cream that had been spread over her wanton body, made her seem ultra sweet and virginal. Daisy had let her use her make up. By one o'clock nobody would have known that a massive orgy had taken place. The house was pristine clean and tidy. The Count had stowed away their outfits for another day and everyone was back in their normal attire. The guests had drifted out into the garden. He had closed up the house.

The sound of the Mardi Gras Mambo by Professor Longhair filled the air. People got up to dance. Ottilie tapped her feet in time with the music. She was wondering what she should do? Sell the Paris apartment and stay permanently in New Orleans? Take back the house from Helmut? Buy out Elmer as she'd planned? She'd noticed he had brought his secretary with him and appeared to be very happy. Or should she continue to let it to Helmut? That would please Elmer. It would also give him an income. Ottilie was deep in thought trying to work out her course of action when Lord Christopher came up to her.

'Ottilie.'

'For fuck's sake Christopher!' she said, angrily. 'Don't you ever get the message. I don't want to know you.'

'Actually old girl, I came over to ask you if you wanted to dance?' he said, thinking on his feet. He'd had every intention of saying the same thing again, but then when he looked at her, he realised that no matter how much Frank Dale had given him, Lord Christopher didn't want Ottilie as his wife. And suddenly he dreaded the idea that she might say 'yes'. There was no doubt that Ottilie looked sexy. But she didn't appeal to him in the slightest.

'Dance?' she said, amazed.

'Yes. You see I don't really know anybody here and that's such a good tune, it makes me want to get up and move.'

'You're asking me to dance with you?'

'Yes, old girl.'

At that moment she saw both Beau and Frank Dale heading in their direction. She forgot to feel angry with him and his stupid expression. She didn't want to talk or see either Frank or Beau. Dancing with Lord Christopher was the less worse option. She stood up and put her arms around Lord Christopher's neck.

'Why not?' she said.

Ottilie's action stopped Frank Dale dead in his tracks. He relaxed. Lord Christopher had obviously won. He'd get the house. Now he could enjoy himself. Frank slapped Beau on the back.

'Boy,' he said, not noticing Beau wince. 'Boy, how did you get on with my daughter today?'

'Good,' said Beau, remembering her beautiful smile.

'Great, that's just great. Because I've a mighty fine plan for you and my beautiful baby girl.'

'You have?'

'I have,' said Frank Dale. 'Beau Maitland you have my permission to court my Mary Lou. She'll make you a damned fine wife. You do have a fancy for her?'

'Yes, I do,' said Beau.

'Well that's sorted,' said Frank. 'And just as soon as you's married we'll talk governors and campaigns. That suit you?'

'Yes sir,' said the ambitious Beau. 'But I was hoping to see her this evening. She said she'd be here.'

'She is ...' said Frank scanning the marquee. 'She must be outside somewhere. Let's go look.'

The two of them wandered out into the soft moonlight.

Mary Lou was in the marquee. She was sitting at the table, partially hidden by a couple of women standing chatting and eating the salmon and corn fritters. Mary Lou was talking to Epps. He was telling her that the Count was furious with her for telling Ottilie that she was his fiancée and had gone to Fort Worth to buy her an engagement ring.

'Aw, shucks, it was just a joke,' she said.

'Not in good taste, Miss Mary Lou,' said Epps.

'Well now me and good taste have never got together,' she replied.

'Ain't that for sure!' said Epps smiling and looking out over the dance floor. 'I don't recognise that man Miss Ottilie's dancing with. Who is he, do you know?'

Mary Lou quickly turned her head, and jealousy pierced her – something Mary Lou thought she'd never feel.

'Why the bitch!' she exclaimed. 'She screws my lover and goes back to her fiancé!'

'Her fiancé!' exclaimed Epps.

'Yes, that's Lord Christopher Furrel. A real English Lord,' said Mary Lou, and in a flash she was gone, charging over to where Ottilie and Christopher were dancing.

'My turn,' she said, butting in and taking Christopher's arm.

Beau was sitting by himself on a bench in one of the small arbours surrounding the swimming pool. Frank had gone to the loo. Beau was staring unseeing into the water. He was trying to work a few things out. Something niggled in his mind. Something he wasn't too happy about. He'd got Frank's permission to marry Mary Lou. Fine. Double fine because that meant Frank's money would be behind him in the race for governor. But he wasn't feeling one hundred per cent about the arrangement. Beau Maitland wasn't a fool. He'd picked up a certain reticence in Mary Lou. It wasn't the reticence of foreplay or courtship either.

Beau had just decided he was feeling hungry when he noticed the ripples in the water. He thought for a moment it was an army of snakes. Strange black and white trails waving over the surface and lit by the moon. Then a hand came up and clasped a step. A naked woman slowly hauled herself out of the water. In the distance Beau could hear the thumping of the Mardi Gras music but in his head he heard Dvořák – Russalka. The glorious music from that opera flooded through his mind, through his body. Yes, he thought, the woman he was gazing at was a water nymph too.

It was Daisy.

Beau sat utterly mesmerised. She shook her head. He saw her incredible tresses. Black and white flowing freely down her back, beyond her waist. Then he saw her rounded bottom. Beau got an instant hard on. She turned and picked up a towel, bent down slightly and began rubbing her hair. Beau mirrored her action by rubbing his prick. She stood up, flicked her hair back and stretched. Beau held his balls. She was magnificent. A beautiful sculptured animal. He wanted to possess her. Beau thought of rushing up and grabbing her, throwing her on to the floor and taking her. He thought of feeling that pink cold body under him; forcing her to

249

open her legs; thrusting into her; biting those pert breasts; sucking on her nipples; screwing her arse; tying her up; whipping her. Beau imagined red and blue weals criss-crossing the pink white flesh of her buttocks. Yes, a woman like that he could string up and whip. Whether she wanted it or not. He would fuck her back and front, whether she wanted it or not. And the more the idea took hold that she didn't want it, the harder Beau got. He undid his flies, brought out his cock and played with it. Rubbing harder, fantasising more as he watched her. Whichever way she moved she appeared to him beautiful. Unattainable. She must be a guest. He'd find out who she was. Nobody could miss her with that extraordinary hair. She wrapped a towel around her body and strode away towards the house.

Beau was rubbing himself into ecstasy when he heard footsteps and soft voices. A man's and a woman's. Jeez, Frank and Mary Lou. He leapt over the back of the bench and into the bushes behind. He didn't want Frank to find him wanking. Neither did he want to stop.

Beau stood hidden by a clump of branches and he brought his cock back to its former tumescent state. He clutched at his balls and jerked madly, images of screwing the unknown girl in a variety of positions pouring into his head. Then he spurted. Feeling intense relief he sank down on to the earth and proceeded to have a dialogue with himself.

What a ridiculous thing to have done. He could have been caught. She was beautiful and highly desirable but he was stupid to have taken his cock out and wanked. He would have been even more stupid to have rushed across and taken her. Where would that have got his ambitions? Women who look like that are not to be touched. In fact, although she didn't know it, he was now engaged to Mary Lou and all women were out of bounds. All. Beau told himself to remember that. He had been incredibly careful. A couple of late teens indiscretions. But as soon as he realised what he wanted, he also realised how to get it – using his good looks to attract the women but keeping his cock well inside his flies. Ottilie was the exception. But she was an old friend and she would keep her mouth shut. She and he came from a similar background. Similar stock. In any case at the time of screwing Ottilie he was thinking of making her his wife. Beau had read too many recent newspaper reports on how ambitious politicians had foundered on the rocks of womanising. Or, once in office had been hounded by old lovers appearing and telling everything to the press. Beau would not allow that to happen to him. He could wank in secret, in the darkness of the night, under the bedclothes, in his own home.

He'd got his life all worked out. He knew exactly where he was going. To the top. Many a man had fucked his way there. He'd do that in the marriage bed with Mary Lou. He'd have her and screw her Daddy's money out of her. Until then Beau knew in the current climate his only option was to wank – all the way.

'What have you done, Elmer?' said a woman's voice, coming through the branches, near Beau. Beau froze. He couldn't get out now. He'd be seen. People would think him odd. He'd have to stay until they'd gone.

'I've been a naughty boy,' said Elmer, who was shaking like a jelly. Ever since she'd felt his buttocks and his prick, discovered his wet patch, he'd been scared she'd take his pants down in front of all the people. She'd threatened to.

'If I find you've wet yourself I might just take that diaper off right there and then.'

That's what she'd said whilst they were drinking their third glass of champagne. But she'd refused to allow him to go to the bathroom. She just kept pouring more drink into him. He'd been at bursting point when she grabbed his arm and took him on the dance floor.

'You gotta dance with me now, Elmer,' she'd said.

It was during the slow dance, she was rubbing her body against him. And he was torn between wanting to get stiff and wanting to pee. She had nuzzled into his neck. And he'd let go. He'd filled that nappy with his

251

own warm water. And she'd brought her hand down and felt the damp patch.

'Elmer, I think your pants should come off,' she'd said.

A look of sheer horror had crossed Elmer's face.

'Don't you think so?'

Elmer didn't know what to think or what to do. He was at her mercy.

'Elmer, I think you and me should take a little walk,' she'd said, guiding him off the dance floor and out of the marquee. 'I have a feeling that somebody lost control.'

'Yes,' he said meekly.

'What's over there,' asked Josephine pointing to the trees and the bushes beyond the firework sculpture.

'A swimming pool,' he said.

'Perfect,' she said, taking hold of his hand and leading him towards it.

Josephine pulled him to a halt when they saw a woman towelling herself. They stood quietly by waiting for her to depart. When she did they walked along by the pool past a bench and Josephine pulled him into the bushes.

'You sure have been a naughty boy. I can feel that damp through your pants. Control, I said Elmer. Control. You know what happens now don't you?'

'Yes, Madam,' said Elmer.

'Tell me Elmer,' said Josephine.

'You're gonna punish me,' he said.

'I sure am, but first you're gonna kneel down in front of me, spread my skirt apart and suck my pussy,' said Josephine.

'Yes, Mam, thank you, Mam,' said Elmer.

Beau could not believe his ears. He couldn't move now even if he wanted to. Although he'd just jerked off, now he had another massive hard on. He rolled over in the dirt and the leaves and the earth to see if he could watch what was happening.

Josephine was leaning against a tree, and Elmer was

kneeling before her. Beau saw him lift the skirt and put the hem in the woman's hands.

'Now, Elmer, I showed you how I liked it. Remember, lick my clit and let that finger of yours go slowly up.'

Beau watched the man's head move up and down drinking at the woman whilst her hips were gyrating and she was sighing. He put his hand down between his legs and began to massage his own cock.

'Yes, yes,' the woman was saying. 'Yes, Elmer, you found the spot. You're a good boy. And I'll let you fuck me – later. Now stand up and take down your pants.'

Elmer stood up. Beau watched them silently and carefully from his hiding place. He was trying to work out what Elmer was wearing.

'Elmer, it's as I thought. You have peed in your diaper. Lie down.'

A diaper! Jeez. Depravity. But he kept watching.

Elmer lay down. Josephine bent over him. She undid the safety pin and removed the wet article and held it up over his face.

'Wet for me means pleasure. Wet for you means punishment,' said Josephine.

Beau heard a sharp snap. He peered through the bushes. The woman was holding some twigs and branches in her hand.

'Okay, put your ass in the air.'

Beau tried to keep his mouth closed and not let out a sound as he rubbed furiously at his cock whilst watching fascinated as the woman brought the branches and twigs down hard, again and again, on Elmer's bare bottom.

Frank Dale was wandering around aimlessly. He couldn't find his daughter or Beau. He'd gone back to the place where he'd left him by the pool but no one was there. He hoped they were together. He thought he'd go find Lord Christopher and Ottilie. Time was getting on. He'd drunk as much orange juice as he could. He'd eaten as much food as he could. There was no one there that appealed to him for a quick fuck. He'd have to wait until he got back to his casino for that. There was a new little hat check girl he had his eye on. Yeah, he'd tell her she was up for promotion, especially if she sucked his dick. Then he'd pull down her panties, bend her over his desk and stick his cock right up. Another notch on his belt. If she made him come real fast he'd give it to her again. If she didn't, he'd replace her. Frank Dale had a quick turnover in hat check girls.

He sat down and lit a cigar. Too much goddamn garlic in that food. Too many goddamn people in the marquee too. Kissing and hugging. Some were talking. He didn't wanna talk to anybody except Lord Christopher. He wanted to hear for himself that he'd hit the jackpot.

'Ottilie, darling, stay the night. I want to have you again.'

Frank couldn't see who said it but he knew the voice. That goddamn Count. Shit. Frank twisted in his chair. There was the Count with his arms around Ottilie, one hand inside her frock holding her breasts. And she was swaying. He was right when he thought she was drunk. Everybody in the place except him seemed to be drunk. He watched with fury as the Count kissed Ottilie on the lips. A long kiss. A possessive, passionate kiss. Not the sort of kiss you give to a woman who's just got engaged to another man.

So where was Lord Christopher? Frank stood up and charged out of the tent. He would go look for him. The first person he met was Beau who seemed shell shocked.

'You talk to my daughter?' asked Frank.

'No,' answered Beau.

'Not at all?'

'No,' said Beau.

'You seen my daughter?'

'Yes but not to talk to,' answered Beau.

'Shit! Why not?' asked Frank.

'Because she was otherwise occupied,' replied Beau, flatly.

'Otherwise occupied? What the fuck does that mean?' asked Frank.

'If you go down by the pool you'll find out,' said Beau. 'But I don't think I'm too interested in continuing our arrangement.'

'Well fuck off then,' said Frank, and stormed across the lawn in the direction of the bushes and the swimming pool. He was beginning to get ideas he didn't like. Images he didn't want. His temperature rose. His blood was boiling. He was in such a temper he almost knocked over Missy Lee and Epps who were carrying the fireworks from the house to the Mardi Gras sculpture.

He heard the sighs and the moans before he saw them.

'Fuck me, fuck me harder.'

It was Mary Lou's voice coming from the bushes.

Tearing down some branches Frank crashed in on them. There they were, Mary Lou and Lord Christopher, naked and writhing on the ground. His cock was firmly embedded in her sex. Frank Dale raised his arm. With as much ferocity as he could muster, which was considerable, Frank Dale began to beat them.

'You animal. You fucking whore,' Frank shouted. 'I'll kill you. I'll kill the both of you.'

With difficulty they managed to evade some of his blows, get up and half-stumble, half-run away from his ever more manic onslaught.

Frank Dale had lost his rag. All sense had gone. Something in his brain had snapped. He went after them, shouting and screaming.

He'd kill them. Everything he'd worked for, everything he planned for, everything he'd aimed for was now ruined. Beau didn't want her as his wife. That sonofabitch the Count had Ottilie.

Now he'd never get the house.

And no way was his whoring daughter gonna get hitched to that goddamn poverty stricken Lord. He'd kill him first. Then he'd kill her.

Naked and hurt, Lord Christopher and Mary Lou carried on running. They ran towards the house. The back door was open.

'Follow me,' said Mary Lou, grabbing Lord Christopher's hand and pulling him inside. They were faced with a mass of doors. 'It's all right, some are false, some are cupboards, but I know which is which and I know the way through.'

Frank was hot on their heels. He didn't run straight in after them. He saw the boxes of fireworks by the back door. That was the answer. If he couldn't have the house nobody was having it. He'd fire it. The whole goddamn thing. Yeah. He tapped his pocket. He had a box of matches. He lifted up as many boxes as he could carry. There'd be some real good fireworks tonight. Then Frank Dale went inside and accidentally slammed the door behind him. It shut fast on a time lock.

Chapter 12

'You weren't joking!' exclaimed Elmer, looking at a letter Josephine had just given him.

'No,' she said. 'But I didn't know it at the time.'

'Design a tomb!' said Elmer.

'So what d'ya say?' asked Josephine, stroking the nape of his neck.

'I dunno . . .' said Elmer.

'Honey it's that or Oklahoma. And Oklahoma ain't New Orleans. And we're broke. How can we marry if we're broke? I say you write back and tell her you'll do it,' said Josephine.

'Okay, you write the letter,' said Elmer.

'But what do I call her?'

'Lady Christopher Furrel,' he said.

Beau Maitland sat in his office in St Cecilia's Chamber Music Hall. He wanted Ottilie to sing at his charity gala, would she do it? He kept picking up the receiver and starting to dial then he put it down again.

He'd set up a good concert. One that he could be proud of. One that people would enjoy. He really did need Ottilie's help. His new sponsor had insisted she sing. Beau had said, 'No problem.' Anything, anything he'd say to get that particular person on his bandwagon.

257

Beau had left the Mardi Gras party as soon as Frank had told him to fuck off. Immediately his mind went into overdrive. He had decided not to wait for the firework display. He had to think how he was going to manage without Frank's backing to get the governorship nomination. Charities. There lay the answer. That was the best, albeit the most circuitous route, of getting what he wanted without anybody realising his blind drive for power.

Beau had got home and had spent the night going through the biographies of the richest men in the state. The very rich usually support a charity close to home. Something that affects their family, especially their children. He found the perfect man. Next morning he telephoned and said he'd like to give a gala concert in his hall in aid of that particular charity. The man, being a nice man, not seeing Beau's machinations, not knowing of his desires, agreed to be the sponsor. With the one proviso. He had known Ottilie and her father. He had heard she was back in New Orleans, heard she had a fabulous voice, all Paris trained, heard she had married a title, and wanted her to sing. Beau had to deliver.

When he did he'd be on a roll. If not this time he'd certainly get the governorship the time after. Beau reckoned he was unstoppable. And never a hint of scandal. No sexploits could crawl out of his woodwork. Because there weren't any. He'd made certain of that.

Beau dialled her number. Ottilie answered.

'Hello?' she said.

'Your Ladyship . . . it's Beau,' he said hesitantly.

'Hi Beau, there's no need to be formal, call me Ottilie, like always,' she said.

'Ottilie, I know you said you wouldn't but I wondered if you would . . . I'd really like you to sing at the gala we're giving in a couple of weeks.' He told her which charity it was for.

'Let me check,' she said.

Beau was elated. She hadn't turned him down.

'We're crossing the Herring Pond soon,' she said,

turning the pages of her diary. 'You're in luck Beau. We're not leaving until the end of the month.'

'So you'll do it?'

'I don't see why not,' she said. 'Is there anything special you'd like me to sing?'

'Um, I hadn't got that far. I wanted to know if you'd do it first. Maybe you could come in and we'll talk about it,' he said.

'Sure, tomorrow, say three o'clock?'

'Fine by me,' he said, 'thank you.'

Ottilie replaced the receiver. Her husband walked into the room.

'Who was that darling?' he asked.

'Beau Maitland,' she replied.

'And what did he want?' he asked, putting his hands over her shoulders and clasping her breasts.

'Me,' she said.

'Oh really!' he exclaimed. 'Well he can't have you.'

'Is that an order?' she asked, smiling.

'It's not an order, it's a command,' he said, running his hands down over her belly and kissing her neck.

'Then I will have to comply,' she said, reaching out a hand and stroking him between his legs.

'I told you once before, my women are only allowed to fuck the men of *my* choice not theirs. And what applied to my women applies even more to my wife,' said Count Helmut.

'He only really wanted a part of me,' said Ottilie.

'Which part?'

'My voice. For a gala concert he's giving in a couple of weeks.'

'In that case I give my Countess my permission,' he said, parting the heavily embroidered beautiful orange silk kimono and touching the top of her bare thighs. Helmut found her utterly desirable. He wanted to take her there and then.

'Helmut . . .?'

'Yes, my darling,' he said.

'Can we be serious for a moment?'

259

'I am, there is nothing I take more seriously in life than sex,' he replied, his fingers opening her labia.

'In that case, can we be frivolous?'

'Maybe. What is it?' he asked.

'We can't stay renting forever. What are we going to do about the house?' she said, pushing Helmut's straying hands away from her body.

'That's easy, there isn't a house to do anything about,' he said, instant images forming in his mind of the terrible night when Frank Dale burnt the house to a cinder. And himself with it. All things considered they were real lucky. Frank had been the only casualty. They'd had some worries about Beau until someone said they'd seen him leaving. And his car had gone.

There was a knock on the door and Epps came in.

'Lord and Lady Christopher Furrel to see you,' he said.

'Invite them in,' said Ottilie. 'And could you tell Missy Lee that we'll be in for dinner tonight but to keep it simple. We'll take it in the bedroom, just some salad and champagne.'

'I'll tell her later,' said Epps. 'She's busy interviewing a maid for you.'

'Oh! How many's that she's seen?'

'Ten, twelve . . .'

'You reckon she likes this one?'

'She's been "interviewing" her for the last hour, so I reckon she does,' said Epps, grinning knowingly as he left the room.

Mary Lou came in with her husband, Lord Christopher. They looked the epitome of happy honeymooners about to go on a sea voyage. He was in grey flannels and a blazer. She was wearing a green and white spotted suit with a short skirt, white very high heels and a big white picture hat.

'And I'd bet my last dollar she's not wearing panties under that,' whispered Helmut to Ottilie, who smiled nodding her head.

'Hi, and what's making you smile? This?' asked Mary Lou, flashing an enormous diamond ring.

'Just you,' said Ottilie.

'Me! Why?' she asked.

'Helmut reckoned you had nothing on underneath,' said Ottilie.

'Goddamn right,' said Ottilie. 'My husband likes to grab a bit of pussy whenever he can and I sure is the last person to stop him, especially if it's mine. Ain't that so, honey?'

'Absolutely correct, Mary Lou,' said Lord Christopher, running his hands up her legs.

'So, to what do we owe the honour of a visit?' asked Ottilie.

'We're going to England,' announced Mary Lou. 'Christopher is taking me to my new home, he says it needs a bit of decorating. That don't bother me. We'll see what needs to be done, get the people in and do it, and we'll go have fun. Won't we darling?'

'That's the general idea,' said Lord Christopher.

'Now I've got my daddy's money we sure can indulge ourselves,' said Mary Lou. 'He made some pretty good investments – legit – so it's fun time.'

'Are you planning on having this fun in England?' asked Helmut.

'Wherever we can find it,' said Mary Lou. 'England, Paris, France . . .'

'Does Christopher know anybody – with the same idea of fun as you Mary Lou?' asked Helmut.

'I don't think he does and that's why we're here. We wanted to ask you . . .' said Mary Lou.

'I have a cousin in Paris with some interesting foibles,' said Helmut. 'But if you wanted to stay in England you could always contact Daisy for a bit of variety. She's studying now at university but I'm sure she'd like a little deviation from time to time.'

'It wasn't a little deviation we was thinking of Helmut,' said Mary Lou.

'You surprise me!' said Helmut, smiling. 'But it just so happens I do know a Russian who runs an extremely interesting establishment not far from London. And he has a tie up with an hotel in Kensington, London.'

'A tie up?' queried Mary Lou.

'I use the words advisedly,' said Helmut.

'Then I think we ought to stay there,' said Mary Lou. 'Have you got the address?'

'Oh yes,' said Helmut. 'But you'll need an introduction. I'll ring the owner for you and tell her you'll be coming.'

'We sure will,' said Mary Lou, smiling. 'Thank you Helmut, we sure appreciate that. Oh and by the way, I asked Elmer if he'd do my daddy's tomb. He's so broke and he wants to marry Josephine. It's a way of helping him out. She's got a good head on her shoulders and it seems like she can keep him in order. Quiet little thing, you'd never think it would you? But he adores her, just does everything she wants. He's stopped gambling you know. Anyhow, we got a ship to catch. See you sometime in Europe?'

'Yes,' said Helmut. 'We might even stay at the same hotel.'

'Oh what are you gonna do about the house?' asked Lord Christopher.

'We were just discussing that when you arrived,' said Ottilie, giving him a farewell peck on the cheek.

After Epps had shown them out he came back and informed them that Missy Lee had taken on the new girl.

'But what we wanna know is, are you gonna stay here or are you gonna get the house rebuilt?' asked Epps.

Helmut and Ottilie looked at one another and smiled. The conversation with Mary Lou and Lord Christopher had triggered the same thought.

'We're gonna have it rebuilt,' said Helmut.

'Great,' said Epps. 'I'll go tell Missy Lee.'

'I had an idea,' said Ottilie, after Epps had closed the door.

'So did I,' said Count Helmut.

'I'll buy Elmer out. That'll please him,' she said. 'He can get on with his own life. And we'll get on with ours. I was thinking Helmut, what about making it a fun place, a leisure centre?'

'My thoughts exactly,' he said, smiling wickedly, taking her in his arms, and slipping off the kimono. 'But we'll make it very special fun and a very special leisure centre.'

OTTILIE'S JUMBALAYA RECIPE 6–8 People

1 Chicken, chopped into small pieces
1 Onion or three shallots
½ Green Pepper
½ Red Pepper
2 tablespoons of Flour, for seasoning
1 teaspoon Salt
Olive oil, preferably virgin (other oils can be used
  but the result is a different taste)
3 medium sized Tomatoes
Shrimps, as many or as few as you like and want
Crayfish when available
1 cup of Long Grain Rice
4 cups of Water
3 teaspoons of Creole seasoning
2 cloves of Garlic
2 stalks of Celery
1 tablespoon of Butter
½ lb skinned Wild Boar Sausages
1 large frying pan, 2 saucepans, one with a lid. A
  glass cloth.

Put chopped celery, whole onion (or the three shallots whole), and the three tomatoes in a saucepan, complete with their skins and boil for five minutes. Drain, keeping the water. Using fresh water, lightly boil shrimps and crayfish until cooked. Drain keeping the water. Mix the two waters together. Measure out two cups of this liquid and boil with half the butter. When boiling add the rice, stir and turn down the heat. Leave to simmer with lid on. When almost finished wrap the lid in a cloth and put back on top of saucepan. This mops up unnecessary moisture and leaves the rice fluffy. Mix the flour with the salt, and two teaspoons of Creole seasoning. Then coat each piece of chicken with the mixture. Put olive oil and rest of the butter in a pan on low heat and when hot put in chopped gloves of garlic. When garlic is a light brown add the chicken pieces. Leave to cook on low heat turning constantly to brown without being burnt. Add the celery and chopped sausages to the frying chicken. Run onions under the tap to cool then remove skin, chop and fry in with the chicken. Peel the tomatoes and mash to a pulp. Cut red and green peppers into thin strips. Fry in with the chicken etc. Remove chicken etc. from the frying pan and put on a plate. Fry the shrimps and crayfish in the chicken and veg oil. Add the fluffy cooked rice to the shrimps and crayfish in the frying pan, turning well. Sprinkle with rest of Creole seasoning. Then add the tomato pulp, mixing it well in with the rice. Return the chicken and vegetables to the frying pan and arrange on top.

Serve hot from the pan.

Visit the Black Lace website at
www.blacklace-books.co.uk

FIND OUT THE LATEST INFORMATION AND TAKE
ADVANTAGE OF OUR FANTASTIC FREE BOOK OFFER!
ALSO VISIT THE SITE FOR . . .

- All Black Lace titles currently available
  and how to order online
- Great new offers
- Writers' guidelines
- Author interviews
- An erotica newsletter
- Features
- Cool links

BLACK LACE — THE LEADING IMPRINT
OF WOMEN'S SEXY FICTION

TAKING YOUR EROTIC READING
PLEASURE TO NEW HORIZONS

LOOK OUT FOR THE ALL-NEW BLACK LACE BOOKS – AVAILABLE NOW!

All books priced £6.99 in the UK. Please note publication dates apply to the UK only. For other territories, please contact your retailer.

SNOW BLONDE
Astrid Fox
ISBN O 352 33732 X

Lilli Sandström is an archaeologist in her mid-thirties; cool blond fisherman Arvak Berg is her good-looking lover. But Lilli has had enough of their tempestuous relationship for the time being so she retreats to the northern forests of her childhood. There, in the beauty of the wilderness, she explores and is seduced by a fellow archaeologist, a pair of bizarre twins, woodcutter Henrik and the glacial but bewitching Malin. And when she comes across old rune carvings she also begins to discover evidence of an old, familiar story. *Snow Blonde* is also an unusual, sexy and romantic novel of fierce northern delights.

QUEEN OF THE ROAD
Lois Phoenix
ISBN O 352 33131 1

Private detective Toni Marconi has one golden rule: always mix business with pleasure. Provided, that is, she can be in charge. When she sets out on the trail of a missing heiress her friends worry she may have bitten off more than she can chew. Toni's leads take her to a nightclub on the edge of the Arizona desert where she meets characters with even stranger sexual appetites than her own. And then there is 'Red' – the enigmatic biker who holds a volatile sexual attraction for her. One thing's for sure, Toni will not give in until she's satisfied, whatever the consequences. **Macho bikers and horny cops get sleazy with a sassy heroine who likes to be in charge.**

Coming in November

NOBLE VICES
Monica Belle
ISBN 0 352 33738 9

Annabelle doesn't want to work. She wants to spend her time riding, attending exotic dinner parties and indulging herself in even more exotic sex, at her father's expense. Unfortunately, Daddy has other ideas, and when she writes off his new Jaguar, it is the final straw. Sent to work in the City, Annabelle quickly finds that it is not easy to fit in, especially when what she thinks of as harmless, playful sex turns out to leave most of her new acquaintances in shock. **Naughty, fresh and kinky, this is a very funny tale of a spoilt rich English girl's fall from grace.**

A MULTITUDE OF SINS
Kit Mason
ISBN 0 352 33737 0

This is a collection of short stories from a fresh and talented new writer. Ms Mason explores settings and periods that haven't previously been covered in Black Lace fiction, and her exquisite attention to detail makes for an unusual and highly arousing collection. Female Japanese pearl divers tangle erotically with tentacled creatures of the deep; an Eastern European puppeteer sexually manipulates everyone around her; the English seaside town of Brighton in the 1950s hides a thrilling network of forbidden lusts. **Kit Mason brings a wonderfully imaginative dimension to her writing and this collection of her erotic short stories will dazzle and delight.**

HANDMAIDEN OF PALMYRA
Fleur Reynolds
ISBN 0 352 32919 X

Palmyra, 3rd century AD: a lush oasis in the heart of the Syrian desert. The inquisitive, beautiful and fiercely independent Samoya takes her place as apprentice priestess in the temple of Antioch. Decadent bachelor Prince Alif has other ideas. He wants a wife, and sends his equally lascivious sister to bring Samoya to the Bacchanalian wedding feast he is preparing. Samoya embarks on a journey that will alter the course of her life. Before reaching her destination, she is to encounter Marcus, the battle-hardened centurion who will unearth the core of her desires. **Lust in the dust and forbidden fruit in Ms Reynolds' most unusual title for the Black Lace series.**

Coming in December

THE HEAT OF THE MOMENT
Tesni Morgan
ISBN 0 352 33742 7

Amber, Sue and Diane – three women from an English market town – are successful in their businesses, but all want more from their private lives. When they become involved in The Silver Banner – an English Civil War re-enactment society – there's plenty of opportunity for them to fraternise with handsome muscular men in historical uniforms. Thing is, the fun-loving Cavaliers are much sexier than the Puritan Roundheads, and tensions and rivalries are played out on the village green and the bedroom. **Great characterisation and oodles of sexy fun in this story of three English friends who love dressing up.**

WICKED WORDS 7
Various
ISBN 0352 33743 5

Hugely popular and immensely entertaining, the *Wicked Words* collections are the freshest and most cutting-edge volumes of women's erotic stories to be found anywhere in the world. The diversity of themes and styles reflects the multi-faceted nature of the female sexual imagination. Combining humour, warmth and attitude with fun, filthy, imaginative writing, these stories sizzle with horny action. Only the most arousing fiction makes it into a *Wicked Words* volume. This is the best in fun, sassy erotica from the UK and USA. **Another sizzling collection of wild fantasies from wicked women!**

OPAL DARKNESS
Cleo Cordell
ISBN 0 352 33033 3

It's the latter part of the nineteenth century and beautiful twins Sidonie and Francis are yearning for adventure. Their newly awakened sexuality needs an outlet. Sent by their father on the Grand Tour of Europe, they swiftly turn cultural exploration into something illicit. When they meet Count Constantin and his decadent friends and are invited to stay at his snow-bound Romanian castle, there is no turning back on the path of depravity. **Another wonderfully decadent piece of historical fiction from a pioneer of female erotica.**

Black Lace Booklist

Information is correct at time of printing. To avoid disappointment
check availability before ordering. Go to www.blacklace-books.co.uk.
All books are priced £6.99 unless another price is given.

To find out the latest information about Black Lace titles, check out the website: www.blacklace-books.co.uk or send for a booklist with complete synopses by writing to:

Black Lace Booklist, Virgin Books Ltd
Thames Wharf Studios
Rainville Road
London W6 9HA

Please include an SAE of decent size. Please note only British stamps are valid.

Our privacy policy
We will not disclose information you supply us to any other parties. We will not disclose any information which identifies you personally to any person without your express consent.

From time to time we may send out information about Black Lace books and special offers. Please tick here if you do not wish to receive Black Lace information. ❑

Please send me the books I have ticked above.

Name ....

Address ....

....

....

....

Post Code ....

Send to: Cash Sales, Black Lace Books, Thames Wharf Studios, Rainville Road, London W6 9HA.

US customers: for prices and details of how to order books for delivery by mail, call 1-800-343-4499.

Please enclose a cheque or postal order, made payable to Virgin Books Ltd, to the value of the books you have ordered plus postage and packing costs as follows:

UK and BFPO – £1.00 for the first book, 50p for each subsequent book.

Overseas (including Republic of Ireland) – £2.00 for the first book, £1.00 for each subsequent book.

If you would prefer to pay by VISA, ACCESS/MASTERCARD, DINERS CLUB, AMEX or SWITCH, please write your card number and expiry date here:

....

Signature ....

Please allow up to 28 days for delivery.